A PEARL BUCK READER

A PEARL BUCK READER

*Selected
and Condensed by
the Editors of
Reader's Digest*

Volume One

The Reader's Digest Association, Inc.
Pleasantville, New York
Cape Town, Hong Kong, London, Montreal, Sydney

READER'S DIGEST CONDENSED BOOKS
Editor-in-Chief: John S. Zinsser, Jr.
Executive Editor: Barbara J. Morgan

Managing Editors: Anne H. Atwater, Tanis H. Erdmann,
Thomas Froncek, Marjorie Palmer
Senior Staff Editors: Jean E. Aptakin, Virginia Rice (Rights),
Ray Sipherd, Angela Weldon
Senior Editors: M. Tracy Brigden, Catherine T. Brown, Linn Carl,
Joseph P. McGrath, James J. Menick, John R. Roberson, Margery D. Thorndike
Associate Editors: Thomas S. Clemmons, Katharine L. Edmonds,
Alice Jones-Miller, Maureen A. Mackey
Senior Copy Editors: Claire A. Bedolis, Jeane Garment, Jane F. Neighbors
Associate Copy Editors: Maxine Bartow, Rosalind H. Campbell, Jean S. Friedman
Assistant Copy Editors: Ainslie Gilligan, Jeanette Gingold, Marilyn J. Knowlton
Art Director: William Gregory
Executive Art Editors: Soren Noring, Angelo Perrone
Associate Art Editors, Research: George Calas, Jr., Katherine Kelleher

CB PROJECTS
Executive Editor: Herbert H. Lieberman
Senior Editor: Dana Adkins

CB INTERNATIONAL EDITIONS
Executive Editor: Francis Schell
Senior Editor: Gary Q. Arpin

Contents

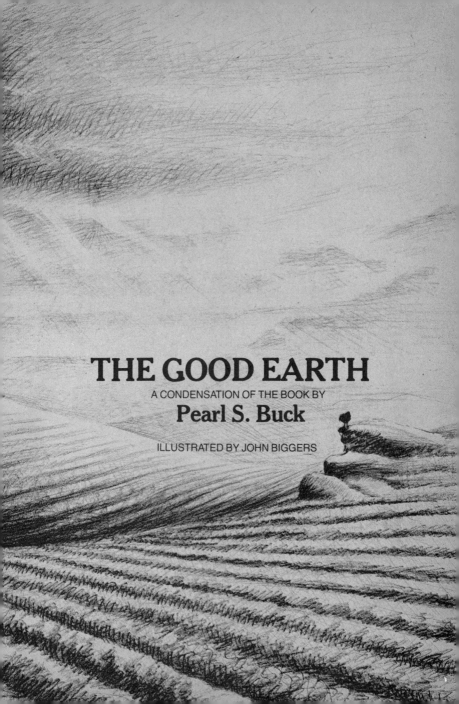

THE GOOD EARTH

A CONDENSATION OF THE BOOK BY

Pearl S. Buck

ILLUSTRATED BY JOHN BIGGERS

The publication of *The Good Earth* in
1931 signaled the arrival of a major new
talent on the American literary scene.
The novel won the Pulitzer Prize the
next year and was the basis for the
award of the Nobel Prize for Literature
to Mrs. Buck in 1938, the first—and
only—time an American woman has
been so honored. The China Pearl Buck
wrote about in *The Good Earth* has
been significantly changed by political
events. But now, as then, this classic
novel has, as one reviewer put it,
"the power to illuminate the destiny
of man as it is in all countries and at all
times by quietly telling the story of one
poor Wang Lung."

I

I T WAS Wang Lung's marriage day. At first, opening his eyes
in the blackness of the curtains about his bed, he could not
think why this dawn seemed different from any other. The
house was still except for the faint, gasping cough of his old
father, whose room was opposite his own across the middle
room. Wang Lung usually lay listening to it, but this morning
he did not wait. He sprang up and he pushed aside the curtains
of his bed. It was a dark, ruddy dawn, and through a small
square hole of a window a bronze sky gleamed. He thrust his
hand out to feel the air. A soft wind blew gently from the east,
mild and murmurous and full of rain. It was a good omen.
Within a few days there would be water. Yesterday he had
said to his father that if this brazen, glittering sunshine continued, the wheat would not fill in the ear. Now it was as if
Heaven had chosen this day to wish him well.

He hurried outside, drawing on his blue outer trousers as he
went, and knotting about his waist a girdle of blue cotton
cloth. He went to the shed leaning against the house that was

the kitchen, and as he entered, the ox lowed at him from its corner next to the door. The kitchen was made of earthen bricks as was the house, great squares of earth dug from their own fields, and thatched with straw from their own wheat. Out of their own earth his grandfather had also fashioned the oven, baked and black with many years of meal preparing. On top of this stood a deep, round iron caldron.

Wang Lung filled this caldron partly with water, dipping it cautiously, for water was precious. But this day he would bathe his whole body. Not since he was a child had anyone looked upon his body. Today one would, and he would have it clean. He selected a handful of dry grass from the corner of the kitchen and arranged it delicately in the mouth of the oven. Then from an old flint and iron he struck a spark and there was a blaze.

This was the last morning he would have to light the fire. Every morning since his mother died six years before, he had lit the fire, boiled water and taken it in a bowl to the room where his father sat on his bed waiting for hot water to ease him of his morning coughing. Now father and son could rest. There was a woman coming into the house. Their house had seemed half empty since his mother's death. They were always having to resist relatives who were more crowded—his uncle, with his endless brood of children, coaxing, "Now how can two lone men need three rooms? Cannot father and son sleep together? The warmth of the young one's body will comfort the old one's cough."

But his father always replied, "I am saving my bed for my grandson. He will warm my bones in my old age."

Now the grandsons were coming—grandsons upon grandsons! They would have to put beds along the walls and in the middle room. The blaze died down while Wang Lung thought of all the beds there would be, and the water began to chill in the caldron.

The shadowy figure of the old man appeared in the doorway, holding his unbuttoned garments about him. He was coughing as he gasped, "How is it that there is not water yet to heat my lungs?"

Wang Lung stared and recalled himself and was ashamed. "This fuel is damp," he muttered. "The damp wind—"

The old man continued to cough until the water boiled. Wang Lung dipped some into a bowl, and then he opened a glazed jar that stood upon a ledge of the oven and took from it a dozen or so of the dried leaves and sprinkled them on the water.

The old man's eyes opened greedily and immediately he began to complain. "Why are you wasteful? Tea is like eating silver." He grasped the bowl in his shriveled, knotty fingers and watched the leaves spread on the surface of the water, unable to bear drinking the precious stuff.

"It will be cold," said Wang Lung.

"True—true—" said the old man in alarm, and he began to take great gulps of the hot tea.

Wang Lung dipped the water recklessly from the caldron into a deep wooden tub. His father stared at him. "Now there is water enough to bring a crop to fruit," he said.

Wang Lung continued to dip the water to the last drop, then he hurried out, carrying the tub to his own room. The door hung loosely in its warped wooden frame, and it did not shut closely.

The old man put his mouth to the opening and bawled, "It will be ill if we start the woman like this—tea in the morning water and all this washing!"

"It is only one day," shouted Wang Lung. And then he added, "I will throw the water on the earth when I am finished."

The old man was silent at this, and Wang Lung unfastened his girdle and stepped out of his clothing. He wrung a small towel from the steaming water and scrubbed his dark, slender body vigorously, passing the towel in and out of the water until a delicate cloud of steam went up from his whole body. Then he drew from a box that had been his mother's a fresh suit of blue cotton cloth. He might be a little cold this day, but the covering of his wadded winter garments was torn and filthy, and he did not want this woman to see him for the first time with the wadding sticking out of his clothes. Later she would have to wash and mend, but not today. Then with swift fingers he unplaited the long braid that hung down his back, took a wooden comb from the drawer of a small, unsteady table and began to comb his hair.

His father again put his mouth to the crack between the door and its frame. "Am I to have nothing to eat this day?" he complained. "At my age the bones are water in the morning until food is given them."

"I am coming," said Wang Lung, braiding his hair quickly and smoothly and weaving into the strands a tasseled, black silk cord. Then he wound the braid about his head and went out, carrying the tub of water. He had quite forgotten breakfast. He would stir a little water into cornmeal and give it to his father. For himself he could not eat anything. He staggered with the tub to the threshold, and as he poured the water upon the earth near the door, he remembered he had used all the hot water in the caldron for his bath, and so he would have to start the fire again. A wave of anger passed over him. "That old head thinks of nothing except his eating," he muttered as he lit the fire again, but aloud he said nothing. He put a little water into the caldron, and it boiled quickly. He stirred the cornmeal into it and took it to the old man.

"We will have rice this night, my father," he said. "Meanwhile, here is cornmeal."

"There is only a little rice left in the basket," said the old man, seating himself at the table in the middle room and stirring the thick yellow gruel with his chopsticks.

"We will eat a little less, then, at the spring festival," said Wang Lung.

And then he went into his own room and drew over his blue cotton coat and trousers a robe made of the same material—his one long robe, which he wore only on feast days. He passed his hand over his cheeks. Perhaps he had better be newly shaven? He could pass through the Street of Barbers before he went to the house where the woman waited for him.

He took from his girdle a small pouch of gray cloth and counted the money in it. There were six silver pieces and a double handful of copper coins. He had asked friends to his wedding feast that night, and he planned to bring back pork, a small pond fish and a handful of chestnuts from town. He might even buy a few bamboo sprouts and a little beef to stew with the cabbage from his garden. But this only if he had money left after his head was shaved.

He went out into the early morning. The sun sparkled on the dew on the rising wheat and barley. The farmer in Wang Lung was diverted for an instant and he stooped to examine the budding heads. He smelled the air and looked anxiously up at the sky. Rain was there, dark in the clouds.

He wound his way in among the fields, following a narrow path. In the near distance the gray city wall arose. Within that gate in the wall stood the great house where the woman had been a slave since childhood, the House of Hwang. There were those who said, "It is better to live alone than to marry a woman who has been a slave." But when he had said to his father, "Am I never to have a woman?" his father had replied, "With every woman wanting gold rings and silk clothes before she will take a man, only slaves remain for the poor."

His father had gone then to the House of Hwang and asked if they had a slave to spare. "Not too young, and above all, not pretty," he had said.

Wang Lung had suffered about that; it would be something to have other men congratulate him for having a pretty wife.

His father, seeing his mutinous face, had cried out at him, "And what will we do with a pretty woman? We must have a woman who will tend the house and bear children as she works in the fields, and will a pretty woman do these things? She will be forever thinking about clothes to go with her face!"

Wang Lung knew his father spoke well. Nevertheless, he had said violently, "At least, I will not have a woman who is pockmarked, nor one who has a split upper lip."

"We will have to see what is to be had," his father had replied.

Well, the woman was not pockmarked, nor did she have a split lip. He and his father had taken silver earrings and two silver rings, washed with gold, to the woman's owner in acknowledgment of betrothal. Beyond this, Wang Lung knew nothing of the woman who was to be his, except that on this day he could go and get her.

He walked into the cool, dark tunnel of the city gate through the thick wall of earth and brick. Water carriers, their wheelbarrows laden with great tubs, passed to and fro, the water splashing out of the tubs onto the stones. Baskets of small, hard green peaches stood along the walls, and the vendors cried out, "The first peaches of spring—the first peaches! Buy, eat, purge your bowels of the poisons of winter!"

Wang Lung said to himself, "If she likes them, I will buy her a handful when we return."

Inside the gate, he turned to the right and was on the Street of Barbers. There were few before him so early, only some farmers who had carried their produce into town the night before in order to sell their vegetables at the dawn markets and return in time for a day's work in the fields. Wang Lung avoided them for fear that some might recognize him, for he wanted none of their joking on this day. All down the street in a long line the barbers stood behind their small stalls. Wang Lung went to the farthest one and sat down on the stool. The barber quickly took a kettle from a pot of burning charcoal and began to pour water into a brass basin.

"Shave everything?" the barber asked.

"My head and my face," said Wang Lung. Then he submitted to the soaping and shaving. When it was finished and the money counted into the barber's wrinkled, water-soaked hand, Wang Lung had a moment of horror. So much money!

But walking down the street again with the wind fresh upon his shaven skin, he said to himself, "It is only once."

He went to the market then and bought two pounds of pork wrapped in a dried lotus leaf. This he placed in the basket he carried, and then, hesitating, he also bought six ounces of beef. When all the rest of the things had been bought, even to fresh squares of bean curd, he went to a candlemaker's shop and bought a pair of incense sticks. Then he turned his steps with great shyness toward the House of Hwang.

Once at the gates of the house he was seized with terror. He had never been in a great house before. How could he go in with his wedding feast on his arm and say, "I have come for the woman"?

He stood there for a long time, looking at the two great wooden gates, painted black and studded with iron, closed fast upon each other. Two lions made of stone stood on guard, one at either side. There was no one else.

He suddenly felt faint. First he would go and buy a little food. He had eaten nothing. He went into a small restaurant, and putting his pennies on the table, he sat down. A dirty serving boy with a shiny black apron came near, and Wang Lung called out to him, "Two bowls of noodles!" When the boy brought them, he ate them greedily.

There was no one Wang Lung knew in the small, dark room. Only a few men sat eating or drinking tea. It was a place for poor men, and among them he looked neat and almost well-to-do, so that a passing beggar whined at him, "Have a good heart, teacher, and give me a small cash—I starve!"

Wang Lung had never had a beggar ask of him before, nor had anyone ever called him teacher. He was pleased and threw into the beggar's bowl two small cash, each equivalent to one fifth of a penny, and the beggar, grasping the cash with his black claw of a hand, fumbled them within his rags.

Wang Lung sat and the sun climbed upward. The serving boy lounged about impatiently. "If you are buying nothing more," he said at last, "you will have to pay rent for the stool."

Incensed at such impudence, Wang Lung would have risen, except that when he thought of the great House of Hwang, sweat broke out over his whole body. "Bring me tea," he said weakly to the boy. Before he could turn, it was there and the boy demanded sharply, "Where is the penny?"

"It is robbery," Wang Lung muttered. Then he saw a neighbor enter, one whom he had invited to his wedding feast. He put the penny hastily upon the table, drank the tea at a gulp and went out quickly by the side door.

"It is to be done," he said to himself desperately, and slowly he turned his steps to the great gates.

This time, since it was after high noon, the gates were ajar and the keeper of the gate idled upon the threshold, picking his teeth with a bamboo sliver. He was a tall fellow with a large mole upon his left cheek, from which hung three long black hairs.

With great difficulty Wang Lung said, "I am Wang Lung, the farmer."

"Well, and Wang Lung, the farmer, what?" retorted the gateman, who was polite to none except the rich.

"I am come—I am come—" faltered Wang Lung.

"That I see," said the gateman with elaborate patience, twisting the long hairs of his mole.

"There is a woman," said Wang Lung, his voice sinking to a whisper.

The gateman gave a great laugh. "So you are he! I was told to expect a bridegroom. But I did not recognize you with a basket on your arm."

"It is only a little meat," said Wang Lung apologetically, waiting for the gateman to lead him within. But the gateman did not move. Wang Lung saw that he wanted money.

"I am a poor man," he said pleadingly.

"Let me see what you have in your girdle," said the gateman.

Wang Lung in his simplicity put his basket down and took out his pouch and shook into his left hand what money was left. There was one silver piece and fourteen copper pennies.

"I will take the silver," said the gateman coolly, and before Wang Lung could protest, the man had taken the silver and was striding through the gate, bawling loudly, "The bridegroom, the bridegroom!"

Wang Lung, in spite of his anger at what had just happened and his horror at this loud announcing of his coming, could do nothing but pick up his basket and follow. With his face burning and his head bowed, he walked through court after court, hearing that voice roaring ahead of him, hearing tinkles of laughter on every side. Then when it seemed to him he had gone through a hundred courts, the gateman fell silent and suddenly pushed him into a small waiting room. The gateman went into some inner place and returned in a moment to say, "The old mistress says you are to appear before her."

Wang Lung started forward, but the gateman stopped him, crying in disgust, "You cannot appear before a great lady with a basket on your arm. How will you bow?"

"True—true—" said Wang Lung in agitation. But he did not dare to put the basket down because he was afraid something might be stolen from it.

The gateman saw his fear and cried out in great contempt, "In a house like this we feed that meat to the dogs!" and he seized the basket and thrust it behind the door, pushing Wang Lung ahead of him.

Down a long, narrow veranda they went, the roof supported by delicately carved posts, and into a hall the likes of which Wang Lung had never seen before. A score of houses such as his could have been put into it, so wide were the spaces, so high the roof. Upon a dais in the center of the room he saw a very old lady, her small, fine body clothed in silvery gray satin. On the low bench beside her was a pipe of opium, burning over its little lamp. She looked at him with small black eyes that were as sharp as a monkey's in her thin and wrinkled face. Wang Lung fell to his knees and knocked his head on the tiled floor.

"Raise him," said the old lady to the gateman. "These

obeisances are not necessary. Has he come for the woman?"

"Yes, Ancient One," replied the gateman.

"Ah, yes—a small affair—he has come for the slave called O-lan. Call her quickly," said the old lady.

And in an instant a slave appeared, leading by the hand a rather tall woman clothed in a clean blue cotton coat and trousers. Wang Lung glanced once and then away, his heart beating wildly. This was his woman.

"Come here, slave," said the old lady carelessly. "This man has come for you."

The woman stood before the lady with bowed head.

"Are you ready?" asked the lady.

The woman answered as slowly as an echo, "Ready."

It was a good enough voice, plain and not ill-tempered. Wang Lung looked at her back as she stood before him, and he saw with an instant's disappointment that her feet were not bound. But this he could not dwell upon, for the old lady called Wang Lung and said, "Stand beside her while I speak."

When Wang Lung came forward, she said to him, "This woman came into our house when she was a child of ten. Now she is twenty years old. I bought her in a year of famine. Her parents came from the north in Shantung. You see she has the strong body and the square cheeks of her kind. She will work well for you in all that you wish. She is not beautiful, but that you do not need. Neither is she clever, but she does well what she is told to do and she has a good temper. Take her and use her well."

And to the woman she said, "Obey him and bear him sons and yet more sons. Bring the first child to me to see."

"Yes, Ancient Mistress," said the woman submissively.

They stood hesitating, and Wang Lung was greatly embarrassed, not knowing whether he should speak or not.

"Well, go, will you!" said the old lady in irritation, and Wang Lung, bowing hastily, went out, the woman after him, and after her the gateman, carrying her box on his shoulder. This box he set down in the room where Wang Lung had left his basket, and then he disappeared, leaving them alone.

Wang Lung turned and looked at the woman. She had a square, honest face and a short, broad nose; her mouth was wide, a gash in her face; her eyes were small and dull black in color, filled with some sadness that was not clearly expressed. She seemed to be habitually silent. She bore Wang Lung's look of appraisal without embarrassment or response. He saw it was true that there was not beauty of any kind in her face—a brown, common, patient face. But on her ears and on her hands he saw the rings he had given her. He turned away with secret exultation. Well, he had his woman!

"Here are this box and this basket," he said gruffly.

Without a word she bent over and placed one end of the box on her shoulder. Then, staggering under its weight, she tried to rise. He watched her at this and suddenly said, "I will take the box. Here is the basket."

He shifted the box to his own back while she, still speechless, took the basket. He thought of the hundred courts he had come through and of his figure, absurd under its burden.

"If only there were a side gate—" he muttered.

After a little thought, O-lan nodded. She led the way through a small unused court that was overgrown with weeds, and there under a bent pine tree was an old round gate. They went through it and into the street.

Once or twice he looked back at her. She plodded along steadily on her big feet, her wide face expressionless. At the gate of the wall he stopped uncertainly and fumbled in his girdle for the pennies he had left. He took out two of them and with these he bought six small green peaches. "Take these and eat them," he said gruffly.

She clutched them greedily as a child might and held them in her hand. When next he looked at her as they walked along the margin of the wheat fields she was nibbling one.

And thus they went on until they reached the western field where stood the temple to the earth. This temple was a small structure, not higher in all than a man's shoulder and made of gray bricks and roofed with tile. Wang Lung's grandfather, who had built it, had covered the walls with plaster, and a village artist had been hired in a good year to paint a scene of hills and bamboo on the walls. But the rain of generations had poured upon this painting until now there was only a faint feathery shadow of the bamboos left.

Within the temple sat two small, solemn earthen figures, the god himself and his lady. They wore robes of red and gilt paper. Each year at the New Year, Wang Lung's father bought sheets of paper and carefully cut and pasted new robes for the pair. And each year rain and snow and the sun of summer spoiled their robes.

At this moment, however, the robes were still new, and Wang Lung was proud of their appearance. He took the basket from the woman's arm and looked under the pork for the sticks of incense he had bought. When he found them, he stuck them side by side in the ashes of incense that had been burned before the gods, for the whole neighborhood worshiped these two small figures. Then he fumbled for his flint and iron, and using a dried leaf for tinder, he struck a flame to light the incense.

Together they stood before the gods of their fields and watched as the ends of the incense reddened and turned gray. When the ash grew heavy, the woman leaned over and with her forefinger pushed the head of ash away. Then, as though fearful for what she had done, she looked quickly at Wang Lung for approval. He nodded. There was something he liked in her action. It showed that she felt the incense belonged to them both; it was a moment of marriage. They stood in complete silence while the incense smoldered into ashes; and then Wang Lung shouldered the box and they went home.

THE OLD MAN stood at the door of the house to catch the last rays of the sun. He made no movement as Wang Lung approached with the woman. It would have been beneath him to notice her. Instead he feigned great interest in the clouds as he cried, "That cloud which hangs upon the left horn of the new moon speaks of rain."

And then as he saw the basket he cried out again, "And have you spent money?"

"There will be guests tonight," Wang Lung said briefly, and he carried the box into the room where he slept and set it down.

The old man said volubly, "There is no end to the money spent in this house!"

Secretly he was pleased that his son had invited guests, but he felt it would not do to give out anything but complaints before his new daughter-in-law lest she be set from the beginning in ways of extravagance. Wang Lung said nothing, but he went into the kitchen, and the woman followed him. He took the food piece by piece from the basket and said to her, "There are seven to eat. Can you prepare food?"

The woman answered in her plain voice, "I have been a kitchen slave in the House of Hwang."

Wang Lung nodded and left her and did not see her again until the guests came crowding in—his uncle, jovial and sly and hungry; his uncle's son, an impudent lad of fifteen; and three farmers, clumsy and grinning with shyness. Two of the farmers came from the village and one was his next-door neighbor, Ching, a small, quiet man. After they had been seated about the middle room, Wang Lung went into the kitchen to bid the woman serve.

"I will hand you the bowls," she said, "if you will place them on the table. I do not like to come out before men."

Wang Lung felt in him a great pride that this woman of his did not fear to appear before him but would not before other men. He took the bowls from her hands at the kitchen door and set them on the table in the middle room and called loudly, "Eat, my uncle and my brothers." And they ate heartily of the good fare, and this one praised the sauce and that one the pork, and Wang Lung said over and over in reply, "It is poor stuff— it is badly prepared."

But in his heart he was proud of the dishes, for with sugar

and vinegar and a little wine and soy sauce the woman had skillfully brought forth all the force of the meat. Wang Lung had never tasted such dishes at the tables of his friends.

That night after the guests had tarried long over their tea and their jokes, the woman still lingered behind the oven. After Wang Lung had seen the last guest away, he went in and found her there in the straw, asleep beside the ox. When he called her, she put up her arm suddenly in her sleep as though to defend herself from a blow. She opened her eyes at last and looked at him with her speechless gaze, and he felt as though he were facing a child. He took her by the hand and led her into the room where that morning he had bathed for her, and he lit a red candle. In this light he was suddenly shy when he found himself alone with the woman, and he was compelled to remind himself, "This woman is mine."

He began to undress. The woman crept around the corner of the curtains and began without a sound to prepare herself for bed.

Wang Lung said gruffly, "When you lie down, put the light out first."

Then he lay down and drew the thick quilt about his shoulders and pretended to sleep. But he was not sleeping. He lay quivering, every nerve of his flesh awake. And when, after a long time, the room went dark and there was the slow, silent, creeping movement of the woman beside him, an exultation filled him fit to break his body.

II

THERE WAS THIS luxury of living. The next morning he lay on his bed and watched the woman who was now wholly his own. She rose and drew her loosened garments about her and fastened them closely at her throat and waist, fitting them to her body as she twisted and turned. Then she put her feet into her cloth shoes and drew them on by the straps at the back. Her face looked unchanged. This astonished Wang

Lung. He felt as though the night must have changed him; yet here was this woman rising from his bed as though she had risen from it every day of her life.

The old man's cough rose querulously out of the dusky dawn and Wang Lung said to the woman, "Take to my father first a bowl of hot water for his lungs."

She asked, her voice exactly as it had been yesterday, "Are there to be tea leaves in it?"

The simple question troubled Wang Lung. He would have liked the woman to think that they made nothing of tea leaves in this house. In the House of Hwang even a slave, perhaps, would not drink only water. But he knew his father would be angry if on the first morning the woman served tea to him. Therefore he replied negligently, "Tea? No—no—it makes his cough worse."

And then he lay in bed warm and satisfied while the woman boiled the water in the kitchen. He would have liked to sleep on, but his foolish body, which he had made arise so early every morning all these years, would not sleep; so he lay there, savoring the luxury of idleness. Part of the time he thought of what his harvest would be if the rains came and of the white turnip seed he wished to buy from his neighbor Ching if they could agree upon a price. But weaving and interweaving between these thoughts there ran new thoughts of what his life now was, and it occurred to him to wonder if this woman of his liked him. This was a new wonder. Before he had only wondered whether he would like her; now he wanted her to like him as her husband.

The door opened and she came in silently, bringing him a steaming bowl. There were tea leaves floating on the surface of the water. He looked up at her quickly.

She was at once afraid and said, "I took no tea to the old one, but to you I—"

Wang Lung answered before she finished, "I like it—I like it," and he drank his tea with pleasure. And he thought, This woman of mine likes me well enough!

During the next months it seemed to Wang Lung that he did nothing except watch this woman of his, O-lan. In reality, he worked as he had always worked. He put his hoe on his shoulder and walked to his plots of land and cultivated the rows of grain. He yoked the ox and plowed the western field for garlic and onions. But the work was luxury, for when the sun struck the zenith, he could go to his house and food would be there ready for him to eat, and the table would be clean, and the bowls and the chopsticks placed neatly on it. Hitherto he had had to prepare the meals when he came in tired. Now the meals were ready for him and he could eat at once.

When he left in the morning, O-lan took the bamboo rake and roamed the countryside, reaping here a bit of grass and there a twig, returning at noon with enough to cook their dinner. It pleased Wang Lung that they no longer needed to buy fuel. In the afternoon, O-lan took a hoe and a basket and went to the road leading into the city, where she picked up the droppings from the mules and donkeys and horses and carried them home for fertilizer for the fields. These things she did without being commanded. And when the end of the day came, she did not rest until the ox had been fed and until she had brought water for it to drink.

And with thread that she herself spun from a wad of cotton on a bamboo spindle she mended the rents in their winter clothes. She took their bedding into the sun and ripped the coverings from the quilts and washed them and hung them to dry, and she picked over the cotton in the quilts that had grown hard and gray, killing the vermin that had flourished in the hidden folds. Day after day she did one thing after another, until the three rooms seemed almost prosperous. The old man's cough grew better, and he sat in the sun by the southern wall of the house, always half asleep and warm and content.

But O-lan never spoke unless it was absolutely necessary. Wang Lung, secretly watching her stolid, square face, the half-fearful look in her eyes, made nothing of her. At night he knew the soft firmness of her body. But during the day she acted like a faithful, silent serving maid. And sometimes, working over the clods in the fields, he would fall to pondering about her. What had she seen in those hundred courts? What had been her life, that life she never shared with him? And then he was ashamed of his own curiosity. She was, after all, only a woman.

But there was not enough work in three rooms and two meals a day to keep a woman who had been a slave in a great house busy.

One day when Wang Lung had been planting wheat until his back throbbed with weariness, O-lan's shadow fell across the furrow over which he worked. There she stood, with a hoe across her shoulder.

"There is nothing to do in the house until nightfall," she said briefly, and she began to work the furrow to the right of him.

The sun beat down upon them, for it was early summer, but as they moved together in perfect rhythm, without a word, hour after hour, he fell into a union with her that took the pain from his labor. There was this perfect sympathy of movement, of turning this earth of theirs over and over to the sun, this earth that gave them their home and fed their bodies. Sometimes they turned up a bit of brick, or a splinter of wood. In some bygone age, bodies of men and women had been buried there; houses had stood there and fallen back into the earth. So also would their bodies—and their house—return into the earth. Each had his turn at this earth. They worked on, moving together—together producing the fruits of the earth.

When the sun had set, Wang Lung straightened his back slowly and looked at the woman. Her face was streaked with the earth. Her wet dark garments clung to her square body. She smoothed the last furrow slowly. Then she said, straight out, her voice more than usually plain in the calm evening air, "I am with child."

Wang Lung stood still. What was there to say to this thing, then! It was as though she had said, "I have brought you tea." It seemed as ordinary as that to her! But to him—he could not say what it was to him. His heart swelled.

He took the hoe suddenly from her hand and said, his voice thick in his throat, "Let it be for now. It is the end of the day. We will tell the old man."

They walked home, O-lan a half a dozen paces behind him as befitted a woman.

The old man stood at the door. He was impatient and called out, "I am too old to wait for my food like this!"

But Wang Lung, passing him into the room, said, "She is with child already."

He tried to say it as easily as he might say, "I have planted the western field today," but he could not. Although he spoke in a low voice it sounded to him as if he had shouted the words.

The old man blinked for a moment and then comprehended

and cackled with laughter. "Heh-heh—" he called to his daughter-in-law, "so the harvest is in sight!"

He could not see her face in the dusk, but she answered evenly, "I shall prepare food now."

"Yes—yes—food—" said the old man eagerly, following her into the kitchen. The thought of food made him forget the child.

But Wang Lung sat by the table in the darkness and put his head upon his folded arms. Out of this body of his, out of his own loins, life!

When the day for birth drew near, he said to O-lan, "We must have someone to help at the time—some woman."

But she shook her head. She was clearing away the bowls

THE GOOD EARTH

after the evening food. The old man had gone to his bed and
the two of them were alone in the night, with only the light
that fell upon them from the flickering flame of a small tin
lamp filled with bean oil.

"No woman?" he asked in consternation. He was beginning
now to be accustomed to these conversations in which her part
was little more than a movement of her head or her hand. He
had even come to feel no lack in such conversing. "But it will
be odd with only two men in the house!" he continued. "Is
there no one in the great house—no old slave with whom you
were friends—who could come?"

It was the first time he had mentioned the house from which
she had come. She turned on him as he had never seen her:
her narrow eyes widened; her face stirred with dull anger.

"None in that house!" she cried out at him.

He stared at her. She had placed the chopsticks down
carefully on the table, and she looked at him and said, "When
I return to that house it will be with my son in my arms. I shall
have a red coat on him and red-flowered trousers and a hat
with a gilded Buddha on the front and on his feet tiger-faced
shoes. And I will wear new shoes and a new coat of black
sateen and I will go and show myself and my son to all of
them."

He had never heard so many words from her before. They
came forth steadily and without a break. How astonishing she
was! He would have said that she had scarcely thought of the
child, so quietly had she gone about her work. Instead she saw
this child, born and fully clothed, and herself as his mother, in
a new coat! He was for once without words himself.

"I suppose you will need some money," he said at last with
apparent gruffness.

"If you will give me three silver pieces . . ." she said
fearfully. "It is a great deal, but I will waste no penny of it. I
shall make the cloth dealer give me the last inch to the foot."

Wang Lung fumbled in his girdle. The day before he had
sold reeds from the pond in the western field. He put the three

silver pieces upon the table. Then, after a little hesitation, he added a fourth piece that he had been saving to gamble some morning at the teahouse. But he had never done more than linger and look at the dice as they clattered on the table, fearful that he might lose if he played.

"You may as well make his coat of a small remnant of silk," he said. "After all, he is the first."

She did not take the money at once but stood looking at it. Then she said in a half whisper, "It is the first time I have had silver money." Suddenly she took it and clenched it in her hand and hurried into the bedroom.

Wang Lung sat there thinking of the silver. It had come out of the earth, this silver, out of his earth that he plowed and turned and spent himself upon. By his sweat he wrung fruit from it, and from the fruit, silver. Each time before this that he had taken the silver out to give to anyone, it had been like giving a piece of his life. But now for the first time the giving was not painful. He saw the silver transmuted into something worth even more than itself—clothes upon the body of his son. And this strange woman of his, who worked about, saying nothing, seeming to see nothing, she had first seen the child thus clothed!

HER HOUR came early one night when the sun had scarcely set. She was working beside him in the harvest field. The wheat had borne and been cut, and the field had been flooded and the young rice set, and now the rice ears were full after the warm ripening sun of early autumn.

Together they had cut the sheaves all day, bending and cutting with short-handled scythes. She stooped stiffly because of the burden she bore, so that they cut unevenly, his row ahead and hers behind. She began to cut more and more slowly as noon wore on to evening, and he turned to look at her with impatience. She stopped and stood up then, dropping her scythe. On her face was a new sweat, the sweat of a new agony.

"It is come," she said. "I will go into the house. Do not come into the room until I call. Only bring me a newly peeled reed, and slit it, that I may cut the child's life from mine."

She walked deliberately across the fields toward the house, carrying her scythe. After he had watched her go, he went to the edge of the pond and chose a slim green reed and peeled it carefully and slit it on the edge of his scythe. The quick autumn darkness was falling as he shouldered his scythe and went home.

When he reached the house, he found his supper hot on the table and the old man eating. She had stopped in her labor to prepare them food! He said to himself that she was a woman such as is not commonly found. Then he went to the door of their room and called out, "Here is the reed!"

Her hand reached out through the crack between the door and the frame and took the reed. She said nothing, but he heard her panting as an animal pants after it has run a long way.

The old man looked up from his bowl to say, "Eat, or all will be cold! It will be a long time. I remember well when the first was born to me it was dawn before it was over. Ah, me, to think that out of all the children I begot and your mother bore, one after the other, a score or so—I forget—only you have lived!" And then he said again, as though he had just thought of it, "By this time tomorrow I may have a grandson." And he stopped his eating and sat chuckling for a long time in the dusk.

But Wang Lung stood listening at the door. O-lan's panting became quick and loud, but when he could bear no more and was about to break into the room, a thin, fierce cry came out and he forgot everything.

"Is it a male?" he cried importunately, forgetting the woman. "Tell me at least this—is it a male?"

And the voice of the woman answered as faintly as an echo, "A male!"

He went and sat down at the table then. The food was long cold and the old man was asleep on his bench, but how quick it had all been! He shook the old man's shoulder.

"It is a boy!" he called triumphantly. "You are a grandfather and I am a father!"

The old man woke with a start and began to laugh as he had been laughing when he fell asleep. "Yes—of course," he cackled. "Grandfather—grandfather—" and he rose and went to his bed, still laughing.

Wang Lung took up the bowl of cold rice and began to eat. He was very hungry all at once. He could hear the woman dragging herself about and the incessant piercing cry of the child. "I suppose we shall have no more peace in this house now," he said to himself proudly.

When he had eaten, he went to the door again and O-lan called to him. He went in. She was lying neatly covered on the bed. Beside her lay his son.

His heart crowded up into his breast as he leaned over the child to look at him. He had a round wrinkled face and his hair was long and damp and black. He had ceased crying and lay with his eyes tightly shut.

Wang Lung looked at his wife and she looked back at him. Her hair was still wet and her dark eyes were sunken. Beyond this, she was as she always was. But to him she was touching, lying there. His heart rushed out to these two, and he said, not knowing what else there was that could be said, "Tomorrow I will go into the city and buy a pound of red sugar and stir it into boiling water for you to drink."

And then, looking at the child again, this burst forth from him as though he had just thought of it: "We shall have to buy a good basketful of eggs and dye them all red for the village so everyone will know I have a son!"

III

THE DAY after the child was born, O-lan rose as usual and prepared food, but she did not go into the fields; Wang Lung worked alone until after the noon hour. Then he dressed himself in his blue robe and went into town. At the market, he bought fifty eggs, not newly laid but still fresh enough, and red paper to boil with them to make them red. At the sweet-shop, he bought a pound of red sugar. The merchant smiled. "It is for the mother of a newborn child, perhaps?"

"A firstborn son," said Wang Lung proudly.

"Ah, good fortune!"

This, of course, the merchant had said many times to others, but to Wang Lung it seemed special, and he was pleased. He bowed and bowed again as he went from the shop. It seemed to him as he walked into the sharp sunshine of the dusty street that there never was a man so filled with good fortune as he.

He thought of this at first with joy and then with a pang of fear. It did not do in this life to be too fortunate. The air and the earth were filled with evil spirits who could not endure the happiness of mortals, especially poor mortals. He turned abruptly into the candlemaker's shop, and there he bought four sticks of incense, one to represent each person in his house. And then he went to the small temple of the gods of the earth and thrust the sticks into the cold ashes of the incense he had burned there before, he and his wife together. He watched until the four sticks were well lit and then, comforted, went home.

ALMOST BEFORE Wang Lung realized it, O-lan was back at work beside him. The harvests were over; they had beaten out the grain with flails in the dooryard of the house and win-nowed it, casting it up from great flat bamboo baskets into the wind and catching the good grain as it fell, while the chaff blew away in a cloud with the wind. Then there were the fields to plant for winter wheat again. When he had yoked the ox and plowed the land, O-lan followed behind with her hoe and broke the clods in the furrows.

She worked all day now and the child lay near her on an old quilt on the ground, asleep. When he cried, the woman stopped and uncovered her bosom, sitting flat upon the ground, and the sun beat down upon them both. The woman and the child were as brown as the soil; they sat like figures made of earth, and out of the woman's great brown breasts the milk gushed forth for the child in abundance.

Winter came on and they were prepared against it. There had never been such harvests before; the small house was bursting. From the rafters of the thatched roof hung strings and strings of dried onions and garlic, and there was even a large salted leg of pork that Wang Lung had bought from his neighbor Ching. There were as well two of their own chickens, drawn and dried and stuffed with salt. There were great jars made of reeds, filled with wheat and rice. Much of this would be sold. Wang Lung was frugal; he did not spend his money at gambling or on delicate foods, and so have to sell the grain at harvest when the price was low. He saved it and sold it at the New Year when people paid well for food.

His uncle always had to sell his grain before it was well ripened. Sometimes he even sold it standing in the field to save himself the trouble of harvesting. But then his uncle's wife was a foolish woman, fat and lazy, and forever clamoring for sweet food and for new shoes bought in the town. O-lan made all their shoes.

When the bitter and biting winds of winter came out of the desert to the northeast of them, they stayed in the house in the midst of all this plenty. And when the child was a month old, they had had the customary feast of noodles to assure him a long life. Wang Lung had given red eggs to all those who came from the village to congratulate him. Everyone envied him his son, a great, fat, moon-faced child with high cheekbones like his mother. Now he sat on the quilt placed on the earthen floor of the house, and they opened the door to the south for the sun, and the wind on the north beat in vain against the thick earthen wall.

The leaves were soon torn from the date tree beside the threshold and from the willow trees and the peach trees near the fields. Only the bamboo leaves still clung in the sparse clump to the east of the house, though the wind wrenched the stems double. And then suddenly on a still gray day when the wind fell and the air was quiet and warm, the rains came, and they all sat in the house filled with well-being, watching the rain fall full and straight and sink into the fields. The child stretched out his hands to catch the silver lines of rain as they fell, and he laughed and they laughed with him, and the old man squatted on the floor beside him and said, "There is not another child like this in a dozen villages. Those brats of my brother notice nothing before they walk."

And in the fields the wheat seed sprouted and pushed spears of delicate green above the wet brown earth.

At a time like this there was visiting, because the farmers felt that for once Heaven was doing the work in the fields without their carrying buckets to and fro; and they gathered at this house and that, drinking tea, going from house to house between the fields under great oiled-paper umbrellas. But Wang Lung and his wife were not among them. There was no house in this village of half a dozen scattered small houses that was so filled with warmth and plenty as their own, and Wang Lung felt that if he became too intimate with the others there would be borrowing. New Year was coming and who had all the money he wanted for new clothes and feasting? He stayed in his house and examined his rakes of split bamboo, and where a string was broken, he wove in new string made of hemp he grew himself, and where a prong was broken out, he cleverly drove in a new bit of bamboo.

And what he did for the farm implements, O-lan did for the house implements. If an earthen jar leaked, she did not—as other women did—cast it aside. Instead she mixed clay and welded the crack and heated it slowly, and it was as good as new.

They sat in their house, therefore, and they rejoiced in each other's approval, although their speech was never anything more than scattered words such as these: "Did you save the seed from the big squash for the new planting?" Or, "We will sell the wheat straw and burn the bean stalks in the kitchen." Or perhaps rarely Wang Lung would say, "This is a good dish of noodles," and O-lan would answer in deprecation, "It is good flour we have this year from the fields."

From the produce, Wang Lung in this good year had a handful of silver pieces over and above what they needed and these he was fearful of keeping in his belt. So O-lan dug a small hole in the wall behind their bed and into this Wang Lung thrust the silver. O-lan covered the hole with a clod of earth, and it looked as if nothing had been disturbed. But to both it gave a sense of secret richness and reserve. And now when Wang Lung walked among his fellows, he walked at ease with himself and with all.

THE NEW YEAR approached and Wang Lung went into town and bought squares of red paper on which the characters for happiness and for riches were brushed in gilt ink. These squares he pasted on his plow and on the ox's yoke and on the two buckets in which he carried his fertilizer and his water, to bring him luck in the new year. And over his doorway he pasted a fringe of red paper cunningly cut into a flower pattern. And the old man made new robes for the gods and Wang Lung burned incense before them. And for his house he bought two red candles to burn on the eve of the new year.

Wang Lung went again into town and bought pork fat and white sugar. O-lan rendered the fat smooth and white and took flour, which the ox had ground from their own rice between their millstones, and made rich New Year's cakes, called moon cakes, such as were eaten in the House of Hwang.

When the cakes were laid out upon the table, Wang Lung felt his heart fit to burst with pride. There was no other woman in the village able to make such cakes. On some of the cakes she had put rows of little red berries and pieces of dried green plums, making flowers and patterns. The old man was hovering about the table, pleased as a child with the bright colors. "Call my brother and his children—let them see!" he said.

But O-lan, her hands all dusty with the fine rice flour, said, "Those are not for us to eat. I am preparing them for the old mistress. I shall take the child on the second day of the new year and carry the cakes as a gift."

The cakes were more important than ever, then, and Wang Lung was pleased that to the great hall where he had stood with so much timidity and in such poverty his wife would now go as a visitor, carrying his son dressed in a red coat and cakes as fine as these.

Everything else that happened that New Year sank into insignificance. His new coat of black sateen that O-lan had made for him only made him say to himself, "I shall wear it when I take them to the great house."

He even bore carelessly the first day of the new year when his uncle and his neighbors came crowding into the house to wish his father and himself well, all boisterous with food and drink, although he found it very hard when the plain white cakes were praised not to cry out, "You should see the colored ones!"

But he did not, for more than anything he wished to enter the great house with pride.

THEN ON the second day of the new year, the day for women to visit one another, they rose at dawn and the woman dressed the child in his red coat and in the tiger-faced shoes she had made. On his head she put the crownless red hat with the small gilt Buddha sewn on front, and she set him on the bed. Then Wang Lung quickly dressed while his wife combed out her long black hair and knotted it with a brass pin that he had bought for her, and she put on her new coat of black that was made from the same piece as his own new robe. Then she picked up the child and he the basket of cakes, and they set out on the path across the fields.

Wang Lung had his reward at the great gate of the House of Hwang, for the gateman opened his eyes wide at all he saw, and he twirled the three long hairs on his mole and cried out, "Ah, Wang the farmer, three this time instead of one! One has no need to wish you more good fortune this year than you have had in the last."

Wang Lung answered negligently, "Good harvests—good harvests—" and he stepped with assurance inside the gate.

"Do sit within my wretched room," the gateman said, "while I announce your woman and son within."

And Wang Lung stood proudly watching them go across the court, his wife and his son, bearing gifts to the head of a great house. It was all to his honor, and when they were gone from his sight down the long vista of the courts, he went into the gateman's house and there he accepted from the gateman's pockmarked wife the honorable seat to the left of the table, and she presented him with a bowl of tea.

It seemed a long time before the gateman returned, bringing back the woman and child. Wang Lung looked closely at O-lan's face to see if all was well, for he had learned now to detect small changes in her countenance that were at first invisible to him. She wore a look of heavy content, and he became impatient to hear her tell of what had happened. With a short bow to the gateman he hurried O-lan away and took the child into his own arms.

"Well?" he called back to her over his shoulder. For once he was impatient with her slowness. She drew a little nearer to him and said in a whisper, "I believe that they are feeling a pinch this year in that house."

"What do you mean?" said Wang Lung, urging her to go on. But she would not be hastened. Words were to her things to be caught one by one and released with difficulty. "The ancient mistress wore the same coat this year as last. I have never seen this happen before." And then after a pause she said, "I saw not one slave with a new coat like mine." And then after a while she said, "As for our son, there was not even a child among the concubines of the old master himself to compare to him in beauty and in dress."

A slow smile spread over her face and Wang Lung laughed aloud and held the child tenderly. How well he had done! And then as he exulted he was smitten with fear. What a foolish thing he was doing, walking like this under an open sky, with a beautiful son for any evil spirit to see! He opened his coat hastily and thrust the child's head into his bosom, and he said in a loud voice, "What a pity our child is a female whom no one could want and covered with smallpox as well! Let us pray she may die."

"Yes—yes—" said his wife as quickly as she could, understanding what a thing they had done.

And being comforted with these precautions, Wang Lung once more urged his wife. "Did you find out why they are poorer?"

"I had but a moment for private talk with the cook," she replied, "but the cook said, 'This house cannot stand forever with all the young lords spending money like waste water in foreign parts, and the old mistress eating enough opium every day to fill two shoes with silver.'"

"Do they indeed?" murmured Wang Lung, spellbound.

"The old mistress herself told me they wished to sell some of the land just outside the city wall, where they have always planted rice each year because it is good land and easily flooded from the moat around the wall."

"Sell their land!" repeated Wang Lung. "Then indeed they are growing poor. Land is one's flesh and blood."

He pondered for a while, and suddenly a thought came to him and he smote the side of his head with his palm. "What I have not thought of!" he cried, turning to the woman. "We will buy the land!"

They stared at each other, he in delight, she in stupefaction.

"Buy the land—the land—" she stammered.

"I will buy it!" he cried in a lordly voice. "I will buy it from the great House of Hwang!"

"It is certainly better than putting money into a mud wall," she said pacifically. "But why not buy a piece of your uncle's land? He is clamoring to sell that strip near the western field."

"That land of my uncle's," said Wang Lung, "I would not have it. He has been dragging a crop out of it for twenty years, and not a bit of manure has he put back. No, I will buy Hwang's land."

He said "Hwang's land" as casually as he might have said "Ching's land." He would be more than equal to those people in the great house. He would go before the old lord with the silver in his hand and say, "I have money. What is the price of the land you wish to sell?"

And it was as though his wife knew his thoughts, for again the slow smile spread over her face, and after a long time she said, "Last year this time I was a slave in that house."

And they walked on, silent with the fullness of this thought.

IV

THIS PIECE of land greatly changed Wang Lung's life. At first, after he had dug the silver from the wall and taken it to the great house, he was overcome with a depression of spirit that was close to regret. After all, this land would take hours of labor, and it was more than a third of a mile away. And again, the buying of it had not been quite so filled with glory as he had anticipated. He had gone too early to the great house. True, it was noon, but when he had said in a loud voice, "Tell the old lord I have important business—tell him money is concerned!" the gateman had answered, "All the money in the world would not tempt me to wake the old tiger."

In the end, it had had to be managed with the old lord's agent, an oily scoundrel whose hands were heavy with the money that stuck to them in passing. When Wang Lung had poured out his silver proudly, the agent had scraped it up carelessly and said, "Enough for a few days of opium for the old lady, at any rate."

Well, but the land was his! Wang Lung set out one gray day in the second month of the new year to look at it, a long rectangle of heavy black clay that stretched beside the moat of the town. He paced the land off carefully, three hundred paces lengthwise and a hundred and twenty across. Four stones still marked the corners, and on each was the great seal of the House of Hwang. Well, he would have that changed. He would put his own name there—not yet, for he was not ready for people to know that he was rich enough to buy land, but later, when he was richer, so that it did not matter what he did. And looking at that long rectangle of land he thought to himself, To those at the great house it means nothing, this handful of earth, but to me it means so much!

And the distance that still lay between him and the great house seemed suddenly as impassable as the moat full of water and as high as the wall beyond. He was filled with an angry determination then, and he said to his heart that he would fill that hole with silver again and again until he had bought from the House of Hwang enough land so that *this* land would seem less than an inch in his sight.

SPRING CAME with blustering winds and clouds of rain, and for Wang Lung the half-idle days of winter were plunged into long days of desperate labor. The old man looked after the child now and O-lan worked with Wang Lung from dawn until sunset. When Wang Lung perceived one day that she was again with child, his first thought was that she would be unable to work during the harvest. He shouted at her, irritable with fatigue, "So you have chosen this time to breed again, have you!"

She answered stoutly, "This time it is nothing. It is only the first that is hard."

Beyond this nothing was said of the second child until one morning in autumn when she laid down her hoe and crept into the house. He did not go back that day even for his noon meal, for the sky was heavy with thunderclouds and his rice lay ripe for gathering. Before sunset she was back beside him, her body flattened, spent, but her face silent and undaunted.

His impulse was to say, "For this day you have had enough. Go and lie upon your bed." But the aching of his own body made him cruel, and he only asked between the strokes of his scythe, "Is it male or female?"

She answered calmly, "It is another male."

They said no more, but he was pleased, and working on until the moon rose above a bank of purple clouds, they finished the field and went home.

After his meal Wang Lung went in to look at his second son. O-lan was lying on the bed with the child beside her—a fat, placid child, well enough but not quite as large as the first one. Wang Lung went back to the middle room well content. Another son, and another and another each year—one could not trouble with red eggs every year; it was enough to do it for the first. The house was full of good fortune; this woman brought him nothing but good fortune. He shouted to his father, "Now, Old One, with another grandson we shall have to put the big one in your bed!"

For a long time the old man had wanted this child to sleep in his bed, but the child would not leave his mother. Now, however, toddling in with feet still unsteady with babyhood, he stared at this new child beside his mother, and seemed to comprehend that another had his place; he allowed himself without protest to be placed in his grandfather's bed.

And again the harvests were good and Wang Lung again hid silver in the wall.

WANG LUNG's uncle began at this time to become the trouble that Wang Lung had always expected he might. This uncle was the younger brother of Wang Lung's father, and by all the claims of relationship he could depend on Wang Lung if he had not enough for himself and his family. So long as Wang Lung and his father were poor, the uncle made muster to scratch about on his own land and gather enough to feed his seven children and his wife and himself. But once fed, none of them worked. The wife would not stir herself to sweep the floor of their hut. As the girls grew older they ran about the village streets and left their hair uncombed, and some-times even talked to men. Wang Lung, meeting his oldest girl cousin thus one day, was so angered for the disgrace done to his family that he dared to go to his uncle's wife and say, "Now, who will marry a girl like my cousin, whom any man may look on? She has been marriageable for three years and today I saw an idle lout lay his hand on her arm and she answered him with brazen laughter!"

His uncle's wife had nothing active in her body except her tongue and this she now loosed upon Wang Lung. "Well, and who will pay for the dowry and for the middleman's fees? It is all very well for those to talk who have more land than they know what to do with, but your uncle is an unfortunate man and he has been so from the first." She broke into easy tears, and began to work herself up into a fury. She snatched at her knot of hair and tore down the loose hair about her face and began to scream, "Ah, it is something you do not know—to have an evil destiny! Where the fields of others bear good rice, ours bear weeds; where the houses of others stand for a hundred years, the earth itself shakes under ours so that the walls crack; where others bear sons, I, although I conceive a son, will yet give birth to a girl—ah, evil destiny! " She shrieked aloud, so that the neighbors rushed out of their houses to see what was the matter.

Wang Lung stood stoutly, however, and would finish what he had come to say. "Nevertheless," he said, "although it is not for me to presume to advise the brother of my father, I will say this: it is better that the girl be married."

Having spoken plainly, he went away and left his uncle's

wife screaming. He had it in his mind to buy more land this year from the House of Hwang, and it angered him as he saw himself and his sons rising into a landed family that this shiftless brood should be running loose, bearing the same name as his own.

The next day his uncle came to the field where he was working. O-lan was not there, for ten moons had passed since the second child was born and a third birth was close upon her, and this time she was not so well. His uncle came slouching along a furrow, his clothes held insecurely with his girdle, so that it seemed that if a gust of wind blew at him he might suddenly stand naked.

Wang Lung said maliciously without looking up, "I ask your pardon, my uncle, for not stopping my work. These beans must, if they are to bear, be cultivated twice and thrice. Yours, doubtless, are finished. I am very slow—a poor farmer—never finishing my work in time to rest."

But his uncle answered smoothly, "I am a man of evil destiny. This year out of twenty seed beans, one came up. There is no use in putting the hoe down. We shall have to buy beans this year if we are to eat them." He sighed heavily.

Wang Lung knew that his uncle had come to ask something of him. He put his hoe down into the ground, breaking up the tiniest clod in the soft earth already well cultivated. The bean plants stood erect in thrifty order, casting little fringes of shadow in the sunshine.

At last his uncle began to speak. "My wife has told me," he said, "of your interest in my worthless oldest slave creature. It is wholly true what you say. She should be married. I am terrified constantly that she might bring shame to our name."

Wang Lung put his hoe down hard into the soil. He would have liked to say, "Why do you not control her, then? Why do you not keep her decently in the house and make her sweep and cook?" But those things could not be said to a member of an older generation. He remained silent, therefore, and waited.

"If it had been my good destiny," continued his uncle

mournfully, "to have married a wife who could work and at the same time produce sons instead of a woman who grows nothing but flesh and gives birth to nothing but females and that one idle son of mine, I, too, might have been rich now as you are. Then I might have—willingly I would have shared my riches with you. I would have wed your daughters to good men; I would have placed your son in a merchant's shop as an apprentice; I would have been delighted to repair your house; and I would have fed you with the best I had—you and your father and your children, for we are of one blood."

Wang Lung answered shortly, "You know I am not rich. I have five mouths to feed, and another mouth is being born in my house at this very moment."

His uncle replied shrilly, "You are rich—rich! Is there another in the village who could have bought land from the great house?"

At this Wang Lung was goaded to anger. He flung down his hoe and shouted suddenly, glaring at his uncle, "If I have a handful of silver it is because I work and my wife works, and we do not—as some do—sit idling over a gambling table or gossiping on doorsteps, letting the fields grow to weeds!"

The blood flew to his uncle's face as he rushed at his nephew and slapped him on both cheeks. "Now that," he cried, "is for speaking so to your father's generation! Have you no religion, no morals? Have you not heard that in the Sacred Edicts it is commanded that no man is ever to correct an elder?"

Wang Lung stood sullen, conscious of his fault but angry to the bottom of his heart.

"I will tell your words to the whole village!" screamed his furious uncle in a high, cracked voice. "Yesterday you attack my house and my daughter; today you reproach me, who, if your father passes on, must be as your own father to you!"

At last Wang Lung said unwillingly, "What do you want me to do?"

His uncle changed immediately. The anger melted out of him. He smiled and put his hand on Wang Lung's arm. "Ah, I know you—good lad—good lad—" he said softly. "A little silver in this poor old palm—say, ten pieces, or even nine— and I could begin to make arrangements with a matchmaker for that slave of mine. Ah, you are right! It is time—it is time!"

Wang Lung picked up his hoe and threw it down again. "Come to the house," he said shortly. "I do not carry silver on me like a prince." And he strode ahead, bitter beyond words because some of the good silver with which he had planned to buy more land was to go in his uncle's palm, from whence it would slip onto the gambling table before nightfall.

He strode into the house, brushing out of his way his two small sons who played naked in the warm sunshine. His uncle, with idle good nature, called to the children and took from some recess in his clothing a copper coin for each child. "Ah, you are two little men," he said, clasping one in either arm.

But Wang Lung went into the room where he slept. It was very dark, and except for the square of light from the hole, he could see nothing. But he heard movement, and so he called out sharply, "What now—has your time come?"

His wife answered from the bed more feebly than he had ever heard her speak, "It is over. It is only a slave this time— not worth mentioning."

Wang Lung stood still. A sense of evil struck him. A girl! A girl was causing all this trouble in his uncle's house. Now a girl had been born into his house as well.

He went without reply then to the wall and removed the clod of earth. He fumbled among the little heap of silver and counted out nine pieces. Then he went out to his uncle, thrust the money at him and walked quickly back to the field. There he fell to working as though he meant to tear the earth from its foundations.

It was evening before his anger was spent. And then he thought of that new mouth come into his house and it struck him with heaviness that the birth of daughters had begun for him, daughters who do not belong to their parents but are

45

born and reared for other families. He had not even thought, in his anger at his uncle, to stop and see the face of this small new creature.

As he stood leaning upon his hoe he was seized with sadness and he groaned aloud. It was an evil omen.

V

IT SEEMS that once the gods turn against a man they will not consider him again. The rains, which should have come in early summer, withheld themselves, and day after day the skies shone with brilliance, and at night the stars hung out of the sky, golden and cruel in their beauty.

The fields dried and cracked although Wang Lung cultivated them desperately, and the young wheat stalks, which had sprung up courageously in the spring, dwindled and yellowed into a barren harvest. The young rice beds were squares of jade upon the brown earth. Wang Lung carried water to them day after day when he had given up the wheat, the heavy wooden buckets slung upon a bamboo pole across his shoulders. But though a furrow marred his flesh, no rain came.

At last the water in the pond dried into a cake of clay and even the water in the well sank so low that O-lan said to him, "If the children drink and the old man has his hot water, then the plants must go dry."

Wang Lung answered with anger that broke into a sob, "Well, and they must all starve if the plants starve."

Only the land by the moat bore harvest, and this was because at last Wang Lung abandoned his other fields and stayed the day out at this one, dipping water from the moat to pour upon the greedy soil. This year for the first time he sold his grain as soon as it was harvested, and when he felt the silver in his palm, he gripped it hard in defiance. He would, in spite of gods and drought, do that which he had determined. And he hurried to the House of Hwang.

Now Wang Lung had heard that for the House of Hwang it had been a year verging upon poverty; there, too, there were no harvests. The old lady had not had her full dole of opium for many days and was like an old tigress in her hunger. Each day she sent for the agent and cursed him and struck his face with her fan, screaming at him, "And are there not acres of land left yet?" until he was beside himself.

As if this were not enough, the old lord took yet another concubine, a girl of sixteen. As with the old mistress and her opium, there was no making him understand there was no money for jade earrings. He could not comprehend the words no money, for all his life he had had but to reach out his hand to fill it.

And the young lords shrugged their shoulders and said there must still be enough for their lifetimes. They united only in berating the agent, so that he who had once been unctuous, a man of plenty and of ease, was now anxious and harried so that his skin hung upon him like an old garment. So when Wang Lung went to the agent saying, "I have silver," it was as though he had said, "I have food," to the hungry. And where before there had been dickering, now the two men spoke in eager whispers; the money passed quickly from one hand to the other and the papers were signed and sealed. The land was Wang Lung's.

Wang Lung did not count the passing of his silver a hard thing. He had now a vast field of good land, for the new field was twice as large as the first. But more to him than its dark fertility was the fact that it had belonged once to the family of a prince.

MONTH PASSED into month and still no rain fell. The sky was empty and barren, and the stately sun rose each morning and made its march and set each night. And the moon in its time shone as brightly as a lesser sun.

From his fields Wang Lung reaped a scanty harvest of hardy beans, and from his cornfield, which he had planted in despair when the rice beds had yellowed and died, he plucked short stubby ears with the grains scattered here and there. There was not a bean lost in the threshing, and he shelled the corn in the middle room, watching sharply every grain that flew wide. When he would have put the cobs away for fuel, his wife spoke out, "No—do not waste them. I remember when I was a child that in years like this, even the cobs we ground and ate. It is better than grass."

When she had spoken they all fell silent. There was foreboding in these strangely brilliant days when the land was failing them. And then, as though there were not enough evil, O-lan was again with child, and her milk dried up, and the house was filled with the frightening sound of a child crying for food.

IF ONE HAD asked Wang Lung, "And how are you eating through the autumn?" he would have answered, "I do not know—a little food here and there." But in the whole countryside no one asked questions of any other. No one asked anything except of himself, "How shall I eat this day?" And parents said, "How shall we eat, we and our children?"

Now Wang Lung had cared for his ox as long as he could. He had given the beast a bit of straw and a handful of vines until winter came and these were gone. Then he turned the ox out to hunt for itself, sending the older boy to sit on its back all day. But lately he had not dared to do this, for fear that men from the village, or even his neighbors, might overcome the lad and seize the ox for food. So he kept the ox on the threshold until it grew as lean as its skeleton.

But there came a day when there were only a few beans left and a meager store of corn, and the ox lowed with hunger.

The old man said, "We will eat the ox next."

Then Wang Lung cried out, for it was to him as if his father had said, "We will eat a man next." The ox was his companion in the fields; he had walked behind it and praised it and cursed it from his youth. And he said, "How can we eat the ox? How shall we plow again?"

But the old man answered tranquilly, "Well, a man can buy an ox again more easily than his own life."

But Wang Lung would not kill it that day. The next day passed and the next, and the children cried out for food and O-lan looked at Wang Lung, beseeching him for the children, and he saw at last that the thing had to be done. So he said roughly, "Let it be killed, then, but I cannot do it." And he laid himself upon the bed and wrapped the quilt about his head so that he could not hear the beast's bellowing when it died.

Then O-lan crept out and took a great iron knife and cut a gash in the beast's neck, severing its life.

But when Wang Lung tried to eat the flesh of his ox, his gorge rose. O-lan said to him, "An ox is but an ox and this one grew old. Eat, for there will be another one day."

Wang Lung was a little comforted then and managed to eat a little with them. But the ox was all too quickly gone.

At first it was supposed in the village that Wang Lung had food stored away. His uncle, who was among the first to be hungry, came importuning to his door. Wang Lung measured unwillingly a small heap of beans and a precious handful of corn into the skirt of his uncle's robe. Then he said with firmness, "It is all I can spare. I have first my old father to consider, even if I had no children."

When his uncle came again, Wang Lung cried out, "Even filial piety will not feed my house!" and he sent his uncle away empty-handed. From that day his uncle turned against him like a dog that has been kicked.

As family after family finished its store and spent its last coin in the scanty markets of the town and as the winds of winter came down, cold as a knife of steel, the hearts of the villagers grew distraught with their hunger. When Wang Lung's uncle shivered about the streets like a lean dog, whispering, "There is one who has food—there is one whose children are still fat," the men took up poles and went to the house of Wang Lung and beat on the door. When Wang Lung opened it, his neighbors pushed him out of the doorway, and then they fell upon every corner to find where he had hidden his food. When they found his wretched store of a few dried beans and a bowlful of dried corn, they gave a great howl of disappointment and seized his bits of furniture, the table, the benches and the bed where the old man lay frightened and weeping.

O-lan came forward and spoke, and her plain, slow voice rose above the men. "Not that—not that yet," she called out. "You have all our food. But out of your own houses you have not yet sold your own table and benches. Leave us ours. We are even. Heaven will strike you if you take more. Now, we will go out together and hunt for grass to eat and bark from the trees, you for your children, and we for our three children, and for this fourth who is to be born in such times." She pressed her hand to her belly as she spoke, and the men were ashamed before her and went out one by one, for they were not evil men except when they starved.

One lingered, the one called Ching. He would have spoken some good word of shame, for only his crying child had forced him to evil. But in his bosom was a handful of beans he had snatched and he was fearful lest he must return them if he spoke, and so he only looked at Wang Lung with haggard, speechless eyes and went out.

Wang Lung stood there in his dooryard where year after year he had threshed his good harvests. There was an anger in him now that he could not express. And he walked, dragging one foot after the other in his famished weakness, to the temple of the earth, and deliberately he spat upon the faces of the gods. There had been no sticks of incense now for many moons, and their paper clothes were tattered. But they sat there unmoved and Wang Lung gnashed his teeth at them and walked back to his house groaning and fell upon his bed.

They scarcely rose at all now, any of them. Fitful sleep took the place of food. They had dried and eaten the cobs of the corn and stripped the bark from trees; all over the countryside people were eating what grass they could find on the wintry hills. There was not an animal anywhere.

One never saw in these days a child playing upon the village street. At most the two boys in Wang Lung's house crept to the door and sat in the cruel sun. Their once rounded bodies were angular and bony now, with sharp small bones like the bones of birds, except for their ponderous bellies, swollen out with empty wind.

Although at first the angry insistence of her crying had filled the house, the girl-child lay uncomplaining, hour after hour, wrapped in an old quilt. Her little hollowed face looked out at them all, little sunken blue lips like a toothless old woman's, and hollow black eyes peering. The persistence of this small life in some way won her father's affection, although if she had been round and merry, he would have been careless because she was a girl. Sometimes, looking at her, he whispered softly, "Poor fool—poor little fool." And once when she essayed a weak smile, he broke into tears and took into his lean, hard hand her small claw and held the tiny grasp of her fingers over his forefinger. Thereafter he would sometimes lift her and thrust her inside his coat against his flesh and sit with her so by the threshold of the house, looking out over the dry, flat fields.

As for the old man, he fared better than any, for if there was anything to eat he was given it. Wang Lung said to himself proudly that no one could say in the hour of death he had forgotten his father.

There was a day when his neighbor Ching, worn now to less than the shadow of a human creature, came to Wang Lung's door and whispered, "We have eaten the beasts and the grass and the bark of trees. What now remains for food?"

Wang Lung shook his head hopelessly, and looked down into the delicate bony face of his daughter, and into the sharp, sad eyes that watched him unceasingly from his breast. When he caught those eyes in his glance, invariably there wavered upon the child's face a flickering smile that broke his heart.

Ching thrust his face nearer. "In the village they are eating human flesh," he whispered. "It is said your uncle and his wife are eating. How else are they living with strength enough to walk about—they who have never had anything?"

Wang Lung drew back from the deathlike head, afraid with a fear he did not understand. He rose quickly as though to cast off some entangling danger. "We will leave this place," he said loudly. "We will go south! We must, lest we forget our nature and eat each other as the wild dogs do."

And then it seemed to him suddenly that what he said was very right, and he called aloud to O-lan, who lay upon the bed, "Come, woman, we will go south!"

There was cheer in his voice that had not been heard in many moons, and the children looked up and the old man hobbled out from his room. O-lan rose feebly from her bed and came to the door of their room, and clinging to the door frame, she said, "It is a good thing to do. One can at least die walking."

The child in her body hung from her lean loins like a knotty fruit and from her face every particle of flesh was gone so that the jagged bones stood forth rocklike under her skin. "Only wait until tomorrow," she said. "I shall have given birth by then."

Then Wang Lung saw his wife's face and he was moved with pity. "How shall you walk, you poor creature!" he muttered, and he said unwillingly to Ching, who still leaned against the house by the door, "If you have any food left, give me a handful to save the life of the mother of my sons, and I will forget that I saw you in my house as a robber."

Ching looked at him ashamed and answered humbly, "I have never thought of you with peace since that hour. It was that dog, your uncle, who enticed me. Before this cruel Heaven I promise you that I have only a handful of dried red beans buried beneath the stone of my doorway. This I and my wife placed there for our last hour, for our daughter and ourselves, that we might die with a little food in our stomachs. But some of it I will give to you. Tomorrow go south, if you can. I stay, I and my household. I have no son, and it does not matter whether I live or die."

And he went away and in a little while he came back, bringing tied in a cotton kerchief a double handful of small red beans, moldy with the soil. The children clambered about at the sight of the food, and the old man's eyes glistened. But Wang Lung pushed them away for once and took the food in to his wife. She ate a little of it, bean by bean, unwillingly except that her hour was upon her and she knew that if she did not have food, she would die in the clutches of her pain.

Wang Lung put a few of the beans into his own mouth and chewed them into a soft pulp. Then he put his lips to the lips of his daughter and pushed the pulp into her mouth. Watching her small lips move, he felt himself fed.

That night he stayed in the middle room, as he had during the birth of his firstborn son. He listened intently for the small sharp cry he knew so well, and he listened with despair. "It would be merciful if there were no breath," he muttered, and then he heard the feeble cry—how feeble a cry!—hang for an instant upon the stillness. "But there is no mercy of any kind in these days," he finished bitterly.

There was no second cry, and over the house the stillness became impenetrable. Wang Lung could not bear it. He was afraid. He rose and went to the door of the room. He called out and the sound of his own voice heartened him a little. "You are safe?" he called to the woman. He listened. Suppose she had died as he sat there! But he could hear a slight rustling, and at last she answered, her voice a sigh, "Come!"

He went in then and she lay there upon the bed, her body scarcely raising the cover. She lay alone.

"Where is the child?" he asked.

She made a slight movement of her hand and he saw on the floor the child's body—a wisp of bone and skin—a girl.

"Dead!" he exclaimed.

"Dead," she whispered.

He was about to say, "But I heard it cry"—and then he looked at O-lan's face. Her eyes were closed and the color of her flesh was the color of ashes and her bones stuck up under the skin. She lay there silently, having endured to the utmost, and there was nothing he could say. After all, during these months he had had only his own body to drag about. What agony of starvation this woman had endured, with the starved creature gnawing at her from within, desperate for its own life! He said nothing, but he took the dead child into the other room and laid her upon the earthen floor and searched until he found a bit of broken mat and this he used to wrap her in. Upon her neck he saw two dark bruised spots, but he finished what he had to do. Then he took the roll of matting, and went as far from the house as he had strength and laid his burden against an old grave at the border of his western field. Now he felt his legs sinking beneath him, and he covered his face with his hands. "It is better as it is," he muttered to himself, and for the first time he was wholly filled with despair.

THE NEXT MORNING, when the sun rose unchanging in its sky of varnished blue, it seemed to him a dream that he could ever have thought of leaving his house. How could they drag their bodies over a hundred miles, even to plenty? He had no money. Long ago the last coin had gone. And who knew whether or not they would wear out all their last strength only to find more starving people and these strangers to them as well? Far better to stay where they could die in their beds. He sat despondent on the threshold of the door and gazed bleakly over the dried and hardened fields.

And then, as he sat there giving up his hope, he saw four men walking across the fields toward him. One was his uncle and with him were three men he did not know.

"I have not seen you these many days," called his uncle with loud and affected good humor. "And how well you have fared! And your father, my elder brother, he is well?"

Wang Lung looked at his uncle. The man was thin, it was true, but not starving, as he should be. Wang Lung felt in his own shriveled body the last remaining strength of life gathering into a devastating anger. "How you have eaten—how you have eaten!" he muttered thickly. He thought nothing of these strangers or of any courtesy. He saw only that his uncle still had flesh on his bones.

His uncle opened wide his eyes and threw up his hands to the sky. "Eaten!" he cried. "If you could see my house! Not even a sparrow could pick up a crumb there. My wife—do you remember how fat she was? Now she is nothing but the poor bones rattling together in her skin. And of our children only four are left—the three little ones gone—gone—and as for me, you see me!" He took the edge of his sleeve and wiped the corner of each eye carefully.

"You have eaten," repeated Wang Lung dully.

"I have borrowed a little food from these good men in the town," retorted his uncle briskly, "on the promise that I would help them to buy some land. And I thought of you first of all, you, the son of my brother. They have come to buy your land and to give you money—food—life!" His uncle, having said these words, stepped back and folded his arms with a flourish of his dirty and ragged robes.

Wang Lung did not rise. But he lifted his head and saw that the men were indeed from the town, dressed in long robes of soiled silk. Their hands were soft and their nails long. He suddenly hated them with an intense hatred. Here were these well-fed men, standing beside him whose children were starving; here they were, come to squeeze his land from him in his extremity. He looked up at them sullenly, his eyes deep in his bony, skull-like face. "I will not sell my land," he said.

His uncle stepped forward. At this instant Wang Lung's younger son came creeping to the doorway on his hands and knees. The child had gone back to crawling because he had so little strength.

"Is that your lad," cried the uncle, "the fat little one I gave a copper to in the summer?"

And they all looked at the child, and suddenly Wang Lung began to weep silently, the tears gathering in great knots of pain in his throat and rolling down his cheeks. "What is your price?" he whispered at last.

One of the men from the city spoke, a man with one eye blind and sunken in his face. Unctuously he said, "My poor man, for the sake of the boy, we will give you a better price than could be got in these times anywhere. We will give you . . ." He paused and then said harshly, "We will give you a hundred pennies an acre!"

Wang Lung laughed bitterly. "Why, that is taking my land for a gift. I pay twenty times that when I buy land."

"Ah, but not when you buy it from men who are starving," said the other man.

Wang Lung looked at them. They were sure of him, these men! What will a man not give for his starving children and his old father! He sprang up and at the men as a dog springs at an enemy. "I shall never sell the land!" he shrieked at them. "I will feed the earth itself to the children, and when they die, I will bury them in the land, and I and my wife and my old father, even he, will die on the land that has given us birth!"

He was weeping violently and his anger went out of him as suddenly as a wind as he stood shaking and weeping. The men stood there smiling slightly, unmoved. His talk was madness, and so they waited until his anger was spent.

Suddenly O-lan came to the door and spoke, her voice flat, as though such things were commonplace. "The land we will not sell, surely," she said, "else when we return from the south we shall have nothing to feed us. But we will sell the table, the beds, the benches and even the caldron. But the rakes and the hoes and the plow we will not sell, nor the land."

The calmness in her voice carried more strength than all Wang Lung's anger, and the one-eyed man spoke to the others, and they muttered among themselves. Then the one-eyed man turned and said, "They are poor things and fit only for fuel. Two silver bits for the lot and take it or leave it."

He spoke with contempt, but O-lan answered tranquilly, "It is less than the cost of one bed, but if you have the silver, give it to me quickly and take the things."

The one-eyed man fumbled in his girdle and dropped the silver into her hand, and the men came into the house and took out the table and the benches and the bed in Wang Lung's room, and they wrenched the caldron from the oven on which it stood. But when they went into the old man's room, Wang Lung's uncle stood outside. He did not wish to be there when his older brother was laid on the floor and the bed taken from under him. When all was finished and the house was empty except for the rakes and the hoes and the plow, O-lan said to her husband, "Let us go while we have the silver and before we must sell the rafters of the house and have no hole into which we can crawl when we return."

And Wang Lung answered heavily, "Let us go."

But looking across the fields at the small figures of the men receding, he muttered over and over, "At least I have the land—I have the land."

VI

THERE WAS nothing to do but to pull the door closed on its wooden hinges and fasten the iron hasp. They were wearing all their clothes. Into each child's hands O-lan thrust a rice bowl and a pair of chopsticks, and the two little boys held them tight as a promise of food to come. Thus they started across the fields, a dreary small procession moving so slowly that it seemed they would never reach the town.

Soon Wang Lung saw that the old man would fall, and he lifted him on his back and carried him, staggering under the old man's light frame. The bitter wind never ceased to blow against them; the two boys cried of its cold. But Wang Lung coaxed them by saying, "You are two big men, traveling south. There is warmth there and white rice every day."

In time they reached the gate of the wall, resting continually every little way, and where Wang Lung had once delighted in its coolness, now he clenched his teeth against the gust of wintry wind that swept furiously through its channel, as icy water will rush between cliffs. Beneath their feet the thick mud was speared with needles of ice. The little boys could make no headway and O-lan was laden with the girl. Wang Lung staggered through with the old man and set him down. Then he went back and carried the children through one by one, and sweat poured out of him like rain, spending all his strength with it. He had to lean for a long time against the wall, with his eyes shut and his breath coming and going quickly, while his family stood shivering and waiting around him.

They were close to the gate of the great house now, but it was locked fast, and on the steps a few men and women lay cowering. When Wang Lung passed with his miserable little procession one cried out in a cracked voice, "The hearts of the rich are hard like the hearts of the gods. They still have rice, and from the rice they are still making wine, while we starve. A thousand curses to the parents that bore the children of Hwang!"

They went on toward the south. When they passed through the town, it was evening, and they found a multitude of people going in the same direction. Wang Lung asked of one, "Where is all this multitude going?"

And the man said, "We are starving people going to catch the fire wagon and ride it to the south. It leaves from the house over there and costs less than a silver piece."

Fire wagons! Wang Lung had heard men in the tea shop tell of these wagons, chained one to the other and drawn neither by man nor beast, but by a machine breathing fire like a dragon. He had said to himself many times that he would go and see it, but with one thing and another there had never been time.

Now, however, he turned doubtfully to O-lan and said, "Shall we go on this fire wagon?"

They drew the old man and the children a little away from the passing crowd and looked at each other anxiously. At the instant's respite the old man and the little boys sank down on the ground. O-lan carried the girl still, but the child's head hung over her arm with such a look of death that Wang Lung, forgetting all else, cried out, "Is the little slave already dead?"

O-lan shook her head. "Not yet. The breath flutters back and forth in her. But she will die this night and all of us unless—" Then, as if she could say no other word, she looked at him, her square face exhausted and gaunt.

Wang Lung said with what cheer there was to be found in his voice, "Up, my sons, and help your grandfather up. We will go on the fire wagon and sit while we walk south."

At that moment there came thundering out of the darkness a

noise like a dragon's voice and two great eyes puffing fire out, and everyone screamed and ran. In the confusion they were pushed hither and thither, but they clung desperately together until they were pushed in the darkness into a boxlike room, and then with a roar the thing tore forth into the darkness, bearing them in its vitals.

With his two pieces of silver Wang Lung paid for a hundred miles of road. The officer who took his silver gave him back a handful of copper pennies, and with a few of these Wang Lung bought from a vendor who thrust his tray of wares in at a hole in the wagon four small loaves of bread and a bowl of soft rice for the girl. It was more than they had had to eat at one time for many days, and although they were starved for food, desire left them when it was in their mouths. It was only by coaxing that the boys could be made to swallow. But the old man sucked perseveringly at the bread between his toothless gums. "One must eat," he cackled forth, very friendly to all who pressed about him as the wagon rocked on its way.

There were some in the wagon who went each year to the rich cities of the south to work and to beg. And Wang Lung, when he had grown used to the astonishment of seeing the land whirl by the holes in the fire wagon, listened to what these men said. They spoke with the loudness of wisdom where others are ignorant.

"First you must buy six mats," said one man. "These are two pennies for one mat, but if you act like a country bumpkin, you will be charged three. I cannot be fooled by the men in the southern cities, even if they are rich."

Wang Lung listened anxiously. "And then?" he urged. He sat squatting upon his haunches on the bottom of the wagon, which was, after all, only an empty room made of wood, with the wind and the dust flying up through the cracks in the floor.

"Then," said the man, "you bind these together into a hut, and you go out to beg, first smearing yourselves with filth to make yourselves piteous."

"One must beg?" Wang Lung disliked this notion.

"Ah, indeed," said the man, "but not until you have eaten. These people in the south have so much rice that each morning you may go to a public kitchen and for a penny hold as much as you can in your belly of the white rice. Then you can beg comfortably and buy bean curd and cabbage and garlic."

Wang Lung withdrew a little from the others and secretly counted out the pennies he had left. There was enough for the six mats and for rice for each. It came over him with comfort that thus they could begin the new life. But the notion of holding up a bowl and begging continued to distress him. It was very well for the old man and for the children and even for the woman, but he had his two hands. "Is there work?" he asked of the man.

"Aye, work!" said the man with contempt, and he spat upon the floor. "You can rent a ricksha and pull a rich man in the ricksha if you like, and sweat your blood out. Give me begging!" And he cursed so that Wang Lung would not ask anything further of him.

But still it was a good thing that he had heard what the man said, for when the fire wagon had carried them as far as it would and had turned them out upon the ground, Wang Lung had a plan ready. He set the old man and the children against a long gray wall of a house and told O-lan to watch them. Then he went off, asking of this one and that where the market streets lay. At first he could scarcely understand what was said to him, so brittle and sharp were the sounds that these southerners made. But he found the mat shop at last and put his pennies down as one who knew the price and carried away a roll of mats. When he returned, the boys cried out at him in relief, and he saw that they had been filled with terror in this strange place.

Wang Lung looked around to see where he could put his hut. There were already other huts clinging to the wall behind them, like fleas to a dog's back. Wang Lung observed the huts, and then he began to shape his own mats this way and that, but they were stiff and clumsy, being made of split reeds. He was despairing when suddenly O-lan said, "That I can do. I remember it from my childhood."

And she placed the girl on the ground and pulled the mats this way and that and shaped a rounded roof high enough for a man to sit under. She placed bricks that were lying about on the edges of the mats that were on the ground. They went within, and they made a floor with the one remaining mat and sat down.

Sitting thus and looking at each other, it seemed less than possible that the day before they had left their own house and land and were now a hundred miles away. The feeling of plenty in this rich land filled them, and when Wang Lung said, "Let us go and seek the public kitchens," they rose up almost cheerfully and went out once more. This time the small boys clattered their chopsticks against their bowls as they walked, for soon there would be something to put into them. Along the street they met many people like themselves carrying bowls, going to the kitchens for the poor. And with them at last they came to two great buildings made of mats.

In the rear of each building were earthen ovens, larger than any Wang Lung had ever seen, and on them were iron caldrons as big as small ponds; and there was the good white rice, bubbling and boiling, and clouds of fragrant steam. Now the fragrance of rice was the sweetest in the world to them, and they all pressed forward in a great mass. Mothers shouted out in anger for fear that their children would be trodden upon and little babies cried. Caught in their midst, Wang Lung could do nothing but cling to his father and his two sons. He was swept in front of the great caldron, and he held out his bowl. It was filled, and he threw down his pennies. It was all he could do not to be swept on before the thing was done.

Then when they had gone out to the street again and stood eating their rice, he ate and was filled. The children tugged at him then, and he led them all back to the hut. There they lay down and slept until the next morning, for it was the first time since summer that they had been filled with food.

The next morning it was necessary that there be more money. Wang Lung looked at O-lan, doubtful as to what should be done, but O-lan answered him steadily, as though this were the life she had known always, "I and the children can beg and the old man also. His gray hairs will move some who will not give to me."

She called the two boys to her and said to them, "Each take your bowl and hold it thus and cry out thus—"

She held out her empty bowl and called piteously, "A heart, good sir—a heart, good lady! Have a kind heart—a good deed for your life in heaven! Feed a starving child!"

The two little boys stared at her, and Wang Lung also. Where had she learned to cry thus? How much of this woman there was that he did not know! She answered his look saying, "So I called when I was a child and so I was fed. In such a year as this I was sold as a slave."

Then the old man awoke, and the four of them went out on the road to beg. The woman thrust the girl into her bosom, and she cried out at every passerby, "Unless you give, good sir, good lady—this child dies—we starve—" And indeed the child looked dead, her head shaking this way and that, and there were some, a few, who tossed her a small cash.

But the boys began to take the begging as play after a while, and then their mother dragged them into the hut. "You talk of starving and laugh at the same time! You fools, starve then!" And she slapped them until the tears were running down their faces, and then she sent them out saying, "Now you are fit to beg! That and more if you laugh again!"

As for Wang Lung, he went into the streets and asked until he found a place where rickshas were for hire. He went in and hired one for the day and dragged the thing out to the street.

Pulling this rickety wooden wagon on its two wheels behind him, it seemed to him that everyone looked at him for a fool. He was as awkward between its shafts as an ox yoked for the first time, and he could scarcely walk; yet he must run if he was to earn his living. He went into a narrow side street where there were no shops and went up and down for a while to accustom himself, and just as he said to himself in despair that he had better beg, a door opened, and an old man, spectacled and garbed as a teacher, stepped forth and hailed him.

Wang Lung began to tell him that he was too new at it to run, but the old man motioned to him tranquilly to lower the shafts and let him step in. Wang Lung obeyed, not knowing what else to do. Then the old man, sitting erect, said, "Take me to the Confucian temple."

Wang Lung had no knowledge of where the temple stood, but as he went, he asked, and since the road lay along crowded streets, with vendors and carriages and many vehicles like his own, there was no possibility of running, and he walked as swiftly as he was able. He was used to loads upon his back, but not to pulling, and before the temple was in sight his arms were aching and his hands blistered. But at last he lowered the ricksha at the temple gates, and the old man stepped forth and drew out a small coin and gave it to Wang Lung, saying, "Now I never pay more than this, and there is no use in complaint." And with this he went into the temple.

Wang Lung had not complained because he had not seen this coin before, but another ricksha puller standing nearby said, "How far did you pull that old man?" And when Wang Lung told him, the man cried out, "He gave you only half the proper fare. How much did you argue for before you started?"

"I did not argue," said Wang Lung. "He said come and I came."

"Now there is a country lout for you, pigtail and all!" the other man called out to bystanders. "Someone says come and he comes, and he never asks, 'How much will you give me if I come?' Know this, idiot, only white foreigners can be taken without argument. They are such fools they do not know the proper price of anything but let the silver run out of their pockets like water."

Wang Lung felt very ignorant in this crowd of city people, and he pulled his ricksha away without a word in answer,

He had one more passenger during the morning and with this one he argued and agreed upon a price. In the afternoon two more called to him. But at night when he counted out his money, he had only a penny above the rent of the ricksha. He went back to his hut in great bitterness, saying to himself that for labor greater than the labor of a day in a harvest field he had earned only one copper penny. Then the memory of his land came flooding over him. The thought of it, lying back there, far away but waiting and his own, filled him with peace, and so he came back to his hut.

When he entered, he found that O-lan had for her day's begging received forty small cash, and of the boys, the elder had eight cash and the younger thirteen, and with these put together there was more than enough to pay for the rice in the morning.

But the old man had received nothing at all. All day long he had sat by the roadside, but he had not begged. He slept and woke and stared at what passed by him, and then he slept again. And being of the older generation, he could not be reproved. He said merely, "I have sown seed, and I have reaped harvest and thus have I filled my rice bowl. And I have beyond this begotten a son." With this he trusted like a child that he would be fed.

VII

Now AFTER the first sharpness of Wang Lung's hunger was over and he saw that his family had something to eat daily, the strangeness of his life passed. Running about the streets all day long he learned that in the morning the women he drew in his vehicle went to the market, and the men to the schools and to the houses of business. And at night he drew men to big teahouses and to places of pleasure. But none of these places did Wang Lung know for himself, since his feet crossed no threshold except that of his own hut. He lived in the rich city as alien as a rat in a rich man's house.

The little village of huts clinging to the wall never became a part of the city, and once when Wang Lung heard a young man haranguing a crowd at a corner and saying that China must rise against the hated foreigners, he was alarmed and slunk away, thinking that he was the foreigner against whom the young man spoke.

It was only one day when he was on the street of the silk markets looking for a passenger that he learned that there were those who were 'more foreign than he in this city. He happened to pass a shop when someone came out suddenly, a creature the likes of which he had never seen before. He had no idea whether it was male or female, but it was tall and dressed in a straight black robe of some rough material, and the skin of a dead animal was wrapped about its neck. As he passed, the person motioned to him sharply to lower the shafts, and he did so. When he stood erect again, dazed at what had befallen him, the person in broken accents directed that he was to go to the Street of Bridges. He began to run hurriedly, scarcely knowing what he did, and he called to another puller whom he was passing, "Look at this—what is this I pull?"

And the man shouted back at him, "A foreigner—a female from America. You are rich—"

But Wang Lung ran as fast as he could for fear of the strange creature behind him, and when he reached the Street of Bridges, he was exhausted and dripping with sweat.

The female stepped out then and said, "You need not have run yourself to death," and left him with double the usual fare.

Then Wang Lung knew that this was indeed a foreigner and more foreign yet than he, and that people of black hair and black eyes are one sort and people of light hair and light eyes of another sort, and after that he was no longer wholly foreign in the city.

In this great, sprawling, opulent city it seemed that there could not be any lack of food. The cobbled streets of the fish market were lined with great baskets of silver fish; at the grain markets there were such baskets of grain that a man might step into them; and at the meat markets whole hogs hung by their necks, split open the length of their great bodies; and from the ceilings hung row upon row of brown baked ducks, white salted ducks, and geese and pheasant and every kind of fowl. As for the vegetables, there was everything that the hand of man could coax from the soil: bright red radishes, lotus root and taro, green cabbages and celery, curling bean sprouts and garnishes of cress. There was nothing that a man might desire that was not to be found in the markets of that city. Going hither and thither were the vendors of sweets and fruits and nuts and of hot delicacies—sweet potatoes

browned in oil and delicately spiced balls of pork wrapped in dough and sugar cakes made from rice—and the children of the city ran out to the vendors with pennies to buy these good things to eat. Yes, one would say that in this city there could be no one who starved.

Still, every morning a little after dawn Wang Lung and his family joined a long procession of people, all shivering in clothes too thin for the damp river fog, walking to the public kitchens. And with all Wang Lung's pulling and with all O-lan's begging, they never could gain enough to cook rice in their own hut. If there was a penny over and above the price of the rice at the kitchens, they bought a bit of cabbage. But the cabbage was dear and the boys had to hunt for fuel to cook it between the bricks O-lan had set up for an oven.

One night he came home late and there in the stew of cabbage was a good round piece of pork. It was the first time they had had meat to eat since they had killed their own ox, and Wang Lung's eyes widened. "You must have begged of a foreigner this day," he said to O-lan. But she said nothing.

Then the younger boy, too young for wisdom and filled with his own pride, said, "I took it—it is mine, this meat. When the butcher looked the other way after he had sliced it off, I seized it and ran into an alley and hid."

"Now I will not eat this meat!" cried Wang Lung angrily. "Beggars we may be, but thieves we are not." He took the meat out of the pot with his fingers and threw it on the ground and was heedless of the lad's howling.

Then O-lan came forward in her stolid fashion and picked up the meat and washed it off and thrust it back into the pot. "Meat is meat," she said quietly.

Wang Lung said nothing then, but he was angry and afraid in his heart because his sons were growing into thieves, and he himself would have none of the meat, contenting himself with the cabbage. But after the meal was over he took his younger son into the street and put the boy's head under his arm and cuffed it soundly. "There and there and there!" he shouted. "That for a thief!" But to himself, when he had let the sniveling lad go home, he said, "We must get back to the land."

THUS DAY by day beneath the opulence of the city Wang Lung lived in the foundations of poverty upon which it was laid. With the food spilling out of the markets and rich men clothed in satin and in velvet, in the part of the city where Wang Lung lived there was not enough food to feed savage hunger, nor enough clothes to cover bones.

Men labored all day at baking bread and cakes for feasts for the rich, and yet they were not given enough money to buy a piece of the rich bread they made for others. And men and women labored with furs and thick brocaded silks, cutting and shaping them into sumptuous robes for the rich, and they themselves snatched a bit of coarse blue cotton cloth and sewed it hastily together to cover their own bareness.

In the huts around Wang Lung's, the women sewed rags together to make clothes for the children, and they wandered about the nearby countryside, snatching at bits of cabbage in the fields and stealing handfuls of rice from the grain markets. And at harvest they followed the reapers like fowl, their eyes sharp for every dropped grain. Through these huts passed children; they were born and died and were born until mothers and fathers scarcely knew how many were living.

The old men and the old women accepted the life they had. But there was talk among the young men, angry, growling talk. The scattered anger of their youth became settled into a fierce despair because all their lives they had labored more severely than beasts for only a handful of food. Listening to such talk one evening, Wang Lung heard for the first time what was on the other side of the wall to which their huts clung.

It was at the end of one of those days in late winter when for the first time it seems possible that spring may come again. The ground about the huts was still muddy with the melting snow and the water ran into the huts so that each family had hunted for a few bricks upon which to sleep. But there was this night a soft mildness in the air that made Wang Lung restless, and there arose within him a mighty longing for his fields. And he said roughly to his wife, "If I had anything to sell, I would sell it and go back to the land."

O-lan had been rinsing their rice bowls with a little water, and now she piled them neatly in a corner of the hut and looked at him. "There is nothing to sell except the girl," she answered slowly.

Wang Lung's breath caught. "Now, I would not sell a child!" he said loudly.

"I was sold," she answered. "I was sold to a great house so that my parents could return to their home."

"And would you sell the child, therefore?"

"If it were only I, she would be killed before she was sold.

But a dead girl brings nothing. I would sell this girl for you—
to take you back to the land."

"Never would I," said Wang Lung stoutly, "even if I spend
my life in this wilderness." And he went out to the street and
stood there idle.

Here his old father habitually sat leaning against the wall
and here he sat now, holding in one hand the end of a loop of
cloth that O-lan had torn from her girdle, and within this loop
the girl toddled to and fro. Thus he spent his days looking after
this child who had now grown rebellious at having to be in her
mother's bosom as she begged. Wang Lung looked at the small
girl, staggering persistently at the end of the loop. She had
grown greatly on the food given her each day, and although
she had as yet said no words at all, her lips that had been like
an old woman's were smiling and red, and as of old she grew
merry when he looked at her and she smiled.

I might have done it, he mused, if she had not lain in my
bosom and smiled like that.

And then he thought again of his land and cried out passionately, "Shall I never see it again! With all this labor and
begging there is never enough to do more than feed us today."

Then out of the dusk there answered him a deep burly
voice, "You are not the only one. There are a hundred hundred like you in the city."

It was the father of the family in the hut next to Wang
Lung's. He was a man seldom seen in the daylight, for he slept
all day and worked at night pulling heavy wagons of merchandise that were too large for the streets by day. Sometimes
Wang Lung saw him come creeping home at dawn. And
sometimes at dusk the man came out and stood with the other
men who were about to go into their hovels to sleep.

"Well, and is it forever?" asked Wang Lung bitterly.

The man puffed at his bamboo pipe. "No, not forever.
When the rich are too rich, there are ways, and when the poor
are too poor, there are ways. Last winter we sold two girls and
endured. This is one way when the poor are too poor. When

the rich are too rich, there is a way, and if I am not mistaken, that way will come soon." He pointed with the stem of his pipe to the wall behind them. "Have you seen inside that wall?"

Wang Lung shook his head, staring.

"I took one of my slaves in there to sell. You would not believe it if I told you how money comes and goes in that house. I will tell you this—even the servants eat with chopsticks of ivory, and even the slave women sew pearls upon their shoes, and when the shoes have a bit of mud upon them, they throw them away, pearls and all!" The man drew hard on his pipe and Wang Lung listened, his mouth open. Over this wall, then, there were such things!

"There is a way when men are too rich," said the man. He was silent for a time; then he added indifferently, "Well, work again," and was gone.

Wang Lung could not sleep that night for thinking of all the silver and gold and pearls on the other side of the wall against which his body rested. But still he understood nothing of what the man had meant when he said, "When the rich are too rich, there is a way."

VIII

SPRING SEETHED in the village of huts. A swarm of ragged women and children issued forth each day to search the countryside for the green dandelions and shepherd's purse that thrust up feeble new leaves, food that they could get without begging and without money. And out with this swarm went O-lan and the two boys.

But the men worked on as before, although the lengthening warm days and sudden rains filled everyone with discontent and longing. In the evening they came out of their huts and talked together in the lingering twilight.

Most of these ragged men had nothing beyond what they took in the day's labor, and thought only of how they might tomorrow eat a bit of fish, or of how they might idle a bit. They talked always of money; of what they had paid for a foot of cloth or a small fish, or of what they could earn in a day, and always of what they would do if they had the money that the man over the wall had in his coffers.

Listening to all that they would do if they had these things, Wang Lung cried out suddenly one evening, "If I had the gold and the silver, I would buy land with it, and I would bring forth harvests."

At this they united in turning on him. "Now here is a pig-tailed country bumpkin who understands nothing of city life and of what may be done with money. He would go on working like a slave behind an ox or an ass!" And each one of them felt he was more worthy to have the money than was Wang Lung, because he knew better how to spend it. But this scorn did not change Wang Lung's mind, and he grew more impatient every day for the land that was already his.

Being possessed continually by this thought, Wang Lung saw as in a dream the things that happened about him in the city every day. He accepted strangeness without questioning. There was, for example, the paper that men gave out here and there, and sometimes even to him.

The first time he had such paper given him, it was given by a foreigner, a man, very tall, with eyes as blue as ice and a hairy face. Wang Lung, although frightened to take anything from his hand, was more frightened to refuse, seeing the man's strange eyes. Then, when he had courage to look at the paper after the foreigner had passed on, he saw on it a picture of a white-skinned man, who hung upon a crosspiece of wood. The man was without clothes except for a bit about his loins, and to all appearances was dead; his head drooped upon his shoulder and his eyes were closed. Wang Lung looked at the pictured man in horror. There were characters beneath, but of these he could make nothing. He carried the picture home at night, and he and the old man and the two boys discussed its possible meaning. The old man said, "Surely this was a very evil man to be thus hung."

But Wang Lung was fearful of the picture and pondered as to why a foreigner had given it to him, whether or not some brother of this foreigner's had not been so treated and the other brethren were seeking revenge. Therefore he avoided the street where he had met the man and after a few days the paper was forgotten.

But the next time a stranger handed a paper freely to Wang Lung it was a man of the city, a young man well clothed, who talked loudly as he distributed the sheets among the crowds on the street. This paper bore also a picture of blood and death, but the man who died this time was not white-skinned but a man like Wang Lung himself, a common fellow, slight, with black hair and eyes and clothed in ragged garments. A great fat one stood upon the dead figure and stabbed the dead figure with a long knife. It was a piteous sight and Wang Lung stared at it as he listened to the young man.

"The dead man is yourselves," proclaimed the young man, "and the murderous one who stabs you is the rich. You are poor and downtrodden because the rich seize everything."

Now, that he was poor Wang Lung knew full well, but he had always blamed it on a Heaven that would not rain in its season. Therefore he listened with interest to hear what the rich men had to do with this thing. And at last he grew bold and asked, "Sir, is there any way whereby the rich who oppress us can make it rain so that I can work on the land?"

At this the young man turned on him with scorn and replied, "Now how ignorant you are! If the rich would share with us what they have, it wouldn't matter whether it rained or not because we would all have money and food."

A great shout went up from those who listened, but Wang Lung turned away unsatisfied, for he desired nothing but his land under his feet again.

Then in this city where something new was always springing at him, Wang Lung saw another thing he did not understand. One day when he pulled his empty ricksha down a street, he saw a man seized by a small band of armed soldiers, and when the man protested, the soldiers brandished knives in his face. Wang Lung watched in amazement as the soldiers seized another and another, and it came to Wang Lung that those who were seized were all common fellows who worked with their hands. While he stared, yet another man was seized, and this one a man who lived in the hut nearest his own against the wall.

Quickly Wang Lung thrust his ricksha into a side alley and darted into a hot-water shop for fear that he might be next, and there he hid behind the great caldrons until the soldiers passed. And he asked the keeper of the shop the meaning of the thing he had seen, and the man, who was old and shriveled with the steam rising continually about him out of the caldrons, answered with indifference, "It is but another war somewhere. Who knows what all this fighting is about?"

"But why do they seize my neighbor, who is as innocent as I who have never heard of this war?" asked Wang Lung in great consternation. And the old man answered, "The soldiers are going to battle somewhere and need carriers for bedding and ammunition, and so they force laborers like you to go with them and do it. It is no new sight in this city."

"Well, but a man's family—" said Wang Lung, aghast.

"Well, what do they care?" said the old man scornfully.

When the sound of the soldiers' boots was gone, Wang Lung darted out. Seizing his ricksha, he ran with it empty to the hut. O-lan had but just returned from gathering greens on the roadside, and he told her in broken, panting words what was happening. He looked at her haggardly and said, "Now am I truly tempted to sell the little slave and go north."

But she mused and said in her plain way, "Wait a few days. There is strange talk about."

Nevertheless, he went out no more in the daytime, but sent the eldest lad to return the ricksha to the place where he had hired it. Then he waited until night came and went to the houses of merchandise and there, for half what he had earned before, he pulled great wagonloads of boxes all night. Each

wagon required a dozen men to pull it, all pulling and strain-
ing and groaning at once. Through the dark streets he strained
all night against the ropes, his body streaming with sweat.
Before them a little boy ran carrying a flaming torch to show
the way, and in its light the faces and the bodies of the men
and the wet cobbles glistened alike. Wang Lung went home
just before dawn, too broken for food until he had slept. But
during the day when the soldiers searched the street, he slept
safely in the furthermost corner of the hut behind a pile of
straw O-lan had gathered to make a shield for him.

With the coming of spring the city became filled with
further unrest. Carriages drawn by horses pulled rich men and
their possessions to the edge of the river where ships carried
them away. Wang Lung's sons came back with their eyes
wide, one crying, "We saw a man as fat and monstrous as a god
in a temple, and such boxes and boxes, and when I asked what
was in them, one said, 'There is gold and silver in them, but
the rich cannot take all they have away, and someday it will all
be ours.' Now, what did he mean by this, my father?"

Wang Lung answered shortly, "How should I know what an
idle city fellow means?"

And the elder son cried wistfully, "Oh, I wish we might go
even now and get it if it is ours. I should like to taste a sweet
cake with sesame seed sprinkled on the top."

And Wang Lung remembered the cakes that O-lan had once
made at the New Year's feast, cakes of rice flour and lard and
sugar, and his heart pained him with longing for that which
had passed. Suddenly it seemed to him that not one more day
could he lie in this wretched hut, nor could he strain the hours
through another night, his body bent against a rope cutting his
flesh, dragging the load over the cobblestones. He had come
to know each stone now as a separate enemy.

"Ah, the fair land!" he cried out suddenly and fell to weeping, so that the children were frightened and the old man
twisted his face this way and that under his sparse beard.

Then Wang Lung took his little girl into his arms and sat

with her, and he looked at her and said, "Little fool, would you like to go to a great house where there is food and drink?"

Then she smiled, not understanding what he said, and put up her small hand to touch with wonder his staring eyes and he could not bear it. He cried out to O-lan, "Tell me, were you beaten in that great house?"

And she answered him flatly and somberly, "Every day I was beaten."

Wang Lung groaned and held the child to him and said over and over to her softly, "Oh, little fool—oh, poor little fool."

Then suddenly there came a noise like the cracking of heaven and they all fell unthinking on the ground and hid their faces, for it seemed as though the hideous roar would catch them all up and crush them. Wang Lung covered the girl's face with his hand.

But O-lan, when silence had fallen as suddenly as it had gone, lifted her head and said, "Now what I have heard of has come to pass. The enemy has broken in the gates of the city." And then they heard shouting, rising voices, at first faint, as the wind of an approaching storm, and then gathering in a deep howl, louder and louder as it filled the streets.

Wang Lung sat erect on the floor of his hut then, and a strange fear crept over his flesh. They all stared at each other waiting for something they knew not. But there was only the noise of the gathering mob and their howling.

Then they heard the sound of a great door groaning upon its hinges, and suddenly the man who had once talked to Wang Lung at dusk thrust his head in at the hut's opening and cried out, "Now do you still sit here? The hour has come—the gates of the rich man are open to us!" And as if by magic O-lan was gone, creeping out under the man's arm as he spoke.

Then Wang Lung rose up, half-dazed, and he set the girl down. He went out and there before the great iron gates of the rich man's house a multitude of clamoring common people pressed forward, howling together the deep, tigerish howl that he had heard rising and swelling out of the streets. He knew that at the gates of all the rich men in the city there pressed a howling multitude of men and women who had been starved and imprisoned and now were for the moment free to do as they would. The great gates were ajar, and the people pressed forward so tightly packed together that foot was on foot and body wedged tightly against body so that the whole mass moved together as one.

Thus Wang Lung was forced along over the threshold of the gates, his feet scarcely touching the ground. He was swept through court after court, and of those men and women who had lived in the house he saw not one. But in the rooms food stood on tables and in the kitchens fires burned. In the inner courts, where the lords and ladies had their dainty beds and their lacquered boxes of gold and their boxes of silken clothing, the crowd fell upon the treasures.

Only Wang Lung in the confusion took nothing. He had never in all his life taken what belonged to another, and not at once could he do it. So he stood in the middle of the crowd at first, dragged this way and that, and then, coming somewhat to his senses, he pushed toward the edge and found himself in the innermost court where the ladies of the rich had dwelt. The back gate was ajar, the gate that the rich kept for their escape in such times, and therefore called the gate of peace. Through this gate they had escaped and were now hidden in the streets, listening to the howling in their courts.

But one man had failed to escape. He had hidden in an empty inner room, and now, thinking he was alone, he was creeping out. Thus Wang Lung, drifting away from the others until he too was alone, came upon him.

He was a great fat fellow, neither old nor young, and his naked body gaped through a purple satin robe he held about him. In the mountains of his cheeks his eyes were as small and sunken as a pig's. When he saw Wang Lung, he shook all over and fell upon his knees and knocked his head on the floor and cried, "Save a life—save a life—do not kill me. I have money for you—much money—"

It was this word money that suddenly brought to Wang Lung's mind a piercing clarity. Money! Yes, he needed that! The girl saved! *The land!*

He cried out in a harsh voice such as he did not himself know he possessed, "Give me the money then!"

And the fat man rose to his knees, sobbing and gibbering, and feeling for the pocket of his robe. He brought forth his hands dripping with silver. Wang Lung held out the end of his coat and received it. And again Wang Lung cried out in that strange voice that was like another man's, "Give me more!"

And again the man's hands came forth dripping with silver, and he whimpered, "Now there is none left and I have nothing but my wretched life," and he fell to weeping.

Wang Lung, looking at him as he shivered and wept, suddenly loathed him as he had loathed nothing in his life, and he cried, "Out of my sight before I kill you for a fat worm!"

And the man ran past him like a cur and was gone.

Then Wang Lung was left alone with the silver. He did not stop to count it but went out of the open gate of peace and across the small back streets to his hut. He hugged the silver and to himself he said over and over, "We go back to the land—tomorrow we go back to the land!"

IX

BEFORE A HANDFUL of days had passed it seemed to Wang Lung that he had never been away from his land, as indeed in his heart he never had. With six pieces of the silver he bought good seed from the south, full grains of wheat and of rice and of corn, and he bought seeds he had never planted before: celery and red radishes and red beans and lotus for his pond.

And even before he reached his own land, he bought an ox from a farmer plowing in a field. He saw the man plowing and they stopped, eager as they were to reach the house and the land. They looked at the ox. Wang Lung was struck with its great strong neck, and he called out, "That is a worthless ox!

What will you sell it for, seeing that I have no animal and am hard put to it and willing to take anything?"

And the farmer called back, "I would sooner sell my wife than this ox that is but three years old and in its prime."

Then it seemed to Wang Lung that of all the oxen the world held he must have this one. He had his heart set on it. With this ox he could plow his fields and cultivate them, and with this ox tied to his mill he could grind the grain. He said to the farmer, "I will give you enough to buy another ox and more, but this ox I will have."

At last after bickering the farmer yielded for half again the

worth of an ox. But silver was suddenly nothing to Wang Lung when he looked at this ox, and he led it away with a rope through its nostrils, his heart burning with his possession.

When they reached the house, they found the door torn away and the thatch from the roof gone, and their hoes and rakes were also gone, so only the bare rafters and the earthen walls remained. But after the first astonishment all this was as nothing to Wang Lung. He went to the town and bought a plow of hardwood and two rakes and two hoes and mats to cover the roof until they could thatch it again.

Then in the evening he stood in the doorway of his house and looked across the land, his own land, lying loose and fresh from the winter's freezing and ready for planting. It was full spring. In the shallow pool the frogs croaked drowsily.

Through the twilight he could see dimly the fringe of trees at the border of the near field. They were peach trees, budded most delicately pink, and willow trees thrusting forth tender green leaves. And up from the quiescent, waiting land a faint mist rose, silver as moonlight, and clung about the tree trunks.

At first it seemed to Wang Lung that he wished only to be alone on his land, and when his neighbors came to him, those who were left of the winter's starving, he was surly with them. "Who has my rakes and my hoes and who burned my roof in his oven?" Thus he bawled at them. And they shook their heads, full of virtue, and said, "In these evil times, how can it be said that this one or that stole anything? Hunger makes a thief of any man."

Then Ching, his neighbor, came creeping forth from his house to see Wang Lung and said, "Through the winter a band of robbers lived in your house and preyed upon the town. Your uncle, it is said, knows more of them than an honest man should. But who knows what is true in these days?"

Ching was nothing but a shadow: his skin stuck to his bones and his hair had grown thin and gray, although he had not yet reached forty-five years of age. Wang Lung stared at him, and then in compassion he said suddenly, "Now you have fared worse than we—what have you eaten?"

And Ching sighed forth in a whisper, "What have I not eaten? Offal from the streets like dogs; my woman brewed some soup from flesh I dared not ask what it was. Then she died, having less strength than I, and I gave the girl to a soldier because I could not see her die also." He fell silent, and after a time he said, "If I had a little seed, I would plant once more."

"Come here!" cried Wang Lung roughly and dragged him into the house by the hand. There he bade the man hold up the ragged tail of his coat and into it Wang Lung poured seeds from the store he had brought from the south, and he said, "Tomorrow I will come and plow your land with my ox."

Then Ching began to weep and Wang Lung rubbed his own

eyes and cried out as if he were angry, "Do you think I have forgotten that you gave me that handful of beans?" But Ching could answer nothing, only he walked away weeping.

It was joy to Wang Lung to find that his uncle was no longer in the village and that no one knew where he was. Some said he had gone to distant parts with his wife and his son. But his uncle's daughters—and this Wang Lung heard with stout anger—had been sold, the prettiest first, for the price they could bring.

Then Wang Lung set himself robustly to the soil, begrudging even the hours he had to spend in the house for food and sleep. He loved rather to take his roll of bread and garlic to the field and stand there eating, planning and thinking, Here shall I put the black-eyed peas and here the young rice beds. And if he grew too weary in the day, he would lie down in a furrow, and there with the good warmth of his own land against his flesh, he would sleep.

And O-lan in the house was not idle. With her own hands she lashed the mats firmly to the rafters and took earth from the fields and mixed it with water and mended the walls of the house. She built again the oven and filled the holes in the floor that the rain had washed away. She went into town one day with Wang Lung and together they bought beds and a table and six benches and a great iron caldron, and then they bought for pleasure a red clay teapot with a black flower marked on it in ink and six bowls to match. Last of all they went into an incense shop and bought a paper god of wealth to hang on the wall over the table in the middle room, and they bought two pewter candlesticks and two red candles to burn before the god.

And with this, Wang Lung thought of the two small gods in the temple to the earth, and on his way home he went and peered in at them, and they were piteous to behold; the clay of their bodies was naked and sticking through the tatters of their paper clothes. No one had paid any heed to them in this dreadful year. Wang Lung looked at them grimly, and he said aloud, as one might speak to a punished child, "Thus it is with gods who do evil to men!"

Nevertheless, when the house was itself again, and the pewter candlesticks were gleaming and the candles burning in them were shining red, and the teapot and the bowls were on the table and the beds were in their places once more, Wang Lung was afraid of his happiness. O-lan grew great with the next child. His children tumbled like brown puppies about his threshold and against the southern wall his old father dozed and smiled as he slept. In his fields the young rice sprouted as green as jade and more beautiful, and the young beans lifted their hooded heads from the soil. And out of the silver there was still enough left to feed them until the harvest. Looking at the blue heaven above him and the white clouds driving across it, Wang Lung muttered unwillingly, "I must stick a little incense before those two in the small temple. After all, they have power over the earth."

ONE NIGHT as Wang Lung lay with his wife he felt a hard lump the size of a man's closed hand between her breasts, and he said, "Now what is this thing you have on your body?"

He put his hand to it and he found a cloth-wrapped bundle. She drew back violently at first, but then she yielded and said, "Well, look at it, then, if you must," and she broke the string that held it to her neck and gave him the thing.

It was wrapped in a bit of rag, and this he tore away. Suddenly into his hand fell a heap of jewels. Wang Lung gazed at them, stupefied. There were such jewels as one had never dreamed could be together, jewels red as the flesh of watermelons, golden as wheat, green as young leaves in spring, clear as water trickling out of the earth. What the names of them were Wang did not know, but holding them there in the hollow of his hand, he knew from the glittering in the half-dark room that he held wealth. Motionless, drunk with color and shape, he and the woman stared at what he held. At last he whispered to her, breathless, "Where—where—"

And she whispered back as softly, "In the rich man's house. I saw a loose brick in the wall. I pulled the brick away, caught the shining and put them into my sleeve. I have lived in a rich man's house. I knew the meaning of a loose brick."

Again they fell silent, staring at the wonder of the stones. Then after a time Wang Lung drew in his breath and said resolutely, "Now treasure like this one cannot keep. It must be sold and put into safety—into land, for nothing else is safe. If any knew of this we should be dead by the next day."

As he wrapped the stones in the rag again, by chance he saw the woman's face. She was sitting cross-legged on the bed and her heavy face was moved with a dim yearning of open lips.

"Well, and now what?" he asked, wondering at her.

"Will you sell them all?" she asked in a hoarse whisper.

"And why not?" he answered, astonished. "Why should we have jewels like this in an earthen house?"

"I wish I could keep two for myself," she said with such helpless wistfulness that he was moved as he might be by one of his children longing for a toy.

"Well, now!" he cried in amazement.

"If I could have two," she went on humbly, "only two small ones—the two small white pearls even . . . I would not wear them." And she dropped her eyes and fell to twisting a bit of the bedding. "I could hold them in my hand sometimes," she added, as if thinking to herself.

Then Wang Lung, without comprehending it, looked for an instant into the heart of this dull and faithful creature who had labored all her life at some task for which she had won no reward and who in the great house had seen others wearing jewels that she had never even felt in her hand once. And, moved by something he did not understand, he handed the jewels to her in silence, and she searched among the glittering colors, her hard brown hand turning over the stones delicately and lingeringly until she found the two smooth white pearls. Then she wrapped them in a bit of cloth and hid them between her breasts and was comforted.

Wang Lung watched her, astonished, and later he would sometimes stop and stare at her and say to himself, "Well now, that woman of mine, she has those two pearls between her breasts still, I suppose." But he never saw her take them out or look at them, and they never spoke of them at all.

As for the other jewels, he decided he would buy more land. He went to the great house, but there was in these days no gateman standing at the gate, twisting the long hairs of his mole. Instead the great gates were locked. Wang Lung pounded against them with both fists and no one came. At last he heard slow footsteps coming, and then he heard the slow drawing of the iron bar and the gate creaked and a cracked voice whispered, "Who is it?"

Wang Lung answered loudly, "It is I, Wang Lung!"

Then the voice said peevishly, "Now who is an accursed Wang Lung?"

And Wang Lung perceived that it was the old lord himself because he cursed as one accustomed to servants. Wang Lung answered, therefore, more humbly than before, "Sir and lord, I am come not to disturb your lordship, but to talk a little business with the agent."

Then the old lord answered through the crack, "Now curse him, that dog left me many months ago—may his mother and his mother's mother be cursed for him—he took all that I had. No debts can be paid."

"No—no—" called Wang Lung hastily. "I came to pay out, not to collect debt."

At this there was a shrill scream from a voice Wang Lung had not yet heard and a woman thrust her face out of the gates. "Now that is a thing I have not heard for a long time," she said sharply. "Come in." She opened the gates wide enough to admit him, and then behind his back, while he stood astonished in the court, she barred them securely again.

The old lord stood there coughing and staring, a dirty gray satin robe wrapped about him, from which hung an edge of bedraggled fur. Wang Lung stared back, curious, yet half afraid, for it seemed impossible that the old lord, of whom he had heard so much, was this old figure, no more dreadful than his old father, and indeed less so, for his father was a cleanly and smiling old man, and the old lord, who had been fat, was now lean and unshaven, and his hand was yellow and trembling as he passed it over his chin.

The woman was clean enough. She had a sharp face, handsome with a sort of hawk's beauty—a high-bridged nose and keen bright black eyes and pale skin stretched too tightly over her bones. Her hair was smooth and shining black, but from her speech one could perceive she was but a slave, sharp-voiced and bitter-tongued. And besides these two, the woman and the old lord, there was not another person in the court where so many had been before.

"Now about money . . . " said the woman sharply. But Wang Lung hesitated. He could not speak comfortably before the old lord. This the woman instantly perceived, and she said to the old man shrilly, "Now off with you!"

And the aged lord, without a word, shambled silently away, his old velvet shoes flapping on and off at his heels. As for Wang Lung, left alone with this woman, he was stupefied with the silence everywhere. In the court he saw heaps of refuse, as though not for a long time had anyone taken a broom to sweep it.

"Now then, woodenhead!" said the woman with exceeding sharpness, and Wang Lung jumped at the shrill sound of her voice. "What is your business? If you have money, let me see it."

"Well, but I cannot speak with a woman," objected Wang Lung mildly. He could make nothing of the situation in which he found himself, and he was still staring about him.

"Well, and why not?" retorted the woman with anger. Then she shouted at him suddenly, "Have you not heard, fool, that there is no one here?"

Wang Lung stared at her, unbelieving, and the woman shouted at him again, "I, Cuckoo, and the old lord—there is no one else!"

"Where then?" asked Wang Lung, too aghast to make sense in his words.

"Have you not heard how bandits swept into the house and how they carried away what they would? And they hung the old lord up by his thumbs and beat him, and the old mistress they tied in a chair, and everyone ran. But I hid. And when I came out, they were gone and the old mistress sat dead in her chair, not from any touch they had given her but from fright."

"And the servants and the slaves?" gasped Wang Lung.

"Oh, those," she answered carelessly, "they were gone long ago—all those who had feet to carry them away, for there was no food and no money by the middle of the winter."

The woman fell silent and the silence of the courts was as heavy as silence is after life has gone. Then she said, "But all this was not a sudden thing. The fall of this house has been coming. In the last generation the lords ceased to see to the land and spent the money as carelessly as water. And the strength of the land has gone from them and bit by bit the land has begun to go also."

"Where are the young lords?" asked Wang Lung, still staring about him, so impossible was it for him to believe these things she had told him.

"Hither and thither," said the woman indifferently. "The elder young lord sent a messenger to take his father when he heard what had befallen, but I persuaded the old head not to go. I said, 'Who will be in the courts, and it is not seemly for me, who am only a woman.'" She pursed her narrow red lips virtuously and cast down her bold eyes as she spoke these words, and again she said, "Besides, I have been my lord's faithful slave for these several years and I have no other house."

Wang Lung looked at her closely then. He began to perceive what this was, a woman who clung to an old and dying man because of what last thing she might get from him. He said with contempt, "Seeing that you are only a slave, how can I do business with you?"

At that she cried out, "He will do anything I tell him."

Wang Lung pondered. Well, there was the land. Others would buy it through this woman if he did not.

"How much land is there left?" he asked her unwillingly, and she saw instantly what his purpose was.

"If you have come to buy land," she said, "there are a hundred acres to the west and two hundred to the south that he will sell."

This she said so readily that Wang Lung perceived that she knew everything the old man had left, even to the last foot of land. But still he was unbelieving and not willing to do business with her. "Into whose hand would I put the money?" he asked.

"Into the old lord's hand," replied the woman smoothly. Wang Lung knew that the old lord's hand would open into hers. But all this time here were these jewels hot and heavy against his body. He could not rest now until they were changed into land, and he said to her, "Will the old lord set his own seal to the deeds of sale?"

And the woman answered eagerly, "He will—he will—on my life!"

Then Wang Lung said plainly, "Will you sell the land for silver or for jewels?"

And her eyes glittered as she spoke. "I will sell it for jewels!"

Now Wang Lung had more land than one man with an ox can plow and harvest, and so he built another small room onto his house, and he said to his neighbor Ching, "Sell me the land you have and come into my house and help me with my land." And Ching was glad to do it.

The heavens rained in season then; and when the wheat was harvested in heavy sheaves, the two men planted the young rice, more rice than Wang Lung had ever planted before, for the rains came in abundance, so that the lands were fit for rice. Then when this harvest came, it was so great that he and Ching alone could not harvest it, and Wang Lung hired as laborers two other men who lived in the village.

He remembered the idle young lords of the fallen great house as he worked on the land he had bought from the House of Hwang, and he bade his two sons sharply each morning to come into the fields with him, and he set them at guiding the ox. If they could accomplish no great labor, at least they came to know the heat of the sun on their bodies and the weariness of walking back and forth along the furrows.

But he would not allow O-lan to work in the fields, for he was no longer a poor man, but a man who could hire laborers if he would, seeing that never had the land given forth such harvests as it had this year. He was compelled to build yet another room onto the house to store his harvests in. And he bought three pigs and a flock of fowls to feed on the grains spilled from the harvests.

So O-lan worked in the house and made new clothes for each one and new shoes, and she made coverings of flowered cloth stuffed with warm new cotton for every bed, and when she was finished, they were rich in clothing and in bedding as they had never been. And once more she lay down on the bed and gave birth again; and though she could hire whom she chose, she chose to be alone.

This time she was long at labor. When Wang Lung came home in the evening, he found his father standing at the door, laughing and saying, "An egg with a double yolk this time!"

And when Wang Lung went in, there was O-lan on the bed with two newborn children, a boy and a girl as alike as two grains of rice. He laughed boisterously at what she had done. "So this is why you bore two jewels in your bosom!"

And he laughed again at what he had thought of to say, and O-lan, seeing how merry he was, smiled her slow, painful smile.

Wang Lung had, therefore, at this time no sorrow of any kind, except that his elder girl neither spoke nor did those things that were right for her age. Whether it was the desperate first year of her life or the starving or what, month after month went past and Wang Lung waited for the first words to come from her lips. But no sound came, only the sweet, empty smile, and when he looked at her, he groaned forth, "Little fool—my poor little fool."

And as if to make amends, he made much of her, and she followed him silently about, smiling when he noticed her.

IN THESE PARTS, where Wang Lung had lived all his life and his father and his father's father had lived upon the land, there were famines once in five years, or, if the gods were lenient, once in seven or eight or even ten years. This was because the heavens rained too much or not at all. Time after time men fled from the land and came back to it, but Wang Lung set himself now to build his fortunes so securely that through the bad years to come he need never leave his land again.

For seven years there were harvests, and every year Wang Lung hired more laborers. He built a new house behind his old one, a large room behind a court and two small rooms on each side of the court beside the large room. This house he covered with tiles, but the walls were still made of the hard tamped earth from the fields, only he had them brushed with lime and they were white and clean. Into these rooms he and his family moved, and the laborers, with Ching at their head, lived in the old house.

Wang Lung had set Ching to be his steward over the men and over the land, and he paid him well, two silver pieces a month besides his food. But with all Wang Lung's urging Ching to eat, the man still put no flesh on his bones, remaining always a small, spare man of great gravity. Nevertheless he labored gladly, pottering silently from dawn until dark, speaking if there was anything to be said, but happiest if he could be silent. Wang Lung knew that if any one of the laborers slept too long or ate more than his share of the bean curd in the common dish, or if any bade his wife or child come secretly to the harvesting and snatch handfuls of the grain, Ching would, at the end of the year when master and man feast together after the harvest, whisper to Wang Lung, "Such a one do not ask back for the next year."

And it seemed that the handful of beans and of seed that had passed between these two men had made them brothers, except that Ching never wholly forgot that he was hired.

By the end of the fifth year, Wang Lung worked very little in his fields himself; he spent his whole time on the marketing of his produce. He was greatly hampered by his lack of book knowledge, and it was a shame to him that when a contract was written for him in a grain shop, he had to say humbly to the haughty dealers in the town, "Sir, and will you read it for me, for I am too stupid."

And it was a shame to him that when he had to set his name to the contract, another, even a paltry clerk, his eyebrows lifted in scorn and his brush pointed on the wet ink block, had to brush hastily the characters of Wang Lung's name.

It was on such a day one harvest time after he had heard the shout of laughter that went up from the clerks in the grain shop that he went home angrily, saying to himself, "Now not one of those town fools has a foot of land, and yet each feels he can laugh a goose cackle at me because I cannot tell the meanings of brushstrokes over paper." But as his indignation wore away, he said in his heart, "I will take my eldest son from the fields and he shall go to a school. And when I go into the grain markets, he will read and write for me so that there may be an end of this hissing laughter against me, a landed man."

That very day he called to him his eldest son, a straight, tall boy of twelve years now, looking like his mother with his wide face bones and his big hands and feet but with his father's quickness of eye, and Wang Lung said, "Come out of the fields from this day on, for I need a scholar in the family."

The boy flushed dark red and his eyes shone. "My father," he said, "so have I wished for these last two years that I might be, but I did not dare to ask it."

Then the younger boy came in crying and complaining when he heard of it, a thing he was wont to do, and now he whined to his father, "It is not fair that my brother can learn and I must work like a hind. I am your son as well as he!"

Wang Lung could not bear his noise. He would give him anything if he cried loudly enough for it, and so he said hastily, "Well, both of you can go, and if Heaven in its evil takes one of you, there will be the other one with knowledge to do the business for me."

Then arrangements were made to send the boys to a small school near the city gate kept by an old man who had in past years gone up for government examinations and failed. For a small sum he taught boys in the classics, beating them with his folded fan if they were idle. And hearing the cracks of his stout fan and the cries of the pupils, the neighbors said, "He is a worthy teacher." And this is why Wang Lung chose the school for his sons.

On the first day when he took them there, he was awed by the old teacher. Wang Lung bowed before him and said, "Sir, here are my two worthless sons. If anything can be driven into their thick brass skulls, it will be only by beating them, and therefore, if you wish to please me, beat them to make them learn." But going home again alone, having left the two lads, Wang Lung's heart was fit to burst with pride.

From that time on the boys were no longer called the elder and the younger but were given names by the teacher; for the elder, Nung En, and for the second, Nung Wen, and the first word of each name signified one whose wealth is from the earth.

X

Thus Wang Lung built the fortunes of his house, and when the seventh year came, the great river to the north, swollen with excessive rain and snow, burst its bounds and came sweeping and flooding all over the lands of that region. All through the late spring and early summer the water rose, and at last it lay like a great sea, lovely and idle, mirroring the moon and clouds and willows and bamboos. Here and there an earthen house fell slowly back into the water and the earth. And so it was with all houses that were not, like Wang Lung's, built upon a hill, and these hills stood up like islands. And men went to and from town by boat and by raft, and, as always, there were those who starved.

But Wang Lung was not afraid. His storerooms were yet filled with harvests of the last two years. But since much of the land could not be planted, he was more idle than he had ever been in his life. There were, besides, the laborers, whom he hired for a year at a time, and it was foolish for him to work when there were those who ate his rice while waiting day after day for the waters to recede. So after he had bade them mend the hoes and the rakes and the plows and to feed the

cattle and to twist hemp into ropes—all those things which in the old days he had done himself when he had tilled his land alone—his own hands were empty and he did not know what to do with himself.

Now a man cannot sit all day and stare at a lake of water covering his fields. The house, as he wandered about it impatiently, was too silent for his vigorous blood. The old man was very feeble now, half-blind and almost wholly deaf, and there was no need of speech with him except to ask if he was warm and fed. There was no telling the old man anything, for he forgot it at once. And it made Wang Lung impatient that the old man could not see how rich his son was and would always mutter if there were tea leaves in his bowl, "A little water is well enough and tea like silver."

The old man and the elder girl, who never spoke at all but sat beside her grandfather hour after hour, twisting a bit of cloth, folding and refolding it and smiling at it, these two had nothing to say to a man prosperous and vigorous. When Wang Lung had poured the old man a bowl of tea and had passed his hand over the girl's cheek and received her sweet, empty smile that passed with such sad swiftness from her face, he always turned away from her with a moment's stillness, which was his daughter's mark of sadness on him, and then he looked to his two youngest children. But a man cannot be satisfied with the foolishness of little children, and after a brief time of laughter and teasing, they went off to their own games and Wang Lung was alone.

Then it was that he looked at O-lan, his wife, as a man looks at the woman who has lived beside him so closely that there is nothing he does not know of her and nothing new that he may expect from her. And it seemed to Wang Lung that he looked at O-lan for the first time in his life, and he saw for the first time that she was a woman whom no man could call other than a dull and common creature. He saw that her hair was rough and unoiled and that her face was large and flat and coarse-skinned. Her eyebrows were scattered and the hairs too few. Her lips were too wide, and her hands and feet were large and spreading. Looking at her thus with strange eyes, he cried out at her, "Now anyone looking at you would say you were the wife of a common fellow. Cannot you buy a little oil for your hair and make yourself a new coat of black cloth? And those shoes you wear are not fit for a land proprietor's wife, such as you now are."

She was sitting on a bench, threading a long needle in and out of a shoe sole, and she stopped and held the needle poised, and her mouth gaped open and showed her blackened teeth. Then, as if she understood at last that he had looked at her as a man at a woman, a red flush crept up over her high cheekbones. But she only looked at him humbly and hid her feet under the bench on which she sat. Then, although in his heart he was ashamed that he reproached this creature who through all these years had followed him faithfully, and although he remembered that when he was poor and labored in the fields, she left her bed even on the day a child was born to help him in the harvest fields, yet he could not stem the irritation in his breast, and he went on ruthlessly, although against his inner will, "I have labored and have grown rich and I would have my wife look less like a hind. And those feet of yours—" He stopped, and looked angrily at her big feet in their loose cotton shoes.

And at last she said in a whisper, "My mother did not bind them, since I was sold so young. But the younger girl's feet I will bind."

He flung himself off because he was ashamed that he was angry, and angry because she would not be angry in return but only frightened. And he drew on his new black robe, saying fretfully, "Well, I will go to the tea shop and see if I can hear anything new. There is nothing in my house except fools and children."

His ill temper grew as he went to the town because he remembered suddenly that all these new lands of his he could not have bought in a lifetime if O-lan had not given him the handful of jewels from the rich man's house. But he said as if to answer his own heart rebelliously, "Well, but she did not know what she did. She seized them for pleasure as a child may seize a handful of sweets, and she would have hidden them forever in her bosom if I had not found it out."

Then he wondered if she still hid the pearls between her breasts. But where before it had been a thing to picture in his mind, now he thought of it with contempt, for her breasts had grown flabby and pearls between them were foolish and a waste.

All this might have been nothing if Wang Lung were still a poor man. But he had money. There was silver hidden in the walls of his house and there was a sack of silver buried under the floor, and silver sewed into the mat under their bed, and his girdle was full of silver. So that now he began to be careless of it and to think what he could do to enjoy the days of his manhood.

Everything seemed not as good to him as it was before. The tea shop that he used to enter timidly now seemed dingy and mean to him, and people nudged each other when he came in, and he once heard a man whisper to another, "There is that man Wang who bought the land from the House of Hwang. He is rich now."

And Wang Lung, hearing this, had sat down with seeming carelessness, though his heart had swelled with pride. But on this day when he had reproached his wife, even the deference he received did not please him. He sat gloomily drinking his tea, and then he thought suddenly to himself, Now why should I drink my tea at this shop, I who have land and whose sons are scholars?

He rose up quickly, threw his money on the table and wandered forth without knowing what it was he wished.

Now there was in the town a great tea shop newly opened by a man from the south, who understood such business, and Wang Lung had before this passed the place by. But now he was compelled by his restlessness to see something new. Thus he stepped across the threshold of the new tea shop into the great glittering room, full of tables and open to the street. He was bold enough in his bearing and trying to be the more bold because he remembered that only in the last few years was he more than a poor man who had even labored at pulling a ricksha.

He bought his tea quietly and looked about him with wonder. This shop was a great hall and the ceiling was set about with gilt and upon the walls there were scrolls of white silk painted with the figures of women. These women Wang Lung looked at secretly, and it seemed to him they were women in dreams, for none on earth had he seen like them.

Now this tea shop was the only building in the town that had an upper floor, except the pagoda outside the West Gate, and at night the sweet strumming of lutes and the high singing of women's voices and light laughter floated out of the upper windows. But where Wang Lung sat the noise of many men drinking tea and the sharp click of dice and dominoes muffled all else.

Thus it was that Wang Lung did not hear behind him a woman's footsteps creaking upon the narrow stairs that led from the upper floor, so he started violently when someone touched him on the shoulder, not expecting that anyone would know him here. When he looked up it was into the narrow, handsome face of Cuckoo, the woman who had helped him to buy the land from the old lord. She laughed when she saw him, and her laughter was a sort of sharp whispering. "Well, Wang the farmer!" she said, lingering with malice on the word farmer. "And who would think to see you here!"

It seemed to Wang Lung then that he must prove to this woman at any cost that he was more than a mere country fellow, and he laughed and said too loudly, "Is not my money as good to spend as another man's? And money I do not lack in these days."

Cuckoo stopped at this, her eyes narrow and bright as a snake's eyes, and her voice as smooth as oil flowing from a vessel. "And who has not heard it? And how shall a man better spend extra money than in a place like this, where rich men and elegant lords gather to take their joy? There is no such wine as ours—have you tasted it, Wang Lung?"

"I have only drunk tea as yet," replied Wang Lung, half-ashamed.

"Tea!" she exclaimed after him, laughing shrilly. "But we have tiger-bone wine and wine of fragrant rice—why need you drink tea?" And as Wang Lung hung his head, she said softly and insidiously, "And I suppose you have not looked at anything else, have you, eh? No pretty little hands, no sweet-smelling cheeks?"

Wang Lung hung his head yet lower and the blood rushed into his face; and the woman laughed again and pointed to the painted scrolls and said, "There they are, their pictures. Choose which one you wish to see and put the silver in my hand, and I will place her before you."

"Those!" said Wang Lung, wondering. "I thought they were pictures of dream women such as the storytellers speak of!"

"So they are dream women," rejoined Cuckoo, with mocking good humor, "but dreams such as a little silver will turn into flesh." And she went on her way.

Wang Lung sat staring at the pictures with a new interest. Up this narrow stairway, then, there were these women in flesh and blood. Before this they had all seemed equally beautiful, but now there were clearly some more beautiful than others, and out of the score and more he chose three of the most beautiful, and out of the three, one, a small, slender thing with a body as light as a bamboo and a little face as pointed as a kitten's face, and one delicate hand clasping the stem of a lotus flower.

"She is like a flower on a quince tree," he said suddenly aloud, and hearing his own voice, he was alarmed and ashamed. He rose hastily and put down his money and went out into the darkness that had now fallen and so to his home.

But over the fields and the water the moonlight hung, a net of silver mist, and in his body his blood ran hot and fast.

Now IF THE waters had at this time receded from Wang Lung's land, leaving it wet and steaming under the sun so that it would need plowing, Wang Lung might have forgotten the painted face on the scroll. But the waters lay placid and unmoving except in the slight summer wind that rose at sunset, and in his house O-lan looked at Wang Lung miserably as he went here and there and flung himself down in a chair and rose from it without drinking the tea she poured for him.

At the end of one long day, when the twilight lingered, murmurous and sweet with the breath of the lake, he stood at the door of his house, and suddenly without a word he turned abruptly and went into his room and put on his new coat that

O-lan had made for feast days. And with no word to anyone he went over the narrow paths along the water's edge and through the city gate until he came to the new tea shop.

There every light was lit, and men sat drinking and talking, their robes open to the evening coolness, and everywhere fans moved to and fro and good laughter flowed out into the street like music.

Wang Lung hesitated upon the threshold, standing in the bright light that streamed from the open doors. He might have stood there and gone away, for he was fearful still, although his blood was rushing through his body fit to burst his veins, but there came out of the shadows on the edge of the light a woman who had been leaning idly against the doorway, and it was Cuckoo. But when she saw who it was, she shrugged her shoulders and said, "Ah, it is only the farmer!"

Wang Lung was stung by the sharp carelessness in her voice, and his sudden anger gave him a courage he had not otherwise, so that he said, "Well, and may I not do as other men?" And he thrust his hand into his girdle and brought it out full of silver.

She stared at the silver and said without further delay, "Come and say which one you wish."

And Wang Lung, without knowing what he said, muttered, "Well, I do not know that I want anything." And then his desire overcame him, and he whispered, "That little one— that one with the pointed chin and a face like a quince blossom of white and pink—she holds a lotus bud in her hand."

The woman nodded easily, and beckoning him to follow, she threaded her way between the crowded tables, and Wang Lung followed her at a distance. At first it seemed to him that every man watched him, but he took courage when he saw that none paid him any heed. By this time they were walking up the narrow stairway, and this Wang Lung did with difficulty, for it was the first time he had ever climbed steps in a house. Nevertheless, when they reached the top, it was the same as a house on the earth, except that it seemed a mighty way up when he passed a window and looked into the sky. The woman led the way down a close dark hall, and at last struck a closed door harshly with the flat palm of her hand and went in. There, on a bed covered with a flowered red quilt, sat a slender girl.

Now if someone had told him there were small hands like these, he would not have believed it, hands so small and fingers so pointed, with long nails stained the color of lotus buds, deep and rosy; nor feet like these, little feet in pink satin shoes no longer than a man's middle finger, swinging childishly over the edge of the bed.

He sat on the bed beside her, and he looked at her as he had looked at the picture; he saw her figure, slender as bamboo in her tight short coat; he saw her small pointed face set in its painted prettiness above the high collar lined with white fur; he saw her round eyes the shape of apricots, so that at last he understood what the storytellers meant when they sang of the apricot eyes of the beauties of old. And he would not have dreamed that she was to be touched.

Then he heard laughter, light, quick, tinkling as a silver bell in a pagoda shaking in the wind, and a little voice like laughter said, "Oh, you great fellow! Shall we sit here the night through while you stare?"

And at that he seized her hand between both of his.

Now WANG LUNG became sick with the sickness that is greater than any man can have. He had suffered under labor in the sun, and he had suffered from starvation, and he had suffered from the despair of laboring without hope in a southern city. But under none of these did he suffer as he now did under this slight girl's hand.

Every day he went to the tea shop; every evening he waited till she would receive him; and every night he went in to her. All during the hot summer he loved her thus. Yet he never had enough of her: he went back to his house every night dazed and unsatisfied, and his days were endless, and his breast was filled with a sweet, sick pain that he could not understand.

If anyone spoke to him, his wife or his children, or if Ching came to him and said, "The waters will soon recede. What seed should we prepare?" he shouted and said, "Why do you trouble me?"

All the time his heart was like to burst. And as the days went on, he would not look at the grave faces of O-lan and of the children, suddenly sober in their play when he approached, nor even at his old father, who peered at him and asked, "What is this sickness that turns you full of evil temper and your skin yellow?"

And all this time the girl Lotus did what she would with him. When she laughed at the braid of his hair and said, "Now the men of the south do not have these monkey tails!" he went without a word and had it cut off.

When O-lan saw what he had done, she burst out in terror, "You have cut off your life!"

But he shouted at her, "And shall I look an old-fashioned fool forever?"

He would have cut off his life if the girl Lotus had commanded it or desired it, because she had every beauty that had ever come into his mind to desire in a woman.

He now washed every day. He bought red scented soap and rubbed it on his flesh, and not for any price now would he eat a stalk of garlic. He bought also new material for his clothes, and although O-lan had always cut his robes, making them wide and long for good measure, now he was scornful of her cutting and sewing, and he took the material to a tailor and had his clothes made as the men in the town had theirs: light gray silk for a robe, cut neatly to fit his body, and over this a black satin sleeveless coat. And he bought black velvet shoes such as the old lord had worn. And beyond this he bought a silver ring washed with gold for his finger, and as his hair grew where it had been shaved above his forehead, he smoothed it with a fragrant foreign oil.

O-lan did not know what to make of all this, except that one day after staring at him for a long time she said heavily, "There is that about you which makes me think of one of the lords in the great house."

Wang Lung laughed loudly then, but in his heart he was greatly pleased, and for that day he was more kindly with her than he had been for many days.

Now THE MONEY, the good silver, went streaming out of his hands. There was not only the price he must pay for his hours with the girl, but there was her pretty demanding of this or that jewel or trinket. And O-lan, who in the old days might have said to him easily enough, "And why do you take the money from the wall?" now said nothing. She watched him in misery, knowing that he was living some life apart from her, but not knowing what life it was. She was afraid to ask him anything because now his anger was always ready for her.

There came a day when Wang Lung returned over the fields and drew near to her as she washed his clothes at the pool. He stood there silent for a while, and then he said to her roughly, because he was ashamed and would not acknowledge his shame, "Where are those pearls you had?"

She answered timidly, looking up from the clothes she was beating upon a smooth, flat stone, "The pearls? I have them."

And he muttered, not looking at her but at her wrinkled, wet hands, "There is no use in keeping pearls for nothing." Then after an instant's silence he cried out suddenly, "Give them to me—I have need of them!"

Slowly she thrust her hand into her bosom and drew forth the small package and gave it to him and watched him as he unwrapped it; the pearls lay in his hand and caught softly the light of the sun. He laughed.

O-lan returned to beating the clothes, and when tears dropped slowly and heavily from her eyes, she did not put up her hand to wipe them away; she only beat the more steadily with her wooden stick upon the clothes spread over the stone.

XI

AND THUS IT might have gone forever until all the silver was spent had not Wang Lung's uncle returned suddenly without explanation. He stood in the doorway as though he had dropped from a cloud, his ragged clothes unbuttoned and girdled loosely as ever. He grinned widely at them all as they sat about the table at their early-morning meal, and Wang Lung sat agape, for it was like a dead man returning to see him. His father blinked and stared and did not recognize the one who had come until he called out, "Well, my elder brother and his son and his sons and my sister-in-law."

Then Wang Lung rose, dismayed in his heart but his voice courteous. "Well, my uncle, and have you eaten?"

"No," replied his uncle easily, "but I will eat with you." He sat down then and ate, and no one spoke until he had supped down three bowls of rice, fish and beans.

And when he had eaten, he said simply, 'Now I will fetch my wife and my son. In this great house of yours what we eat will never be missed."

Wang Lung, in great consternation, could do nothing but answer with sullen looks, for it is a shame to a man when he has enough and to spare to drive his own father's brother from the house. And that very evening his uncle came, bringing his wife and his son. Wang Lung was exceedingly angry and the more angry because he had to answer with smiles and welcome his relatives.

When they were all accustomed to what had taken place and when O-lan had said to him, "Cease to be angry. It is a thing to be borne," Wang Lung saw that his uncle and his uncle's wife and son would be courteous enough for the sake of their food and their shelter. Then his thoughts turned more violently than ever to the girl Lotus, and he muttered to himself, "When a man's house is full of wild dogs, he must seek peace elsewhere."

Now what O-lan had not seen in her simplicity and the old

man had not seen because of the dimness of his age, the wife of Wang Lung's uncle saw at once, and she cried out to O-lan, the laughter slanting her eyes, "Now Wang Lung is seeking to pluck a flower somewhere."

When O-lan looked at her humbly, not understanding, she laughed and said, "The melon must always be split wide open before you can see the seeds, eh? Well then, plainly, your man is mad over another woman!".

This Wang Lung heard his uncle's wife say in the court outside his window as he lay dozing one morning. He was quickly awake, and he listened, aghast at the sharpness of this woman's eyes. The thick voice rumbled on, pouring like oil from her fat throat, "When a man smooths his hair and buys new clothes, then there is a new woman and that is sure."

There came a broken sound from O-lan, what it was she said he could not hear, but his uncle's wife said, "You, poor fool, have never been fit for a man's fancy and little better than an ox for his labor. And it is not for you to repine when he buys himself another to bring her to his house, for all men are so, and so would my old do-nothing also, except the poor wretch has never had enough silver in his life to feed himself even."

No more than this did Wang Lung hear upon his bed, for now suddenly he saw how to satisfy his thirst after this girl he loved. He would buy her and bring her to his house and make her his own. He rose up at once from his bed and went out and motioned secretly to the wife of his uncle, and when she had followed him outside the gate he said, "I listened and heard what you said in the courts, and you are right. I have need of more than that one and why should I not, seeing that I have land to feed us all?"

She answered volubly and eagerly, "And why not, indeed? It is only the poor man who has to drink from one cup." Thus she spoke, knowing what he would say next.

He went on as she had planned. "But who will negotiate for me and be the middleman? A man cannot go to a woman and say, 'Come to my house.'"

To this she answered instantly, "Now you leave this affair in my hands. Only tell me which woman it is, and I will manage the affair."

Then Wang Lung answered unwillingly and timidly, for he had never spoken her name aloud before to anyone, "It is the woman called Lotus, in the great tea shop on the main street of town."

She mused awhile, fingering her lower lip, and said at last, "I do not know anyone there. Who is the keeper of this woman?"

And when he told her, she laughed and said, "Oh, Cuckoo? But it is a simple matter, indeed. That one would do anything for enough silver in her palm."

And Wang Lung, hearing this, felt his mouth become suddenly dry and parched. His voice came from him in a whisper. "Silver, then! Silver and gold! Anything to the very price of my land!"

THEN FROM a strange and contrary fever of love Wang Lung would not go again to the teahouse until the affair was arranged. Suddenly he saw the house as Lotus might see it. He hurried O-lan into this and that, sweeping and washing and moving chairs, so that she, poor woman, grew more and more terror-stricken, for well she knew by now, although he had said nothing, what was to come to her.

Wang Lung said to himself that with two women in the house there must be another court where he could go with his love and be separate. So while he waited for his uncle's wife to complete the matter, he called laborers and commanded them to build another court behind the middle room, and then three rooms around the court. He superintended the laborers himself, so that he need not talk with Ching of what he did. And in the new little court he built a pool and went into the city and bought five goldfish for it. He bought red cloth to hang at the doors for curtains and a new table and two carved chairs and painted scrolls of hills and water to hang on the wall, and then he bought a wide carved bed and flowered curtains to hang around it.

During all this time he said nothing to anyone except to scold the children if they were filthy or to roar out at O-lan that she had not brushed her hair for three days, so that at last one morning O-lan burst into tears and wept aloud as he had never seen her weep before. He said harshly, therefore, "Now what, woman? Cannot I say comb out your horse's tail of hair without this trouble over it?"

But she answered nothing except to say over and over, moaning, "I have borne you sons—I have borne you sons—"

He was silenced and uneasy and muttered to himself because he was ashamed, and so he let her alone.

Thus it went until one day his uncle's wife came and said, "The thing is complete. The girl will come for jade earrings and a ring of jade and a ring of gold and two suits of satin clothes and two suits of silk and a dozen pairs of shoes and two silken quilts."

Of all this Wang Lung heard only "The thing is complete—" and he cried out, "Let it be done!" He ran and got out silver and poured it into her hands and said, "And for yourself take a good ten pieces of silver."

Then she made a feint of refusal, drawing up her fat body and crying, "No, we are one family and this I do for you and not for silver." But Wang Lung saw her hand outstretched as she denied, and into it he poured the silver.

Then he bought pork and beef and mandarin fish, and he bought a snarl of dried birds' nests from the south to brew for soup. He bought every delicacy he knew, and then he waited. At last on a shining fiery day at the end of summer, she came to his house.

Wang Lung saw her coming from afar. She rode in a closed sedan chair borne upon men's shoulders, and behind that sedan followed a second one containing the woman Cuckoo. For an instant Wang Lung knew fear, and he said to himself, "What am I taking into my house?"

Scarcely knowing what he did, he went quickly into the room where he had slept for so many years with his wife and shut the door. There in the darkness he waited in confusion until he heard his uncle's wife calling loudly for him to come out. Then he went slowly out, abashed, his head hanging over his fine clothes, and his eyes looking here and there but never ahead.

But Cuckoo hailed him merrily. "Well, I did not know we would be doing business like this!"

Then she went to the chair, which the men had set down, and lifted the curtain and clucked her tongue and said,

"Come, my Lotus Flower, here is your house and your lord."

Then the curtain lifted and Wang Lung looked and saw sitting in the shadowy recess of the chair, painted and cool as a lily, the girl Lotus. He forgot everything, everything but that she had come to his house forever. He stood stiff and trembling, watching as she rose, graceful as though a wind had passed over a flower. Then she took Cuckoo's hand and stepped out, keeping her eyelids dropped as she walked, tottering and swaying upon her little feet. She did not speak to him as she passed him but whispered to Cuckoo, faintly, "Where is my apartment?"

Then his uncle's wife came forward and they led the girl into the court that Wang Lung had built for her.

After a time Wang Lung's uncle's wife came out, laughing a

little maliciously, and dusted her hands together as though to free them of something that clung to them. "She reeks of perfume and paint, that one," she said, still laughing. "Like a regular bad one she smells." And then she said with a deeper malice, "She is not as young as she looks, my nephew!" Then, seeing the anger on Wang Lung's face, she added hastily, "But I have never seen another more beautiful. It will be as sweet as the eight-jeweled rice at a feast after your years with the thick-boned slave."

Wang Lung answered nothing, only at last he dared to lift the red curtain and go into the court he had built for Lotus and then into the darkened room where she was. There he was beside her for the whole day until night.

All this time O-lan had not come near the house. At dawn she had taken a hoe from the wall and called the children and wrapped a little cold food in a cabbage leaf and had not returned. But when night came on she entered, silent and earth-stained and dark with weariness, and the children were silent behind her. She said nothing to anyone but went into the kitchen and prepared food and set it on the table as she always did. She called the old man and put the chopsticks in his hand, and she fed the poor fool. Then she ate a little with the children. Then when they had gone to bed and Wang Lung still sat at the table dreaming, she washed herself for sleeping, and at last she went into her accustomed room and slept alone upon the bed.

Then did Wang Lung eat and drink of his love night and day. Day after day he sat beside Lotus and watched her at all she did. She never came forth in the heat of the early autumn days but lay while Cuckoo bathed her slender body with lukewarm water and perfume and rubbed oil into her hair. For Lotus had said, "Let me have this woman for my servant, seeing that I am altogether alone in the world, for my father and my mother died when I could not yet talk, and my uncle sold me as soon as I was pretty to a life such as I have had, and I have no one." This she said with her tears, always abundant and ready and glittering in the corners of her pretty eyes, and Wang Lung could have denied her nothing when she looked up at him so. Besides, it was true that the girl would be alone in his house, for it was plain enough that O-lan would not serve the second one or notice that she was in the house at all. So Cuckoo and Lotus, her mistress, dwelt apart from the others in the new court that Wang Lung had made.

And he ate and drank of his love and was satisfied.

WANG LUNG was prepared for O-lan to hate Lotus, having heard many times of such things. Some women, he had heard, would even hang themselves when the man brought a second woman into the house, and others would scold. He was glad that O-lan was a silent woman, for at least she could not think of words against him. But he had not foreseen that whereas she would be silent about Lotus, her anger would find its vent against Cuckoo.

Cuckoo was willing enough to be friends, albeit she did not forget that in the great House of Hwang she had been in the lord's chamber and O-lan had been a kitchen slave. She called out to O-lan when first she saw her, "Well, my old friend, here we are in a house together again, and you mistress and first wife—how things are changed!"

But O-lan only stared at her and answered nothing. Then she put down the jar of water she carried, and she went to Wang Lung and she said to him plainly, "What is this slave woman doing in our house?"

Wang Lung would have liked to say in a surly voice, "It is my house and whoever I say may come in shall come in, and who are you to ask?" But he could not because of some shame in him when O-lan was there before him. O-lan stood there solidly on her big feet and waited.

Then Wang Lung, seeing she would have an answer, said feebly, "And what is it to you?"

And O-lan said, "I bore her haughty looks all during my youth in the great house. She used to run into the kitchen a score of times a day crying out, 'Now tea for the lord'—'Now food for the lord'—and it was always this is too hot and that is too cold, and that is badly cooked, and I was too ugly and too slow and too this and too that . . ." Then O-lan waited, and when he did not speak, the hot, scanty tears welled slowly into her eyes, and at last she crept away, groping for the door because her tears blinded her.

Wang Lung was glad to be alone, but still he was ashamed and angry that he was ashamed, and he said to himself restlessly, "Well, I have been good enough to her, and there are men worse than I." And he said at last that O-lan must bear it.

But O-lan was not finished with it, and she went her way silently. In the morning she heated water and presented it to the old man, and to Wang Lung—if he was not in the inner court—she presented tea, but when Cuckoo went to find hot water for her mistress, the caldron was empty. O-lan would go steadily about her cooking, answering nothing to Cuckoo's loud crying, "And is my delicate lady to lie thirsting and gasping in her bed for a swallow of water in the morning?"

But O-lan would not hear her. Then Cuckoo went complaining to Wang Lung, and he was angry that his love must be marred by such things. He went to O-lan to reproach her and shouted, "And cannot you add a dipperful of water to the caldron?"

But she answered with sullenness deep upon her face, "I am not the slave of slaves in this house at least." Then he was angry beyond bearing, and he seized O-lan's shoulder and shook her and said, "Do not be yet more of a fool. It is not for the servant but for the mistress."

And she bore his violence and looked at him and said, "And to that one you gave my two pearls!"

Then his hand dropped and he was speechless, and he went away ashamed.

And so he bade the laborers build another kitchen, and Cuckoo was pleased because he said, "You shall cook what you please in it." And he said to himself that at last his affairs

were settled. It seemed to him that he could never tire of Lotus and of the way she pouted at him with the lids drooped like lily petals over her great eyes, and of the way laughter gleamed out of her eyes when she glanced up at him.

But after all this matter of the new kitchen became a thorn in his body, for Cuckoo went to town every day and bought expensive foods imported from the southern cities. This all cost more money than he liked to give out, and yet he was afraid to say no for fear it would displease Lotus.

There was yet another small thorn that sprang from the first, and it was that his uncle's wife went often into the inner court at mealtimes, and she grew free there, and Wang Lung was not pleased that Lotus chose this woman for a friend. But when he said gently, "Now, Lotus, my flower, do not waste your sweetness on an old, fat hag like that one," Lotus was fretful.

She answered peevishly, hanging her head away from him, "Now I am used to a merry house and in yours there is no one except the first wife who hates me. You do not love me—if you did, you would wish me to be happy."

Then Wang Lung, humbled and anxious, said, "Let it be only as you wish and forever."

Then she forgave him, but after that when he came to her, if she was drinking tea with his uncle's wife, she would bid him wait, and he would stride away angry. And so his love was not as whole and perfect as it had been before. It was pierced through and through with small angers that were the more sharp because he could no longer go to O-lan freely to talk about them, seeing that now their life was sundered.

Then like a field of thorns spreading from one root here and there, there was yet more to trouble Wang Lung. One day his father, who was so drowsy with age one would say he saw nothing, woke suddenly out of his sleeping in the sun and tottered, leaning on his dragon-headed staff that Wang Lung had bought for him on his seventieth birthday, to the doorway between the main room and the court where Lotus walked. It happened that it was at an hour when Wang Lung walked with Lotus in the court, and they stood beside the pool and looked at the fish.

When the old man saw his son standing beside the slender painted girl, he cried out in his shrill voice, "There is a harlot in the house!" And he would not be silent.

Wang Lung, fearing that Lotus would grow angry—for this small creature could shriek and scream and beat her hands together if she was angered at all—led the old man away, saying, "Now calm your heart, my father. It is not a harlot but a second woman in the house."

But the old man would not be silent, and he said suddenly, "I had one woman, and my father had one woman, and we farmed the land." And again he cried out, "I say it is a harlot!"

And so the old man, with a sort of cunning hatred against Lotus, would go to the doorway of her court and shout into the air, "Harlot!"

One day Wang Lung heard a shriek from the inner court and

ran there to find the two younger children, and between them his elder daughter, his poor fool. Now the children were constantly curious about this woman who lived in the inner court. The two elder boys were shy and knew well enough why she was there, although they never spoke of her, but the two younger children could never be satisfied with their peepings and exclamations. On this day, they had conceived the notion that the elder girl must also see the woman, and they had dragged her into the court and there she stood before Lotus. When the fool saw the bright silk of the coat Lotus wore, she put out her hands and laughed aloud, a laugh that was only sound and meaningless. But Lotus was frightened and screamed out, so that Wang Lung came running in, and Lotus shook with anger and leaped up and down and pointed her finger at the poor laughing girl and cried out, "I will not stay in this house if that one comes near me. If I had known that I should have accursed idiots to endure, I would not have come," and she pushed the gaping little boy who stood nearest her, clasping his twin sister's hand.

Then the anger awoke in Wang Lung, for he loved his children, and he said roughly, "I will not hear my children cursed. No—not by anyone!" And he gathered the children together and said to them, "Now go out, my son and my daughter, and come no more to this woman's court, for she does not love you." And to the elder girl he said with great gentleness, "And you, my poor fool, come back to your place in the sun." And he took her by the hand and led her away.

For he was most angry that Lotus had dared to curse this child of his and call her idiot, and a load of fresh pain for the girl fell upon his heart, so that for two days he would not go near Lotus but played with his children. He went into the town and bought a circle of barley candy for his poor fool and comforted himself with her baby pleasure in the sweet stuff.

When at last he went in to Lotus again, she took special trouble to please him. But he, although he loved her again, did not love her as wholly as before.

There came a day when summer was ended, and the sky in the early morning was clear and cold and blue as seawater, and a clean autumn wind blew hard over the land, and Wang Lung woke as from a sleep. He went to his door and looked over his fields. The waters had receded.

Then a voice cried out in him, a voice deeper than love cried out for his land. And he tore off his long robe and his velvet shoes and rolled his trousers to his knees and stood forth, robust and eager. He shouted, "Where is the hoe and the plow? And where is the seed for the wheat planting? Come, Ching, my friend—call the men—I go out to the land!"

XII

As he had been healed of his sickness of heart when he came from the southern city, so now again Wang Lung was healed of his sickness of love by the good dark earth of his fields. For he stood first behind the oxen and saw the earth turning as the plow went into the soil, and then he himself took a hoe and broke up the soil into fine loamy stuff, soft as black sugar, and still dark with the wetness of the land upon it. This he did for the sheer joy he had in it, and when he was weary, he lay down on his land.

When night came, he strode into his house, his body aching and weary and triumphant, and tore aside the curtain to the inner court. When Lotus saw him, she cried out at the earth upon his clothes. But he laughed and seized her small, curling hands in his soiled ones and laughed again and said, "Now you see that your lord is but a farmer and you are a farmer's wife!"

Then she cried out with spirit, "A farmer's wife am I not, be you what you like!"

He laughed again and went out from her easily, and he laughed because he was free. All stained as he was with the earth, he ate well of the food that O-lan prepared for him, good rice and cabbage and bean curd, and fresh garlic rolled into wheat bread. The earth had healed him of his sickness.

So these two women took their places in his house: Lotus, his toy and his pleasure, and O-lan, the mother who had borne his sons, who kept his house and fed him. And it was a pride to Wang Lung that men mentioned with envy the woman in his inner court; it was as if he had a rare jewel that was useless except as a sign and symbol of a man who had passed beyond the necessity of caring only to be fed and clothed and could spend his money on joy if he wished. The men of the village now looked upon Wang Lung no more as one of themselves, but they came to borrow money from him at interest and to ask his advice concerning marriages. If any two had a dispute over the boundary of a field, Wang Lung was asked to settle the dispute and his decision was accepted, whatever it was.

Then the year turned to winter and Wang Lung took his harvest to the markets, and this time he took with him his eldest son. There is a pride a man has when he sees his eldest son reading aloud the letters upon a paper, and this pride Wang Lung now had. He would not pretend it was anything uncommon, although when the boy said sharply, "Here is a letter that has the wood radical when it should have the water radical," Wang Lung's heart was fit to burst with pride, so that he was compelled to turn aside and cough. And when a murmur of surprise ran among the clerks at his son's wisdom, he called out merely, "Change it, then! We will not put our name to anything wrongly written."

When it was finished and his son had written his father's name on the deed of sale, the two walked home together.

The year deepened into snow and the New Year's festival came, and now not only from the countryside but from the town also men came to see Wang Lung to wish him good fortune, and they said, "There is no fortune we can wish you greater than you have, sons in your house and women and money and land."

And Wang Lung, dressed in his silken robe with his sons in good robes beside him, and sweet cakes and watermelon seeds and nuts upon the table, knew that his fortune was good.

But when the year turned to spring and the willow trees sprouted their leaves fully and unfolded them and the earth was moist and steaming and pregnant with harvest, the eldest son of Wang Lung changed suddenly and ceased to be a child. He grew moody and would not eat and there was no correcting him at all, for if his father said to him with anything beyond coaxing, "Now eat of the good meat and rice," he turned stubborn, and if Wang Lung was angry at all, he burst into tears and fled from the room.

Moreover, he would not rise out of his bed in the mornings to go to school unless Wang Lung bawled at him, and then he went sullenly, and sometimes he spent whole days idling about the streets. Wang Lung only knew about it when the younger boy said spitefully, "Elder Brother was not in school today."

Wang Lung was angry at his eldest son then and shouted, "Am I to spend good silver for nothing?"

In his anger he fell upon the boy with a bamboo and beat him until O-lan heard it and rushed in from the kitchen and stood between her son and his father. She said, "It is useless for you to beat him. I have seen this melancholy come upon the young lords in the great house."

"It need not be so," answered Wang Lung in argument. "When I was a lad, I had no such melancholy and no such weepings."

O-lan answered slowly, "I have not seen it except with young lords. You worked on the land."

After he had pondered awhile, Wang Lung saw truth in what she said. When he himself was a young man, there was no time for melancholy, for he had to be up at dawn and out with the plow, and if he wept, no one heard him, and he could not run away, for if he did, there would be nothing for him to eat on return. He remembered all this, and he said to himself, "But my son is not the same. He is more delicate than I was, and his father is rich, and there is no need for his labor. Besides, one cannot take a scholar and set him to the plow."

And he was secretly proud that he had a son like this, and so he said to O-lan, "Well, if he is like a young lord, it is another matter. I will betroth him, and we will marry him early."

Then he went into the inner court.

Now Lotus, seeing that Wang Lung was thinking of things other than her beauty, pouted and said, "If I had known that you could look at me and not see me, I would have stayed in the teahouse."

She looked at him out of the corner of her eyes, so that he laughed and seized her hand and answered, "Well, and a man cannot always think of the jewel he has sewn on his coat, but if it were lost, he could not bear it. These days I think of how my eldest son is restless with desire and must be wed, and I do not know how to find the one he should wed."

Now Lotus, since the eldest son had grown tall and graceful with young manhood, looked on him with favor, and so she replied, musing, "There was a man who used to come to the great teahouse, and he often spoke of his daughter. He said she was small and fine but still only a child."

"What sort of man was this?" asked Wang Lung.

And she answered, "I know nothing except that he was named Liu, and I think that he was the owner of a grain market in the Street of the Stone Bridge."

Before she finished the words Wang Lung struck his hands together in delight and said, "Now then, that is where I sell my grain! It is a propitious thing."

"That is true," Lotus said gaily, "and Cuckoo shall go and ask Liu, and she shall have the matchmaker's fee if it is well done."

But the matter was not to be decided so quickly as that. Wang Lung said, "No, for I have decided nothing. I must think of the matter for some days."

And so he might have waited for many days, thinking, had not his eldest son come home in the dawn with his face hot and red from drinking wine. Wang Lung heard him stumbling in the court and ran out to see who it was. His son was sick and vomited before him, and then he fell and lay on the ground, for he was unaccustomed to more than the pale mild wine they made from their own fermented rice. Wang Lung was frightened and called for O-lan. Together they lifted him up and laid him on the bed in O-lan's room. O-lan brought vinegar in warm water and washed him gently, as she had seen others wash the young lords in the great house when they drank too much.

Then, seeing his delicate childish face and the drunken sleep that even the washing would not awaken, Wang Lung went into the room where the two boys slept together. The younger one was yawning and tying his books in a cloth to carry to school, and Wang Lung said to him, "Where was your elder brother?" And when the boy would not answer, he took him by the neck and shook him and cried, "Now tell me all, you small dog!"

The boy was frightened at this and broke out sobbing and

said between his sobs, "He has been away to the town three nights now. He goes with the son of your uncle, our cousin."

Then Wang Lung flung the boy aside and strode forth and said to Lotus, "Let it be as we have said. Let Cuckoo go to the grain merchant and arrange the marriage. Let the dowry be good but not too great—if the girl is suitable."

When he had said this, he went in his anger to his uncle's room and shouted, "Now I have harbored an ungrateful nest of snakes and they have bitten me!"

His uncle was sitting eating his breakfast, and he looked up at these words and said lazily, "How now?"

Then Wang Lung told him, half choking, what had happened, and his uncle only laughed.

When Wang Lung heard this laughter he remembered in one crowded space of time all that he had endured because of his uncle: how his uncle had tried to force him to sell his land; how they lived here, these three, eating and drinking and idle; and how his uncle's wife ate of the expensive foods Cuckoo bought for Lotus; and now, how his uncle's son had spoiled his own son. He bit his tongue between his teeth and said, "Out of my house, you and yours. I will burn the house down rather than have it shelter you. You have no gratitude even in your idleness!"

But his uncle sat where he was and ate on, now from this bowl and now from that, and then turned and said, "Drive me out if you dare."

And when Wang Lung stammered and blustered, not understanding, "Well—what—" his uncle opened his coat and showed him what was against its lining.

Then Wang Lung stood still and rigid, for he saw there a false beard of red hair and a length of red cloth, and the anger went out of him like water. He began to shake because there was no strength left in him.

These things—the red beard and the red length of cloth— were a sign and symbol of a band of robbers who marauded toward the northwest. Many were the houses they had burned and many were the women they had carried away. They bound good farmers with ropes to the thresholds of their own houses, to be found there the next day, raving mad if alive and burned and crisp as roasted meat if dead. Wang Lung stared, and then he turned and went away without a word. And as he went he heard his uncle's laughter.

Now Wang Lung found himself in such a predicament as he had never dreamed of. His uncle came and went as before, grinning a little under the sparse and scattered hairs of his gray beard, but Wang Lung dared not speak anything except courteous words. It was true that bandits had never come to his house during all his years of prosperity, although he had been afraid many times and had barred the doors stoutly at night. Now suddenly he saw why he had been safe and why he would be safe as long as his uncle and his uncle's wife and their son lived in his house. When he thought of this he broke into a cold sweat. He dared tell no one what his uncle had hidden in his coat.

Then—as if this were not enough—Cuckoo came back with news that although the affair of the betrothal had gone well, the merchant Liu was not willing for the marriage to take place now, because his daughter was too young, being but fourteen years old; the marriage must wait for another three years.

Wang Lung was dismayed at three more years of his eldest son's anger and idleness and mooning eyes. The next morning, as was his wont when the affairs of his house became too deep for him, he took a hoe and went out to his fields. And he went out to his fields day after day for many days.

Again, the good land healed him, and the warm winds of summer wrapped him with peace. One day, as if to cure him of his ceaseless thoughts of his own troubles, there came out of the south a small, slight cloud that began to spread fanwise up into the sky. The men of the village watched the horizon and talked of it, for they were afraid that locusts had come out of the south to devour what was planted in the fields. Wang Lung stood there also, and he watched, and at last the wind blew something to their feet. One man stooped and picked it up. It was a dead locust, dead and lighter than the living hosts behind.

Then Wang Lung forgot everything that troubled him. Women and sons and uncle, he forgot them all as he rushed among the frightened villagers, shouting at them, "Now we will fight these enemies from the skies!"

But there were some who shook their heads and said, "No, Heaven has ordained that this year we shall starve, and why should we waste ourselves in struggle against it?"

And weeping women went to town to buy incense to thrust before the earth gods in the little temple. But still the locusts spread over the land.

Then Wang Lung called his own laborers and Ching, and with their own hands they set fire to certain fields, burning the wheat, and they dug wide moats and ran water into them from the wells, and they worked without sleeping. O-lan and the women brought them food, and the men ate standing in the field.

Then the sky grew black and the air was filled with the deep roar of many wings, and the locusts fell upon the land, flying over this field and leaving it whole, and falling upon that field and eating it as bare as winter. The men sighed and said, "So Heaven wills." But Wang Lung was furious. He and his men beat the locusts and trampled on them and flailed at them. The locusts fell into the fires they kindled and floated dead on the water in the moats they dug. Many millions of them died, but measured against those that were left, it was nothing.

Nevertheless, for all his fighting Wang Lung had this as his reward: when the cloud moved on, the best of his fields had been spared. He was content. Many people ate the roasted bodies of the locusts, but Wang Lung himself would not eat them, for to him they were filthy because of what they had done to his land.

But for seven days he thought of nothing but his land, and he was healed of his troubles and his fears. He said to himself

calmly, "Well, every man has his troubles, and I must make shift to live with mine as I can. My uncle is older than I and will die, and three years must pass as they can with my son."

And he reaped his wheat. The rains came and the young green rice was set into the flooded fields, and again it was summer.

ONE DAY AFTER Wang Lung had said to himself that peace was in his house, his eldest son came to him as he returned from the land, and said, "Father, if I am to be a scholar, there is no more that that old head in the town can teach me."

Wang Lung dipped a towel into a basin of boiling water and wrung it and held it steaming against his face as he said, "Well, and how now?"

His eldest son went on, "I would like to go south to the city and enter a great school where I can learn what is to be learned."

Wang Lung rubbed the towel about his eyes and answered

his son sharply, for his body ached from his labor in the fields, "What nonsense is this? You have learning enough for these parts." And he dipped the cloth in the water again and wrung it.

But the young man stood there and muttered something, and Wang Lung was angry for he could not hear what it was, so he bawled at his son, "Speak out what you have to say!"

Then the young man flared at his father's voice and said, "Well, I will, then, go south. I will not stay in this stupid house and be watched like a child, and in this little town that is no better than a village!"

Wang Lung looked at his son standing there in a long robe of pale silver-gray linen, thin and cool for the summer's heat; his skin was smooth and golden and his hands under his long sleeves were as soft and fine as a woman's. Then Wang Lung looked at himself, thick and stained with earth, wearing only trousers of blue cotton cloth. One would have said he was his son's servant rather than his father. And this thought made him scornful, and he shouted out, "Now then, get into the fields and rub a little good earth on yourself before men take you for a woman!"

Wang Lung forgot that he had ever had pride in his son's cleverness, and he went out, stamping his bare feet as he walked and spitting upon the floor coarsely. His son stood and looked at him with hatred, but Wang Lung did not turn back.

Then for many days nothing was said and his son seemed suddenly content again, but he would not go to school anymore; he read in his own room. This Wang Lung allowed him, and Wang Lung was content and thought to himself, It was a whim of his youth. He does not know what he wants and there are only three years—maybe a little extra silver will make it two years.

Then Wang Lung forgot his eldest son, for the harvests were fair enough. But late one night when he sat alone, reckoning on his fingers what he could sell of his corn and of his rice, O-lan came softly into the room. With the passing years she had grown gaunt and the rocklike bones of her face stood out and her eyes were sunken. If asked how she did, she never said more than this: "There is a fire in my vitals."

For the past three years her belly was as great as it had been when she was with child, only there was no birth. Wang Lung saw her only as he saw his chair or a tree in the court, never even as keenly as he might see one of the oxen drooping its head. She did her work alone and spoke no more than she could escape speaking. She cooked their meals and washed their clothes at the pool, even in the winter when the water was stiff with ice. But Wang Lung never thought to say, "Well, why do you not hire a servant?"

On this evening, then, when he sat alone with only the red candles in the pewter stands alight, she stood before him and looked this way and that, and at last she said in a harsh whisper, "When you are away, the eldest son goes too often into the inner court."

Now Wang Lung could not at first grasp what she said and he leaned forward with his mouth agape. Finally he said, "You dream!"

She shook her head at this and said further, "Come home unexpectedly." And again, after a silence, "It is better to send him away, even to the south." Then she went away and left him sitting there agape.

"Well, this woman is jealous," he said to himself, laughing at the small thoughts of women.

But when he went in that night to Lotus, she was petulant and pushed him away. Then the words of O-lan stood out sharply, and he flung himself out of the room and walked among the bamboos beside the house wall. At last he watched the dawn come ruddy over his land, and he went in and ate. Then he went out to oversee his men, as was his custom in times of harvest, and he shouted loudly, so that anyone in his house might hear, "Now I am going to the piece by the moat and I shall not be back early," and he set his face to the town.

But when he had gone halfway he turned back to his house. He went in and stood at the red curtain that hung in the door to the inner court. And listening, he heard the murmuring of a man's voice. It was the voice of his own son.

The anger that arose in Wang Lung's heart now was an anger he had never known in all his life before. This anger was the anger of one man against another who steals away the woman he loves, and when Wang Lung remembered that the other man was his own son, he was filled with sickness.

And then he went out and chose a slim, supple bamboo from the grove and stripped off the branches. He went back in softly and suddenly tore aside the curtain. There was his son, standing in the court and looking down at Lotus, who sat on a small stool at the edge of the pool. At that Wang Lung leaped forward and fell on his son, lashing him. When Lotus screamed and dragged at his arm, he shook her off, and beat her also until she fled. He beat the young man until he stooped, cowering, to the ground and covered his torn face in his hands.

Then Wang Lung paused; he was weak as with an illness. He threw down his bamboo and whispered to the boy, panting, "Now get to your room, put your things in a box, and tomorrow go south to what you will and do not come home until I send for you."

The boy rose without a word and left. Then, wearily, Wang Lung went back to the old court. O-lan was sitting there, sewing some garment, and when he passed, she said nothing. If she had heard the beating and the screaming, she made no sign. And he went on out to his fields, spent as with the labor of a whole day.

XIII

WHEN HIS ELDEST son was gone, Wang Lung said to himself that it was a good thing; now he could look to his other children, for what with his troubles, he hardly knew what he had for children after this eldest son.

Now the second son of Wang Lung was as unlike the eldest

as two sons in a house may be. Where the eldest was big-boned and ruddy-faced like his mother, this second one was short and slight and yellow-skinned, and there was that in him that reminded Wang Lung of his own father, a crafty, sharp eye, and a turn for malice if the moment came for it. Wang Lung said, "This boy will make a good merchant. I will see if he can be apprenticed to Liu in the grain market. It will be a convenient thing to have a son where I sell my harvests so he can watch the scales and tip the weight a little in my favor. And the youngest boy I will keep for the land."

Therefore Wang Lung put on his silk coat and set out across the fields. He went first to the Street of the Stone Bridge and there before a gate that bore the name of Liu he stopped. Not that he knew the word himself, but he asked one who passed. It was a respectable gate built plainly of wood, and Wang Lung struck it with the palm of his hand.

Immediately it was opened and a woman servant stood there, asking who he was, and when he answered his name, she led him into the first court and bade him seat himself. Then she went out to call her master. Wang Lung examined the curtains and the table, and was pleased, for there was evidence of good living but not of extreme wealth. He did not want a rich daughter-in-law lest she be haughty and cry for this and that.

Suddenly there was a heavy step and a stout elderly man entered, and Wang Lung rose, and they both bowed, looking secretly at each other, each respecting the other for what he was, a man of worth and prosperity. Then they seated themselves and drank hot wine, which the servant woman poured out for them, and talked slowly of crops and prices.

And at last Wang Lung said, "Well, I have come for a thing, and if it is not your wish, let us talk of other things. But if you have need for a servant in your market, there is my second son, and a sharp one he is."

Then the merchant said with great good humor, "And so I have such need of a sharp young man, if he reads and writes."

And Wang Lung answered proudly, "My sons are both good scholars, and they can each tell when a letter is wrongly written."

"That is good," said Liu. "Let him come. His wages are his food until he learns the business, and then if he does well, he may have a piece of silver at the end of every moon, and at the end of three years, three pieces. After that he is no longer an apprentice, but he may rise as he is able in the business. And besides this wage, there is whatever fee he may extract from this buyer and that seller. About this I will say nothing if he is able to get it."

Wang Lung rose then, well pleased, and he laughed and said, "Now we are friends, and have you no son for my second daughter?"

Then the merchant laughed richly, for he was fat and well fed, and he said, "I have a second son of ten whom I have not betrothed yet. How old is the girl?"

"She will be ten on her next birthday and she is a pretty flower," Wang Lung answered.

Then Wang Lung said no more, for it was not a thing that could be discussed face to face beyond this. But after he had bowed and gone away well pleased, he said to himself, "The thing may be done," and he looked at his young daughter when he came home. She was a pretty child and moved about with small, graceful steps.

But when Wang Lung looked at her closely, he saw the marks of tears on her cheeks, and her face was a shade too pale for her years. He drew her to him by her little hand and said, "Now why have you wept?"

She hung her head and toyed with a button on her coat and said, shy and half murmuring, "Because my mother binds a cloth about my feet more tightly every day and I cannot sleep at night."

"I have not heard you weep," he said, wondering.

"No," she said simply, "my mother said I was not to weep aloud because you are too kind and you might say to leave me as I am, and then my husband would not love me, even as you do not love her."

This she said as simply as a child recites a tale, and Wang Lung was stabbed at hearing it, because with all her dimness O-lan had seen the truth in him.

In the days after this he sent his second son away into town and signed the papers for the second girl's betrothal. He would have been content except that now, whether he would or not, he fell to thinking of his life and of how O-lan had been the first woman he had known and how she had been a faithful servant beside him. He saw now that she had grown thin and her skin was sere and yellow. She moved more and more slowly about, and he remembered, now that he thought of it, that sometimes he heard her groaning when she stooped to the oven, and only when he asked, "Well, what is it?" did she cease suddenly.

So, he was stricken with remorse, although he did not know why, and he argued with himself, "Well, it is not my fault if I have not loved her as one loves a concubine, since men do not. I have not beaten her, and I have given her silver when she asked for it."

But still he could not forget what the child had said, and he kept looking at her as she brought in his food or as she moved about. One day when she stooped to sweep the floor, he saw her face turn gray with some inner pain, and she put her hand to her belly.

He asked her sharply, "What is it?"

But she averted her face and answered meekly, "It is only the old pain in my vitals."

Then he stared at her and he called to the younger girl, "Take the broom. Your mother is ill." And to O-lan he said more kindly than he had spoken to her in many years, "Go in and lie on your bed, and I will bid the girl bring you hot water."

She obeyed him slowly, and without answering him, she went to her room.

Wang Lung heard her dragging about. At last she lay down and moaned softly. Then he sat listening until he could not bear it. He rose and went into the town to a doctor's shop.

The doctor sat idle over a pot of tea. He was an old man with a long gray beard and brass spectacles over his nose. When Wang Lung told him what his wife's signs were, he pursed his lips and said, "I will come."

When they came to O-lan's bed, she had fallen into a light sleep, and the sweat stood like dew on her forehead. The old doctor shook his head to see it. He put forth a hand and felt her pulse, and then he shook his head again gravely, saying, "The spleen is enlarged and the liver diseased. There is a rock as large as a man's head in the womb; the stomach is disintegrated. It is a difficult case. For ten pieces of silver I will give you a prescription of herbs and a tiger's heart. But if you wish complete recovery guaranteed, then five hundred pieces of silver."

Now when Wang Lung heard this all, his old remorse smote him, and he answered fiercely, "I will have no death in my house; I can pay the silver."

The old doctor's eyes shone greedily, but he knew the penalty of the law if the woman died, and so he said, although with regret, "No. As I look at the color of the whites of her eyes, I see I was mistaken. Five thousand pieces of silver must I have to guarantee full recovery."

Then Wang Lung looked at the doctor in silence and in sad understanding; it was simply that the doctor had said, "The woman will die."

He went out with the doctor, therefore, and paid him ten pieces of silver. When he was gone, Wang Lung went into the dark kitchen where O-lan had lived her life, and he turned his face to the blackened wall and wept.

BUT THERE was no sudden dying of life in O-lan's body. She was scarcely past the middle of her span of years, and her life would not easily pass from her body. All through the long months of winter she lay dying on her bed. For the first time

Wang Lung and his children knew what she had been in the house, and how she had made it comfortable for them all and they had not known it.

It seemed now that no one knew how to light the oven, and no one knew how to turn a fish in the caldron without breaking it, and no one knew whether it was the sesame oil or the bean that was right for frying this vegetable or that. Dropped food lay under the table and no one swept it unless Wang Lung grew impatient and called in a dog from the court to lick it up or shouted at the younger girl to scrape it up and throw it out.

The youngest boy did this and that to fill his mother's place with his grandfather, who was as helpless as a little child now and could not understand why O-lan no longer came to bring him hot water and to help him. He was peevish because he called her and she did not come, and he threw his bowl of tea on the ground like a willful child.

Only the poor fool knew nothing. Yet one had to think to bring her in at night and to feed her and to set her in the sun and to lead her in if it rained. Once they left her outside through a whole night, and the next morning the poor wretch was shivering and crying in the dawn, and Wang Lung cursed his son and daughter that they had forgotten their sister. Then he saw that they were but children trying to take their mother's place, and after that he saw to the poor fool himself.

Wang Lung turned over the work to Ching, and Ching labored faithfully, and night and morning he came and asked how O-lan did. At last Wang Lung could not bear it because he could only say, "Today she drank a little soup," or "Today she ate a little thin gruel of rice."

All during the cold dark winter Wang Lung sat beside O-lan's bed. If she was cold, he lit an earthen pot of charcoal and set it beside her bed. At last one day he burst forth, "I cannot bear this! I would sell my land if it could heal you."

She smiled at this and said in gasps, whispering, "No, and I would not—let you. For I must die—sometime anyway. But the land is there after me."

But he would not talk of her death. He rose and went out when she spoke of it.

Nevertheless, because he knew she would die and it was his duty, he went one day into the town and chose a good black coffin made from heavy and hard wood. Then the carpenter said cunningly, "The price is a third off for two. Why do you not buy one for yourself and know that you are provided for?"

"No, for my sons can do it for me," answered Wang Lung, and then he thought of his own father, and he said, "I will take the two."

And Wang Lung told O-lan what he had done, and she was pleased that he had provided well for her death.

Thus he sat by her. They did not talk much, for she was faint, and besides there had never been much talk between them. Often she forgot where she was and murmured of her childhood, and for the first time Wang Lung saw into her heart.

"I will bring the meats to the door only—and well I know I am ugly and cannot appear before the great lord—" And again she said, panting, "Do not beat me—I will never eat of the dish again—" And she said over and over, "My father—my mother—my father—my mother—" and again and again, "Well I know I am ugly and cannot be loved—"

When she said this, Wang Lung could not bear it. He took her hand and soothed it, a big, hard hand, stiff as though it were dead already. And he wondered and grieved at himself most of all because what she said was true, and even when he took her hand, he was ashamed because he could feel no tenderness, no melting of the heart such as Lotus could win from him with a pout of her lips.

But because of this, he was kinder to her. He brought her special food and delicate soups. Moreover, when he went in to Lotus to distract his mind from its despair, he could not forget O-lan even as he held Lotus.

There were times when O-lan woke to herself and to what was about her. Once she said to him, "After I am dead, neither that slave nor her mistress is to come into my room or touch my things, and if they do, I will send my spirit back for a curse." Then she fell into her fitful sleep, and her head dropped upon the pillow.

But one day before the new year, she was suddenly better, as a candle flickers brightly at its end. She was herself as she had not been. She sat up in bed and twisted her hair for herself and asked for tea to drink.

When Wang Lung came, she said, "There is a thing I must see before I can die."

To this he replied angrily, "You cannot speak of dying and please me!"

She smiled slowly then, the same slow smile that ended before it reached her eyes, and she answered, "Die I must, for I feel it waiting in my vitals, but I will not die before my eldest son comes home and weds, so that I may die easily, knowing your grandson is stirred into life and there will be a great-grandson for the old one."

Now Wang Lung was cheered at the strength in her voice, and he would not cross her, although he would have liked more time for a great wedding for his eldest son. Therefore he said to her, "Well, we will do this thing. Today I will send a man south to search for my son and bring him home to be wed. Then you must promise me that you will gather your strength again and grow well, for the house is like a cave for beasts without you."

This he said to please her and it pleased her, although she did not speak again, but lay back and closed her eyes, smiling a little.

And as Wang Lung said, so he did. He bade Cuckoo to provide a feast and call in cooks from the town. He poured silver into her hands and said, "Do as it would have been done in the great house."

Then he went into the village and into town and invited everyone he knew.

On the night of the day before his marriage, Wang Lung's eldest son came home and Wang Lung forgot that the young man had troubled him. For two years had passed since he had seen this son, and here he was a tall man and a goodly one, with a great square body and short black hair, shining and oiled. He wore a long dark-red gown of satin such as one finds in the shops in the south, and a short black velvet jacket without sleeves.

Then the young man sat beside his mother's bed and the tears stood in his eyes to see her thus, but he would not say anything except cheerful things such as, "You look twice as well as they said."

But O-lan said simply, "I will see you wed, then I must die."

Now the bride who was to be wed must not be seen by the young man, so when her mother brought her from town, Lotus took her into the inner court to prepare her for marriage, and no one could do this better than Lotus and Cuckoo.

On the morning of her wedding day, they washed her and dressed her in garments she had brought from home: white-flowered silk, a light coat of sheep's wool, and then the red satin garments of marriage. Then they painted her with powder and with red paint and set the bride's crown and the beaded veil upon her head. To everything the maid was acquiescent but properly reluctant and shy.

Then Wang Lung and the guests waited in the middle room and the bride came in, supported by her own slave and by the wife of Wang Lung's uncle. She came in modestly and correctly with her head bowed and walked as though she were unwilling to wed and must be supported to it. This showed her great modesty and Wang Lung was pleased.

After this Wang Lung's eldest son came in, dressed in his red robe and his black jacket. Behind him came his two brothers, and Wang Lung, seeing them, was fit to burst with pride at this procession of his goodly sons. Then the old man, who had not understood at all what was happening, now suddenly understood and cackled out with cracked laughter and said over and over, "There is a marriage—children again and grandchildren!"

And he laughed so heartily that the guests all laughed to see his mirth, and Wang Lung thought to himself that if only O-lan had been up from her bed, it would have been a merry day.

All this time Wang Lung looked sharply at his son to see if he glanced at the bride, and the young man did glance secretly from the corner of his eyes, but it was enough, for he grew pleased and merry in his ways. Wang Lung said proudly to himself, "Well, I have chosen one he likes for him."

Then the young man and the bride together bowed to the old man and to Wang Lung and went into the room where O-lan lay. She was sitting up, dressed in her good black coat. They bowed to her, and she patted the bed and said, "Sit here and drink the wine and eat the rice of your marriage, for I would see it all."

The two sat down side by side and in silence, shy of each other. The wife of Wang Lung's uncle came in, fat and important with the occasion, bearing two bowls of hot wine, and the two drank separately, and then mingled the wine of the two bowls and drank again. They ate rice and then mingled their rice together. This signified that their life was now one, and thus they were wed. Then they bowed again to O-lan and to Wang Lung and went out, and together they bowed to the assembled guests.

Then the feasting began. The rooms and the courts were filled with the smell of cooking and with the sound of laughter, for the guests Wang Lung had invited came from far and wide. With them were many whom Wang Lung had never seen, since it was known that he was a rich man and food would never be missed in his house at such a time.

O-lan would have all the doors open so that she could hear the laughter and smell the food, and she said again and again to Wang Lung, who came in often to see how she did, "Has everyone wine? Is the sweet rice dish in the middle of the feast very hot, and have they put the full measure of lard and sugar into it and the eight fruits?"

He assured her that everything was as she wished.

Then it was over, and the guests were gone, and night came. With the silence over the house and the ebbing of merriment, strength passed from O-lan. She grew weary and seemed to fall into a fitful sleep. When she spoke, it was as though she did not know where she was, for she said, muttering and turning her head this way and that, "Well, if I am ugly, still I have borne a son." And again she said, "How can that one care for him as I do?"

Then Wang Lung sat beside her while she slept, and he looked at her. As he looked, she opened her eyes. There was some strange mist over them, for she stared at him as though she wondered who he was. Suddenly her head dropped off the round pillow where it lay, and she shuddered and was dead.

ONCE SHE LAY dead it seemed to Wang Lung that he could not bear to be near her. But to comfort himself he busied himself, calling men to seal the coffin according to custom. He went to a geomancer and asked him to find a lucky day for burials, and the geomancer chose one three months hence. Then he called for mourning for himself and for his children. Their shoes were made of coarse white cloth, the color of mourning, and about their ankles they bound bands of white cloth, and the women in the house bound their hair with white cord.

After this Wang Lung could not bear to sleep in the room where O-lan had died. He took his possessions and moved altogether into the inner court where Lotus lived. He said to his eldest son, "Go with your wife into that room where your mother lived and died, and beget there your own sons."

So the two moved into it and were content.

Then as though death could not easily leave the house where it had come once, the old man, Wang Lung's father, who had been distraught ever since he saw them putting the dead body of O-lan into the coffin, lay down on his bed one night, and when the second daughter came in the morning to bring him his tea, there he was, his scattered old beard thrust up into the air, and his head thrown back in death.

She cried out at the sight and ran to her father. Wang Lung came in and found the old man so; his light, stiff old body was as dry and cold and thin as a gnarled pine tree. Then Wang Lung washed the old man himself and laid him gently in the coffin he had bought for him and had it sealed. He said, "On the same day we will bury these two dead from our house. I will take a good piece of my hill land, and we will bury them there together. When I die, I will be laid there also."

So he did what he said he would do. On the day appointed by the geomancer in the spring, Wang Lung called priests from the Taoist temple, and they came dressed in their yellow robes; and he called priests from the Buddhist temple, and they came in their long gray robes; and these priests beat drums and chanted the whole night through for the two who were dead. Whenever they stopped their chanting, Wang Lung poured silver into their hands and they took breath again and chanted and did not cease until dawn rose.

Now Wang Lung had chosen a good place in his fields

under a date tree upon a hill to set the graves, and Ching had had the graves dug and a wall of earth built. This land Wang Lung did not begrudge, even though it was high land and good for wheat, because it was a sign of the establishment of his family. Dead and alive, they would rest upon their own land.

After the priests had finished the night of chanting, Wang Lung stood beside the two graves and watched the burial. His grief was hard and dry, and he would not cry out loud as others did, because it seemed to him that there was nothing to be done more than he had done. But when the graves were covered over, he turned away silently and walked home alone. And out of his heaviness there stood out strangely but one clear thought and it was painful to him: he wished he had not taken the two pearls from O-lan. He would not again bear to see Lotus put them in her ears. And he said to himself, "There in that land of mine is buried the first good half of my life and more. It is as though half of me were buried there."

And suddenly he wept a little, and he dried his eyes with the back of his hand, as a child does.

XIV

DURING ALL this time Wang Lung knew that if it had not been for his uncle's power, he would have been robbed and sacked for his money and for the women in his house. So his uncle and his uncle's son and his uncle's wife were like guests in his house. They drank tea before others and dipped first with their chopsticks into the bowls at mealtime. They saw that Wang Lung was afraid of them and they grew haughty and demanded this and that and complained daily of what they ate and drank.

Now Wang Lung's eldest son, engrossed in his marriage, scarcely saw what happened except that he guarded his wife jealously from the gaze of his cousin, so that now these two were no longer friends but enemies. But when he saw these three doing as they would with his father, he grew angry, for he was of a quick temper, and he said, "If you care more for these three tigers than you do for your son and his wife, we had better set up our house elsewhere."

Wang Lung told him plainly then what he had told no one. "I hate these three, but your uncle is lord of a horde of wild robbers, and if I coddle him, we are safe."

When the eldest son heard this, he stared until his eyes hung out of his head, and the two of them fell silent, each thinking heavily what to do. And Wang Lung spoke aloud at last, musing, "If there was a way that we could keep them here but make them harmless and undesiring, what a thing it would be."

Then the young man struck his two hands together and cried out, "Well, you have told me! Let us buy them opium to enjoy, and let them have their will of it as rich people do."

But Wang Lung, since he had not thought of the thing first himself, was doubtful. "Opium is as dear as jade," he said.

"It is dearer than jade to have them at us like this," the young man argued, "and to endure their haughtiness and my cousin peeping at my wife."

So Wang Lung went the next day into the town to a tobacco shop. Half unwillingly he said to the clerk, "And how much is your opium if you have it?"

And the clerk said, "It is not lawful in these days to sell it over the counter, but if you wish to buy it and have the silver, it is weighed out in the room behind this, an ounce for a silver piece."

Then Wang Lung would not think further what he did, but said quickly, "I will take six ounces of it."

Then one day Wang Lung said to his uncle, "Since you are my father's brother, here is a little better tobacco for you."

And he opened the jar of opium. Wang Lung's uncle smelled it and laughed with pleasure. He said, "Well now, I have smoked it a little but not often before this, for it is too dear, but I like it well enough."

And Wang Lung answered him, pretending to be careless,

"It is only a little I bought once for my father when he could not sleep at night, and I found it today unused and I thought, There is my father's brother. Why should he not have it as I am younger and do not need it yet?"

Then Wang Lung's uncle took it greedily, for it was sweet to smell and a thing that only rich men used. He smoked the opium, lying all day on his bed. Wang Lung saw to it that there were pipes bought and left here and there. He pretended to smoke himself, but he only took a pipe to his room and left it there cold. He would not allow his sons and Lotus to touch the opium, saying as his excuse that it was too dear, but he urged it upon his uncle and upon his uncle's wife and son, and Wang Lung did not begrudge the silver for it because it bought him peace.

Now as the winter wore away, it happened one day that his eldest son followed him and said to him proudly, "There will soon be another mouth in the house."

Wang Lung, when he heard this, turned himself about and laughed and rubbed his hands together and said, "Here is a good day indeed!"

And he went to find Ching and tell him to go to town to buy fish and good food. When it arrived, he sent it in to his son's wife, saying, "Eat, make strong the body of my grandson."

All during the spring Wang Lung had this knowledge for his comfort. And thinking constantly of the child to come and of others to come from his sons when they were all wed, he bought six slaves, two about twelve years of age with big feet and strong bodies, and three younger to wait upon them all, and one, a small, delicate maid of seven years, to wait on the person of Lotus, for Cuckoo had grown old.

Summer came and the land was to be planted. Wang Lung walked hither and thither and discussed with Ching the quality of each piece of soil and what changes of crops there should be for the fertility of the land. When everything was planned, Wang Lung went back to his house well content and said to his own heart, "I am no longer young and it is not necessary for me to work anymore with my hands since I have men on my land and my sons."

Yet although he had given his son a wife and although he had bought slaves for them all, and although his uncle and his uncle's wife were given enough opium for their pleasure all day, there was still no peace, for his uncle's son did not yield to opium as easily as the two old ones had.

One day when Wang Lung entered from the fields, his eldest son drew his father aside, and he said, "I will not endure my cousin in the house anymore with his peepings and his lounging about with his eyes on the slaves."

Wang Lung had come in from the fields in high humor, and he answered, angry at this fresh trouble, "Well, you are a foolish child to be forever thinking of this. You have grown too fond of your wife; it is not seemly for a man to love his wife with a foolish love, as though she were a concubine."

The young man was stung by this rebuke, for more than anything he feared anyone who accused him of behavior that was not correct. He answered quickly, "It is not for my wife. It is because it is unseemly in my father's house. I wish that we could go into the town and live. We could leave my uncle and his wife and my cousin here and still live safely in the town behind the gates."

Wang Lung laughed bitterly and shortly, and then he threw the desire of the young man aside for something worthless. "This is my house," he said stoutly, "and you may live in it or not." And Wang Lung tramped about loudly and spat upon the floor and acted as a farmer may, although one side of his heart triumphed in his son's fineness.

But the eldest son was not ready to give over. He followed his father saying, "Well, there is the old great house of the Hwangs. The front part of it is rented out and filled with common people, but the inner courts are locked. We could rent them and live there peacefully." Then he forced the tears to come into his eyes and said again, "I try to be a good son. I do not gamble and smoke opium and I am content with the woman you have given me. I only ask a little of you and it is all."

Wang Lung was not moved by the tears alone, but he was moved by the words of his son when he had spoken of the great house of the Hwangs.

Never had Wang Lung forgotten that once he had gone crawling into that great house and stood so ashamed in the presence of those who lived there that he was frightened of even the gateman, and this memory of shame had remained with him all his life, and he hated it. So when his son proposed that they live in the great house, he saw it actually happening before his eyes. I could sit on that seat where that old one sat and call another into my presence, he mused. And he said to himself again, "This I could do if I wished."

One day Wang Lung went into town to see his second son at the grain market, and he asked him, "Well, my second son, what say you of the thing your elder brother desires—that we move into town to the great house if we can rent part of it?"

The second son was a young man by now, although still of small stature, and he answered smoothly, "It is an excellent thing and it would suit me well, for then I could wed and have my wife there also and we would all be under one roof as a great family is."

Wang Lung said in some shame, for he knew he had not done well by his second son, "I have said to myself for a long time that you should be wed, but what with this thing and that I have not had time—but now the thing shall be done." And he cast about secretly in his mind for the first steps he would take to find a bride.

The second son said, "Well, wed I will, then, for it is right for a man to have sons. But do not get me a wife from a house in town, such as my brother has, for she will talk forever of what was in her father's house and make me spend money."

Wang Lung heard this with astonishment, for he had not known that his daughter-in-law was thus, seeing only that she was a woman careful to be correct in her behavior and fair enough in her looks. But it seemed to him wise talk and he rejoiced that his son was clever about saving money. And he said, "What sort of a bride would you have, then?"

The young man answered as smoothly and steadily as if he had had the thing planned, "I desire one from a village, of good landed family and without poor relatives, neither plain nor fair to look upon, and a good cook, so that even though there are servants in the kitchen, she may watch them. And she must be such a one that if she buys cloth, the garment will be well cut so that the scraps of cloth left over should lie in the palm of her hand."

Now Wang Lung was astonished, for it was not such blood as this that ran in his own lusty body when he was young, nor in the body of his eldest son; yet he admired the wisdom of the young man. He said, laughing, "Well, I shall seek such a one and Ching shall look for her among the villages."

Still laughing, he went away down the street of the great house. He hesitated between the stone lions and then, since there was no one to stop him, he went in. In the front courts the trees were hung with drying clothes and women sat everywhere gossiping. Children rolled naked on the tiles, and the place reeked with the smell of common people who swarm into the courts of the great when the great are gone.

Now Wang Lung in the old days would have felt himself one of these common people and against the great. But now that he had land and silver, he said to himself that they were filthy. He picked his way among them with his nose up and breathing lightly because of the stink they made, as though he himself belonged to the great house.

He went on through the courts, although it was for idle curiosity and not because he had decided anything, and at the back he found a gate locked and beside it an old woman drowsing. He saw that she was the pockmarked wife of the man who had been gateman. This astonished him, for he remembered her as buxom and middle-aged and she was now haggard and wrinkled and white-haired. Thus he saw in a moment how many and how swift were the years that had passed since he was a young man with his firstborn son in his arms. For the first time in his life, Wang Lung felt his age creeping up on him. Then he said somewhat sadly to the old woman, "Wake and let me into the gate."

And the old woman started up blinking and said, "I am not to open except to such as may rent the courts."

And Wang Lung said, "And so I may, if the place pleases me."

He went in after her and remembered the way well, for there stood the little room where he had left his basket; here the long veranda supported by the delicately carved pillars. He followed her into the great hall itself, and there before him was the dais where the old lady had sat, her fragile, tended body wrapped in silvery gray satin.

Moved by some strange impulse, he went forward and sat where she had sat and looked down on the bleary face of the old hag, who blinked at him and waited in silence for what he would do. Then some satisfaction that he had longed for all his days without knowing it welled up in his heart and he struck the table with his hand and said suddenly, "This house I will have!"

IN THESE DAYS when Wang Lung had decided a thing, he could not do it quickly enough. So he told his eldest son to arrange the matter, and he sent for his second son to help with the moving, and they moved, first Lotus and Cuckoo and their slaves, and then Wang Lung's eldest son and his wife and their slaves.

But Wang Lung himself, when the moment came for leaving the land on which he was born, could not do it as quickly as he had thought. He said to his sons when they urged him, "Well then, prepare a court for me and I will come when the maid is found who is to wed my second son, for it is easier to stay here where Ching is until the matter is completed."

Left in the house, then, were the uncle and his wife and son and Ching and the laboring men, besides Wang Lung and his youngest son and the poor fool. His second daughter was now wed to the son of Liu, and Wang Lung stirred himself to bid Ching find a bride for his second son.

Now Ching had grown old and withered and lean as a reed, but there was the strength of an old and faithful dog in him yet, although Wang Lung would no longer let him lift a hoe or follow the plow. Still he was useful, for he watched the labor of others and he stood by when the grain was weighed. So when he heard what Wang Lung wished, he put on his good blue cotton coat and went to this village and that and looked at many young girls. At last he came back and said, "I would sooner choose a wife for myself than for your son. But if it were I and I were young, there is a girl three villages away, a buxom, careful girl with no fault except a ready laugh, and her father is glad to be tied to your family by his daughter. And the dowry is good for these times."

It seemed to Wang Lung then that this was good enough. He was relieved, and he said, "Now there is only one more son and I will be finished with all this marrying."

When it was done and the wedding day set, he rested and sat in the sun and slept even as his father had before him.

Then, as if the gods were kind for once, his uncle's son grew restless, and he said to Wang Lung, "There is a war to the north. I will go and join it if you will give me silver to buy more clothes and a foreign fire stick to put over my shoulder."

Then Wang Lung's heart leaped with pleasure, but he hid his pleasure artfully as he gave him the silver. Then he said to himself, "If he likes it, there is an end to this curse in my house, for there is always a war somewhere in the nation." Again he said to himself, "He may even be killed, if my good fortune holds, for in wars there are those who die." He was in high good humor then, although he concealed it, and he comforted his uncle's wife when she wept to hear of her son's going, and he lit her opium pipe for her and said, "Doubtless he will rise to be an official and honor will come to us all through him."

Now Wang Lung, as the hour drew near for the birth of his grandson, stayed more and more in the house in town. He could never have his fill of wonder at this, that here in these courts where the family of Hwang had once lived, now he lived with his sons and a child was to be born of a third generation.

And nothing was too good for his money to buy. He bought lengths of satin and of silk for them all, for it looked ill to see common cotton robes upon the carved chairs of southern black wood. And he was pleased when the friends that his eldest son had found in town came into the courts and proud that they should see all that was. And Wang Lung himself, who once had been well satisfied with good wheat bread wrapped about a stick of garlic, now tasted winter bamboo and shrimp roe and shellfish and pigeon eggs and all those things that rich men use to force their lagging appetites. And Cuckoo, seeing all that had come about, laughed and said, "It is like the old days when I was in these courts."

So with this idle and luxurious living, rising when he would and sleeping when he would, Wang Lung waited for his grandson. Then one morning he heard the groans of a woman, and his eldest son said, "The hour is come, but Cuckoo says it will be long, for the woman is narrowly made and it is a hard birth."

So Wang Lung sat and listened to the cries, and for the first time in many years he felt the need of some spirit's aid. He rose and bought incense and went to the temple in town where the goddess of mercy dwelt in a gilded alcove. He summoned an idling priest and gave him money and bade him thrust the incense before the goddess.

Then, as he watched the priest thrust it in the ashes of the urn before the goddess, he thought with sudden horror, And what if it be not a grandson but a girl, and he called out hastily, "If it is a grandson, I will pay for a new red robe for the goddess, but nothing will I do if it is a girl!"

He went out in agitation because he had not thought of this.

And then, having done all he could, he went back to the courts. He sat down and wished for a slave to bring him tea, but though he clapped his hands, no one came. There was much running to and fro, but he dared stop no one to ask what was happening. He sat there dusty and spent and no one spoke to him.

Then at last when he had waited so long it seemed to him it must soon be night, Lotus came in and laughed and said loudly, "Well, there is a son in the house of your son. And he is fair and sound."

Then Wang Lung laughed also and rose and slapped his hands together. When Lotus had gone on to her room, he fell to musing again and thought to himself, Well, I did not fear like this when my first wife bore her first, my son. And he sat silent and remembered how she had gone into the small dark room alone and silently she had borne him sons, and how she had come then to the fields and worked beside him. And here was this one who cried like a child with her pains, and who had all the slaves running in the house, and her husband there by her door. And he remembered as one remembers a dream long past how O-lan had fed the child richly out of her breast.

Then his son came in, smiling and important, and said loudly, "Your grandson is born, my father, and now we must find a woman to nurse him, for I will not have my wife's beauty spoiled with the nursing."

And Wang Lung said sadly, although why he was sad he did not know, "Well, let it be so if she cannot nurse her own child."

When the child was a month old, his father gave the birth feast. He had many hundreds of eggs dyed red, and these he gave to every guest, and there was feasting and joy, for the child had passed his tenth day and lived.

And when it was over, Wang Lung's son said to his father, "Now that there are the three generations in this house, we should have the tablets of ancestors that great families have, for we are an established family now."

This pleased Wang Lung greatly, and there in the great hall

the tablets were set up, his grandfather's name on one and then his father's, and spaces were left for Wang Lung's name and his son's when they should die. And Wang Lung's son bought an incense urn and set it before the tablets.

When this was finished Wang Lung remembered the red robe he had promised the goddess of mercy, and so he went to the temple to give the money for it.

And then, on his way back, as if the gods cannot bear to give freely, a man came running from the harvest fields to tell him that Ching lay dying. And although his noon meal stood ready, and although Lotus called loudly to him to wait until after the evening sun, he would not stay. Then Lotus sent a slave after him with an umbrella of oiled paper, but so fast did Wang Lung run that the stout woman had difficulty in holding the umbrella over his head.

Wang Lung went at once to the room where Ching had been laid, and he called out loudly, "Now how did all this come about?"

The room was full of laborers, and they answered in confusion, "He would work himself at the threshing . . ." "We told him not at his age . . ." "There was a laborer who could not hold the flail rightly and Ching would show him. . . ."

Then Wang Lung called out in a terrible voice, "Bring me this laborer."

And they pushed a young man in front before Wang Lung, and he stood there trembling, his bare knees knocking together, a great, ruddy, coarse lad. But Wang Lung had no pity for him. He slapped the man on both his cheeks and took the umbrella from the woman to beat him. No one dared stop him for fear that his anger would go into his blood and at his age poison him. And the bumpkin stood the beating humbly, blubbering a little.

Then Ching moaned from the bed where he lay. Wang Lung threw down the umbrella and cried out, "Now this one will die while I am beating a fool!"

And he sat down beside Ching and took his hand and held

it. Ching's face was dark and spotted with his scanty blood, and his half-opened eyes were filmed and his breath came in gusts. Wang Lung leaned down to him and said loudly in his ear, "Here am I and I will buy you a coffin second to my father's only!"

But Ching's ears were filled with blood, and if he heard Wang Lung, he made no sign but only lay there panting and so he died.

Wang Lung wept as he had not wept when his own father died. He hired priests for the funeral and walked behind them wearing white mourning. And if Wang Lung had had his way, he would have buried Ching inside the earthen wall.

But his sons would not have it and said, "Shall our mother and grandfather lie with a servant?"

Then Wang Lung, because at his age he would have peace in his house, buried Ching at the entrance to the wall, and he said, "It is meet, for he has ever stood guardian to me against evil." And he directed his sons that when he himself died, he should lie nearest to Ching.

Then less than ever did Wang Lung go to see his lands. Now that Ching was gone, it pained him to go alone, and his bones ached when he walked over the rough fields. So he rented out all his land that he could, and men took it eagerly, for it was known to be good land. But Wang Lung would never talk of selling a foot of any piece. He would only rent for a year at a time. Thus he felt it was all his own and still in his hand.

He appointed one of the laborers and his wife to live in the country house and to care for his uncle and his uncle's wife.

Then seeing his youngest son's wistful eyes, he said, "Well, you may come with me into town, and I will take my poor fool with me too, for now that Ching is gone, I am not sure that they will be kind to her. And there is no one to teach you concerning the land now that Ching is gone."

So Wang Lung took his youngest son and his poor fool with him, and thereafter he went scarcely at all to the house on his land.

147

XV

To WANG LUNG it now seemed there was nothing left to be desired; he could sit in the sun beside his poor fool and be at peace.

And so it might have been if it had not been for that eldest son of his, who came to his father saying, "We must not think we can be a great family just because we live in these inner courts. It is a shame to ask guests to come through that common swarm with their stinks; and with my brother to wed and his children and mine to come we need the outer courts also."

Then Wang Lung looked at his son standing there in his handsome raiment, and he shut his eyes and growled, "Do as you like, only do not trouble me with it!"

Hearing this, the son went away quickly before his father changed his mind, and he went well pleased. And when the day came when rents are decided upon, the common people found that the rent for the courts where they lived had been greatly raised because another would pay that much for them. They knew it was Wang Lung's eldest son who had done this, although he said nothing and did it all by letters to the son of the old Lord Hwang, who lived in foreign parts and cared for nothing except getting the most money he could for the old house. Then the common people packed their tattered possessions and went away swelling with anger and muttering that one day they would come back.

But all this Wang Lung did not hear, since he was in the inner courts and seldom came forth. His son called carpenters and masons to repair the rooms and the courts that the common people had ruined with their coarse ways of living; they repaired the pools and his son bought golden fish to put in them. And it was all made beautiful as far as his son knew beauty. He planted lotus and lilies in the pools, and the scarlet-berried bamboo of India and everything he could remember that he had seen in the south.

Wang Lung saw all this, and he spoke to his eldest son, saying, "Have done with all this painting and polishing. It is enough. We are, after all, countryfolk."

But the young man answered proudly, "That we are not. Men in the town are beginning to call us the great family Wang."

Now Wang Lung had not known that men so called his house, but it pleased him secretly, and so he said, "Well, even great families are from the land and rooted in the land."

But the young man answered smartly, "Yes, but they do not stay there. They branch forth and bear flowers and fruits."

Wang Lung would not have his son answering him too easily like this, so he said, "I have said what I have said. Have done with pouring out silver. And roots, if they are to bear fruit, must be kept well in the soil of the land."

Then since evening came on, he wished his son would go away. But there was no peace for him with this son of his, for he began again. "Well, let it be enough, but there is another thing. It concerns my youngest brother. It is not fit that he grow up so ignorant. He should be taught. For this he weeps in the night."

Now Wang Lung had never thought to ask his youngest son what he wished to do with his life, since he had decided one son must be on the land, and what his eldest son had said struck him between the brows. He was silent, pondering about his third son. He was a lad not like either of his brothers, a lad as silent as his mother, and because he was silent, no one paid any attention to him.

"Well, but one lad must be on the land," said Wang Lung suddenly in argument, his voice very loud.

"But why, my father?" urged the young man. "You are a man who need not have any sons like serfs. People will say that there is a man who makes his son into a hind while he lives like a prince." The young man knew that his father cared mightily about what people said of him.

Wang Lung said at last, "Send him here to me."

The third son came and Wang Lung looked at him to see

what he was. He saw a tall and slender youth who had his mother's gravity and silence. But there was more beauty in him than there had been in his mother, and for beauty alone he had more of it than any of Wang Lung's children except the second girl. But across the boy's forehead and almost a mar to his beauty were his two black brows, too heavy and black for his young, pale face, and when he frowned, these brows met, heavy and straight.

And after Wang Lung had seen him well, he said, "Your eldest brother says you wish to learn to read."

And the boy said, "Yes," scarcely stirring his lips.

"Well, I suppose that means I shall not have a son on my own land, and I with sons to spare."

This Wang Lung said with bitterness, feeling that these sons of his were too much for him in his old age. But the boy said nothing. He stood there straight and still in his long white robe of summer linen, and at last Wang Lung was angry at his silence, so he shouted at him, "What is it to me what you do? Get away from me!"

Then the boy went away swiftly, and Wang Lung sat alone, and he said to himself that his two girls were better after all than his sons; one, poor fool that she was, never wanted anything more than a bit of food and her length of cloth to play with, and the other one was married and away from his house. And the twilight came down over the court.

But as Wang Lung always did when his anger passed, he let his sons have their way. He called his eldest son and said, "Engage a tutor for the third one if he wants it, and let him do as he likes, only I am not to be troubled about it."

And he called his second son and said, "Since I am not to have a son on the land, it is your duty to see to the rents. You shall be my steward."

The second son was pleased, for this meant the money would pass through his hands; he would know what came in and could complain to his father if more than enough was spent in the house.

Now this second son of his seemed more strange to Wang than any of his sons, for even at his wedding day, which came on, he was careful of the money, and kept the best meats for his friends in town who knew the cost of the dishes, and to the tenants and the country people he gave only the second best, since they ate coarse fare daily, and to them a little better was very good. He gave to the slaves and servants the least that could be given to them, so that Cuckoo sneered, and she said in the hearing of many, "Now a truly great family is not so careful of its silver. One can see that this family does not belong in these courts."

The eldest son heard this, and he was ashamed and angry with his second brother. Thus there was trouble between them even on the wedding day, and when the bride's chair was entering the courts, the eldest son stood aside scornfully and said, "My brother has chosen an earthen pot when he might—with my father's position—have had a cup of jade." And he was scornful and nodded stiffly when the pair came and bowed before him and his wife.

The wife of the eldest son was correct and haughty and bowed only the least that could be considered proper for her position.

Now of all of them who lived in these courts it seemed that there was no one wholly at peace there except the small grandson. To this small one the great house was neither great nor small but only his house, and here was his mother and here his father and grandfather and all those who lived but to serve him. And from this one did Wang Lung secure peace. He could never have enough of watching him and laughing at him and picking him up when he fell. He remembered also what his own father had done, and he delighted to take a girdle and put it about the child and hold him thus from falling. They went from court to court, and the child pointed at the darting fish in the pools and jabbered this and that and snatched the head of a flower and was at his ease in the midst of everything, and only thus did Wang Lung find peace.

Nor was there only this one. In the space of five years Wang

Lung had four grandsons and three granddaughters and the courts were filled with their laughter and their weeping. And when one said to him, "There is to be another mouth again," he only laughed and said, "Well, there is rice enough for all since we have the good land."

Now FIVE YEARS is nothing in a man's life except when he is very young and very old, and if it gave to Wang Lung these others, it took away also that old dreamer, his uncle, whom he had almost forgotten except to see that he and his old wife were fed and clothed and had what they wished of opium. Wang Lung's uncle and his wife had long since smoked all the flesh off their bones and lay day in and day out on their beds like two old, dry sticks.

Then Wang Lung heard that his uncle lay dead one evening when the serving woman went in to take him a bowl of soup. Wang Lung buried him beside his father, only a little lower than his father's grave but above the place where his own was to be. He moved his uncle's wife into the town and gave her a room for her own. The old woman sucked her opium pipe and lay on her bed in great content. Wang Lung marveled to think that once he had feared her, this woman who had been a great, fat, blowsy countrywoman and who lay there now as shriveled and yellow as the old mistress had been in the fallen House of Hwang.

ONE DAY Wang Lung's second son came home from the market for his noon rice and said to his father, "The war to the north is nearer and nearer every day, and we must hold our stores of grain until later, for the price will go higher and higher as the armies come nearer to us."

Wang Lung listened to this as he ate, and he said, "Well, it is a curious thing. I shall be glad to see a war for what it is, for I have heard of it all my life and never seen it."

He remembered that once he had been afraid because he would have been seized, but now he was too old for use and he was rich and the rich need not fear anything. So he paid no great heed to the matter beyond this.

In the days to come he played with his grandchildren, and sometimes he went to see his poor fool who sat in a far corner of his court.

One day in early summer a horde of men came sweeping out of the northwest like a swarm of locusts. One of Wang Lung's small grandsons stood at the gate with a manservant to see what passed, and when he saw the long ranks of gray-coated men, he ran back to his grandfather and cried out, "See what comes, Old One!"

Then Wang Lung went back to the gate with him to humor him, and there the men were filling the street. Wang Lung felt as though air and sunlight had been suddenly cut off because of the gray men tramping heavily through the town. He looked at them closely and saw that every man held a fire stick with a knife sticking out of the end, and the face of every man was wild and fierce and coarse. Wang Lung drew the child to him hastily and murmured, "Let us lock the gate. They are not good men, my little heart."

But suddenly, before he could turn, one saw him and shouted out, "Ho there, my old father's nephew!"

Wang Lung looked up, and he saw the son of his uncle, and he was clad like the others and dusty and gray, but his face was wilder and more fierce than any. And he laughed harshly and called out to his fellows, "Here we may stop, my comrades, for this is a rich man and my relative!"

Before Wang Lung could move, the horde was pouring past him into his own courts, like evil, filthy water, filling every corner and crack. They lay down on the floors and dipped their hands in the pools and drank, and they clattered their knives down on the carved tables, and they spat and shouted at each other. Then Wang Lung in despair ran back with the child into his eldest son's courts, and there his son sat reading a book; when he heard what Wang Lung gasped forth, he began to groan and went out.

When he saw his cousin, he did not know whether to curse him or to be courteous, but he looked and he groaned forth to his father who was behind him, "Every man with a knife!"

So he was courteous then and said, "Well, my cousin, welcome to your home again."

And the cousin grinned widely and said, "I have brought a few guests."

"They are welcome, being yours," said Wang Lung's eldest son, "and we will prepare a meal so that they may eat before they go."

Then the cousin said, still grinning, "Do, but make no haste afterward, for we will rest a handful of days or a month or a year, for we are to be quartered on the town until the war calls."

Now when Wang Lung and his son heard this, they could scarcely conceal their dismay, but it had to be concealed because of the knives, so they smiled what poor smiles they could muster, and said, "We are fortunate—we are fortunate!"

And the eldest son pretended he must go to prepare for his guests. He took his father's hand, and the two of them rushed into the inner court where the eldest son barred the door. Then father and son stared at each other in consternation, and neither knew what to do.

Then the second son came running and beat upon the door. When they let him in, he panted, "There are soldiers every-where in every house—and I came running to say you must not protest, for today a clerk in my shop—I knew him well—went to his house and there were soldiers in the room where his wife lay ill. He protested and they ran a knife through him as though he were made of lard—as smoothly as that—it came through him clean to the other side! Whatever they wish we must give, but let us pray that the war moves on."

Then the three of them looked at each other heavily, and thought of their women and of these lusty, hungry men. The eldest son said, "We must put the women in the innermost court and keep the gates barred and the gate of peace ready to be opened."

Thus they did. They put the women and children all into the court where Lotus lived, and there in discomfort and crowding they lived. Wang Lung and his sons watched the gate day and night.

But there was one who could not be lawfully kept out because he was a relative—the cousin. He would come in and walk about at will, carrying his knife glittering and open in his hand. The eldest son followed him about, his face full of bitterness, but still not daring to say anything, and the cousin looked at this and that and appraised each woman.

Then when the cousin had seen everything, he went to see his mother, and Wang Lung went with him to show where she was. There she lay on her bed, so asleep that her son could hardly wake her, but wake her he did, clapping the thick end of his gun on the tiles of the floor. She woke and stared at him out of a dream, and he said impatiently, "Here is your son and yet you sleep on!"

She raised herself then in her bed and stared at him again, and she said, wondering, "My son—it is my son—" and she looked at him for a long time, and at last, as though she did not know what else to do, she proffered him her opium pipe.

Wang Lung was afraid for fear that this man would turn on him and say, "What have you done to my mother that she is like this?"

So Wang Lung said hastily himself, "I wish she were content with less, for her opium runs into a handful of silver a day, but at her age we do not dare to cross her." And he sighed as he spoke and glanced secretly at his uncle's son, but the man only stared to see what his mother had become. When she fell back and into her sleep again, he rose and clattered forth, using his gun as a walking stick in his hand.

None of the horde of idle men did Wang Lung and his family hate and fear as they did this cousin of theirs; this, although the men tore at the trees and the flowering shrubs, and though they crushed the delicate carved chairs with their great boots, and though they sullied the pools with filth so that the fish died and floated on the water with their white bellies upturned.

For the cousin ran in and out as he would, and he cast eyes at the women, and Wang Lung and his sons looked at each other out of eyes haggard and sunken because they dared not sleep. Then Cuckoo saw it and she said, "Now there is only one thing to do, he must be given a slave while he is here, or else he will be taking where he should not."

And Wang Lung seized eagerly on what she said. He bade her ask the cousin what slave he would have. So Cuckoo did then, and she came back and she said, "He says he will have the little pale one who sleeps on the bed of the mistress."

Now this pale slave was called Pear Blossom and because she was delicate they had petted her and allowed her only to do the lesser things about Lotus, pouring her tea and such, and it was thus the cousin had seen her.

When Pear Blossom heard this as she poured the tea for Lotus, she dropped the pot and it broke into pieces. She threw herself down before Lotus and knocked her head on the tiles and moaned, "Oh, my mistress, not I—I am afraid of him for my life—"

Lotus was displeased and answered pettishly, "He is only a man, and what is this ado?" And she turned to Cuckoo and said, "Take this slave and give her to him."

The young maid put her hands together and cried, her little body trembling with her fear, and she looked from this face to that, beseeching with her weeping. Then the girl saw Wang Lung and she ran and knelt at his feet. He looked down at her and saw how small her shoulders were and how they shook. And he remembered the great coarse body of his cousin, now long past his youth. A distaste for the thing seized him, and he said to Lotus, "Well now, it is ill to force the girl. Let me buy for you another slave. Let me see what can be done."

Then Lotus, who had long been minded for a foreign clock and a ruby ring, was silent, and Wang Lung said to Cuckoo, "Go and tell my cousin the girl has a vile and incurable disease, and if he fears it as we all do, then tell him we have another and a sound one."

And he cast his eyes over the slaves who stood about and they turned away their faces, all except one stout wench, and she said with her face red and laughing, "Well, he is not as hideous a man as some."

Then Wang Lung answered in relief, "Well, go then!"

And Cuckoo said, "Follow close behind me." And they went out.

But Lotus was still angry, and she went into her room. Then Wang Lung raised the little slave gently and she stood before him. He saw that she had a little soft oval face, exceedingly delicate, and a little pink mouth. He said kindly, "Now keep away from your mistress for a day or two, my child, until she is past her anger, and hide when that other one comes in, lest he desire you again."

She lifted her eyes and looked at him gratefully, and she passed him, silent as a shadow, and was gone.

The cousin lived there for a month and a half. The stout wench conceived by him and boasted of it. Then suddenly the war called and the horde went away as quickly as chaff driven by the wind, and there was nothing left except the filth and destruction they had wrought. Wang Lung's cousin stood before them with his gun over his shoulder and said mockingly, "Well, if I do not come back, I have left you my second self and a grandson for my mother. It is one of the benefits of the soldier's life—his seed springs up behind him and others must tend it!"

And laughing at them all, he went his way with the others.

XVI

WHEN THE SOLDIERS were gone Wang Lung and his two elder sons for once agreed on something—it was that all trace of what had just passed must be wiped away. They called in carpenters and masons and within a year the place was fresh and flowering again and there was order everywhere.

Wang Lung commanded the slave who had conceived by the son of his uncle to wait upon his uncle's wife as long as she lived, which could not be long now. And it was a matter for joy to Wang Lung that this slave gave birth only to a girl, for if it had been a boy, she would have been able to claim a place in the family, but since it was a girl, it was only slave bearing slave, and she was no more than before.

Nevertheless, Wang Lung was just to her, and he gave her a little silver and the woman was content except for one thing. "Hold the silver as a dowry for me, my master," she said. "And if it is not a trouble to you, wed me to a farmer."

Wang Lung promised easily, "When the old dreamer dies, I will find a man for you." He was struck with a thought and it was this: here was he promising a woman to a poor man, and once he had been a poor man who came into these courts for his woman. He had not for a long time thought of O-lan, and now he thought of her with a sadness that was heavy with the memory of things long gone.

And the woman came to him one morning and said, "Now redeem your promise, my master, for the old one died in the early morning, and I have put her in her coffin."

And Wang Lung remembered the laborer who had caused Ching's death, and he said, "Well, he did not mean the thing he did; he is as good as any and the only one I can think of now."

So he sent for the laborer and he came. It was Wang Lung's whim to sit on the dais in the great hall and to call the two before him. He said slowly, so that he might taste the whole flavor of the strange moment, "Here, young man, is this woman, and she is yours if you will have her, and no one has known her except the son of my own uncle."

The man took her gratefully, for she was a good-natured wench, and he was too poor to wed except to such a one.

Then Wang Lung came down off the dais. It seemed to him that now his life was rounded off—he had done more than he had ever dreamed he could—and that peace could truly come to him and he could sleep in the sun. It was time for it, also, for he was close to sixty-five years of age. Well, there was the third son to wed one day soon, and with that over, there would be nothing left to trouble him in his life and he could be at peace.

His youngest son had lived among the soldiers when they were there, and he had listened to their tales of war and battle, and he had begged novels of his tutor and read stories of the wars of the Three Kingdoms, and his head was full of dreams. So now he went to his father and said, "I know what I will do. I will go to be a soldier."

When Wang Lung heard this, he cried out in great dismay, "Now what madness is this, my son! It is said from ancient times that men do not take good iron to make a nail, nor a good man to make a soldier, and you are my little son. How shall I sleep with you wandering over the earth here and there in a war?"

But the boy was determined. He looked at his father and drew down his black brows, his eyes alight under his brows. "There is to be a war such as we have not heard of," he said. "There is to be a revolution and our land is to be free!"

Wang Lung listened to this in the greatest astonishment he had yet had from his three sons. "What all this stuff is, I do not know," he said, wondering. "Our land is free already—all our good land is free. You are clothed and are fed with it. I do not know what freedom you desire more than you have."

But the boy only muttered bitterly, "You do not understand—you are too old—you understand nothing."

And Wang Lung pondered and looked at this son of his and saw the suffering young face. He saw that he was as tall as a man already, though still reedy with youth. Wang Lung said doubtfully, muttering and half aloud, "Well, it may be he needs one thing more." And then he said aloud slowly, "If there is a woman you desire . . ."

The boy answered with lofty looks and with dignity, folding his arms on his breast, "I am not the ordinary young man. I wish for glory. There are women everywhere."

And then as though he remembered something he had

forgotten, he said, "Besides, there never were uglier slaves than we have. If I cared—but I do not—well, there is not a beauty in the courts except perhaps the little pale slave who waits on the one in the inner courts."

Then Wang knew he spoke of Pear Blossom, and he was smitten with a strange jealousy. Until the day when he had protected her from the son of his uncle, Wang Lung had not thought of the girl except as a child. But since that day he had thought of the pretty young maid more than he himself would believe he did.

Suddenly he felt himself older than he was—a man too thick of girth and with whitening hair, and he saw his son as a man now slim and young. It was not at this moment father and son, but two men, one old and one young. Wang Lung said angrily, "Now keep off the slaves—I will not have the rotten ways of young lords in my house."

Then the boy lifted his black brows and shrugged his shoulders. "You spoke of it first!" he said and turned and went out.

Then Wang Lung sat there alone in his room, confused with many angers, but, although he could not understand why, this anger stood forth most clearly: his youngest son had dared to look on a little pale young slave in the house and he had found her fair.

AFTER THAT he could not cease thinking about what his youngest son had said of Pear Blossom. He watched the girl incessantly as she came and went. The thought of her filled his mind, and he doted on her.

One night in the early summer of that year, at the time when the night air is thick and soft with mists of warmth and fragrance, he sat in his own court alone under a flowering cassia tree. The sweet heavy scent of the flowers filled his nostrils, and his blood ran full and hot like the blood of a young man. So he stayed away from Lotus, because well she knew when a man was restless. He remembered that he himself would be seventy before many years, and he was ashamed of his coursing blood. It would be a good thing to give the little slave to the lad, he thought, and this he said to himself again and again. Every time he said it the thing stabbed like a thrust on flesh already sore, and yet he could not but stab. And there was not one in all his house to whom he could go as friend.

Then as he sat there in the darkness, someone passed the gate of his court; he looked quickly and it was Pear Blossom.

"Pear Blossom!" he called, his voice a whisper.

She stopped suddenly, her head bent in listening.

Then he called again, "Come here to me!"

She crept timidly through the gate and stood before him. He put out his hand and laid hold of her little coat and said, half choking, "Child—!"

There he stopped with the word. He said to himself that it was a disgraceful thing for a man with grandsons nearer to this child's age than he was. Then she, waiting, caught from him the heat of his blood, and she bent over and slipped, like a flower crumpling on its stalk, to the ground, and she lay there.

And he said slowly, "Child—I am an old man—a very old man. A little maid like you should have a tall, straight youth."

And her voice came out of the darkness like the very breath of the cassia tree. "I like old men—they are so kind—young men are only fierce—"

Hearing her childish voice quavering up from about his feet, his heart welled up in a great wave of love, and he raised her gently and then led her into his own courts.

Now THE EYE of Cuckoo marked first what Wang Lung had done; she saw the girl slipping at dawn out of his court and she laid hold of her and laughed, her old hawk's eyes glittering. "Well!" she said. "And so it is the old lord all over again!"

And Wang Lung in his room, hearing her, girded his robe about him quickly and came out, smiling sheepishly and half proudly. He muttered, "Well, I said she had better take a young man and she would have the old one!"

"It will be a pretty thing to tell the mistress," Cuckoo said then, and her eyes sparkled with malice.

Wang Lung, fearing the anger of Lotus more than anything, begged Cuckoo, "You tell her, and if you can manage it without anger to my face, I will give you a handful of money."

So Cuckoo, still laughing and shaking her head, promised, and Wang Lung went back to his court and would not come forth until Cuckoo came back and said, "The thing is told, and she was angry enough until I reminded her she has wanted for a long time the foreign clock you promised her, and she will have ruby rings and other things as she thinks of them and a slave to take Pear Blossom's place, and Pear Blossom is not to come to her anymore, and you are not to come soon either, because the sight of you sickens her."

And Wang Lung promised eagerly, saying, "Get her what she wills. I do not begrudge anything."

He was pleased that he need not see Lotus until her anger was cooled with the fulfillment of her wishes.

That night, Wang Lung sat in his middle room on the court. The red candles were lit on the table and Pear Blossom sat silently on the other side of the table from him, her hands folded and quiet in her lap. Sometimes she looked at Wang Lung fully and without coquetry as a child does, and as he watched her, the shame went out of him.

Then suddenly there was his youngest son standing before him, sprung out of the darkness of the court. Wang Lung was reminded in a flash of a panther he had once seen the men of the village bring in from the hills.

The boy's eyes gleamed as he fixed them upon his father's face. Thus he stood, and at last he said in a low and surcharged voice, "Now I will go for a soldier—I will go for a soldier—"

But he did not look at the girl, only at his father, and Wang Lung was suddenly afraid of this son, whom he had scarcely considered from his birth up. He would have spoken, but no sound came. And his son repeated again and again, "Now I will go—now I will go—"

Suddenly he turned and looked at the girl once, and she looked back at him, shrinking, her hands at her face. Then the young man tore his eyes from her and went out through the door into the black summer night, and he was gone. There was silence everywhere.

At last Wang Lung turned to the girl and said humbly and gently and with great sadness, "I am too old for you, my heart, and well I know it."

But the girl dropped her hands from her face and cried more passionately than he had ever heard her cry, "Young men are cruel—I like old men best!"

The morning of the next day Wang Lung's youngest son was gone and where he was gone no one knew.

As AUTUMN flares with the false heat of summer before it dies into the winter, so it was with the quick love Wang Lung had for Pear Blossom. With the passing of the flame out of him he was suddenly cold with age and an old man. Nevertheless, he was fond of her, and it was a comfort to him that she was in his court. She served him faithfully and with patience beyond her years, and he was kind to her with a perfect kindness, and his love for her became the love of father for daughter.

For his sake, she was even kind to his poor fool, and this was a comfort to him. Now Wang Lung had thought many times of what would become of his poor fool when he was dead; so he bought a little packet of white poison at the medicine shop, and he called Pear Blossom to him one day and said, "There is no one other than you to whom I can leave this poor fool of mine when I am gone, and she will live on after me, seeing that her mind has no troubles of its own to kill her. Well I know that no one will think when I am gone to feed her or to bring her out of the rain. Now there is a gate of peace for her in this packet; when I die, you are to mix it in her rice and let her eat it, so that she may follow me where I am. And so shall I be at ease."

But Pear Blossom shrank from the thing he held and said, "I can scarcely kill an insect, so how could I take this life? No, my lord, but I will take this poor fool for mine when you go because you have been kind to me—the only kind one."

Wang Lung could have wept for what she said because no one had ever requited him like this, and he said, "Nevertheless, take it, my child, for even you must die one day, and after you there is no one—no one."

When she saw his meaning, Pear Blossom took the packet from him and said no more. Wang Lung trusted her and was comforted for the fate of his poor fool.

Wang Lung then lived more and more alone except for the two in his courts—his poor fool and Pear Blossom. Sometimes he roused himself and looked at Pear Blossom and said, "It is too quiet a life for you, my child."

But she always answered gently and in great gratitude, "It is quiet and safe."

Once when she said this, Wang Lung was curious and asked, "What was it in your tender years that made you so fearful of young men? Now I should have said you had lived quietly and easily in my courts."

And when he looked at her, waiting for her answer, he saw terror in her eyes. She covered them with her hands and whispered, "I hate every man except you—I have hated every man, even my father who sold me."

She would say nothing more, and he mused on it, but then he sighed and gave over his questions, because above everything now he would have peace; he wished only to sit in his court near these two.

XVII

So Wang Lung sat, and so his age came on him day by day and year by year, and he slept fitfully in the sun as his father had done, and he said to himself that his life was finished and he was satisfied with it.

Sometimes, but seldom, he went into the other courts and sometimes he saw Lotus. She never mentioned Pear Blossom, but she greeted him well enough, for she too was old now and satisfied with the food and the wine she loved. And now she and Cuckoo sat together as friends, no longer as mistress and servant, and they talked and ate and slept, and woke to gossip again.

When Wang Lung went, and it was very seldom, into his sons' courts, they treated him courteously and ran to get tea for him.

Then he would sit awhile and look at the children gathering around him to stare. His grandsons were tall boys now, and he looked at them, and often he muttered to himself, "Now that one has the look of his great-grandfather, and there is a small merchant Liu, and this one is myself when young."

And he asked them, "Do you go to school?"

"Yes, Grandfather," they answered in a scattered chorus, and he said again, "Do you study the Four Books?"

Then they all laughed with clear young scorn at him, and one said, "No, Grandfather. No one studies the Four Books since the revolution."

And he answered, musing, "Ah, I have heard of a revolution, but I have been too busy in my life to attend to it. There was always the land."

But the boys snickered at this, and at last Wang Lung rose, feeling himself after all but a guest in his sons' courts.

Then after a time he went no more to see his sons, but sometimes he would ask Cuckoo, "Does anyone ever hear from that youngest son of mine where he is this long time?"

And Cuckoo answered, for there was nothing she did not know in these courts, "It is said that he is a military official and great enough in a thing they call a revolution, but what it is I do not know—perhaps some sort of business."

And Wang Lung said, "Ah?"

He would have thought about it, but the evening was falling and his bones ached in the chill air. For his mind now went where it would and he could not hold it long to any one thing.

And the needs of his old body for food and for hot tea were more keen than for anything.

THUS SPRING wore on again and again, and as these years passed, still one thing remained to him—it was his love for his land. He had gone away from it and set up his house in a town, but his roots were in his land. Although he forgot it for months together, when spring came each year he had to go out onto the land. And he went. Sometimes he took a servant and slept again in the old earthen house where O-lan had died. When he woke in the dawn, he went out and with trembling hands reached and plucked a bit of budding willow and a spray of peach bloom and held them all day.

Thus he wandered one day in a late spring. He went over his fields a little way and came to the place on the low hill where he had buried his dead. He stood trembling on his staff and looked at the graves and remembered them, every one. They were more clear to him now than the sons who lived in his own house. Then he mused and thought suddenly, Well, I shall be the next.

He stared at the bit of earth where he was to lie and muttered, "I must see to the coffin."

This thought he held fast and painfully in his mind. He went back to the town and sent for his eldest son and said, "There is something I have to say."

"Then say on," answered the son, "I am here."

But when Wang Lung would have spoken, he suddenly could not remember what it was, and the tears stood in his eyes because he had held the matter so painfully in his mind and now it had slipped away from him. So he called Pear Blossom and said to her, "Child, what was it I wanted to say?"

Pear Blossom answered gently, "Where were you this day?"

"I was on the land," Wang Lung replied. Then suddenly the thing flew into his mind again, and he cried, laughing out of his wet eyes, "Well, I *do* remember. My son, I have chosen my place in the earth. It is below my father and his brother and above your mother and near to Ching, and I would see my coffin before I die."

Then Wang Lung's eldest son cried out dutifully and properly, "Do not say that word, my father, but I will do as you say."

Then his son bought a carved coffin hewn from a great log of fragrant wood that was supposed to be as lasting as iron, and Wang Lung was comforted. He said, "I would have it moved out to the earthen house and there I will live out my few days and there I will die."

When they saw how he had set his heart, they did what he wished. And then he and Pear Blossom and the poor fool and the servants they needed went back to the house on the land, leaving the house in the town to the family he had founded.

SPRING PASSED and summer passed into harvest and in the hot autumn sun Wang Lung sat where his father had sat against the wall. He thought no more about anything now except his food and his land. Sometimes he stooped and gathered some of the earth up in his hand, and it seemed full of life between his fingers. And he was content, holding it thus. He thought of his good coffin, and the kind earth waited without haste until he came to it.

His sons were proper enough to him. They came to him every day or so, and they sent him delicate food fit for his age, but he liked best to have one stir up cornmeal in hot water and eat it as his father had done.

One day after his two sons had greeted him courteously, they went out and walked about the land. Now Wang Lung followed them silently, and they did not hear the sound of his footsteps or his staff on the soft earth. Wang Lung heard his second son say, "We will sell the land, and we will divide the money between us evenly, for now with the railroad straight through I can ship rice to the sea . . ."

But the old man heard only the words *sell the land*, and he cried out and could not keep his voice from trembling with his anger, "Now, evil, idle sons—sell the land?" He choked and would have fallen, and they caught him and held him up, and he began to weep.

Then they soothed him and said, "No, no, we will never sell the land—"

"It is the end of a family—when they begin to sell the land," he said brokenly. "Out of the land we came and into it we must go—if you will hold your land, you can live—no one can rob you of land—"

And the old man let his scanty tears dry upon his cheeks, and they left salty stains there. He stooped and took up a handful of the soil and muttered, "If you sell the land, it is the end."

And his two sons held him, one on either side, and he held the warm, loose earth fast in his hand. They soothed him, saying over and over, the eldest son and the second son, "Rest assured, our father. The land is not to be sold."

But over the old man's head they looked at each other and smiled.

IMPERIAL
WOMAN

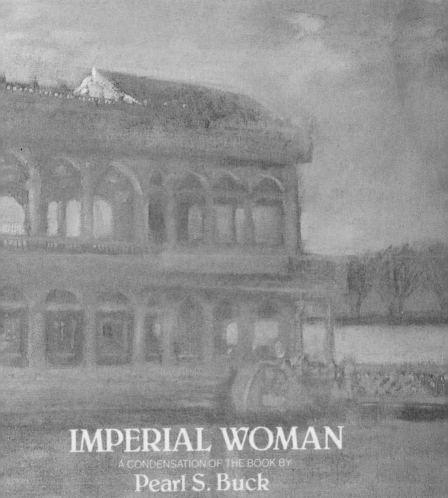

IMPERIAL WOMAN

A CONDENSATION OF THE BOOK BY

Pearl S. Buck

ILLUSTRATED BY RICHARD SPARKS

"Tzu Hsi, the last empress of China, was a woman so diverse in her gifts, so contradictory in her behavior, so rich in her personality," Pearl Buck once wrote, "that it is difficult to comprehend and convey her whole self.

"I have tried to portray Tzu Hsi as accurately as possible from available resources and from my own memories of how the Chinese I knew felt about her. Decades after her death in 1908 I came upon villages in inland China where people thought she was still alive. They were frightened when they heard she was dead. 'Who will care for us now?' they asked.

"This, perhaps, is the final judgment of a ruler."

I

YEHONALA

IT WAS MAY in the city of Peking in the year 1852, the two hundred and eighth year of the Manchu, the great Ch'ing Dynasty. Summer was late, and the northern winds, carrying their load of fine yellow sand from the Gobi desert, still blew cold over the housetops. Sand whirled in the streets and filtered through doors and windows. It lay on tables and chairs and in the crevices of garments; it dried on the faces of children and in the wrinkles of old people.

In Pewter Lane, in the house of Muyanga, a Manchu bannerman, Orchid—the eldest child of Muyanga's brother—sat up in the large bed she shared with her younger sister and frowned when she saw sand lying on the red quilt. Creeping softly out from under the bedclothes, she felt sand beneath her bare feet and sighed. Only yesterday she had swept the house clean, and now it all had to be swept again.

She was a handsome girl, this Orchid, seeming taller than she was because she was slender and held herself erect. Her features were strong, her nose straight, her mouth well shaped. Her eyes were her great beauty, large and exceedingly clear, the black and the white pure and separate.

She dressed herself swiftly and made her way to the kitchen. Steam rose from the large caldron set on the earthen stove. She greeted her serving woman. "You are early, Lu Ma."

From behind the stove a cracked voice replied. "I could not sleep, Young Mistress. What shall we do when you leave us?"

Orchid smiled. "The emperor's mother may not choose me—my cousin Sakota is far more beautiful than I am."

Lu Ma fed wisps of dry grass into the stove. "You will be chosen," she said. She looked desolate, a small hunchbacked Chinese, her face a network of brown wrinkles. "This house cannot do without you," she moaned. "Second Sister will not so much as sew a seam. Your brothers wear out a pair of shoes apiece every month. And what of your kinsman Jung Lu? Are you not as good as betrothed to him?"

"In a manner we are betrothed," Orchid replied. She took a basin and dipped hot water from the caldron. With a small towel, she wiped her face and neck, then her wrists and hands.

"*Ai*," the old woman said, staring at her. "I did always say that you have a destiny. It is in your eyes. When you are empress, my precious, you will remember us and send help."

Orchid laughed softly. "I shall be only a concubine, one of hundreds!"

"Comb your hair, Young Mistress," Lu Ma said. "Jung Lu said that today he might be the bearer of the golden summons."

In their bedroom, her sister was still sleeping under the quilt. Quietly, Orchid unwound her long black hair and combed it with a perfumed wooden comb. Then she braided it in two coils over her ears and put a small flower of seed pearls in each coil. Before she had finished she heard the deep voice of Jung Lu in the next room asking for her. For the first time in her life she did not go to him at once.

They were Manchu, and therefore the ancient Chinese law forbidding the meeting of male and female beyond the age of seven had not kept them apart. She and Jung Lu had been playmates in childhood and friends when childhood was past. Though he was now a guardsman at the gates of the Forbidden City, he was always at Muyanga's house on feast days and birthdays. Two months ago he had spoken to her of marriage.

On that day she had smiled and said, "You must speak to my uncle." Thus she had replied without saying yes or no.

Now she put aside the curtain. There in the main room stood Jung Lu, tall and sturdy, and in his hand he held a packet wrapped in yellow silk. She saw it at once.

"You recognize the imperial summons," he said, his eyes not moving from hers.

"Lu Ma, wake my uncle!" she called. "Jung Lu must have his signature before he returns to the palace."

"*Ai-ya*," the old woman sighed.

"I know what the packet says. I am to go to the palace with my cousin Sakota nine days from now. How many of us are there this year?"

"Sixty," he said.

She lifted her eyes. "I am one of sixty?"

"I have no doubt that in the end you will be first," he said.

His voice, so deep, so quiet, went to her heart with prophetic force. "Where I am," she said, "you will be near me. That I shall insist upon. Are you not my kinsman?"

They were gazing at each other again. He said sternly, "I came here intending to ask your uncle to arrange for you to be my wife. Now I do not know what he will do."

"Can he refuse the imperial summons?" she asked. With smooth grace she walked to the long black wood table that stood against the wall. Between two high brass candlesticks, a pot of yellow orchids bloomed. "They opened this morning—the imperial color. It is an omen," she murmured.

"Everything is an omen now in your mind," he said.

She turned to him, her black eyes angry. "Is it not my duty

to serve the emperor if I am chosen?" She looked away from him and said gently, "If I am not chosen, certainly I will be your wife."

Lu Ma came in, peering first at one young face and then the other. "Your uncle is awake now, Young Mistress. Your kinsman is to enter his bedroom."

The house was beginning to stir. Orchid heard her sister's plaintive call. "Orchid! I am not well! My head aches—"

"Orchid," Jung Lu repeated. "It is too childish a name for you now."

She stamped her foot. "It is still my name! And why do you stay? Do your duty and I will do mine."

In that brief moment of anger her will was set: she would go to the imperial city of the emperor and she would be chosen.

ON THE FOURTEENTH day of the sixth month Orchid woke for the first time in the Winter Palace in the imperial city. The day had arrived that she had been secretly waiting for ever since as a small child she had watched Sakota's elder sister leave home to become an imperial consort. But Sakota's sister had died before she could become the empress.

That last night at home Orchid had been sleepless with excitement. Sakota, too, was wakeful. Somewhere in the silent hours Sakota's soft hand felt her face. "Orchid, I am frightened! Let me come into your bed." Her hands and feet were cold and she was trembling. "Are you not afraid?" she whispered.

"No," Orchid said. She wrapped her strong arms about Sakota's body. "I shall be there with you," she reassured her.

"What if we are not chosen for the same class?" Sakota asked.

In the morning instead of farewell her mother gave Orchid these final words: "Keep yourself apart. Among the virgins you are only one. Since Sakota is the younger sister of the dead consort, certainly she must be favored above you. But whatever place is given you, it is possible for you to rise beyond it."

And during her first night at the Winter Palace Orchid had not wept when she heard the others weeping, for fear that they would be chosen and never see home and family again.

Yesterday what Sakota feared had happened. They were separated. When the virgins had appeared before the dowager mother, she had chosen twenty-eight from the sixty. Sakota, because she was the sister of the dead consort, was placed in the first group, and Orchid in the third. "She has a bad temper," the shrewd old dowager had said, staring at Orchid. "It is better if my son, the emperor, does not notice her."

Now a voice called through the sleeping hall, the voice of the chief tiring woman. "Young ladies, it is time to rise. This is your day of good fortune."

At this summons the others rose at once, but Orchid did not. She lay motionless and watched the young girls shivering under the hands of women servants.

"All must bathe," the chief tiring woman commanded. She sat in a wide bamboo chair, fat and severe. The young girls, now naked, stepped into the shallow wooden tubs, and serving women rubbed their bodies with perfumed soap. Suddenly the tiring woman spoke. "Twenty-eight were chosen. I count only twenty-seven." She examined the paper in her hand and called the names of the twenty-eight virgins. One did not answer. "Yehonala!" the old woman called out.

It was Orchid's childhood name. Yesterday Muyanga, her uncle, had summoned her into his library. "Now that you are about to enter into the city of the emperor," he said, "you must leave behind your little name, Orchid. From this day you will be called Yehonala."

"Yehonala!" the chief tiring woman shouted again.

"Mistress, she lies in bed sleeping," a serving woman answered.

"What hard heart is this?" the old woman cried. "Waken her! Pinch her arms!"

The servant obeyed, and Yehonala opened her eyes. "What is it?" she asked, feigning drowsiness. She sat up, her hands flying to her cheeks. "Oh, oh—" she stammered. "How could I forget?"

"How, indeed!" the chief tiring woman said. "In two hours you must be all ready in the Audience Hall, bathed and perfumed and robed, your hair coiled, your breakfast eaten."

Yehonala yawned behind her hand and, rising, stepped out on the tiled floor, her feet bare and strong. The virgins were all Manchu, not Chinese, and so their feet were unbound and free.

"Hasten yourself, Yehonala! The others are nearly dressed."

"Yes, Venerable," she said. But she took her time as she allowed a woman to undress her.

The chief tiring woman was urging them to hurry. "They had better eat first," she was saying to the serving women. "Then what time is left can be spent on their hair."

Food was brought in by kitchen maids, but the virgins had no appetite and some were weeping again. Seeing such distress around her, Yehonala was the more calm. She sat down at a table and ate heartily.

"I swear I have not seen so hard a heart," the chief tiring woman said in a loud voice. After a moment she whispered to one of the serving women. "Look at her great eyes! She has a fierce heart, this one."

"A tiger heart," the woman agreed. "Truly, a tiger heart."

IT WAS still early when the eunuchs came for them, led by the chief eunuch, An Teh-hai. He was a handsome figure wrapped in a long pale-blue satin robe. His face was smooth, his nose curved downward, and his eyes were black and proud. He gave orders for the virgins to pass before him. Beside him on a table were placed his tally book, his ink brush and box. He marked the name of each virgin as she passed. "There is one not here," he announced.

"Here I am," Yehonala said. She moved forward shyly.

"That one has been late all day," the chief tiring woman said.

"Yehonala," the chief eunuch read in a high harsh voice,

"eldest niece of the bannerman Muyanga." He lifted his head and stared at Yehonala. "Pass on," he ordered, but his eyes followed her. Then he rose and commanded the lesser eunuchs. "Let the virgins be led into the Hall of Waiting."

Four hours the virgins waited. Then at noon a stir in distant courtyards roused them. Horns sounded, drums beat and a gong was struck to the rhythm of footsteps coming nearer. An Teh-hai came again into the Hall of Waiting with the lesser eunuchs. "Young ladies," he said, "you will wait here until your class is called. As you approach the throne, you are not to look upon the imperial face. It is he who looks at you."

The virgins stood in silence. Yehonala had placed herself last, as though the most modest of them all. Within an hour or less, she might reach the supreme moment of her life. The emperor would look at her, weigh her shape and color, and in that little moment she must make him feel her charm.

Soon a murmur fluttered over the group of waiting virgins. Someone caught a whisper—Sakota had been chosen from the first class to be the emperor's new consort. The second class was not as large as the first. In less than an hour the chief eunuch returned. "It is now the time for the third class," he announced. "Arrange yourselves, young ladies. The emperor grows weary."

The tiring women put the last touches on their hair and lips and eyebrows. Silence fell. In the Audience Hall the chief eunuch was already calling out their names and ages. One by one they passed before the emperor and the dowager mother. But Yehonala, the last, drifted away from her place to pet a small palace dog who had come running through an open door, one of those minute beasts that the court ladies liked to hide within their wide embroidered sleeves. At the door the chief eunuch waited. "Yehonala!" he called.

She held back the dog's long ears and laughed into its wrinkled face. She had heard of these little royal dogs that looked like lions, but she had never seen one until now.

"Yehonala!" An Teh-hai's voice roared. He rushed at her and

seized her arm. "Are you mad? The emperor waits! Why, you deserve to die for this!" He hurried to the door and shouted out her name again. "Yehonala, eldest niece of the bannerman Muyanga. Seventeen years, six months and fifteen days—"

She entered and walked slowly down the length of the immense hall, her long coat of rose satin touching the tip of her embroidered Manchu shoes, set high on white soles. She did not turn her head toward the throne.

"Let her pass again," the emperor said.

"I warn you," the dowager mother said, "this girl has a very fierce temper. I see it in her face. She is too strong for a woman."

"She is beautiful," the emperor said. "What does it matter if she has a temper? She can scarcely be angry with me." He had a thin, petulant voice.

"It is better not to choose a strong woman who is also beautiful," his mother reasoned.

Yehonala was now directly in front of him. "Stay," he commanded her. She stopped, her face and body in profile, her eyes gazing into the distance.

"Turn your face to me," he commanded.

Slowly, as though indifferent, she obeyed. In modesty, a virgin does not fix her eyes higher than a man's breast. But Yehonala looked full into the emperor's face. He sat immobile for a long instant. Then he spoke. "This one I choose."

"IF YOU ARE chosen by the Son of Heaven," her mother had said, "serve first the dowager mother. Let her believe that you think of her day and night. Learn what she enjoys, seek out her comfort. She has not many years to live. There will be plenty of years left for you."

On that first night after she had been chosen, Yehonala went to her own small bedroom, one of the three rooms given her to use. Here she must live alone except when the emperor sent for her. A concubine could live within the four walls of this imperial city until she died, forgotten by the emperor. But she,

Yehonala, would not be forgotten. When he was weary of Sakota, he must think of her.

She lay on the bed and considered. She must now plan her life and not one day could be wasted. She must be useful to the dowager empress, unfailing in small and constant attentions. Beyond this she would ask to be taught by tutors. She knew already how to read and write, thanks to her uncle's goodness, but she would ask to be taught history and poetry, music and painting. She would care for her body, too, rub her hands soft with mutton fat and perfume herself with dried oranges and musk, so that the emperor would be pleased. But she would shape her mind to please herself.

She had not slept for two nights, but tonight all her fears were over. Her three rooms were small but luxurious, the walls hung with scrolls, the chair seats covered with red satin cushions, and the beams overhead painted with bright designs. The latticed windows opened into a court with a round pool where goldfish shone under the sun. Her woman servant slept outside her door. She had no one to fear.

No one? Ah, the eunuchs. Her wise mother had warned her of the eunuchs: "They destroy themselves as men before they are allowed to enter the Forbidden City. Their maleness, denied, becomes malice and bitterness and cruelty. Avoid them—from the highest to the lowest."

Suddenly, she thought of her kinsman Jung Lu. She had not seen him since she entered the palace. Neither could she know when they might meet again. Within the walls of the Forbidden City a man and a woman might live out their lives and never meet. She sighed and wept a few tears, surprised that she did. Then, being young and very weary, she slept.

THE VAST palace library was cool even in midsummer. No sound disturbed the stillness except the low murmur of Yehonala's voice as she read aloud from *The Book of Changes* to the aged eunuch who was her tutor. Glancing upward as she turned a page, she saw the old scholar asleep, his head sunk upon his breast. She read on steadily to herself. At her feet a little dog slept. It was her own, given her by the imperial keeper when she sent her serving woman to beg for a pet.

She had been in the palace for months now, and she had not yet received a summons from the emperor. She had not even seen Sakota. She might have been unhappy in this strange isolation except for her busy dreams of the days to come.

She studied in the library each day for five hours with her tutor. Before he had been made a eunuch, he had been a famous writer of poems in the T'ang style. Then he had been commanded to become a eunuch in order to teach the young prince, now the emperor, and after him, his concubines. Among these no one, the old tutor declared, learned as Yehonala did. He gave such good reports of her to the dowager mother that one day when Yehonala waited upon her, the dowager mother said, "You do well to learn the books. My son, the emperor, wearies easily and you must be able to amuse him."

At this moment, while musing upon a page, Yehonala felt a touch on her shoulder and, turning her head, she saw the end of a folded fan. It belonged to a young eunuch, Li Lien-ying. She had been aware for some time that he was determined to be her servant. He was only one among the lesser eunuchs, but he had made himself useful to her in many small ways, and through him she heard the gossip of the Forbidden City. It was not enough for her to read books; to acquire power she must know also every detail of intrigue within these walls.

She raised her eyebrows in question. Li Lien-ying motioned to her with his fan. Silently, she followed him into the pavilion outside until they were beyond danger of rousing the sleeping tutor.

"I have news for you," Li Lien-ying said. He towered above her, his shoulders immense, his head square and large, his features coarse. She might have been afraid of him except that she allowed herself to be afraid of no one.

"What news?" she inquired.

"The young consort has conceived!"

Sakota had fulfilled her duty. If she bore a son, he would be heir to the Dragon Throne and Sakota would become empress mother. And she, Yehonala, would still be only a concubine. And for such a small price she would have cast away her life.

But fate might still be her savior. Sakota might give birth to a girl. There would be no heirs until a son was born. Then his mother would be raised to empress. And I might be that mother, she thought. Her brain grew calm, her heart grew still.

"The emperor's duty to his dead lady is done," the eunuch went on. "Now his fancy will wander. You must be ready. Within six or seven days he may think of a concubine."

"How do you know everything?" she asked.

"Eunuchs know such things," he said, leering down into her face.

She spoke with dignity. "You forget yourself before me."

"I offend you," he said quickly. "I am wrong. I am your servant, your slave."

She accepted his assurances. "Yet why," she inquired, "do you wish to serve me? I have no money to reward you." Although daily she ate of the most delicate dishes and the chests in her bedchamber were filled with beautiful robes, she could not buy so much as a packet of sweets for herself.

"Do you think I ask for gifts?" Li Lien-ying said. "Then you misjudge me. I know what your destiny is. You have a power in you that is in none of the others. I perceived it as soon as my eyes fell upon you. When you rise to the Dragon Throne, as surely you will some day, I will rise with you, always your servant and your slave."

She returned to the library. The old tutor was still asleep as she sat down in the chair she had left.

THE GOSSIP flew from courtyard to courtyard and excitement rose like the wind. The emperor had never had a child, and if there was no heir, then an heir must be chosen from among the great Manchu clans. Princes watched each other jealously. Since Sakota, the new consort, had conceived, they could only wait. If she had a daughter, the strife would begin again.

Yehonala herself belonged to the most powerful of these clans. From her clan three empresses had already risen. Should she not be a fourth?

She began from that day on to read the edicts that came from the throne, studying every word the emperor sent forth. Slowly she began to comprehend the vastness of the country and its people. She knew her ruling people, the Manchu, had seized power over the Chinese two hundred years ago, and had built its heart here in the Forbidden City, where the drums beat at twilight to warn all men to depart and the emperor remained alone among his women and his eunuchs.

This inner city, Yehonala now comprehended, was the ruling center of a country mighty in its mountains and rivers, in the endless numbers of its cities and villages, and in its hundreds of millions of people. Yehonala's bright imagination traveled everywhere the printed pages of her books led her. From the imperial edicts she learned that a mighty rebellion was rising in the south. The rebels were called Taipings, and they were led by a fanatic named Hung, who imagined himself a brother of the one called Christ. Under the banner of this religion the discontents were gathering and even threatening to overthrow the Manchu Dynasty.

Hsien Fêng, like his father, was a weak emperor, whom the dowager mother commanded as though he were a child. Through the dowager mother, then, Yehonala must find her access, and she made it her duty to wait upon the elder lady every day. It was now the season of summer melons, and the dowager mother loved very well the small yellow-fleshed fruit. Yehonala walked daily in the melon rows and tested them for ripeness with her thumb and forefinger. One day when she heard a melon sound as empty as a drum, she picked it and carried it to the courtyards of the dowager mother.

"Our venerable mother is asleep," a serving woman said.

"Then the dowager mother must be ill. It is long past the hour when she wakes." Yehonala's voice reached the ears of the dowager mother, who sat in her bedroom embroidering a gold dragon on a black girdle. She called, "Yehonala, come here! Whoever says I am sleeping is a liar!"

Yehonala made a coaxing smile for the serving woman. "No one says you sleep, Venerable," she answered. "It is I who heard it wrong." With this courteous lie she tripped through the rooms to the bedchamber of the dowager mother and presented the melon with both hands.

"Ah," the old lady cried, "and I sat here thinking of sweet melons and you come at the very moment!"

Yehonala took a knife that a serving woman brought and sliced the melon delicately. The dowager mother began to eat it as greedily as a child, the juice dripping from her chin.

"Save half of it," the dowager mother commanded, when she had eaten as much as she could. "When my son comes to present himself this evening, I will give it to him."

While Yehonala worked in her ways, Li Lien-ying worked in his. He bribed the menservants in the emperor's private courts so that when the monarch appeared restless, his eyes moving this way and that after a woman, they would speak the name of Yehonala. Thus the very day after the presentation of the melon, Yehonala found in the pages of her book a sheet of folded paper. Upon it were written two lines:

> The dragon awakes again,
> The day of the phoenix has come.

How did Li Lien-ying know? She would not ask him. What he did to fulfill her purposes must be secret even from herself.

This was the day when she received her painting lesson, and she had to keep her mind fixed on painting, for her teacher was very exacting. She was Lady Miao, a Chinese widow. Because she was perfect in her art, she was allowed to unbind her feet, to comb her hair as high as the Manchu ladies did, and to put on Manchu robes. When Lady Miao discovered that Yehonala was talented, she devoted herself to her. Lady Miao had not as yet allowed her to paint anything from life.

Instead she had her study the prints of dead masters, the strokes they had made, the colors they had mixed.

Now Yehonala saw from yet another window the vast country at whose center she lived. The art of centuries stretched out before her as her teacher spoke. She loved especially the paintings of Ku K'ai-chih, who had lived some fifteen centuries before. He had painted pictures of imperial palaces on a long roll of silk, on which the imperial ancestor Ch'ien-lung had written a hundred years ago with his own hand: The picture has not lost its freshness. Of the nine royal scenes on the scroll Yehonala's favorite was the one that portrayed a bear rushing toward the emperor and a lady who had thrust herself across its path to save the Son of Heaven. She stood before the beast with folded arms and a fearless look while guardsmen ran forward with their outthrust spears.

This day Lady Miao arrived in the imperial library as usual upon the exact hour of four. A eunuch followed her with brushes and colors. Yehonala rose and remained standing in the presence of her teacher.

"Be seated, be seated," Lady Miao commanded.

"I would ask my teacher a question," Yehonala said. "When may I paint a picture of my own?"

Lady Miao cast a sidelong look from her narrowed eyes. "When I can no longer command you."

The meaning was clear. When she was chosen by the emperor, she would be raised so high that no one could command her save the emperor himself.

SOMETIME THAT night, she was awakened by hands shaking her shoulders. "Wake, wake, Yehonala! You are summoned! The Son of Heaven calls—"

Yehonala pushed back the silken quilts and stepped down from the high bed.

"I have your bath ready," her serving woman whispered. "I have poured perfume into the water. I have put out your best robe, the lilac satin—"

"Not lilac," Yehonala said. "I shall wear the peach-pink."

Other women were coming into the chamber yawning—the tiring woman, the hairdresser and the keeper of the jewels. Yehonala submitted to them without a word. Haste was a necessity. The emperor was awake; he was drinking wine and eating hot breads. The news was brought to the door by Li Lien-ying.

"Do not delay," he hissed in a hoarse voice. "His temper is easily roused, I can tell you."

"She is ready," the serving woman cried and pushed Yehonala out the door. "Go, my precious pet," she whispered.

"Oh, my little dog," Yehonala cried. The small creature was at her heels.

"No, no," Li Lien-ying shouted. "You may not take him!"

But Yehonala stooped and gathered the beast into her arms. "I will take him," she cried and stamped her foot.

In the dark summer night Yehonala, with her serving woman, followed Li Lien-ying through the narrow passageways of the inner city. He held an oiled-paper lantern to guide her over the damp cobblestones. Silence surrounded them. She passed the triple shrine, the Tower of Rain and Flowers, where all the emperors had worshiped alone since the time of the great K'ang-hsi, and came at last to the emperor's private palace. At the high double gates, carved with golden dragons, the chief eunuch, An Teh-hai himself, stood waiting. His long robe of purple brocaded satin glittered in the candlelight. Suddenly he saw the head of the little dog peering out from Yehonala's sleeve. "You may not take the dog into the emperor's bedchamber," he said sternly.

Yehonala fixed her great eyes upon him. "Then I will not enter, either," she said. She spoke in a soft, indifferent voice.

An Teh-hai looked surprised. "Can you defy the Son of Heaven?" he demanded.

She made no reply and stroked the head of the little dog.

"Elder Brother," Li Lien-ying now said to An Teh-hai, "this concubine is very troublesome. Truly it is not worthwhile to compel her, for her mind is more stubborn than a stone. Let her go in with the dog."

Yehonala continued to gaze at the chief eunuch with her great eyes wide and innocent. What could he do but yield?

She followed him through room after room. They came at last to satin curtains of imperial yellow around heavy doors of carved wood. The chief eunuch opened the doors and motioned to her to enter. Now she went alone.

The emperor sat upright in a huge bed on a raised platform. The bed was made of bronze, and climbing dragons were carved on the bronze bedposts. The emperor sat under a quilt of yellow satin embroidered with dragons. He wore a bed shirt of red silk, high about his neck, with sleeves to his wrists. She had seen him before only in his royal headdress. Now his head was bare. His face was long and narrow, sunken beneath an overhanging forehead. They looked at each other, and he motioned to her to come near. She walked to him slowly, her eyes fixed on his face.

"You are the first woman who ever came into this chamber with her head lifted," he said in a high thin voice. "They are always afraid to look at me."

"I am not afraid," Yehonala said in her soft definite voice. "See, I have brought my little dog."

She had been told how to address the Son of Heaven: Lord of Ten Thousand Years, Highest, Most Venerable—these were the words of address. But Yehonala behaved toward the emperor as though he were a man. She stroked the little dog's smooth head again and looked down. "Until I came here," she said, "I never had a dog like this. I used to hear about lion dogs, and now I have one for my own."

The emperor stared at her. He did not know what to say to such childish talk. "Come, sit on the bed beside me," he commanded her. "Tell me why you are not afraid of me."

She sat on the edge of the bed, facing him. His eyes were upon her, searching her face, and she trembled with a sudden chill. She forced herself to speak shyly. "I know my destiny."

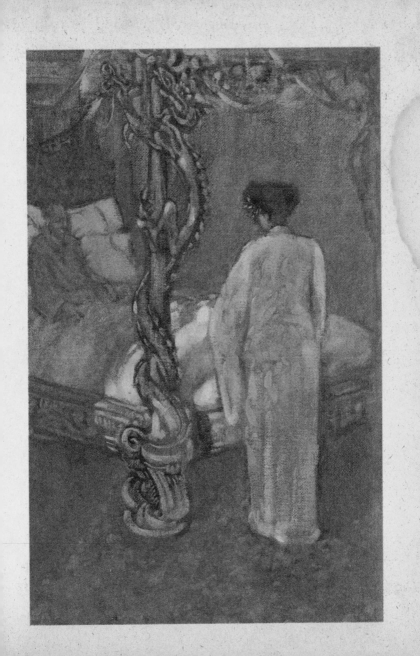

"And how do you know your destiny?" He began to be amused, his thin lips curving upward.

"When I was summoned from my home," she said, "I went to the shrine of Kuan Yin and lit the incense, and then—" She paused, her lips quivered, she tried to smile.

"And then?" the emperor inquired, enchanted by her beautiful face, so soft, so young.

"There was no wind that day," she said. "The smoke from the burning incense rose straight heavenward from the altar. In the fragrant clouds I saw a face—"

"A man's face?"

She nodded, as a child does when too shy to speak.

"Was it my face?" he asked.

"Yes, Majesty," she said. "Your imperial face!"

Two DAYS, two nights, and Yehonala was still in the royal bedchamber. Each time the emperor slept, she went to the door and beckoned to her serving woman. In the dressing room the eunuchs had prepared a caldron of hot water so that the serving woman needed only to dip the hot water into the vast porcelain tub to make her mistress fresh again. She had brought clean garments and different robes.

She knew now what this man was inside the imperial bedroom, a weak and fitful being, possessed by a passion he could not satisfy. When he was defeated, he wept upon her breast. This was the Son of Heaven! Yet when he woke, she was all duty and gentleness. She sent for the chief eunuch and bade him bring the dishes that his sovereign enjoyed. When the meal was over, the emperor commanded his chief eunuch once more to draw the curtains over the window and leave him alone. He said he would not meet his ministers that day or the next.

An Teh-hai looked grave. "Majesty, the Taiping rebels have seized half of another province in the south. Your ministers and princes are waiting impatiently for you."

"I will not come," the Son of Heaven said peevishly, and

the chief eunuch could do nothing then but leave the room.

The emperor was staring at Yehonala with fearful desire. "Come here," he muttered. "I am strong now. The meat has made me strong."

This time it was true that he was strong, and she remembered something the ladies in the Palace of Forgotten Concubines had told her. They said that if the emperor delayed too long in his bedchamber, a powerful herb that gave him sudden and unusual strength was mixed in his favorite dish. Yet so dangerous was this herb that he must not be roused too far, for then the exhaustion that followed could end in death.

On the third morning, this exhaustion fell. The emperor sank, half fainting, on his pillow. His lips were blue, his eyes half closed, and his narrow face slowly took on a greenish pallor. In great fear Yehonala went to summon help.

When she returned to the bedside, she looked down on the emperor's unconscious face, and suddenly she shivered with a strange chill that had fallen upon her again and again in these two days and three nights. She opened the door. Outside her serving woman sat, weary with waiting.

"Come, come with me," the woman said. "Take your old woman's hand—"

And Yehonala let herself be led down the narrow passageways to her solitary home. And while the serving woman made herself busy, she talked to comfort her mistress.

"They are saying everywhere that never has a concubine stayed so long with the Son of Heaven. You are the favorite now. You have nothing more to fear."

Yehonala smiled. "Do they say so?" she said. Yet when she was bathed and clothed in sleeping robes of softest silk in her own bed, she fell into a deathly chill. Never had she dreamed of such loneliness as now was hers. What friend had she? There was no one—

No one? Was Jung Lu not still her kinsman? The ties of blood cannot be broken. She sat up in her bed and clapped her hands for her serving woman.

"What now?" the woman asked at the door.

"Send to me the eunuch Li Lien-ying."

The woman went away to find the eunuch, who came in great haste and elation. "What, what, my lady?" he inquired.

Yehonala had dressed herself in a somber robe. Her face was grave. "Bring to me my kinsman Jung Lu," she said.

After she let the curtain fall and heard the eunuch's footsteps go away, she felt such a yearning arise in her heart that she was frightened for herself. Oh, but she was wrong to send for him, for could she beg him now to help her escape from the Forbidden City? She sank to the floor and closed her eyes. She hoped he would not come.

Li Lien-ying called through the curtain, "My lady, your kinsman is here!" She rose and put aside the curtain, and he was there.

"Come in," she said.

"Come out," he said. "We must not meet inside your chamber."

"Yet I must speak with you alone," she said, for Li Lien-ying waited, his ears outstretched.

But Jung Lu would not come in, and so she was forced to leave her chamber for the courtyard. Her serving woman stood on the steps nearby so that no one could say that she was alone with a man. She sat down on a porcelain garden seat at the far end of the courtyard. "Seat yourself," she said.

But Jung Lu stood before her, straight and stiff.

"Will you not sit down?" she asked again.

"No," he said. "I am here only because you sent for me."

She yielded. "Have you heard?" she asked softly.

"I have heard," he said, not looking at her.

"I am the new favorite."

"That, too, I have heard."

It was all told in these few words. She kept looking at his face, comparing it with the sickly face on the imperial pillow. This face was young and handsome, the dark eyes large and powerful, the mouth set firm above the strong chin.

"I have been a fool," she said. "I want to go home."

He folded his arms and looked carefully above her head into the trees. "This is your home," he said.

She bit her lower lip. "I want you to save me."

He did not move, but he let his eyes slide down to her lovely face, and in those eyes she saw his answer. "Oh, my heart, if I could save you, I would. But I cannot."

The heavy pain inside her vitals suddenly eased. "Then you do not forget me!"

"Night and day I do not forget," he said.

Tears shone silver in her black eyes. "I did not know how it would be," she faltered.

"There is no undoing what is done," he said. "No going back, no being what you were."

She bent her head to keep the tears from running on her cheeks, for fear that Li Lien-ying lurked near enough to see.

"You have chosen greatness," he said in her silence. "Therefore you must be great."

"Only if you promise," she said, her voice small and trembling.

"Promise what?" he asked.

"That you will come when I send for you," she said. "I must have that comfort. I cannot always be alone."

She saw the sweat start out on his forehead. "I will come to you when you call," he said, not moving. "If you must, then send for me. But do not send unless you must."

She gave him one long look. "I have your promise?" she asked.

"You do," he said.

FOR SEVEN DAYS Yehonala would not leave her bed. The palace corridors were busy with whispers that she was angry, that she had tried to swallow her gold earrings. For as soon as the emperor recovered, he sent for her. She would not obey. Never in history had an imperial concubine refused herself. Yehonala would not speak except to her serving woman. "Let them think I want to die," she told her woman.

The woman told this to Li Lien-ying and he gnashed his teeth. "If the emperor were not beside himself with love, it would be easy enough," he snarled. "She could be poisoned, but he wants her whole and sound—and now!"

At last the chief eunuch himself came. Yehonala kept her earrings on a small table beside her bed. "Let the chief eunuch step over the threshold," she declared in a voice raised to reach his ears, "and I swallow my gold earrings!"

So it went until the emperor grew distrustful, believing that some eunuch was delaying her coming in hope of a bribe. "She was very obedient to me," he insisted. "She did all that I asked."

No one dared to say that His Majesty had been hateful to the beautiful girl, and it would not have come to the imperial mind to imagine this. Instead, knowing that with other women his passion had died early, he was pleased that after seven days he longed for her presence more than ever.

By night of the third day, An Teh-hai, too, was beside himself, and he went to the dowager mother.

"I have never heard of such a woman," the dowager mother exclaimed. "Let the eunuchs take her by force to my son!"

The chief eunuch hesitated. "Venerable," he said, "I question this method. She must be won and persuaded. She is so strong, though slender as a young willow tree, that she will not hesitate to bite the Son of Heaven or scratch his face."

"What horror!" the dowager mother exclaimed. "Is there no one inside the palace who can persuade her?"

"Venerable, the consort is her cousin," the chief eunuch suggested.

The dowager mother said, "Well, then, suggest to her that Yehonala is ill and should be visited."

"Yes, Venerable," the chief eunuch said. "Sleep in peace, Venerable."

"Go away," the dowager mother replied. "I am too old for the troubles of men and women."

He went at once to the palace of the consort and there found Sakota embroidering tiger faces on a pair of shoes for her child. With a gesture of her hand she bade him sit.

"I come before you, my lady," he said, still standing, "at the command of the dowager mother."

She lifted her pretty eyes. "Oh?"

The chief eunuch coughed. "Your cousin gives us much trouble. She will not obey the imperial summons."

Sakota blushed as pink as a peach blossom. "What has this to do with me?" she asked.

"It is thought that she might listen to you, the consort."

Sakota pondered this, embroidering slowly. "Is this a proper request to make of me?" she inquired at last.

The chief eunuch was blunt. "Indeed, it is not, my lady. Yet we all must remember that the Son of Heaven is not a common man."

"He likes her so much!" Sakota murmured. She folded her embroidery and put it on the table near her. "We have always been as close as sisters, she and I," she said in her sweetly plaintive voice. "If she needs me, I will go to her."

"Thank you, my lady," the chief eunuch said. "I will escort you there myself."

So it happened that Yehonala, lying on her bed tearless and in despair, looked up and saw her cousin standing in the doorway. "Sakota!" she wailed and held out both her arms. The two young women clasped each other and wept together. Neither dared to speak of what both remembered. "Oh, poor sister," Sakota wept.

"I will not return to him," Yehonala whispered. She all but strangled her cousin, so tightly did she hold her.

"Oh, but you must!" she cried. "Else what will they do to you, my dear? We are not our own now."

Then Yehonala, whispering, revealed her heart. "Here is the misery! If I did not love, I would not care. What is a woman's body? It is only a thing, to be kept or given away. It is only priceless when one loves and is loved in return." She had no need to speak the name. Sakota knew it was Jung Lu.

"It is too late," Sakota said. She stroked Yehonala's smooth wet cheeks. "There is no escape now."

Yehonala pushed her hands away. "Then I must die," she said, her voice breaking, "for truly I will not live." And she put her head down on her cousin's shoulder again and wept.

While Sakota soothed Yehonala with her hands, she pondered in her heart as to what she could do to help her. To leave the Forbidden City was not possible. There was no place in the known world for an escaped concubine. Whatever help, whatever comfort she might have, must be found only within the walls themselves. Though no man could sleep within the walls of this city at night, save the Son of Heaven, nevertheless women had their lovers by day.

Yehonala sat up in bed and pushed her hair away from her face. "I cannot ask my kinsman Jung Lu to come to me—you know that, Sakota! Gossip would flare from court to court. But you may send for him, Sakota. He is your kinsman, too. Send for him and tell him, or I will surely kill myself in this prison."

Sakota sat silent for a long moment. Then, knowing that she had no comfort for this young and stormy woman, she rose. "Cousin, my dear," she said in her most coaxing voice, "I will go away now so that you can be bathed and dressed, and then you must eat some food. I will send for Jung Lu, and if there is gossip, then I will say that it is I who bade him come."

When she was gone, Yehonala lay stone still, staring into the canopy above her. A fantasy wove itself in her mind, a plan, a plot, possible only if Sakota protected her, Sakota who was the imperial consort, whom no one could accuse.

When her serving woman peered in, Yehonala turned her head. "I will have my bath now," she said. "And I will put on my green robe, the apple green—and then I will eat."

"Yes, yes, my pet," the woman said, well pleased.

SOMETIME IN the afternoon of that day, two hours before all men had to leave the emperor's city, Yehonala heard the footsteps for which she waited. Her serving woman sat outside the door. To her, Yehonala had said honestly, "I am in sore trouble. My cousin, the consort, knows my woe. She has commanded our kinsman to come to me, and to carry my trouble to my uncle. While he is here, you are to stay by the door. You are not to let anyone so much as peer into my court. You understand that it is by the consort's command that he comes."

"My lady, I do understand," the woman said.

When he came at last, she heard the door open and close, and she saw his hand lay hold of the inner curtain and hesitate. She sat waiting and motionless in her chair of carved black wood. Then he put the curtain aside and stood there looking at her. Her heart leaped in her breast, and tears welled in her eyes and her mouth began to quiver. His will was shaken. He had seen her weep in pain and he had heard her sob with rage, but he had never seen her sit motionless and weep without a sound, as though her very life were broken.

He gave a great groan and his arms went out to her. She rose blindly from her chair and ran to him and felt his arms enclose her. They stood in silence and in fearful ecstasy until their lips met by instinct. Then he tore his mouth away.

"You know you cannot leave this place," he groaned. "You must find your freedom here within these walls, for there is no other freedom for you now."

She listened, hearing his voice from afar, knowing only that she stood within his arms.

"The higher you rise," he told her, "the greater will your freedom be. Rise high, my love—the power is yours. Only an empress can command."

"But will you love me?" she asked, her voice catching.

"How can I not love you?" he replied. "To love you is my only life."

"Then—seal me your love!" She spoke these bold words in so soft a whisper that he might not have heard them, except she knew that he had. She felt his shoulders shiver and his bones yield. "If once I am made yours," she continued bravely, "even here I can live."

No answer yet. He could not speak. His soul was still not yielding.

She lifted her head and looked into his face. "I know you speak the truth. There is no escape for me except by death. Well, I can choose death. I swear I will die unless you make me yours! If I am yours, I will do what you say—forever and my whole life long. I will be empress."

Her voice was pleading, warm and sweet as honey in the summer sun. He was young and fervent, still virgin. He had loved no one but her. He felt his conscience die, and then he lifted the beautiful girl in his arms and carried her to her bed. . . .

The drums of curfew beat through the courtyards of the Forbidden City. It was the hour of sunset when every man must leave. The ancient command fell upon the ears of lovers hidden deep within the secret rooms. In Yehonala's bedchamber Jung Lu rose and drew his garments about him while she lay half asleep and smiling.

He leaned over her. "Are we sworn?" he asked.

"Sworn." She drew his face down to hers. "Forever, forever!"

He made haste, and she rose quickly and smoothed her robe and brushed back her hair. When her serving woman coughed at the door, she was sitting in her chair. "Enter," she said, pretending to wipe her eyes.

"Are you weeping again, my lady?" the woman asked.

"I am finished weeping," Yehonala said in a small voice. "I know what I must do. My kinsman has made me see my duty."

The woman stood there, her head cocked to one side like a bird's. "Your duty, my lady?" she repeated.

"When the Son of Heaven summons me," Yehonala said, "I shall go to him. I must do his will."

THE HEAT OF summer lingered late. One brilliant day followed upon another. Princesses and court ladies, eunuchs and concubines—all went to the caves in the imperial gardens to spend the hours of the full heat. Crouching pine trees hung over the entrances, and hidden fountains made pools inside where goldfish played.

But Yehonala did not go with them to the caves. She was now always busy with her lessons, always smiling, silent more often than speaking. Seemingly her rebellion was forgotten. When the emperor summoned her, she obeyed him.

Each day she went first to the dowager mother to inquire of her health and happiness. The old lady was often ill, and Yehonala brewed herbs in tea to soothe her. Soon all perceived that the handsome girl was not only the favorite of the Son of Heaven, but of his mother too.

Meanwhile she had a secret until one day her serving woman spoke out. "Mistress, have you not marked that the full moon has come and gone and you have had no show of crimson?"

"Is it so?" Yehonala asked as if she did not care.

"It is so," the woman said proudly. "The seed of the dragon is in you, my lady. Shall I not carry the good news to the mother of the Son of Heaven?"

"Wait," Yehonala commanded. "Wait until the consort has borne her child. If it is a son, does it matter what I bear?"

The court waited, then, for the consort. And still Sakota's child was not born. The court physicians grew anxious about her. She was worn out with waiting and could not eat or sleep. Once Yehonala went to see her, but Sakota would not receive her. She was too ill, the eunuch in attendance said. And Yehonala went away in doubt. Illness? How could Sakota be too ill to see her own cousin? For the first time she wished Sakota did not know that Jung Lu had come to her in private. Never again would she put a weapon of secret knowledge into another's hand.

The days went on, and all omens were dire. Strange swift winds blew down upon the city. On the last day of the month a thunderstorm struck the city at noon. The elders said they had never seen such lightning nor heard such roaring thunder. When rain fell at last, it came with such lashing fury that torrents ate the earth away. On that day Sakota felt the pains of birth begin, and no sooner did she cry out than the news spread everywhere through the palaces.

Yehonala was at that time in the library with her tutor. The sky had grown so dark that the eunuchs lit the lamps. Li Lien-ying appeared at the curtain and made signs to Yehonala.

"Sir," she said to her tutor, "I must hasten to the dowager mother, who has sudden need of me."

Long ago she had planned to go to the dowager mother and stay with her until it was known whether the birth was of a female or a male. She left the library and walked ahead of the eunuch to the palace. The old lady had gone to bed as she did always in a thunderstorm, and now she lay raised on her pillows, her hands clasped about her jeweled Buddhist prayer beads. When she saw Yehonala, she said, "How can a sound child be born at such a time? Heaven itself rages above our heads."

Yehonala knelt beside the bed. "Be soothed, Imperial Mother," she coaxed. "It is not because of us that Heaven rages. Evil men have rebelled against the throne. Heaven is angry on the child's behalf."

"Do you believe so?"

"I do," Yehonala said, and she went on speaking soothing words, rising only to fetch hot broth for the dowager mother.

At sunset the wind died down and a strange yellow light suffused the palaces and courtyards. Yehonala drew the curtains and lit the candles and waited. When night fell, the chief eunuch arrived. Yehonala went to meet him, and from his face she saw the news was evil.

"It is a girl, a sickly female," he said heavily.

Yehonala covered her eyes. "Oh, cruel Heaven!"

"Will you tell the venerable mother?" he asked. "I must hasten again to the emperor. He is ill with anger."

"I will tell her," Yehonala promised.

"And you," the chief eunuch continued, "make yourself ready to be summoned. The emperor will surely need you."

Slowly she went back to the dowager's bedchamber. The dowager mother saw her face and knew all. "It is not a male child," she said, her voice weary.

"It is a female," Yehonala said gently.

She took the dowager mother's hands. "Why do I live?" the old lady inquired piteously.

"You must live, Venerable Mother," Yehonala said, her voice tender. "You must live—until my son is born."

"Is it true?" the dowager mother asked, her old face breaking into a wrinkled smile. "Can this be Heaven's will? From your strong body the child will be a son! Buddha hears!"

Looking up, Yehonala saw adoration in the dowager mother's eyes. "It is true that I am strong," she said. "And I shall bear a son."

The venerable lady rose out of her bed with such energy that those around her were frightened. "Send eunuchs to my son," she exclaimed. "Tell him I have good news." She turned again to Yehonala. "And you, my heart," she exclaimed, "you are more precious to me now than anyone except my son himself. I shall have you moved to the Western Palace. And let the court physicians be summoned without delay!"

"But I am not ill, Venerable," Yehonala said, laughing. "Look at me!" She stretched out her arms and lifted her head. Her cheeks were red, her dark eyes bright.

The dowager mother stared at her. "Beautiful, beautiful," she murmured.

Yehonala made her obeisance and retired from the chamber. Outside the doors her own woman waited with Li Lien-ying. "Let the new empress command me," he declared.

"Be quiet," Yehonala said. "You speak too soon."

"Have I not seen destiny over your head?" he cried.

"Leave me," Yehonala said. And she went on her way.

In her own bedchamber as her woman brushed her hair in expectation of the imperial summons, a sudden noise of wailing voices rose above the walls.

"What evil has befallen?" the serving woman cried.

She ran out, and at the gate she fell against the eunuch Li Lien-ying. His face was as green as a sour peach. "The dowager mother is dead," he gasped.

"Dead!" the serving woman screamed.

"Dead," Li Lien-ying repeated. "She came tottering to the Audience Hall, supported by her ladies, and when the emperor hastened there, she cried out that he would have a son, and these were her last words, for she fell dead into her ladies' arms. Her soul has gone to the eternal Yellow Springs."

Yehonala, hastening to the outer door, had already heard. "I brought the imperial mother too much joy," she said sadly.

"No, but joy came too quickly after sorrow, and her soul was divided," her serving woman said.

Yehonala went back to her bedroom and stood looking at the two robes the serving woman had spread out before her. "Put them away," she said at last. "I shall not be summoned now until the emperor's days of mourning are ended."

THE MONTHS slipped quietly into the Season of the First Cold. The Son of Heaven, wearing white mourning robes, lived without women. Yehonala was free, but by the emperor's command she was also guarded. Each morning before she had eaten, the physicians waited upon her, to feel her pulse and peer under her eyelids and examine her tongue. Then they prescribed bowls of green mixtures and black drafts. She ate heartily and slept well and kept the medicine down somehow.

Meanwhile Yehonala herself was changed. Until the day when she knew she had conceived, she had been willful and mischievous, in spite of her ambition to learn. Now whatever she learned she wove around herself and the child within her. Thus when one day in the library she came upon the words of Lao-tzu: "Of all the dangers, the greatest is to think lightly of the foe," these words seemed as fresh to her as if they had been spoken on that very day.

"Tell me," she said to her tutor, "who are our present foes?"

The old eunuch shook his head. "My lady," he replied, "I have no learning in affairs of state."

"Send me one who can teach me," she said.

The aged eunuch reported her command to An Teh-hai,

who went to Prince Kung, the sixth son of the last emperor, half-brother by blood to the present emperor. Prince Kung's wisdom and intelligence were so great that ministers, princes and eunuchs consulted him secretly instead of the emperor. The chief eunuch therefore begged Prince Kung himself to teach the young favorite.

"She is so strong," he said, "and her mind is as clever as a man's. We do not doubt she will bear a son, our next emperor."

Prince Kung pondered this. He was a young man, and it was not seemly for him to come near a concubine. But the emperor was dissolute and weak, his court corrupt and idle. The treasury was empty; frequent famines swept the land, and in their hunger, the people were plotting against the Dragon Throne. Drive out the Manchu emperors! Restore the ancient Chinese dynasty of Ming! What hope, then, except to hold hard the remnants of the empire until an heir was born?

"I myself will teach the favorite," he said, "but ask her aged tutor to stay in her presence while I am there."

The next day, then, when Yehonala went as usual to the imperial library, she saw there beside her tutor a man, tall, young and powerfully handsome. With him was An Teh-hai, who presented him.

"Be seated, Elder Brother," Yehonala said. The old tutor took his place at the end of the table. The chief eunuch stood behind the prince, and four ladies behind Yehonala.

With his face turned away, Prince Kung thus began the lessons that he continued, one day in seven, for many months. He described how the weakness of the throne invited the rebellion of its subjects and invasion from enemies beyond the seas. He told her that three hundred years before, the first foreign invaders were men from Portugal, seeking trade in spices. After them, Spanish conquerors came and Dutch, and then the English, making war for their opium trade, and after these the French, the Germans.

Yehonala's face was pale and red by turns and her hands clenched. "And we did nothing?" she cried.

"What could we do?" Prince Kung retorted. And he told how continuously the English had made their wars, and how each time they had been victorious.

"I have heard enough," Yehonala said abruptly.

"Yet not enough, Most Favored," Prince Kung said courteously. "In the time of Chia Ch'ing, the British sent an envoy, Amherst by name. This man, when summoned to the Audience Hall at the usual hour of dawn, refused to come, saying that he was ill. The Son of Heaven sent his own physicians to examine the foreigner, and they reported that Amherst feigned illness. The Son of Heaven was angry and ordered the Englishman to go home. The white men are stubborn, Most Favored. They will not kneel before our Sons of Heaven. They tell us that they kneel before no one but gods—and women."

"Women?" Yehonala repeated. She put up her hand to hide her laughter, but the sound escaped her nonetheless, and Prince Kung turned and caught the mischief in her eyes.

"What now?" she asked.

"We must resist," Prince Kung continued, "though not by arms, for we have not such means. But we can resist by obstructions and delays. Now these Americans insist, too, upon the treaties we have been forced to make with the others."

"What is the end?" Yehonala asked.

"Who knows?" Prince Kung replied, sighing heavily. He rose and bowed. "I have brushed a few lines from history for you, Most Favored. If you will, I shall proceed to fill them out until all the truth is plain."

"I pray you do so," Yehonala said.

That night she could not sleep, thinking how her son must take the empire back and drive his foreign foes into the sea.

YEHONALA NO longer felt that she was a prisoner within the palace. She was the center of the people's hope. What she ate, her color, her laughter, her whims—all were matters of concern. In the glow of such importance, a mild mood pervaded her spirit, and never had she felt her body so sound and whole. Strangest of all, she no longer hated the Son of Heaven. She pitied him, a shell of a man, wrapped in the golden robes of office. At night she cradled him in her arms, and by day she showed him extravagant respect, for was he not the father of her son? Yet secretly in her own heart she thought of Jung Lu and the hour when he had come at her desire.

Two streams fed into her life: the first, her deepening pride that she bore within her the heir to the throne, and the other, her secret love. For the first, she studied zealously the history of the people whom her son would rule. Because of the other, she perceived anew the beauty of the world. To her, even in winter the gardens were beautiful; the northern bamboo was green under the snow and the Indian bamboo bore scarlet berries. Palace by palace, she learned to know the sacred city, the center of the earth even as the north star is center of the sky. Ah, she had chosen well to make this her son's birthplace and his home!

In the spring of the new year, Yehonala gave birth to a son in the presence of the elder ladies of the court. While she crouched, a midwife caught the child and held him up before the ladies. "See, Venerables," she announced. "A male child, in full health and strength!" And Yehonala, half fainting, looked up and saw her son.

When night fell, the courtyard outside her little private palace was lit by the light of lanterns set on an altar of sacrifice. From her bed Yehonala looked through the low latticed windows on the assembly of princes and ladies and eunuchs. It was the hour of the birth sacrifice to Heaven, and the emperor stood before the altar to give thanks. On the altar were three offerings: the steamed head of a pig, a steamed cock and between them a live fish, struggling in a net of scarlet silk.

The rite was difficult, for this fish had been taken alive from a lotus pond, and it must be returned alive again to that same water, or the heir would not live to reach his manhood. There was deep silence in the courtyard. The imperial father knelt

before Heaven and chanted his prayers. Then seizing the still-living fish, he gave it to the chief eunuch, who hastened to the pool and threw it in. An Teh-hai peered into the water, a lantern held high behind him, and in silence the court waited. The light fell upon a flash of silver in the water. "The fish lives, Majesty," he shouted.

The assembly now began to laugh and talk. Firecrackers were set off, and rockets sprayed the sky with light. While Yehonala leaned on her elbow, from the center of the sky she saw floating against the sparkling darkness a huge golden orchid, its petals touched with purple. "My lady, this is in your honor!" her serving woman cried. A roar rose up from the city when the people saw the sight, and Yehonala laughed and threw herself upon her pillows. How glad she was to be a woman! What man could know such triumph as hers? "Is my cousin the consort in the courtyard, too?" she asked.

"I see her standing with her ladies," the old woman replied.

"Go out to her," Yehonala commanded. "Invite her to come in. Tell her I long to see her."

But Sakota shook her head when asked. "I rose from my bed to attend the sacrifice," she said, "and to my bed I must return. Indeed, I am not well." Leaning upon two ladies, she walked into the darkness.

The serving woman went back to Yehonala to report. "My lady, the consort will not come. She says she is ill, but I think she is not."

"Then why did she not come?" Yehonala demanded.

"Who can tell how the heart of a consort changes?" the woman replied. "She has a daughter. The son is yours."

"Sakota is not so small in heart," Yehonala insisted, and yet while she spoke, she remembered that her cousin held over her head the dagger of secret knowledge.

The courtyard was empty now. Everywhere that night the people feasted. The doors of the prisons were opened and the prisoners were freed. No shops were opened. No beasts were killed for food. This was in honor of her newborn child.

Lying in the shelter of the great curtained bed, her son curled into the hollow of her arm, Yehonala pondered her destiny and his. They were alone against the world, she and her son. The man she loved could never be her husband. The emperor was weak, and her son had only her to keep him safe amid the intrigues within the palaces. In that night and in as many nights as she was to live, there came the dark hours when she faced her destiny with naked eyes. She must defy them, enemies and friends. This child, her son, must forever be the son of the emperor and heir to the Dragon Throne!

II

TZU HSI

FOR HIS FIRST month, by ancient tradition, her son remained in his mother's palace. Here in this cluster of rooms around the courtyard bright with peonies, Yehonala spent the hours of day and night. Everyone came to look at the child and exclaim about his size, his handsome face, his strong hands and feet. Everyone, that is, except Sakota. The consort should have been the first to see the child and acknowledge him the heir, and yet she did not come.

Yehonala hid her anger, but three days before the month was over she sent Li Lien-ying to Sakota with this message: "Since you, Cousin, have not come to visit me, I must come to you to ask your favor and protection for my son, for he belongs to us both, according to law and tradition."

Thus before the end of her son's first month Yehonala went to Sakota's palace. She wore a new robe of imperial-yellow satin and a headdress of black satin, beaded with pearls. Her fine eyebrows were drawn with a brush dipped in inked oil. Her mouth, full and tender, was painted a smooth red. From her ears hung earrings of jade and pearls.

She took her son in her arms then, he in scarlet satin from head to foot, and with him she sat in her palanquin and they were borne to the consort's palace. There in the reception hall she saw Sakota. Before this timid small creature, Yehonala stood as strong and handsome as a young cedar tree.

"I come to you, Cousin," she said, after greeting her. "I come on behalf of our son. True, I gave him birth, but your duty, Cousin, is even greater to him than my own, for is not his father the Son of Heaven, who is your lord before he is mine? I ask your protection for our son."

"But—but why?" Sakota stammered. "Why do you speak to me so? Are we not kin? Is not the emperor our mutual lord?"

"It is for our son that I ask your favor," Yehonala said. "I must be sure that you are for our son and not against him."

Each knew what the other meant. Yehonala was saying that she must be certain Sakota would not plot to set another on the Dragon Throne. By her silence Sakota announced that she did not wish to give her promise.

Yehonala stepped forward. "Give me your hands, Cousin." Her voice was smooth and resolute. "Promise me that no one can divide us. We must live out our lives together here within these walls. Let us be friends and not enemies."

Sakota hesitated. Then suddenly, her great eyes furious, Yehonala leaned down and crushed Sakota's two small soft hands so fiercely that the tears rushed to her eyes. So Yehonala had done when they were children whenever Sakota had pouted and rebelled.

"I—I promise," Sakota said in a broken voice.

"And I promise," Yehonala said firmly. Then she saw what all the waiting ladies saw: the thin gold shields of her finger-nails had cut red stripes into Sakota's tender flesh.

"I will not stay, Cousin," Yehonala said. "I came for this promise and now I have it. Nor will I forget that I, too, have given my own promise." With surpassing pride, she swept her imperial-yellow robe about her, took her son and went away.

That night she sent for Li Lien-ying and commanded him to bring to her the chief eunuch, An Teh-hai. "Tell him I have a trouble that I brood upon," she said.

When An Teh-hai arrived, Yehonala pointed at the chair on which he was to sit, and she sat down in her own thronelike chair. She had dismissed her ladies, and Li Lien-ying made a pretense of withdrawing, but Yehonala bade him stay.

"What I have to say is for both of you. Are there those who plot to seize the throne from my son? If . . ." She paused, for no one who spoke of the emperor could mention death.

"My lady, all is true." The chief eunuch nodded his handsome head. "You must know," he said, "that when the consort gave birth to a sickly girl, certain princes plotted how they would steal the imperial seal the moment the emperor departed for the Yellow Springs."

Again he shook his head. "We may not expect a long reign. The emperor is young, but before he was twelve years of age he was debauched by eunuchs and by sixteen he was exhausted by women. Let me speak the truth," he said in a lowered voice, his wide face solemn. "We must now count our friends and enemies."

Yehonala looked at him without a sign of fear. "Who are our enemies?" she asked.

"First, the grand councillor Su Shun," the chief eunuch whispered.

"He!" she exclaimed. "And I have taken his daughter, Lady Mei, as my court lady and my favorite!"

"Even he," the chief eunuch said gravely, "and with him the emperor's own nephew, Prince Yi, and after him Prince Cheng. These three, Venerable, are your first enemies, because you have given us an heir."

The danger was as great as she had imagined. These were mighty lords and princes, and she was but a woman. She lifted her head proudly. "And who are my friends?"

"Above all others, Venerable, Prince Kung, the younger brother of the Son of Heaven. When Prince Kung saw you," the chief eunuch declared, "he said that you were a woman so clever that either you would bring good fortune to the realm or you would destroy the Dragon Throne."

"Return to the emperor," Yehonala commanded. "Put into his mind that the heir is in danger and that only I can protect our child. Put into his mind that he must raise my rank to equal that of the consort so that she cannot be used by those who crave power over the heir."

The chief eunuch smiled at such cleverness. "My lady," he said, "I will put it into the emperor's mind that he so reward you on the heir's first month's birthday. What day could be more auspicious?"

"None," she agreed. Suddenly she smiled and her eyes shone with triumph.

At the end of his first month, the heir was fit and healthy, his will already imperious, and his hunger constant. To celebrate his birthday, the emperor had decreed that feasts be held throughout the nation. Here in the Forbidden City the day was to be given over entirely to feasting and to music.

When he sent the chief eunuch to inquire what Yehonala would like for her own pleasure, she put her private craving into words. "I do long to see a good play," she told An Teh-hai.

But first on the day of feasting the gifts were to be presented and received. For these rites the emperor chose the throne room named the Palace of Surpassing Brightness. Here in silence they waited for the coming of the Son of Heaven, and when dawn broke across the sky, the imperial procession appeared, its banners carried by the guardsmen in their scarlet tunics. Next came the princes, then the eunuchs, marching slowly two by two, in robes of purple, belted with gold. In their midst twelve bearers bore the sacred yellow dragon palanquin in which sat the Son of Heaven himself. Within the Throne Hall they fell upon their knees and knocked their heads nine times upon the floor, shouting their greeting, "Ten thousand years! Ten thousand years! Ten thousand years!"

The emperor mounted the golden throne. There, seated in dignity, he received the princes and the ministers who presented gifts for the heir. Prince Kung read the list of gifts and from whence they came, and the chief eunuch marked down the name of the giver and its worth.

A scented wood screen stood behind the throne as usual, and behind it, shielded from the eyes of the men, Yehonala and the consort sat with their ladies. When all the gifts had been accepted, the emperor summoned Yehonala to receive his own reward. She stood before the Dragon Throne for one instant, her head high; then she sank slowly to her knees in obeisance and put her forehead on her crossed hands.

Above her the emperor began to speak. "I do this day decree that the mother of the imperial heir, here kneeling, is to be raised to the rank of consort, equal in all ways to the present consort. That there be no confusion, the present consort shall be known as Tzu An, the empress of the Eastern Palace, and the fortunate mother shall be known as Tzu Hsi, the empress of the Western Palace."

Yehonala's blood ran strong and joyful to her heart. Three times and three times and yet three times more she touched her forehead to her hands. Then, rising, she stood until the chief eunuch escorted her to her place behind the scented wood screen. And from that day she was no longer called Yehonala. Tzu Hsi was her imperial name.

That same night she was summoned to the emperor. She welcomed the call, not only for her son's sake but for her own. Well she knew that during the three months surrounding her son's birth the emperor had made use of one concubine and another. Tonight would tell her whether any of them had succeeded in displacing her.

Ah, but now how hard it was to leave the child! Ready and robed in soft pink satin, she could not force herself away from the sleeping boy. Two women sat beside him, one the wet nurse, and the other her own woman. "You are not to leave him for one breath of time," she warned them. "If when I return, he is hurt or weeping, I will have you both beaten."

Still Tzu Hsi could not go away. She leaned above her

sleeping child and saw his rosy face, the pouting lips soft and red, the eyes full and large. Whence did her child receive his beauty? Hers alone, surely, was not enough for this perfection. His father—

"Venerable!" She heard An Teh-hai's voice rumbling impatiently from the outer room. From her dressing table she chose two gifts, a ring of gold and a thin bracelet set with seed pearls. These she gave to the two women, thus bribing them to their duty. Then she hastened out and there was Li Lien-ying, waiting with An Teh-hai. To her eunuch she gave a piece of gold without a word. Inside the bosom of her robe she held gold in a packet for the chief eunuch, too, but she would not give it to him until she saw how the emperor received her. If the night went well, then he would have his prize.

"COME HERE to me," the emperor said.

She stood at the threshold of his vast chamber, and walked slowly toward him, swaying gracefully as she went and hastening the last few steps to the imperial bed. "Ah," she cried in sudden pity, "you are ill and no one told me, my lord."

Indeed by the light of the great candles he looked so wan that he seemed a living skeleton propped there against the pillows. His hands lay lifeless on the quilts. She sat down on the bed and put out her warm, strong hands. "Have you pain?" she asked anxiously.

"No pain," he said. "A weakness—"

"But this hand," she insisted. She took up his left hand. "It feels different from the other—colder, more stiff."

"I cannot use it as once I did," he said unwillingly.

She put back his sleeve and saw his bare arm, thin and yellow as old ivory. "Ah," she moaned, "why was I not told?"

"What is there to tell?" he said. "Come," he said, "come into my bed. None of them has been enough. Only you—"

She saw the old hot light come creeping back into his sunken eyes. And yet as the dark hours passed, she felt a sadness she had never known before. The chill of death had struck the emperor's inward life and he was a man no more. "Help me," he besought her again and again. "Help me—lest I die of this dreadful heat unslaked."

But she could not help him, and when she saw this, she sat by his pillow and took him in her arms as though he were a child. Like a child he sobbed upon her breast. Though his third decade had not yet come, he was an old man.

"You are weary," she said. "You are beset by worries. Let me help you, my lord. Let me always sit behind the screen in the Throne Hall at dawn and listen to your ministers. When they are gone, I will tell you what I think, leaving all decisions to you, my lord, as is my duty."

Thus she wooed him away from his unsatisfied desire to the affairs of the nation and the strengthening of the throne.

"There is no end to my troubles," he complained. "In the days of my forefathers the enemy came always from the north and the Great Wall stopped them. But now these white men swarm up from the seas. And they are never satisfied. Now the Americans are here, too. Where did they come from? This is the year when they wish to renew their treaty with us. But I do not wish to renew any treaty with white men."

"Then do not renew it," Tzu Hsi said impetuously. "Bid your ministers refuse."

"The white men's weapons are very fearful," he moaned.

"Delay, delay," she said. "Do not answer their pleadings. This gives us time. Do not say yes or no."

The emperor was struck with such wisdom. "You are worth more to me than any man," he declared, "even more than my brother. It is he who frightens me by telling me about their big ships. Negotiate, he says—"

Tzu Hsi laughed. "Do not allow yourself to be frightened, my lord, even by Prince Kung. The sea is very far from here."

He wished to believe what she said, and his heart clung to her more than ever. He fell asleep at last, and she sat beside him until dawn. At that hour the chief eunuch came to waken the emperor for the usual early audience. Tzu Hsi rose while the emperor still slept. "From this day on," she said, "I am to sit behind the screen in the Throne Hall."

An Teh-hai bowed down to the floor before her. "Venerable," he exclaimed, "now I am happy."

Tzu Hsi rose in darkness and entered her curtained sedan. Li Lien-ying went before her with a lantern to the Throne Hall, and she sat behind the great carved screen behind the Dragon Throne. Li Lien-ying stood near her, a dagger ready in his hand.

From that day, too, the heir was moved into his own palace and the chief eunuch was made his servant. Prince Kung was appointed his guardian.

THE COLD CAME soon that year. Already by midautumn bitter winds blew from the northwest, scattering pale sand from the distant desert. When the sun went away at nightfall, the cold congealed the blood of young and old alike. Beggars in the streets ran hither and thither to keep alive, and even wild dogs could not sleep.

Tzu Hsi rose one day in a cold and silent hour to take her usual place in the Throne Hall. When the watchman's brass gong sounded through the streets, the serving woman got up from her pallet and made tea in a silver pot. Tzu Hsi drank her tea slowly. Hot water was ready in the porcelain tub in the bathing room. Her woman washed her gently and dressed her in a long robe of rose satin lined with northern sable.

Tzu Hsi did not require that any of her ladies rise early to accompany her. Yet one lady often rose, and it was Lady Mei, the young daughter of Su Shun, a prince and grand councillor. This morning she stood at the door, fresh as a white gardenia flower.

Tzu Hsi smiled now at the young girl. "Are you not early?"

"Venerable, I was so cold I could not sleep."

"One of these days I must get you a husband to warm your bed," Tzu Hsi said, still smiling.

She spoke these words with casual kindness, but she knew from the gossip of the women in the courts that Lady Mei had been seen to look more than once at Jung Lu, the handsome chief of the imperial guard.

"Venerable, please, I want no husband," Lady Mei now murmured. "Let me stay with you always."

"Why not?" Tzu Hsi replied. "This is not to say you shall not have a husband."

Lady Mei went pale. It was unlucky to talk of marriage! The empress of the Western Palace had only to command her marriage and she must obey, whereas her whole heart was—

Li Lien-ying appeared. "Venerable, the hour grows late," he said. She entered her sedan and six bearers lifted the poles to their shoulders and marched to the Throne Hall. Prince Kung stood waiting to receive her. He bowed and led the way to the space behind the Dragon Throne. Here, shielded by the immense carved screen, Tzu Hsi took her seat. On her right stood Lady Mei, and on her left Li Lien-ying.

The terrace in front of the Audience Hall was already filled with princes and ministers who had brought petitions and memorials to the emperor. At the four corners of the terrace stood bronze elephants filled with oil that fed the torches in their uplifted trunks, casting a fierce light upon the scene.

In the Audience Hall itself a hundred eunuchs moved to and fro. A strange silence brooded over all as the hour, fixed by the board of astrologers, drew near. In the last moment before dawn, a courier blew his brass trumpet. This was a sign that the emperor had left his palace and his imperial procession was moving slowly to arrive at the exact hour of dawn.

As the imperial procession appeared at the entrance to the lower courtyard, the couriers cried out together, "Behold the Lord of Ten Thousand Years!" Next came the imperial guard in tunics of red and gold, and at their head Jung Lu walked alone. Behind the guard, bearers in yellow uniforms carried the emperor's palanquin of heavy gold.

Everyone shouted the sacred greeting, "Ten thousand years! Ten thousand years!" while the bearers carried the imperial sedan up the marble steps to the Dragon Terrace. There the emperor descended, wrapped in his robes of imperial yellow, mounted its few steps and sat on the Dragon Throne.

Tzu Hsi, behind the screen, saw only the head and shoulders of the emperor above the back of the throne. Beneath the imperial tasseled hat his neck showed thin and yellow. Tzu Hsi felt mixed pity and repulsion. How could she keep her eyes from reaching beyond the throne? There Jung Lu stood in the full strength of his youth and manhood.

Suddenly, guided by some instinct, her eyes slid toward Lady Mei. The girl stood with her face pressed on the screen, staring at Jung Lu. "Stand back!" Tzu Hsi commanded as she seized Lady Mei by the wrist. The lady turned her head in fright and met Tzu Hsi's eyes, great and black and fierce with anger. The girl's head drooped, and the tears ran down her cheeks. Only then did Tzu Hsi turn her eyes away. Her will rose hard within her. She would not let her heart beguile her mind. This was the hour of learning how to rule. She would not yearn for love.

At this moment Yeh, the viceroy of the Kwang provinces in the south, was kneeling before the throne, reading aloud from a scroll. He was saying that the traders from the West, led by the Englishmen, were angry over so small an affair that he, the viceroy, was ashamed to mention it now before the Dragon Throne. Yet in the past from such small matters wars had been fought and lost, and he, appointed by the Son of Heaven, could not risk the danger of yet another war. The trouble was over nothing more than a flag.

Prince Kung spoke for the emperor. "The Son of Heaven inquires why the Englishmen should be angry over what is nothing more, after all, than a piece of cloth?"

"Most High," the viceroy explained, "the English attach magic qualities to it. It is sacred to some god they worship. Wherever they place it, it designates possession. In this case, it was attached to a pole on a small trading vessel carrying Chinese pirates. The captain of this boat had paid a sum of money to the Englishmen to allow him to fly the flag. I arrested the vessel and put the captain in chains. But the Englishman, John Bowring, the commissioner of trade for the British in Canton, declared that I had insulted the flag, and he demanded that I apologize on behalf of the throne."

Horror rushed over the entire assembly. Even the emperor was aroused. He sat up in his throne and spoke for himself. "Apologize? For what?"

"Most High," the viceroy said, "those were my words."

"Stand," the emperor commanded.

It was unusual, but the viceroy obeyed. He was a tall, aging Chinese scholar, loyal as all scholars were to the Manchu throne, since the throne employed them as administrators of government.

"Did you apologize?" the emperor asked, again speaking directly to signify his deep concern.

The viceroy replied, "Most High, how could I apologize when I am the appointed of the Dragon Throne? I sent the pirate captain and his crew to apologize to the Englishmen. That haughty and ignorant Bowring sent them back to me, declaring that it was I whom he wanted. Whereupon, in extreme vexation, I had the pirates beheaded for causing confusion."

"Did this not satisfy the Englishman Bowring?"

"It did not, Most High," the viceroy replied. "This Bowring enlarges every cause for quarrel. Thus he encourages smuggling opium from India across our borders, saying that as long as any Chinese trader smuggles, foreigners may be allowed to. More than that, guns also are now being smuggled in to sell to the southern Chinese rebels. And he continues to insist that the English are not satisfied with the land we have allowed them to build their houses on. No, Most High, these Englishmen demand that the gates of Canton itself must be opened to them and to their families. Is this not to destroy our traditions and corrupt the people?"

The emperor agreed. "We cannot allow strangers the freedom of our streets. Have you presented this opinion to the

Englishman?" He raised his voice to a feeble shout, alarming the viceroy, who turned his head toward Prince Kung.

"Most High," he said, "Bowring insists that he be allowed to call upon me as an equal. Yet how can he be my equal when I am the appointed of the Dragon Throne? This would be to insult the throne itself. I have replied that he must approach me on his knees. This he will not do."

"You are correct," the emperor said angrily, and from the kneeling multitude of ministers and princes approval rose in a subdued roar. The viceroy bowed his head nine times to the floor and gave way to the next minister.

That night the emperor received Tzu Hsi eagerly, and in his eagerness she read his fear. While he held her right hand in both his hands, he asked her the question that he had waited to put to her. "What shall we do with this Englishman Bowring? Does he not deserve to die?"

"He does," she said gently, "as any man deserves to die who insults the Son of Heaven. But you know, my lord, that when one strikes a viper, the head must be severed at the first blow, or else the creature will turn and attack. Therefore your weapon must be sharp and certain. We do not know yet what the weapon should be. Therefore I beg you to delay, never yielding but never refusing, until the way is clear."

Every word she spoke he received as though he heard it from Heaven. Indeed, when she had finished, he said very fervently, "You are Kuan Yin herself, the goddess of mercy, sent to me at this dreadful moment to guide me."

He had spoken many words of love to her, but what he had just said pleased her beyond anything she had ever heard. "Kuan Yin is my own favorite among the heavenly beings," she replied, and her voice was tender.

The emperor sat up in his bed with sudden energy. "Bid the chief eunuch call my brother," he exclaimed.

When Prince Kung came in, Tzu Hsi felt again as she looked at his grave and handsome face that this was a man she could trust.

"Sit down—sit down," the emperor said impatiently.

"Allow me to stand," Prince Kung replied in courtesy.

The emperor spoke in a high voice, nervous, stammering. "We have—I have—decided not to attack the white strangers with one blow. When one steps on a viper—a viper should be killed instantly, you understand, his head cut off—the question being—"

"I do understand, Most High," Prince Kung said. "It is better not to attack unless we can be sure of destroying the enemy instantly."

"It is what I am saying," the emperor said peevishly. "Someday, of course, it is what we must do. Meanwhile delay, you comprehend, not yielding but not refusing."

Prince Kung reflected. Had his brother made such decisions alone, he might have believed that this one was a result of his habitual lethargy and dread of trouble. But he knew that this was Tzu Hsi's advice. A powerful brain was hidden inside her beautiful head. Yet she was very young—and a woman! Could this be wisdom? "Most High," he began patiently.

But the emperor refused to hear him. "I have spoken!" he cried in a high and angry voice.

Prince Kung bowed his head. "Let it be so, Most High. I will myself take your commands to Viceroy Yeh."

ON A WINTER's morning when her son was nine months old, Tzu Hsi awoke and breathed a mighty sigh. She felt a loneliness so heavy that it seemed some monstrous danger from which she could not escape. Who in this vast tangle of courtyards and palaces cared whether she lived or died? "Ah, my mother," she moaned softly into her satin pillows.

She lifted her head and saw the gray dawn steal over the walls of the courtyard outside her window. Snow lay thickly over the tiled garden. I am too sad, she thought. If only I could see my mother. . . .

"And why," the emperor asked her that night, "why is your mind so far from me? I am not deceived by you. Your body is here but it is lifeless."

"I have been sad today," she said. "I have spoken to no one. I have not even sent for the child."

He continued to stroke the hand he held. "Now why," he asked, "when you have everything, should you be sad?"

Tears filled her eyes against her will. The emperor saw them glitter and he was frightened. "What is this?" he cried. "I have never seen you weep."

She drew her hand away and wiped her eyes gracefully on the edge of her sleeve. "I have yearned all day for my mother," she said. "I have not looked upon her face since I entered these walls at your command."

The emperor was all eagerness to please her. "You must visit her," he urged. "Why did you not tell me? Go, go, my heart, go tomorrow! But you must come back again by twilight. I cannot have you gone for a night."

So Tzu Hsi returned to her mother for a day. Her visit was announced beforehand so that her uncle's house could be prepared. What excitement now prevailed in Pewter Lane!

Tzu Hsi rose on the chosen morning and spent an hour deciding what she should wear. "I do not wish to be splendid," she explained to her woman, "for then they will think I have grown proud."

"Venerable, you must be somewhat splendid," the woman remonstrated, "or they will think you do not give them honor."

"A middling splendor," Tzu Hsi agreed. She selected a satin robe of a delicate orchid, lined with gray fur, its beauty in the perfection of its embroidered sleeves and hem.

At last, she entered her sedan, and the bearers drew the yellow satin curtains closed. For a mile the journey lay within the walls of the Forbidden City. Outside the gate she heard the commander of the imperial guard shout to his guardsmen. How well she knew that voice! She put aside the curtains and saw Jung Lu standing not ten feet from her, his face averted, his body taut and straight.

It was high noon when Tzu Hsi reached the entrance to Pewter Lane. As her sedan approached the gate to her uncle's house, she put her eye to the space between the curtains and saw a girl who was her younger sister and her two brothers, and behind them, Lu Ma. Against the walls on either side stood their neighbors and friends of Pewter Lane.

When she saw their faces grave and welcoming, tears filled her eyes. Oh, she was the same to them, and somehow she must make them know it! Yet she could not cry out their names, for she was now Tzu Hsi, the empress of the Western Palace, and mother of the imperial heir. Up the steps and through the open gate the six bearers carried her. Then they crossed the entrance courtyard and set the sedan down before the house. There the chief eunuch himself put aside the satin curtains. Tzu Hsi stepped out into the sunlight and saw before her the open doors of her old home. The familiar room was there, the main hall, its tables and chairs polished and clean and its tiled floor swept.

The chief eunuch led her to the highest seat to the right of the square tables and arranged her skirts. She folded her hands in her lap. Then he returned to the gate and announced that now the family could approach the empress of the Western Palace. One by one they came, her uncle first and then her mother, and bowed down before her.

When the ceremonies were complete, no one knew what to say next. They had to wait for the empress to speak first. She longed to come down from her high place and run about the house and talk as she used to do. But the chief eunuch stood there watching all she did. Suddenly she tapped her shielded fingernails on the polished table and nodded to signify that she had something to say to him. He came near and leaned down. "You are to stand aside! How can I enjoy myself when you hear every word I speak?"

The chief eunuch was already tired of standing on his feet and so he welcomed the chance to withdraw to another room. Seeing him gone, Tzu Hsi came down from her high seat and bowed to her uncle and put her arms about her mother. "Oh, me," she murmured, "how lonely I am in the palace!"

All were in consternation at this complaint. Even her mother did not know what to say and could only hold her daughter close. And in this long moment Tzu Hsi understood that even those she loved were helpless. She lifted up her head again and laughed, her eyes still wet, and she cried out to her sister, "Come, take this heavy thing from my head!"

Her sister came and lifted off the headdress and set it carefully on a table. They all saw now that Tzu Hsi was the same gay girl that she had ever been. The women examined her rings and bracelets and exclaimed at her beauty. "Your skin is white and soft," they said. "What do you rub in your skin?"

"An ointment from India," she told them. "It is made of fresh cream and pounded orange peel."

Such small questions they asked, but no one dared to ask about her life in the Forbidden City, or how her lord dealt with her, or about the heir, for fear that by chance they might use a word that would bring ill luck. But Tzu Hsi could not hide her joy in her child, and she said happily, "I did wish indeed that I might bring my little son to show you, but it could not be, lest some cruel spirit do the child damage. But I assure you, my mother, that he is such a child as would delight your soul. His eyes are big like this"—here she measured two circles with her thumbs and forefingers—"and he is so fat, his flesh so fragrant—and he never cries. He is always greedy for his food and his teeth are whiter than these pearls, and though he is still so small, he wants to stand on his legs."

"Hush!" her mother cried. "Hush! What if the gods hear you, reckless one? Will they not seek to destroy such a child?" And she cried out in a loud voice, "Nothing is as you say! I have heard that he is puny and weak and—"

Tzu Hsi laughed and put her hand over her mother's mouth. "I am not afraid!"

Soon Tzu Hsi was walking everywhere, looking at the rooms she knew so well. Alone with her mother, she proposed that she would find a good husband for her sister among the young noblemen.

Her mother was grateful. "If you can so do," she said, "it will be a filial deed, and very pious."

So the hours passed, and all in the family were merry because Tzu Hsi was merry. In midafternoon a good feast was set. Lu Ma was busy everywhere bawling at the hired cooks. When the day was nearing night, the chief eunuch returned to his duty. "The time has come, Venerable," he said to Tzu Hsi. "I have the command of the Most High."

She knew there was no escape. Once more she became the empress. Her sister put her headdress back on, and Tzu Hsi took her seat again in the main room. One by one the family came forward and made their obeisances. At last all the farewells were said. It had been a day of deep happiness, and yet she knew that nothing was the same. They loved her still, but their love was entangled with hopes of what she could do for them. Her uncle hinted at debts unpaid, her brothers yearned for amusements, and her mother bade her not forget her promise for her sister. She made promises for all and she would fulfill them, but her loneliness returned and lay ten times more heavy on her heart.

With firm steps she walked across the room and entered her sedan chair for her return to the Forbidden City.

THE HALTING SPRING was delayed by evil sandstorms that blew down from the north. Nor was the news good from the south. Viceroy Yeh had dallied and delayed. He had not replied to the many messages from the Englishman Sir John Bowring. Yet, he now reported to the Dragon Throne, instead of being subdued by such neglect the white men were more restless than before. What if war broke out again? It was rumored that the Englishman Elgin, a noble lord, was threatening to sail English ships northward along the seacoast and attack the Taku forts that protected the capital itself.

After the emperor read this memorial, he handed the document to his brother, Prince Kung, and he commanded that Tzu Hsi read it also and that the two of them present their advice. Then he took to his bed in silence and would not eat.

Now for the first time Tzu Hsi fell into open disagreement with Prince Kung.

"Venerable," Prince Kung said reasonably, "again I tell you that it is not wise to anger these white men. They have guns and warships, and they are barbarians at heart."

"Let them return to their own lands. We have tried patience and now patience fails," Tzu Hsi exclaimed.

"We have not the means to force their return," he reminded her.

"We can kill them while they are still few and throw their bodies into the sea."

He exclaimed at such recklessness. "When their peoples hear of it, they will send a thousand white men for each one that dies."

"I do not fear them," Tzu Hsi declared.

"But I do," Prince Kung said quickly. "When they are attacked, they always return ten blows for one. No, no—mediation and delays are the safe ways, as you wisely did advise before. We must weary them and discourage them, seeming courteously to yield but never yielding."

So in the end it was decided, and that Tzu Hsi might be diverted, Prince Kung advised the emperor that she be permitted to spend the hot season at the Summer Palace outside the city of Peking. There she could forget the troubles of the nation. "Meanwhile," said Prince Kung, "I will consider with the councillors what reply shall be sent south."

Tzu Hsi herself had coaxed the emperor on a summer night when the moon was full. "My lord," she said, "the coolness of the hills will restore you to health." The emperor was sorely in need of such restoration. The slow paralysis that had weakened him lay heavy upon his limbs. Some days he could not raise his hands to his head. His dead left side was his constant affliction. He had yielded therefore and decided that a month hence, the court would journey to the Summer Palace, some nine miles outside the city walls.

Now Tzu Hsi was still so young that the thought of a holiday permeated her heart like warm wine. She did not yet love the severe and noble palaces in which she was doomed to live, although in her own palace she had her pets, a little dog and her pups, crickets in cages, and birds of many colors. The pets she loved best, however, were the wild creatures who settled sometimes in the trees and near the pools. With much patience she learned to call a nightingale so that the creature fluttered happily about her head. But though four square miles lay within the Forbidden City, she longed to be outside all walls.

The Summer Palace had first been built for pleasure several centuries earlier. The original Summer Palace had been destroyed in a war and rebuilt again two centuries ago by the imperial ancestor K'ang-hsi. When his son, Ch'ien-lung, heard that the king of France also had such pleasure grounds, he inquired of the French ministers what the French king had that he had not, and then added Western beauty to the Summer Palace as well. For emperors in those days were diverted by Western men and even welcomed them, not dreaming that they could later have such evil intentions.

For a long time, however, the Summer Palace had been closed, for Tao Kuang, the father of the present emperor, was a miser and would not allow the court to move in the hot season because he feared the expense.

In a high mood, therefore, the court set forth one fine summer day, the bannermen going first, then the princes and their families, and at last a thousand imperial guards on horseback, Jung Lu at their head on a great white stallion. Behind them, Tzu Hsi followed with her son and his nurse.

Toward sunset the imperial procession approached the gate of the Summer Palace itself and, peering through the space between the curtains, Tzu Hsi saw the lofty gate of carved white marble, guarded by two golden lions. She was carried over the high threshold into the quiet of the vast park. Now she opened the curtains and saw a dreamlike scene. Pagodas hung as though suspended on the green hillsides; clear brooks ran rippling beside winding roads paved with marble; and bridges led the way to a hundred pavilions. A lifetime would not be enough to know it all.

She felt her palanquin set down, and the curtains were put aside by Li Lien-ying. She looked about her and by chance her look fell on Jung Lu. He stood alone, his men behind the emperor, whose palanquin was already at the great Hall of Entrance. Unprepared, he lifted up his head and looked into her eyes. She caught his look, and for one instant their hearts entangled. They turned their heads in haste, the moment passed, and Tzu Hsi entered her assigned palace. A sudden happiness sprang up in her. She overflowed with joy at all she saw as she went from one room to another. This ancient palace, now hers, was named the Palace of Contentment. When she had seen all that could be seen, she returned to its entrance and stretched out her arms to the landscape, exquisite and calm in the clear brightness of the evening sun as it slipped down behind the spires of the pagodas, the afterglow fading from the lakes and streams. "I shall retire early," Tzu Hsi said, "and I shall rise at dawn. However many tomorrows are allotted to this joyful place, they will not be enough to take our fill of pleasure."

The moon was rising when Tzu Hsi went to her apartments. A light meal was served to her. She drank her favorite green tea, and then, bathed and in fresh silk garments, she lay down to sleep. But twice, after her weary women slept, she rose from her bed to look from the open windows at the distant mountains, pale in the moonlight. Her loneliness subsided, her troubles died away, her thoughts grew kindly. Beyond the terrace, to the right, stood the Palace of the Floating Cloud, which had been assigned to Sakota. Tomorrow—no, not tomorrow, but someday soon—she would renew their sisterly friendship.

And she thought of Jung Lu and how their unwary eyes had met today, had clung and then had parted again, unwillingly.

She longed fiercely, all of a sudden, to hear his voice and know him near. And why should she not summon him as her kinsman—say, for some advice she needed? Her mind roamed in search of its excuse.

The moonlight grew more golden, the air more fragrant than it had been, and she sighed with happiness. Here in this magic place, could not magic be accomplished?

The morning dawned clear again and calm, and she let this day pass, forgetful of everything except her childlike pleasure in what she saw about her when she visited the palaces and lakes and gardens. And in the evening, by the emperor's command, a play was presented to the court by the imperial players, and for the first time Tzu Hsi could fully indulge her love of theater. And yet whatever she did in the next days, she did not forget her enchanting plan to speak again with Jung Lu. It lay in her brain, the germ within a seed, ready to come to life when she so chose.

One day, reckless with freedom and incessant pleasure, she beckoned Li Lien-ying to her side. "I find my mind troubled," she said in her clear imperious voice. "I cannot forget a promise I made to my birth mother concerning the marriage of my younger sister. Yet the months pass and I do nothing. To whom can I turn for good advice? Yesterday I remembered that the commander of the imperial guard is our kinsman. It is he alone who can help me in this family matter. Summon him to come to me." She said this purposely before her ladies, for she who was so high could have no secrets. Li Lien-ying obeyed at once.

Now, seated on her throne in the great hall of her palace, Tzu Hsi waited with her ladies for Jung Lu. Magnificence became her, as always. The walls were hung with painted scrolls, and porcelain pots of blooming trees stood to her right and left. Her little dogs gamboled with four white kittens on the floor, and Tzu Hsi laughed at them so much that at last she came down from her throne, possessed by mirth and playfulness. She trailed her silken kerchief to make the kittens follow her, and only when she heard the eunuch's footsteps did she make haste to sit upon her throne again, while her ladies smiled behind their fans.

Her face was grave, her lips demure, but her great eyes sparkled when Jung Lu entered. "Welcome, Cousin," Tzu Hsi said. "It has been a long time since we met."

"A long time, Venerable," he said and waited, kneeling.

She gazed down on him from her throne. "I have something to ask your advice about, and so I have summoned you."

"Command me, Venerable," he said.

"My younger sister is old enough to wed," she went on. "Do you remember that child? A naughty little thing, do you remember? Always clinging to me and wailing?"

"Venerable, I forget nothing," he said, his head still bowed.

Tzu Hsi received the secret meaning in these words and hid the treasure in her heart. "Well, now my sister needs a husband," she went on. "She is a woman, very nearly, a slender pretty thing—with fine eyebrows—like mine!"

Here she paused to smooth her eyebrows, shaped like the leaves of a willow tree. "And I promised her a prince, but what prince, Cousin? Name me the princes!"

"Venerable," Jung Lu replied carefully, "how can I know princes as well as you do?"

She turned upon her ladies. "Go—all of you," she commanded. "You see my cousin will not speak before you!"

They fluttered off like frightened butterflies, and she laughed and came down from her throne. She stooped and touched his shoulder. "Rise, Cousin! There is no one near to see us, except my eunuch—and what is he?"

Jung Lu rose unwillingly and kept his distance.

"Sit down yonder on that marble chair," she commanded, "and I will sit here—the distance is enough, I think?" She lifted her dark lashes at him, innocently. "Of my lord's seven brothers, to which one shall I give my little sister?" she asked.

"It is not fitting that the sister of an empress be a concubine—even to a prince," Jung Lu said firmly.

"Then I must choose the seventh prince," she said. "He only has no wife. Alas, he is the least handsome of all the princes. I hope my sister does not love beauty in a face as well as I do!" She looked sidewise at him from beneath her lashes.

"Prince Ch'un's face is not evil," he rejoined. "It is lucky if a prince be at least not evil."

She shrugged her shoulders. "Well, kinsman, if Prince Ch'un be your advice, I will send a letter to my mother." She rose to signify the audience was ended, then paused. "And you," she said carelessly, "I suppose you are wed by now?"

He had risen with her, and now stood before her, tall and calm. "You know I am not wed."

"Ah, but you must," she insisted. A sudden happiness made her face soft and young. "I wish you would wed," she said wistfully.

"It is not possible." He bowed and left her presence without farewell.

She stood there alone, surprised. Then her quick eyes caught the movement of a curtain in a doorway. A spy? She stepped forward and twitched the curtain and saw a shrinking figure. It was Lady Mei, her pretty favorite.

"You?" Then Tzu Hsi demanded, "Why do you spy on me?"

"Venerable, not on you." This in the smallest whisper.

"Then on whom?" Tzu Hsi demanded.

The lady would not speak. Tzu Hsi stared at the childish drooping figure, and then she took the lady by her ears and shook her vehemently. "On him, then!" she whispered fiercely. "You love him, I daresay—" Again she shook with all her strength. "You dare to love him!"

Lady Mei broke into sobs and Tzu Hsi let go of her ears.

"Do you think he loves you?" Tzu Hsi asked scornfully.

"I know he does not, Venerable," the lady sobbed. "He loves only you. We all know—only you—"

Tzu Hsi knew that she ought to punish her for such a charge and yet she was so pleased to hear it said that she did not know whether to smile or slap the girl. She did both. "There—and

231

there," she said heartily. "Go from me before I kill you out of shame! Do not let me see you for seven full days."

From that day on, the face and figure of Jung Lu were in her thoughts day and night, wherever she went. Yet she was not one to be content with dreams, and she let herself proceed with a plan. She would raise Jung Lu high enough so that she could keep him near her always. How could she raise him without drawing all eyes toward her? She recalled her enemies, Su Shun, the grand councillor who hated her, and his friends, the princes Cheng and Yi.

This led her on to thinking of Lady Mei again, who, it could not be forgotten, was Su Shun's child. She must not let that lady hate her, too. Well, then, was it not useful to know that the lady loved Jung Lu? She would send for Lady Mei and bid her take heart, for she, the empress of the Western Palace, would herself speak for her to the commander of the imperial guard. Such a marriage would serve a double purpose, for it would give an excuse to raise Jung Lu to a high place. Yes, here, she saw all at once, was her means to raise up her beloved.

When the forbidden seven days had passed, she sent for Lady Mei. When she had let the lady kneel awhile in silence, she came down from her throne and lifted her up. "You have grown thin these seven days," she said kindly.

"Venerable," Lady Mei said, her eyes piteous, "when you are angry with me, I cannot eat or sleep."

"I am not angry now," Tzu Hsi replied. "Sit down, poor child. Let me see how you are." She took the lady's soft narrow hand and smoothed it between her own and went on talking. "Child, it is nothing to me whom you love. Why should you not wed the commander of the imperial guard? A handsome man, and young—"

Lady Mei's tears came to her dark eyes, and she clung to the kind hands. "Venerable, I do adore you—"

Tzu Hsi smiled serenely. "Now, now—no flattery, child! But I have a plan."

"Whatever you say, Venerable."

"Well, then, when the heir completes his first full year, I will myself invite my kinsman to the great feast so that all may see my intent to raise him. When this is clear, then step can follow step. It is for your sake I raise him, so that his rank may equal your own."

"But, Venerable—"

Tzu Hsi examined the lady's pretty face, still pink. "You think it is too long to wait so many months?"

The lady hid her face behind her sleeve. Tzu Hsi laughed. "Before one journeys to a new place the road must be built!"

THE AUTUMN WAS half gone, and in the library Tzu Hsi gazed pensively beyond the wide doors open to the sun of mid-afternoon.

Prince Kung spoke sharply to recall her from her dreaming. "Recall then, Empress, that the Opium Wars left us defeated. The greedy men of the West can become our masters through the brute force of their evil engines of war."

She woke from her dreaming memories of the summer now gone. How hateful it was to return again to these high walls and locked gates! "Our masters?" she repeated.

"Our masters, unless we keep our wits awake," the prince said firmly. "We have yielded, alas, to every demand—the vast indemnities, the many new ports opened by force to this hateful foreign trade. Force—force is their talisman."

"What is our weakness?" Tzu Hsi demanded.

Prince Kung looked sidewise at her. How could he shape her so that she could save the dynasty? She was still too young, and, alas, forever only a woman. Yet she had no equal.

"The Chinese were too civilized for our times," he said. "Their sages taught that force is evil, the soldier to be despised; but they knew nothing of these wild tribes in the West. Even now, when our subjects rebel against the Manchu Dynasty, they do not see that it is not we who are their enemies, but the men out of the West."

Instantly Tzu Hsi caught the fearful meaning. "Has Viceroy Yeh let these white men enter the city of Canton?"

"Not yet, Empress, and we must prevent it."

"We must put them off until we are strong," Tzu Hsi said.

"You speak too simply, Empress," Prince Kung replied. "It is not a matter of white men alone. The knowledge of foreign weapons is changing even the Chinese people in subtle ways. Force, they say now, is stronger than reason; only weapons can make us free. This concept hides a change so mighty in our nation that unless we can change with it, our dynasty will end before the heir can sit upon the Dragon Throne."

"Give them weapons, then," Tzu Hsi said.

"Alas," Prince Kung sighed, "if we give the Chinese weapons against the enemy from the West, they will turn first on us. Empress, the throne is trembling on its foundations."

Could she comprehend the peril of the times? To her it was not the dynasty alone the white men threatened, it was herself and her son, the imperial heir. And now her instinct rose to save him. From that hour she applied herself with fresh will to read the memorials presented to the throne, especially those from that place where the white men quarreled to gain entrance, the southern city of Canton.

WHEN THE FIRST snow fell, news came by courier that new ships of war had anchored in the harbor near Canton, and these ships brought not only weapons of greater strength than before, but also envoys of high rank from England.

The viceroy did not dare to leave his city; therefore the emperor could only call his government to consultation. Day after day at bitter dawn in the Audience Hall, the Grand Secretariat—half Manchu and half Chinese—joined with the Council of State to hear Prince Kung read the memorial before the Dragon Throne. After much discussion each body separated to decide what advice to give to the Son of Heaven. He received it the next day to return it with his own comment, written with the imperial vermilion brush.

Now everyone knew that it was not the emperor who used the vermilion brush, for each night Tzu Hsi was summoned to the royal bedchamber, and not for love. No, while the emperor lay in his bed, half sleeping in an opium dream, she pondered the written pages, studying every word. And when she had decided what her will was, she lifted the vermilion brush. "Delay," she still commanded. "Promise, and break the promises. Is not our land vast and mighty? Shall we destroy the body because a mosquito stings a toe?"

No one dared to disobey, for to her handwriting she set the imperial seal. All that she commanded was printed in the Court Gazette as imperial decrees. For eight hundred years this gazette had been sent by messenger to every province and its viceroy so that everywhere the people could know the royal will. And this will now was the will of one woman, young and beautiful.

Prince Kung, reading the vermilion words, was sick with fear. "Empress," he said when next they met in the wintry shadows of the imperial library, "I must warn you again that the temper of these white men is short and savage. Delays and promises not kept will only anger them."

Tzu Hsi flashed her splendid eyes at him. "Pray, what can they do? Can their ships sail a thousand miles up our long coast? Let them harass a southern city. Does this mean that they can threaten the Son of Heaven himself?"

"I think it possible," he said gravely.

She pitied his careworn looks, too grave for a man still young and handsome, and she coaxed him with pleasant words. "You make your own load heavy. You should take pleasure as other men do. I never see you at the theater."

To this Prince Kung made no reply except to take his leave.

WITH THE FIRST flowering of the tree peonies the court prepared to enjoy the birthday feast of the heir. The spring was favorable. The rains fell early, and the air was mild and warm. A slumberous peace pervaded every province and Prince

Kung wondered if the empress of the Western Palace had a private wisdom of her own. The ships of the white men delayed at the port near Canton. The viceroy still ruled the city; he had not yet received the present envoy from England, Elgin, who still would not bow himself to the floor.

In this vague and shallow peace the people seized upon the chance to make a feast while the court made ready the birthday of the heir. For Tzu Hsi this birthday gala had another meaning, too. All through the winter while she had resolutely studied and read her books, she had remembered Jung Lu and her plan to advance his rank. One day she chanced to see that Lady Mei looked pensive. She put up her hand and stroked the lady's smooth cheek. "Do not think I have forgotten, child!" She gazed into the startled eyes and knew that Lady Mei understood her meaning.

Thus a few nights before the heir's birthday, as she lay in the emperor's arms, seeming half asleep, she murmured, "Almost I forgot—"

"Forgot what, my heart?" he inquired. He was in good humor—this night he had found enough satisfaction to make him feel himself still a man.

"You know, my lord, that the commander of the imperial guard is my kinsman?" She still seemed half asleep.

"I know—that is, I have so heard."

"Long ago I made my uncle Muyanga a promise concerning him and I have never kept that promise—oh, me!"

"So?"

"If you invite him to our son's birthday feast, my lord, my conscience will not tease me."

The emperor was languidly surprised. "What—a guardsman? Will it not stir jealousy among the lesser princes?"

"There is always jealousy among the small, my lord. But do as you will, my lord." So she murmured.

Nevertheless, in a little while she made slight movements of withdrawal from him. Then she yawned and said that she was tired. She slipped from the bed and said, "Do not summon me tomorrow night, my lord, for I would not like to tell the chief eunuch that I will not come."

"I wish I did not love so troublesome a woman," he complained to his chief eunuch next day.

An Teh-hai complained, too, to show respect. "We all wish it, Most High, and yet we all love her—except some few who hate her!"

Now again the emperor yielded and waited until the night before the birthday feast before summoning Tzu Hsi. She came, being generous when she could have her way, and she gave him full reward. That same night Jung Lu received the imperial invitation to the birthday feast.

The day of the feast dawned fine and fair, and Tzu Hsi woke to noise and music. In every courtyard in the city families set off firecrackers when the sun rose, and they beat gongs and drums and blew trumpets. For three days no one was to work.

She rose from her bed early, was bathed, and allowed herself to be dressed. She ate her morning sweetmeats. The heir was then presented to her in his royal robes of scarlet satin. She took him in her arms, her heart near breaking with love and pride. She smelled his perfumed cheeks and the palms of his plump little hands, and to him she whispered, "I am most fortunate of all women born upon this earth today."

Now, the hour having come, she summoned her ladies and, preceding the heir in her palace sedan, went to the Supreme Throne Hall, the very center of the Forbidden City. This most sacred hall was in the largest of all the palaces, its roof shining golden in the sun.

Alas, so sacred was this Supreme Throne Hall that no woman had ever entered it. Tzu Hsi withdrew into a lesser hall, the Hall of Central Harmony. Yet the emperor was mindful of her. When he had seated himself on the Dragon Throne, with the heir beside him in the arms of Prince Kung, he commanded that all the gifts be taken to the Hall of Central Harmony. Thus Tzu Hsi was able to see them, although she could not express her pleasure at their magnificence.

The day was not long enough for all of the gifts to be received, so when the sun set, the remaining gifts from lesser persons were put aside. This was the hour for the feast in the imperial banquet hall. Here the emperor and his two empresses sat at a table set apart, and at a table near them the heir sat upon the knees of his uncle, Prince Kung. The little boy was in the gayest mood. His large eyes, so like his mother's, traveled from one tasseled lantern to another as they swayed above the tables, and he pointed at them and clapped his hands and laughed. All admired the heir, but no one spoke aloud their praise, in case cruel demons were hovering near. Only Sakota, the empress of the Eastern Palace, looked at him sadly, and mild though she was, she could not refrain from a peevish word or two. She sat there at the feast table declining to eat, though she was thin as a bird, her face pale and pinched under her high headdress. Tzu Hsi replied with the most perfect patience to Sakota's peevishness, and all who saw her felt the largeness of her spirit.

Eunuchs garbed in bright robes moved in silent swiftness among the low tables set for the thousand guests to serve them all. At the far end of the hall were the court ladies, and at the other the noblemen. At Tzu Hsi's right hand, Lady Mei had her seat, and Tzu Hsi looked down upon her and smiled. Both knew where Jung Lu sat at a distant table. To anyone who wondered why the commander of the guard had been so honored, passing eunuchs had the answer ready: "He is the kinsman of the empress of the Western Palace and here by her command." To this no further question could be made.

Meanwhile musicians played their ancient harps, flutes and drums, and the theater went on for those who cared to see. The heir fell fast asleep at last, and the chief eunuch carried him away. The feast drew near its end.

"Tea for the nobles," Prince Kung commanded. Then eunuchs served tea to all the nobles, but none was served to the commander of the guard, who was not noble. Tzu Hsi beckoned with her jeweled hand, and Li Lien-ying, always watching, moved quickly to her side. "Take this bowl of tea from me to my kinsman," Tzu Hsi commanded in her clearest voice. She gave her own bowl with both hands to the eunuch. And Li Lien-ying carried it to Jung Lu, who rose to receive it. Turning toward the empress of the Western Palace, he bowed nine times to signify his thanks. All talk ceased, but Tzu Hsi seemed not to notice. Instead, she looked down at Lady Mei and smiled again.

The moon was high; the hour was late. They waited for the emperor to rise and make his way again to the terrace. But instead he clapped his hands. Silence fell once more.

The Son of Heaven leaned toward his beloved. "My heart," he whispered, "look toward the great doors!"

Tzu Hsi looked and she saw six eunuchs bearing a tray of gold so heavy that they crouched beneath it. On this tray stood a huge golden peach, the symbol of long life.

Prince Kung rose. "The gift of the Son of Heaven to the fortunate mother of the heir!"

All rose and bowed, while the eunuchs brought the tray to Tzu Hsi. "Take the peach with your hands," the Son of Heaven now commanded. As she put her hands on the giant fruit it split and fell apart. Inside she saw a pair of pink satin shoes embroidered with flowers of gold and silver thread. The heels, set in the Manchu fashion beneath the middle of the soles, were encrusted with pink pearls.

Tzu Hsi lifted brilliant eyes to the Son of Heaven. "For me, my lord?"

"For you alone," he said. It was a daring gift, a symbol of man's lustful love for woman.

EVIL NEWS came up from the south. Yeh, the viceroy of the Kwang provinces, sent couriers saying that the English Lord Elgin was again making threats to attack the city of Canton, this time with six thousand warriors waiting on his battleships at the mouth of the Pearl River. Even if there were no Chinese rebels hidden in the city, the imperial armies could not hold the gates. Alas, the city was rotten with these rebels under the leadership of the madman Hung, who declared that he was sent by a foreign god named Jesus to overthrow the Manchu throne.

Prince Kung received this news, but he did not dare to present it to the emperor, who after the heir's birthday feast had smoked opium until now he could not tell day from night. Prince Kung sent word therefore to Tzu Hsi, asking for an audience at once. He did not come alone to the imperial library. With him were the grand councillor Su Shun and his ally, Prince Cheng, and with them Prince Yi, a younger brother of the Son of Heaven. These four now heard the news, which Prince Kung read from a scroll.

"Very grave—very grave," Su Shun muttered. He was a tall, broad man, his face powerful and coarse, and Tzu Hsi wondered how he could be the father of so delicate a beauty as her favorite, Lady Mei.

"We cannot prevail," Prince Kung declared. "This time the French, desiring to seize our possession Indochina, have promised to aid the English against us, using the excuse of a French priest tortured and killed in Kwangsi. Moreover, it is said that this Lord Elgin has received instructions from his ruler, the queen of England, to demand residence here in our capital for a minister from her court."

Tzu Hsi spoke courteously. "Surely my sister-queen of the West does not know what this lord demands in her name. Or why is it that all this did not happen to us before?"

Prince Kung explained patiently. "The delay, Empress, has been caused only by the Indian mutiny of which I told you some months ago. When rebellion rose there recently and many English men and women were killed, the English armies put it down with frightful force. Now they come here for further conquest. I fear it is their intent to possess our country as they do India. This we must prevent at any cost."

"We must, indeed," Tzu Hsi agreed. "Yet the distances are great, and I think disaster cannot happen soon or easily. Soon we must leave the city for the summer. Let action be postponed until we have returned from the Summer Palace. Send word to the viceroy to tell the English to memorialize the throne and present their demands. Then we will send word that the Son of Heaven is ill and we must wait until he is well enough to make decisions."

"Wisdom," the grand councillor cried.

"Wisdom, indeed," Prince Cheng now said, and Prince Yi nodded his head up and down. Prince Kung sighed heavily.

IN THESE MONTHS before the summer Tzu Hsi arranged for the marriage of her sister to the seventh prince, Ch'un. Although he had an ugly face and a head too large for his body, she found him to be honest and simple, grateful to her for the alliance with her sister. The marriage was made before the departure of the court for the Summer Palace, but there was no feasting, in respect for the illness of the emperor.

The court returned from the Summer Palace to the Forbidden City early in the autumn. As the peaceful months passed by, Tzu Hsi believed that she had decided wisely not to allow a war against the foreigners. For the viceroy Yeh reported that the English leader, Lord Elgin, "passed the days at Hong Kong stamping his feet and sighing."

Only the emperor's ill health made Tzu Hsi sad. She did not pretend to love the pallid figure that lay all but speechless on his yellow satin cushions, but she feared the turmoil of his death. The heir was still so young that were the Dragon Throne to fall to him now, there would be mighty quarrels over who should be regent. Strong men in the Manchu clans would come forward to assert their claims. The heir might even be set aside and a new ruler take his place. Ah, there were plots everywhere. Her good fortune was that her adviser, Prince Kung, was honorable and that the chief eunuch, An Teh-hai, was loyal to her because she was the beloved of his master. He perceived her perfect patience, and he began to transfer to her the same devotion that he had given the emperor since first he came into the gates, a child of twelve, castrated by his own father that he might serve inside the imperial city.

No one was prepared for the hideous news that reached the palace gates one day at twilight, in the early winter of that year. Tzu Hsi had spent the day in painting. Lady Miao, her teacher, stayed by her side watching while her imperial pupil brushed a picture of the branches of a peach tree in bloom. Tzu Hsi took pains and worked in silence. She must ink her brush in such a way that at one stroke she could give the branch its outline and also its shading.

Lady Miao commended her. "Well done, Venerable."

"I am not finished," Tzu Hsi replied. With equal care she drew another branch, intertwining with the first. At this Lady Miao remained silent. Tzu Hsi frowned. "You do not like what I have done?"

"Venerable, it is not what I like or do not like," the lady said mildly. "The time has come when you paint as you wish."

While Tzu Hsi listened, the chief eunuch burst into the pavilion. His eyes were rolling and ready to burst, his breath coming out of him in gasps. "Venerable," he bawled, "Venerable, prepare yourself—a messenger from Canton—the city's lost—the foreigners have seized it—the viceroy is taken!"

It was disaster but not death. "Collect your wits," she said sternly. "I thought from your looks that the enemy was inside the palace gates." Nevertheless, she put down her brushes, and Lady Miao withdrew silently. "Invite Prince Kung to join me here," she commanded.

In a few minutes Prince Kung came alone. He himself had received the memorial from the exhausted courier and had brought it with him.

"Read it to me," Tzu Hsi said. She listened as he read slowly, her eyes thoughtful. Six thousand Western warriors had landed and marched to the gates of Canton. The imperial forces had made a show of bravery and then had fled, and the Chinese rebels hiding inside the city had opened the gates and let the foreign enemy in. The viceroy had run to the city wall to escape, but the enemy had taken him prisoner and sent him to Calcutta. Then the Westerners set up a new government, all Chinese, thus defying the Manchu Dynasty. Still worse, the memorial continued, the Englishmen declared that they had new demands from their own queen. They would appear before the emperor in Peking and tell him what these were.

Prince Kung waited patiently for Tzu Hsi to speak. "We cannot receive these hateful strangers at our court," she said at last. "And I do still believe they use Victoria's name without her knowledge. Yet I cannot reach her distant throne, nor reveal to our people the mortal illness of the emperor. The heir is still too young, the succession is not clear. At any cost, we must still promise and delay again, making winter our excuse."

He spoke gently. "Empress, I say what I have already said. You do not understand the nature of these men. It is too late. Their patience is at an end."

"Let us see," she said, black shadows creeping beneath her tragic eyes; and that was all she would say.

HEAVEN HELPS ME, Tzu Hsi told herself, and indeed the snow that winter lay deeper every day than the day before, and it was months before her reply could reach Canton. Winter crept slowly by and spring came again, bitter and uneasy, and deepened into summer, and still Tzu Hsi could not decide if it was safe to go to the Summer Palace. Never before had she longed for the sight of the lakes and mountains as she did now when all was uncertainty about her. When she slept at night she dreamed of the peacefulness of moonlight on distant hills, of pine forests or bamboo groves. When she awoke, she wept, for these dreams were as real as memories.

But one day, as suddenly as a storm comes down, rumors of evil came rushing northward and instantly she put aside all hope of going to the Summer Palace. The emperor commanded his grand councillors and ministers and princes to gather in the Audience Hall and summoned the two consorts to seat themselves behind the wood screen.

The assembly listened in silence to Prince Kung as he stood to announce the news. "In spite of all the throne has done to prevent them, the aliens have not remained in the south. They are even now on their way up our coast, their ships armed and carrying warriors. We must hope they will halt at the forts of Taku, and not enter into the city proper at Tientsin, from whence it would be but a short march to this sacred place."

A groan burst from the kneeling assembly. Prince Kung faltered and went on. "It is too soon for me to speak. Yet I fear that these barbarians will obey neither our laws nor our etiquette! The least delay, and they will come even to the gates of the imperial palaces. Let us face the worst, let us cease dreaming. The last hour is come. Ahead is only sorrow."

The emperor ended the audience, commanding the assembly to withdraw and consider its judgment and advice. He was about to come down from the throne when suddenly Tzu Hsi's clear voice rose from behind the screen. "I who should not speak must nevertheless break my proper silence!"

The emperor stood uncertain, turning his head left and right. Before him the assembly knelt with heads bowed to the floor. In the silence Tzu Hsi's voice rose again. "It is I who have counseled patience with these Western barbarians, and now it is I who say I have been wrong. I declare against patience and delay. I cry war against the Western enemy—war and death to them all—men, women and children!"

Had her voice been that of a man, they would have shouted yea or nay. But it was the voice of a woman, and so no one spoke. The emperor waited, his head drooping, and then, supported by his brothers, he came down from the throne and entered his yellow palanquin.

After him the two consorts also withdrew. Tzu Hsi returned to her own apartment to wait for the imperial summons. In silence she pored over her books, her mind distracted. When evening came near, Li Lien-ying told her that the emperor had dallied all day with one and another of his lesser concubines and had not mentioned her name.

"Venerable," he said, "be sure the Son of Heaven has not forgotten you, but he is afraid now of what may happen. He waits for the judgment of his ministers."

"Then I am defeated!" Tzu Hsi exclaimed.

Li Lien-ying bustled away with the teapot in his hands, his face blank and unsmiling.

The next day Tzu Hsi heard the news she had foreseen. On the advice of his councillors and ministers, the emperor appointed three honorable men to go to Tientsin to negotiate with Lord Elgin. The chief among these three was Kwei Liang, the father of Prince Kung's wife, a man known for his good sense and his caution. "Ah, alas!" Tzu Hsi cried when she heard his name. "This excellent man will never oppose the enemy. He is too old, too careful and too yielding."

She was right indeed. In the sixth month of the year 1858, Kwei Liang signed a treaty with the Western warriors, to be sealed a year from that day by the emperor himself. At swords' points, the English and the French, supported by the Americans and the Russians, had gained their demands. Their governments were to be allowed ministers in Peking; their priests and traders could travel throughout the realm without submitting to its laws. Opium was to be called the stuff of legal trade, and the great river city of Hankow, a thousand miles from the sea, was named a treaty port where white men could live.

After Tzu Hsi heard the news, she retired to her bedchamber, and planned her secret ways. She would subdue herself wholly to the emperor, sparing him the smallest reproach, and she would wait. And with this she made her will as hard as iron.

Meanwhile, content with their victorious treaty, the Western men did not move northward. The year passed as other years had passed, and the summer of the next year brought the day for the treaty to be sealed. Now Tzu Hsi had determined to win her way against the sealing by seducing the emperor. During this year he found her always gentle, always willing, and he became her captive again. On her subtle advice, he sent ministers to the white men to urge them not to come north again because the treaty was not officially sealed. "Let them be content with their southern trade," the emperor commanded.

"What if they refuse?" Prince Kung asked.

The emperor replied, "Tell them, if you must, that we will meet them later at Shanghai to seal the treaty. Can they complain that we are not generous?"

In the spring the emperor commanded that the Taku forts near Tientsin be manned with guns and cannons bought from Americans. This was to be done secretly, so that the English knew nothing of it. Such plans were seeded into his mind in idle hours while Tzu Hsi made dutiful love to him.

What dismay, then, in early summer when couriers brought news that the Western men were sailing northward up the coast far past Shanghai, this time under the Englishman Admiral Hope! But the Taku forts were strong and this time, with the help of Heaven, they repulsed the enemy, destroying three ships of war and killing three hundred men. The emperor was overjoyed. He praised Tzu Hsi, and she encouraged him to refuse everything to the invaders. The treaty negotiated at Tientsin was not sealed.

The whole nation marveled at the wisdom of the Son of Heaven, who, they declared, had known when to delay and when to make war. Only Prince Kung was still fearful. He said, "The Western men are tigers who retire when they are wounded and return again to attack."

A year passed, another strangely quiet year. The heir grew strong and willful. He learned to ride his horse, a black Arabian. He loved to sing and laugh, for everywhere he looked he saw only friendly faces. Summer came again, and Tzu Hsi made her plans to go to the Summer Palace.

Alas, who could know what was to come? The court had only just made its summer journey when warriors from England and France came roaring in full force up the coast, furious for revenge. Two hundred vessels of war carrying twenty thousand armed men landed at the port of Chefoo and prepared to invade the capital. In the Forbidden City there was no time for reproach or for delay. Kwei Liang, that wise old man, accompanied by other noblemen, was sent to persuade the invaders to stand. "Make promises," the frightened emperor commanded. "Concede and yield! We are outdone!"

Tzu Hsi stood at the emperor's side. "No, no, my lord," she cried. "That's shameful! Do you forget your victory? More soldiers, my lord—now is the time for battle, my lord!"

With his arm suddenly grown strong, he pushed her back. "You hear what I have said," he told Kwei Liang.

"I hear and obey, Most High," the old man replied. With this command he and his escorts made haste to Tientsin, for, alas, the invaders had now seized the forts of Taku.

When Kwei Liang was gone, Tzu Hsi, anxious for the safety of her son, used her coaxing lips and tender eyes to make the emperor uncertain again. "What if the white men will not be persuaded?" she argued in the night. And then she induced the emperor to order his brave Mongol general Prince Seng to lead the imperial armies against the white men.

Prince Seng organized his men into an ambush near the Taku forts, determined that he would drive the white men into the sea. Meanwhile, the English and French emissaries came forward to meet the imperial commission under Kwei Liang, their leader bearing a white flag of truce. But this flag Prince Seng took to be a sign of surrender. His men fell upon the Western contingent and took the two leaders captive, and then seized all who were with them. The flag was torn and stamped into the dust, and the captives were imprisoned and tortured.

This good news was carried back to the capital. Once again the Westerners had been routed. The emperor praised Tzu Hsi heartily, and he announced seven days of feasting.

The joy was planned too soon. When the Westerners heard of the treachery done to their comrades, they attacked so strongly that Prince Seng's men were killed as they fled, for they had no foreign guns. The invaders then marched in triumph toward the capital until they came to a marble bridge that crossed the river Peiho, which was only ten miles away from Peking itself. At this bridge they were met by imperial soldiers, sent in haste by the emperor. A battle took place, a sad battle in which the imperial soldiers were routed. They ran back to the capital. The whole city was soon in turmoil. Merchants put up boards over their shop fronts, and all citizens who had young wives and daughters hastened to leave the city.

In the Summer Palace all was in like confusion. The princes gathered in haste to decide how to save the throne and the heir, while the emperor wept and declared he would swallow opium. Prince Kung alone remained himself. He went to the emperor's chambers and found Tzu Hsi there with the heir, surrounded by eunuchs and courtiers, all protesting the decision of the emperor to kill himself. "Ah, you have come," Tzu Hsi cried when she saw the prince. What comfort indeed to see this man, his face composed, his manner calm!

Prince Kung made his obeisance and spoke to the emperor. "I dare to give advice to the Son of Heaven," he said.

"Speak—speak," the emperor groaned.

"I beg to be allowed to write a letter to the leader of the approaching enemy and ask for a truce. To this letter I will set the imperial seal."

Holding her child in her arms, Tzu Hsi heard and could not speak. What this prince had foretold had come to pass. The tiger had returned for revenge.

"And you, Sire," Prince Kung went on, "must escape to Jehol with the heir and the two empresses and the court."

"Yes—yes," the emperor agreed eagerly.

At this Tzu Hsi cried out against Prince Kung. "No! What will the people think if the emperor deserts them now? They will yield themselves to the enemy and be utterly destroyed. Let the heir be taken away and hidden, but the Son of Heaven must remain, and I will stay at his side to serve him."

"Empress," Prince Kung said in his gentlest voice, "I must protect you from your own courage. Let the people be told only that the emperor is going north on a hunting trip to his palaces in Jehol. Let the departure be a few days hence, without haste. Meanwhile, I will hold the invaders with my plea for a truce and promises to punish the Mongol general."

Tzu Hsi was defeated and she knew it. They were against her, from the emperor himself to the lowliest eunuch. In silence she gave her child to his nurse and withdrew from the hall.

Within five days the gates were locked against the enemy and the long imperial procession of sedans and mule carts set forth toward Mongolia on their journey of a hundred miles, a thousand souls in all. Ahead of the imperial array marched the bannermen, carrying their banners of many hues, and behind them came the imperial guard on horseback, led by their commander, Jung Lu. "Gain what you can," the emperor had whispered to Prince Kung when he crept into his palanquin. He was weary, and the chief eunuch lifted him as though he were a child to put him in the cart.

Soon the procession halted for the midday meal, and Tzu Hsi looked backward to the city. There on the edge of sky she saw a mass of darkening smoke. She cried out, "Can it be our city is afire?" They looked back and saw the black, curling clouds mounting against the sky.

That night in her tent Tzu Hsi could not rest. Time and time again she sent Li Lien-ying to see if there was word concerning the beloved city. At last, a courier came running. Li Lien-ying caught him by the collar and hauled him before his imperial mistress. She fixed her great eyes on the frightened man. "What news do you bring?"

"Venerable," the man gasped, "the truce holds as of tonight. But this whole day the barbarians have spent in doing evil to punish Prince Seng because he tortured those prisoners he took and because he tore down that white cloth banner."

Tzu Hsi's heart slowed with dread. She asked, "What was that smoke I saw against the sky today?"

"Venerable," he said, "the Summer Palace is no more. The barbarians looted all its treasures. Then they burned the palaces. Prince Kung almost lost his life trying to stop them."

Her mind whirled, she saw flames and smoke and porcelain towers and golden rooftops crashing down. "Is nothing left?" she whispered.

"Ashes," the courier muttered, "only ashes."

A HOT DRY wind blew steadily from the northwest over Jehol. The flowers in the courtyard were dead and the leaves of the date trees were torn to shreds. Even the needles of the gnarled pines were yellowing. And the emperor had not once sent for Tzu Hsi since they had reached this fortress palace. Who had taken her place? On the emperor's last birthday, now a month ago, he had received good wishes and gifts from the whole court. Only she had not been summoned. Through the hours she had waited, and then she had torn off her robe and had lain sleepless on her bed all night.

Since then the emperor had been ill, but still she had not been summoned. Now he lay dying, so she heard. Were Prince Kung here, she could ask his advice, but he was still in the capital. Peking was now in the hands of the barbarians while he begged and bargained for a truce. She must know what went on in the emperor's bedchamber.

"Fetch me the chief eunuch," she commanded Li Lien-ying.

"Venerable, he is not allowed to leave the bedchamber."

"Who forbids him?" she demanded.

"Venerable, the Three." The Three—Prince Yi, Prince Cheng, and the grand councillor Su Shun—her enemies. Well she knew now what the plot was. Su Shun and his allies had fled with the emperor, but they had seen to it that the councillors who might have helped her were left behind. She was helpless and alone.

No, she had one ally, for even Su Shun could not prevent the imperial guard from doing its duty to protect the emperor. She turned to Li Lien-ying. "Summon my kinsman the commander of the imperial guard! I would ask his counsel."

Li Lien-ying fell upon his knees before her. "Venerable,"

he begged, "do not compel me to obey this one command."

"Why not?" she asked severely.

"Venerable, I dare not say," Li Lien-ying stammered. "You will have my tongue cut out if I speak."

She could not pull the words out of him until at last she flew into a great rage and threatened to have him beheaded. Thus beset, he whispered that the emperor would not summon her because her enemies had told him that—that she and Jung Lu . . .

"Do they say we are lovers?" she demanded.

He nodded his head and hid his face in his hands.

"Liars," she muttered, "liars, liars—"

She had to vent her anger somehow, and she struck the kneeling eunuch with her foot. He fell over and lay there motionless while she went raging up and down the great hall.

"Get up," she commanded suddenly. "I daresay you have not told me all. What else do you know that I am not told?"

He crawled to his feet. "Venerable," he faltered. "I cannot speak the traitorous words. Those three plot—they plot to seize the regency themselves, and then—"

"Kill my son!" she shrieked.

"Venerable, I promise you—I did not hear that. I beg you, calm yourself—"

"When did you hear it?"

"Venerable, I heard a first small rumor many months ago—"

She cried out, "And you were silent!"

"Venerable," he said, pleading, "if I told you every rumor I hear, you would cast me in prison."

"You should have used that stupid brain of yours," she cried. Suddenly she stood up and slapped Li Lien-ying first on one cheek and then on the other until his eyes watered. But he said nothing, for to bear such anger was his duty. "There," she cried, "and there and there—not to tell me at once!"

With this she sat down again and put her palms to her cheeks, while Li Lien-ying knelt like a stone before her. At last her mind cleared. She rose and walked to her writing table. She took a piece of silk parchment and on it wrote a letter to Prince Kung, telling him of her plight and asking his immediate help. She folded it and pressed her own seal upon it and beckoned Li Lien-ying to her side. "You are to go to the capital this very hour," she commanded. "You are to deliver this parchment into the hands of Prince Kung and from him bring a reply, and all this is to take no longer than four days."

"Venerable," he protested, "how can I—"

She cut him off. "You can because you must."

At the end of four days Prince Kung himself arrived, dusty and travel-worn. Never had a gaunt face looked so kind to her, nor a man so powerful and trustworthy. "I have come," he said, "but secretly, for I should have gone first to the emperor. Yet I had already news from the chief eunuch, telling me that these infamous Three have told my elder brother that I am plotting against him, that I am bribed by the enemy's promises to let me take his place. When your letter came, Venerable, I could only hasten to untie this mighty tangle."

Suddenly Tzu Hsi's serving woman came running from the outer courtyard. "Venerable," she sobbed, "your son—"

"What?" Tzu Hsi shrieked. "What have they done to him?"

"Speak, woman!" Prince Kung shouted.

"He has been stolen away," the woman sobbed. "He has been given to the wife of Prince Yi! She and her women, they have him—"

At this Tzu Hsi fell back in her chair. But the prince would not let her yield to fright. "Venerable," he said firmly, "you cannot allow yourself the luxury of fear."

He did not need to speak again. "We must move first!" she cried. "The seal—we must find the great imperial seal first of all—then we have the power with us."

He cried out his admiration. "Was there ever such a mind? I bow myself before you."

She rose, not hearing, from her chair. But the prince put up his hand. "Do not leave these rooms, I beg you. I must find out first the full danger to the heir. The plot has swelled beyond our knowledge. Wait, Venerable, for my return."

She stood motionless when Prince Kung had gone, listening to the merciless wind howling among the towers of the palace. Then she went swiftly to her writing table and wet her camel's-hair brush until it was pointed sharp. And she began to write in bold black strokes a decree of imperial succession.

"I, Hsien Fêng," she wrote, "emperor of the Middle Kingdom, am this day summoned to join my imperial ancestors. I, Hsien Fêng, do hereby declare that the heir is the male child borne to me by Tzu Hsi, empress of the Western Palace, and that he shall be known to all as the new emperor, who shall sit upon the Dragon Throne after me. And as regents, until he shall have reached the age of sixteen years, I do appoint my two consorts, the empress of the Western Palace and the empress of the Eastern Palace, on this day of my death."

Here Tzu Hsi left a space, and after it she added these words: "And I set my name and the imperial dynastic seal to this my will and my decree." Here again she left a space.

She rolled the parchment and put it in her sleeve. Yes, she would take Sakota as regent with her, compel her to be her ally, and thus prevent her from being an enemy. Meanwhile, her serving woman and Li Lien-ying stood watching her and waiting for her commands. Suddenly the woman turned her head toward the closed door. "I hear footsteps," she muttered.

The eunuch opened the door a crack and looked through. "Venerable," he said softly, "it is your kinsman."

Tzu Hsi turned her head sharply. "Let him come in."

Jung Lu walked forward and made a swift obeisance.

"Kinsman, greeting," Tzu Hsi said. Her voice was smooth and sweet. "Do not kneel. Sit down and let us be as we have always been."

But Jung Lu would not sit. He rose and, fixing his eyes on the floor between them, began to speak. "Venerable, the emperor is dying and the chief eunuch sent me to tell you. Su Shun was there less than an hour ago and with him were the princes Yi and Cheng. They had a decree for the emperor to sign, appointing them as regents for the heir! He would not sign it and fell unconscious when they tried to force him, but they will come again."

She did not pause a moment. She flew past him. He followed her swiftly and Li Lien-ying came after. She tossed commands over her shoulder as she went. "Announce me— tell the Son of Heaven that I bring the heir with me!"

As though the winds bore her, she went to the Hunting Lodge. She burst into the door and no one dared to stop her. She heard a child crying nearby and recognized her son's voice. She pushed aside the frightened women and ran through the rooms until she found the room where a woman was trying to comfort her son. She swept him in her arms and carried him away, he clinging to her neck with both his arms, but not afraid. She hastened through corridors, up steps of stone, through halls and chambers until she reached the door that the chief eunuch held open for her.

"Does the Son of Heaven still live?" she cried.

"He breathes," the chief eunuch said. Around the great bronze bed the eunuchs knelt, weeping in their hands. She went straight to the emperor's side, her child in her arms. "My lord!" she called in a loud clear voice. He did not answer. "My lord!" she called again. Ah, would the old magic work?

The emperor heard, his heavy eyelids lifted. He turned his head, his dying eyes looked up and saw her face.

"My lord," she said, "here is your heir."

The child stared down, his eyes big and dark.

"My lord," she said, "you must declare he is your heir. If you hear me, raise your right hand."

His hand lay motionless, yellow skin and bones. Then it moved with such effort that those watching groaned.

"My lord," she said imperiously, "I must be the child's regent. No one but I can guard his life against those who would destroy him. Move your hand once more to signify your wish."

Again they saw the slow, slight movement.

She stepped forward to the bed and lifted his hand. "My

lord," she called, "my lord, come back for one more moment!"

With great effort did his soul return. He moved his dim eyes to rest upon her face. She took the parchment from her sleeve, and as quickly as her own wish, Jung Lu brought the vermilion brush from the writing table nearby. Then he took the child from her arms.

"You must sign your will, my lord," Tzu Hsi said. "I take your hand—so. Your fingers about the brush—so."

He yielded her his hand, and the fingers moved, or seemed to move, to make his name. "Thank you, my lord," she said, and put the parchment in her bosom. "Rest now, dear lord."

She motioned with her hand for all to withdraw. Jung Lu carried the child from the room, and the eunuchs stood at the far end. She sat down then upon the bed, and lifted the emperor's head to rest upon her arm. He opened his eyes wide, and drew in his breath. "Your perfume—sweet!" He held his breath an instant, it quivered in his throat, and then he blew it out in a great sigh and with it died.

She put his head down gently on the pillow and leaned over him and moaned twice, and then she wept a little, her tears pure pity that a man should die so young and never loved. Oh, that she could have loved him! Then she rose and walked from the imperial chamber, slowly, as a widowed empress walks.

THE NEWS OF death swept swiftly through the palace. The emperor lay in state in the Audience Hall, with the gates barred against the living. Silence lay deep along the corridors whose walls hid the struggle for power.

Tzu Hsi was now the empress mother, the mother of the heir. She was not yet thirty years of age. Princes of the blood surrounded her and heads of strong and jealous Manchu clans. All knew that Su Shun was her enemy, and with him were two brothers of the dead emperor. Was Prince Kung still her ally? The court waited irresolute. Each courtier kept to himself.

Meanwhile Su Shun had summoned the chief eunuch and bade him take a message to the empress mother. "Tell her,"

Su Shun said arrogantly, "that I and Prince Yi were appointed regents by the Son of Heaven himself before his spirit left us. Say that we come to announce ourselves to her."

The chief eunuch hastened to obey. Yet on the way he paused to whisper his business to Jung Lu, who waited on guard. Jung Lu took command at once. "Proceed as quickly as you can to bring the Three to the empress mother. I'll hide myself outside her door."

Meanwhile Tzu Hsi sat in her own palace hall, white-robed from head to foot in deepest mourning. Her hands were folded in her lap, her great eyes fixed on distance.

When the chief eunuch came, she spoke wearily. "Bring the three great ones here, and tell them that surely my lord, now dwelling in the Yellow Springs, must be obeyed."

In less time than can be told, she saw the grand councillor come in, and with him the two princes. She turned her head and spoke softly to her favorite, Lady Mei. "Leave us, child. It is not seemly that you stand here by me in the presence of your father." She waited until the girl had slipped away. Then she accepted the obeisances of the princes, and to show that she was not proud, she rose and bowed to them in turn.

Su Shun stroked his short beard and lifted his head to look at her with bold and arrogant eyes. She noted this breach of propriety, but she did not speak to correct it. "My lady," he said, "I have come to announce the decree of regency. In his last hour the Son of Heaven—"

Here she stopped him. "Wait, good prince. If you have a parchment and it bears his imperial signature, I will obey his will, in duty."

"I have no parchment," Su Shun said, "but I have witnesses. Prince Yi—"

Again she stopped him. "I have such a parchment, signed in the presence of many eunuchs." She drew it from her bosom, and in a smooth calm voice, she read the decree from the beginning to the end.

"Let me see the signature," Su Shun snarled. She held the

parchment where he could see the name. "There is no seal," he cried. "A decree without the imperial seal is worthless."

He did not wait to see the look of consternation on her face. He turned and fled, the princes his following shadows. She knew that the imperial seal was locked within its coffer in the death chamber. Whoever seized it first was victor.

"Stupid!" she shrieked against herself, beside herself with rage. "Oh, stupid, stupid woman." She ran to the door and jerked it open, but no one stood outside to give chase, not even Li Lien-ying. She threw herself upon the floor and wept.

At this moment Lady Mei, peeking through the brocaded curtains, saw her mistress lying there. "Oh, my lady," she moaned, "are you wounded?" She could not lift her mistress and so ran to the open door and met there Jung Lu, and behind him the eunuch Li Lien-ying, just arrived.

"Oh," she cried, blood flooding into her cheeks. But Jung Lu did not see her. He carried something in his hands, a lump wrapped in yellow silk. He set it down when he saw the empress lying on the stones, and he stooped and lifted her in his arms. "I have brought the seal," he said.

She got to her feet then, and he stood tall and straight beside her. Avoiding her direct gaze, he took up the seal again in both his hands, a solid rock of jade whereon was carved the imperial symbol of the Son of Heaven. This was the seal of the Dragon Throne and had been for eighteen hundred years and more.

"I heard Su Shun," he said, "while I stood at the door to guard you. It was a race between us. I went one way and sent your eunuch by another."

Here Li Lien-ying put in his own tale. "I crept into the death chamber through a vent, for you know the great gate is padlocked, and I smashed the wooden coffer and took out the seal even as I heard the princes forcing the key into the lock."

Tzu Hsi's woman had all this time been standing at the door, her ear pressed against the panel. Suddenly she opened it. Prince Kung came in. "Venerable," he cried, "the seal is gone! I went myself to the death chamber. But the doors were open already at the order of Su Shun, and when I went in, the coffer was empty." At this moment his eyes fell on the imperial seal covered with yellow silk. "Now I see," he said with a rare smile. "Now I know why Su Shun says that such a woman as you must be killed or she will rule the world."

They looked at one another—Tzu Hsi, Jung Lu, Prince Kung and Li Lien-ying—and they broke into triumphant mirth.

WITH THE SEAL secure, her feverish restlessness left her. Everyone guessed that she had taken the seal, and now her three enemies kept far from her. Amid this consternation she went sweetly and at ease.

Her first deed was to go to her cousin, there to sit beside her and smile tenderly at her. "You and I, dear cousin," she said, "will now be sisters. Our lord willed us to be united for his sake, and I swear my loyalty and love to you so long as we both live." Sakota smiled back again, and with something like her old childish honesty she said, "To tell the truth, Cousin, I am glad to be friends."

"Sisters," Tzu Hsi said.

"Sisters," Sakota amended, "for I always feared Su Shun."

Tzu Hsi pressed Sakota's hand between her hands. "Let us have no secrets from each other, Sister. And fear nothing, for these plotters do not have the imperial seal."

She looked so pure and calm that Sakota bowed her head and murmured in a faint voice, "Yes, Sister."

Meanwhile Prince Kung returned to the capital to prepare a truce with the enemy that would allow the return of the dead emperor for his imperial funeral. "I have but one warning," the prince told her in parting. "Do not, Majesty, allow any meeting between yourself and your kinsman the commander of the guard. Your enemies will have their eyes upon you now to see if there be truth in the old gossip."

Tzu Hsi cast a reproachful look toward the prince. "Do you think me stupid?" Yet his advice was good. For now that the emperor was dead, she did often in the night let her secret thoughts circle about Jung Lu. But she must not give comfort to her enemies, nor freedom to herself until the throne was hers to hold for her son.

Prince Kung sent word that since a truce had been made with the invaders, the cortege of the dead emperor could now set forth on the homeward journey. It was the custom of centuries that when an emperor died away from his burial place, the consorts had to travel ahead so that they could welcome the imperial dead to his final home. Tzu Hsi hid her joy that this was so, for the Three were forced by duty to follow with the imperial catafalque, whose great weight compelled so slow a pace that the journey to the capital would take them ten days. But in her simple mulecart the empress mother would reach the city in half the time and there establish her place and power.

"Venerable, your enemies despair," the chief eunuch told her the night before departure. "This is their plot. Instead of our loyal Manchu guards, Su Shun has ordered his own soldiers to accompany you on the plea that the imperial guards are needed for the dead emperor. And even I have been commanded to attend the bier, and with me your own eunuch, Li Lien-ying."

She cried out, "Alas—"

The chief eunuch put up his huge hand. "I have worse to tell. Jung Lu is ordered to remain behind to guard this Jehol palace."

"What shall I do?" she asked. "This means I am to die in some lonely mountain pass."

"Venerable, be sure your kinsman has his own plan. He says you are to trust him. He will be near you."

With this faith only to uphold her, she set forth the next morning at dawn, her son's cart in front, then hers and Sakota's surrounded by Su Shun's guards. Yet all saw her calm and courteous, directing here and there and asking last, as though she had all but forgot, that her large toilet case be put beside her. In it was hidden the imperial seal.

Rain fell steadily as the day went on, a clean hard rain that swelled the mountain streams and choked the narrow roads between the mountains. By nightfall, the rivers were so high that they were forced to stop in a gorge and make shelter as best they could in tents. Here in darkness, the captain of Su Shun's guard declared that the empress mother and the heir must have their tent set well apart from all the rest because their station was so high.

"I will myself be your guard, Venerable," he said.

Her eyes chanced to fall upon his right hand, which he had placed on his sword. Shining in the lantern light, she saw a ring of pure red jade. Its color caught in her mind. "I thank you," she said calmly, "and when our journey is ended, I will reward you well."

The river thundered past the tent where Tzu Hsi sat beside her sleeping child. His nurse slept and at last her own serving woman slept, but Tzu Hsi could not while she guarded the imperial seal. The seal was the treasure, and for it she might lose her life. This was the hour for her enemy. If she cried out, who would hear her? She could only wait, each moment a separate torture.

At midnight the guard beat the hour on a brass gong to signify that all was well. Her gaze, which had been fixed on the child's sleeping face, at that moment caught the movement of the leather curtain of the tent. It was the wind, doubtless, or the rain pouring down. But while she watched, a short, sharp dagger cut the leather silently, and then she saw a man's hand and on the thumb was a red jade ring. In that same instant another hand reached out and seized the hand that held the dagger and forced it back. The slit fell shut again. Ah, she knew well that saving hand! She listened and heard men struggle. There was a moan, then silence. "Let that be an end to you," she heard Jung Lu mutter.

Such comfort now came flowing into her being that she was shaken to the heart. She stole across the carpet to the door of the tent. Jung Lu stepped toward her and they gazed at each other. "I knew that you would come," she said.

"I will not leave you."

"Is the man dead?"

"Dead. I have thrown the body down the gorge."

They stood, eyes meeting eyes, yet neither took the next step toward the other. "When I know what reward is great enough," she said, "then I will give it to you."

"Because you live I am rewarded," he replied.

Again they stood until he said, "Venerable, we must not linger. Everywhere we are surrounded by our enemies."

"Are you alone?" she asked.

"No, twenty of my own men are with me. You have the seal?"

"Here."

He turned and went out into the darkness. She let the curtain fall and stole back to her bed. Outside her tent he stood on guard. For the first time in many weeks she slept deeply and in peace.

At dawn it was seen by all that the captain's place had been taken by Jung Lu and that he was surrounded by twenty of his own men. No questions could be asked, but everyone knew that Tzu Hsi had won a victory, and each stepped more quickly to do his duty. The journey began again. Jung Lu rode a high white horse beside the heir and his imperial mother, and his men rode with him, ten on each side.

On the fifth day the walls of the capital rose from the surrounding plains. Behind the gates the city lay silent in suspense, for the poorest citizen knew that tigers were at war, and victory was uncertain. At such times the people wait.

Tzu Hsi had planned her course. Dressed in deep mourning, looking neither to the right nor to the left, she descended from her cart while eunuchs knelt on either side. Then in perfect courtesy she went to Sakota's cart and helped her to descend, escorting her coregent to her Eastern Palace before she went to her own.

Scarcely had an hour passed before she had a message: "Prince Kung asks pardon, for he knows the empress mother is weary. Yet so urgent are the affairs of state that he is waiting for audience in the imperial library, and with him are his brother princes and the noble headmen of the Manchu clans."

Without waiting to change her garments, she went again to Sakota's palace, and the two ladies went swiftly to the imperial library and entered side by side. Everyone rose and then knelt in obeisance. Prince Kung gravely led the ladies to their thrones.

"Our problem is severe," Prince Kung said at last. "Nevertheless, we have one great strength. The empress mother has the imperial seal in her secret keeping. The legitimate succession is therefore hers as regent for her son, together with the empress dowager of the Eastern Palace. Yet we must move with all decorum and propriety. How, then, shall we seize the traitors? Shall violence be used while the emperor comes to his own funeral scene? It would indeed be impious. The heir's reign would begin under an evil cloud."

All agreed that Prince Kung spoke well. It was decided that each step would be taken slowly, with caution and dignity, conforming to the ancient traditions of the dynasty.

Three days passed, and Tzu Hsi spent them in meditation, planning every motion of what she would do. In the palace all was mournful quiet. When it was known that the imperial cortege was near, the empress dowagers set forth to meet their dead lord, and with them went the heir.

At the East Flowered Gate of the Forbidden City they halted and knelt as the huge coffin appeared, carried by its hundred bearers. In front knelt the heir, and behind him Tzu Hsi and Sakota, the princes and the heads of clans and officials, each in his rank. Loud lamentations rose into the air.

Prince Yi, Prince Cheng and the grand councillor Su Shun would now report to the heir, and for this rite a great pavilion had been built inside the gate. There Tzu Hsi now went with her son, and Sakota obediently went with them. The princes and the officials of the court gathered around. Tzu Hsi sat at the right hand of the heir, and on his left sat Sakota. Without delay, Tzu Hsi calmly began to speak. "We thank you, Prince

Yi, Prince Cheng and Grand Councillor Su Shun, for your care of him we hold most dear. In the name of our new emperor, the Son of Heaven now ruling, we give you thanks, since we, the two consorts of the late emperor, are the duly appointed regents, by decree of the late emperor himself. Your duties are now fulfilled and it is our will that you be relieved of further cares." They all understood the immovable will behind the courteous words.

Behind the handsome child sitting on the throne and his beautiful, powerful mother stood the royal Manchu clans, and behind these again the imperial guard. Prince Yi looked at Jung Lu and his heart shook within him.

Su Shun leaned to whisper in his ear, "Had that female fiend been killed early, then would we be safe at this hour! You are the leader now, and if you fail, we die."

Prince Yi stepped nearer to the child emperor, and trying boldness, he thus addressed the throne: "It is we, Most High, who are your appointed regents. Our imperial ancestor, your father, did appoint me and Prince Cheng and the grand councillor Su Shun, we three, to act on your behalf. As regents, we hereby decree that the two consorts have no authority beyond their station and they are not to be present at audiences, except by our permission." While Prince Yi spoke in a trembling voice the little emperor yawned and played with the cord that tied his garments.

When Prince Yi stepped back, Tzu Hsi lifted her right hand, and thrusting her thumb downward, she commanded, "Seize the three traitors!" Immediately Jung Lu strode forward with his guardsmen and seized the Three and tied ropes about them. Who dared to aid them now? No one spoke. In dignity and order the funeral procession formed again behind the great catafalque. The traitors walked last in the dust, their faces downcast. For them remained no hope.

Thus did the emperor Hsien Fêng come home again. His bier rested in the sacred hall, guarded night and day by his imperial guardsmen, while Buddhist priests prayed his three souls to Heaven and placated his seven earthly spirits by chanting and burning incense.

Tzu Hsi sent forth an edict. The realm, she declared, had been disturbed too much by enemies, and this was the fault of Prince Yi and his allies, who had brought shame upon their country by tricking the white men. These white men had then burned the Summer Palace in revenge. Yet the traitors persisted in their evil, she declared, and they pretended that the late emperor had appointed them as regents and had set themselves up in power, disregarding the express wish of the emperor no longer ruling. "Let Prince Kung," the edict ended, "in consultation with the grand secretaries, the six boards and the nine ministries, consider the proper punishment to be inflicted upon these traitors, in proportion to their offenses." To this edict, the empress mother affixed the imperial seal.

Then she prepared another edict: "Su Shun is guilty of high treason. He has usurped authority. He has accepted bribes and has committed every wickedness. Moreover, he kept his wife and concubines with him while he escorted the imperial catafalque from Jehol, although it is known to be a crime to be punished by death. Therefore we decree that Su Shun shall die by slicing, his flesh to be cut into a thousand thousand strips. His property shall be confiscated, and no mercy shall be shown to his family."

Prince Kung alone dared to raise his voice to oppose Tzu Hsi's vengeance against Su Shun. "Majesty," he said, "it would become the empress dowagers to show some mercy. Let Su Shun be beheaded rather than sliced."

Minutes passed before Tzu Hsi answered. "Let it be by our mercy, then," she said at last, "but the beheading shall be public."

On a fair and sunny morning, the people made a holiday to come and see Su Shun die in the marketplace. He walked bravely before the throng, villain though he was. Proud to the end, he laid his head upon the block. With a single blow, his head was severed from his body, and when it rolled into the dust, the people howled with joy, for he had injured many.

Since the princes Yi and Cheng belonged to the imperial house, they were ordered to the Empty Chamber, and there were told to hang themselves. Jung Lu gave to each a silken rope, and he stood by while each did hang himself upon a beam.

So died the Three, and those who had hoped to rise with them were sent into exile. Thus began the reign of the young emperor, but everyone knew that, whatever her propriety and her courtesy to all, the empress mother reigned supreme.

III

THE EMPRESS MOTHER

WINTER CREPT DOWN from the north and the city of Peking shriveled in the cold. Now that the succession was decided, the years stretched somberly before the nation and sensible minds did not deceive themselves. The treaty that Prince Kung had made with the white invaders was a treaty that acknowledged the victory of the enemy.

From now on, forevermore, there would be men in Peking from England and France and other alien countries. And there would be their wives and their children, their servants and their families. Doubtless, white men would find ways to lie with lovely Chinese women, and there would be confusion under Heaven.

Moreover, the treaty said, thousands of pounds of gold must be found for the foreigners as recompense for the war that the invaders had forced. Was this justice?

Furthermore, the treaty said, new ports were to be opened to these men and their goods from the West, even the port of Tientsin, which was less than a hundred miles from the capital itself. When the people saw foreign goods, would not false desires rise in their unenlightened hearts?

Of these and many like evils the empress mother read during one dark winter day in her lonely palace. The young emperor, her son, was but six years old. He could not sit upon the Dragon Throne before his sixteenth birthday. For nearly ten years she must rule in her son's place. And what was her realm? A country vaster than she could guess, a nation older than history. Rebellion raged, and the country was divided, for the rebel Hung ruled in Nanking, the southern capital of the last Chinese Ming Dynasty. The imperial armies fought incessantly against him but were seldom paid, and to keep from starving, they robbed the people until the country folk hated rebels and imperial soldiers equally.

Greatest of all her burdens was the burden of herself. She knew her own faults and the danger that, still young and of passionate heart, she could be betrayed by her own desires. Well she knew that a score of various women hid within her frame, and not all were strong and calm. She had her softness, her fears, her longing for one stronger than she, a man whom she could trust. Where was he now?

As though to cut herself off from the past, she moved to a distant palace in the imperial city, the Winter Palace, its six halls and many gardens built by the ancestor Ch'ien-lung. Near to it was a vast library, in which were enshrined the minds and memories of all great scholars. At the entrance to the palaces there stood a spirit screen on which were nine imperial dragons made of colored porcelain. Behind this screen the largest hall was the Audience Hall, opening upon a wide marble terrace. Behind this hall were the other halls, each with its courtyard—one her private throne room, the next her living place, another her secret shrine. Behind the shrine was a long room where her eunuchs stayed on guard. These rooms were furnished with the luxury the empress loved. Here were her many clocks, her flowers and birds, her embroidered pallets for her dogs, her cabinets of scrolls.

None but the strong could endure the life that the young empress mother now set for herself in this silent ancient place. She rose daily in the cold and bitter dawn and went in her imperial-yellow sedan to the Audience Hall. She would not go alone, however, for she commanded her sister-regent to sit with her on a second throne behind a silken curtain. The Dragon Throne was empty and would be until the young emperor could himself rule the nation. To the right of the empty throne Prince Kung stood and heard the memorials of princes and ministers.

Foremost among the suppliants were those who came one winter's day to beseech the regents to end the rule of the rebel Hung in the southern city of Nanking. The elder viceroy, who had long ruled the province of Kiangsu, was old and fat. He knelt uneasily, the cold of the marble floor creeping through the horsehair cushions to his knees.

"This rebel Hung's father," he declared, "was an ignorant farmer, but this Hung studied and went up for imperial examination. Three times he failed, but somewhere as he came and went he met a Christian who told him of the descent to earth of the foreign god Jesus and his incarnation as a human being, so that after he was killed by enemies he rose again and ascended once more on high. Thereafter Hung began to have dreams and visions. He declared himself the reincarnation of Jesus. He summoned all malcontents to follow him so that he could set up a new kingdom under his own rule in which the rich would all be made poor and the poor would become rich. With such promises the numbers of his followers has swelled into the millions. By robbery and murder he has taken lands and gold, and he has bought guns from the white men. Good people everywhere are distracted with terror. Indeed, our whole country will be lost unless this devil is destroyed."

The empress mother heard this memorial with increasing anger. Was this man to destroy the nation while her son was but a child? The imperial armies must be reorganized, new generals raised up. She would not tolerate this rebel.

After the audience that day, when Prince Kung came as usual to her private throne room, he found a woman cold, haughty, determined. "Where is General Tsêng Kuo-fan?" she demanded from her throne.

When the rebellion first rose, Tsêng Kuo-fan, already experienced in the affairs of government, was appointed by the throne to organize the imperial armies that were now being routed in the south by the rebel Hung. He trained an army called the Hunan Braves, and before he sent them against the rebels he seasoned them in war against local bandits. "This Tsêng Kuo-fan," she told Prince Kung, "it is his duty to send the Braves everywhere and anywhere that the rebels threaten to break through our ranks."

"Most High," the prince said coldly, "I venture to say that I doubt it wise for you to advise Tsêng Kuo-fan in matters of war."

She flashed her great eyes at him sidewise. "I do not ask for your advice, Prince." Her voice was gentle, but he saw her face grow white with rage. He bowed his head, controlling his own anger, and immediately withdrew. When he was gone, she went to her writing table and wrote to the distant general.

"It is time now to put forth all strength," she wrote. "We know that the provincial capital, Nanking, has been held for nine years by the rebels. Dislodge them with the help of your brother in Kiangsi. Next, recall from his guerrilla warfare the general Pao Ch'ao. This man is fearless and loyal to the throne. Keep him flexible, ready to move swiftly, so that when you move on to encircle the central city of Nanking, he may fly to the rear if the rebels rise again behind you. You have a double task—to kill the leader Hung, and while you press toward this end, to suppress every uprising that may spring up behind you. Reward will be generous when the rebel Hung is dead."

With her own hands the empress mother stamped the imperial seal upon the parchment and, summoning the chief eunuch, she sent the edict to Prince Kung to be copied and then taken south by courier to Tsêng Kuo-fan.

When the chief eunuch returned with the jade emblem that was Prince Kung's reply, the empress mother smiled and asked, "Did he say a word?"

"Benevolent," the eunuch replied, "the prince read the

edict line by line, and then he said, 'An emperor sits inside this woman's brain.' "

The empress mother laughed softly behind her embroidered sleeve. "Did he—did he, indeed!"

SHE HAD WON the people's faith. Affairs large and small of the whole realm were brought daily to her Audience Hall. The empress mother found patience for such small matters as the curbing of a distant magistrate who oppressed his region cruelly, or the price of rice in a city where speculators had driven it too high, as well as for the great ones of protecting coastlines from foreign enemies and regulating the hateful opium trade. She remembered also her vast household in the palaces. She scanned the household bills, the records of silks received and stored, and not one bolt was taken from the storehouses without her private seal. She knew well how thievery within a palace spreads to all the nation, and she let every serving man and every minister feel the coldness of her watching eyes upon him.

Yet she rewarded richly and often. A eunuch who obeyed her well was given silver, and a faithful serving woman gained a satin jacket. No one knew except herself the great rewards she planned for Jung Lu and Prince Kung. Jung Lu had saved her life and the emperor's and for this he deserved whatever she willed to give him. But Prince Kung had saved the capital by the skill of his bargaining with the enemy. She had resolutely forgotten the Summer Palace until she remembered against her will the gardens and the lakes, the treasure houses of tribute. At such times her heart hardened against Prince Kung. Could he not have prevented somehow the fearful loss? Then Jung Lu she would reward first. Yet prudence told her that she must summon Prince Kung and pretend to ask his advice.

On a day in late winter, then, so near to spring that a warm mist hung over the city, the empress mother summoned Prince Kung to her private Audience Hall. He looked so proud, so stately, as he approached her throne that she was displeased. He bowed, she fancied, somewhat slightly, as though he grew familiar. A thrust of secret anger stabbed her breast, but she put it aside. She had the task of winning him over to something that she wished.

"I pray you let us not stand on ceremony," she said, her voice pure music, and invited him to sit in her presence.

"I have in my mind," she said, "to bestow a reward upon the commander of the imperial guard. I do not forget that he saved my life when the traitors would have taken it. Had I died, those traitors would have kept the throne for themselves, and never would the heir have been the emperor."

Prince Kung did not look at her face while she spoke. "Most High," he said, "what reward have you in mind?"

She seized the moment boldly. "The post of a grand councillor has been empty since Su Shun's death. It is my will to put Jung Lu there."

He felt her powerful gaze upon him, and he returned the look. "It is impossible."

"Nothing is impossible if I will it."

Her eyes flamed, but he was ruthless. "You know that gossip creeps unending through the court. Deny rumor as I do always for the honor of the throne, yet I cannot kill it."

She made her eyes innocent. "What gossip?"

Having said so much, he spoke plainly. "Some doubt the young emperor's paternity."

Her lips trembled and she put a silk kerchief to her mouth. "Oh," she moaned, "and I thought my enemies were dead! You should have put to death the ones who spoke such filth against me! You should not have let them live an hour."

Was she innocent? He did not know and would never know. He stayed silent.

She drew herself erect upon her throne. "I ask advice no more. Today I shall proclaim Jung Lu a grand councillor. And if anyone dares to speak against him"—she leaned forward and forgot courtesy—"I'll silence them! And I bid you, Prince, be silent!"

Never in all their years had these two come to open anger. Then they recalled the mutual need of loyalty. The prince was first. "Most High, forgive me." He rose to his feet and made his obeisance.

She replied in her gentlest voice, "I do not know why I spoke so to you, who have taught me all I know. It is I who must ask you to forgive me. And I have long had it in my mind to give to you the best reward of all. You shall receive the noble title of prince adviser to the throne with full emolument. And the title of duke of Ch'in, which my late lord bestowed upon you, shall now be made hereditary."

These were high honors, and Prince Kung was bewildered by the sudden bestowal. He said in his usual mellow fashion, "Most High, I wish no reward for what was my duty."

"Indeed, you must accept," the empress mother said. "Yet I ask a gift from you, too, most honored prince."

"It is given," Prince Kung promised.

"Let me adopt your daughter, Jung-chun, as princess royal. Give me this happiness to comfort me and let me feel you have some small reward for your true and loyal aid against the traitors at Jehol."

Now the prince yielded, and he did so with magnanimity.

IT WAS summer again, a pleasant season bringing mists and gentle rain and even the scent of the salt seas, which the empress mother had never seen. As the heat of high summer crept behind the walls of the Forbidden City, she longed for the Summer Palace that was no more. Yet, she told herself, there remained the Sea Palaces. Why should she not make for herself there a place of repose and pleasure?

Not more than half a mile away, the three lakes called seas were first made by the emperors of the Nurchen Tartars five hundred years earlier. Yet those emperors could not dream of the beauty that Yung-lo, the third emperor of the Chinese dynasty of Ming, had later added. He caused the lakes to be deepened and bridges to be built to small pavilioned islands.

Mighty rocks, curiously shaped by rivers, were brought to make gardens, and palaces and halls were built in these gardens. Ancient twisted trees were planted and tended as carefully as though they were human.

For her own residence the empress mother now chose the Palace of Compassion near the Middle Sea. She loved especially the rock gardens, and there for the first time since the death of the emperor, she allowed herself to look at plays—sad, quiet plays, that portrayed the wisdom of the soul. In an unused courtyard she ordered those eunuchs who were carpenters and painters to make a great stage. She had her royal box raised beyond a narrow brook that ran through the courtyard, and this flowing water softened the voices of the actors and made music of their words.

To this place one day, the empress mother commanded Jung Lu to be summoned. It was her way never to tie two deeds too close, lest anyone comprehend by chance her private mind. She let a full two months pass by after she had made Prince Kung's daughter her adopted child before she sent for Jung Lu as though on a day's whim.

The play was going on before her eyes, as she sat with her ladies in their places around her. In a few minutes, Lady Mei saw that the empress mother was looking at her with thoughtful eyes. The empress mother beckoned with her down-turned hand.

The singing on the stage silenced her sovereign's voice to all but the lady herself. "I have not forgot my promise to you, child. This day I will fulfill it." Lady Mei continued to stand, her head bowed to hide her blushing face. The empress mother smiled. "I see you know what promise."

"Can I forget a promise that Majesty has made?" This was Lady Mei's reply.

"Prettily said, child! Well, you shall see—"

By this time Jung Lu was walking to the royal box. The afternoon sun shone down upon his tall figure. He approached the dais and made his obeisance. The empress mother inclined her head and motioned to a seat near her low throne. He hesitated and sat down.

For a while she seemed not to heed him. The star of the play came on the stage to sing and all eyes were upon him. Suddenly she began to speak, not turning her eyes from the stage. "Kinsman, I have had in mind all this while a good reward for your service to me and to the young emperor."

"Majesty—" he began, but she put up her hand.

"You must accept," she said, still gazing at the stage. "I need you near me. Whom can I trust? Prince Kung, yes—I know his name is on your lips. Well, I trust him! But does he love me? Or—do I love him?"

"You must not speak so," he muttered.

The voice upon the stage soared high, the drums beat, the ladies cried out their praises.

She smiled and her great eyes shone. "When you are a grand councillor, I may summon you as often as need be, for the burden of the realm will fall upon you, too."

"I shall not obey such summons save in company with all the councillors."

"Yes, you shall," she said willfully.

"And spoil your name?"

"I'll save my own name and by this means: if you have a wife young and beautiful, who can speak evil?"

"I will wed no one!" His voice was bitter between his teeth.

She spoke sharply. "I command you to wed Lady Mei. No, you shall not speak. She is the gentlest woman in our court, the truest soul, and she loves you."

"Can you command my heart?" he cried beneath his breath.

"You need not love her," she said cruelly.

"If she is what you say, then I would do her great injustice."

"Not if she knows you do not love her and still longs to be your wife."

He pondered this while serving eunuchs brought trays of sweetmeats to feed the throng. Heads turned toward the empress mother and she knew she must dismiss Jung Lu. She spoke between her teeth. "You may not disobey me. It is decreed that you shall accept this marriage, and on the same day you shall take your seat among the councillors. And now retire!"

He rose and made his deep obeisance. His silence gave assent. With careful grace she lifted her head again and seemed intent upon the stage.

That night when she was alone, the scene returned to her. After Jung Lu left, the stage had been a blur before her eyes while pain pervaded all her being. Jung Lu was the lover whom she craved, the husband she denied herself.

She lay motionless while pain lodged deep and hard inside her bosom. Why was she not all woman? Why could she not be content to yield the throne and be his wife? How did it serve her if a dynasty held or fell? She saw herself at last, a woman in her secret need and longing; yet pride of place and power—these, too, were her necessity. She turned upon her pillow and wept with pity for herself. I cannot love enough, she thought, to yield myself to love. And why? Because I know myself too well. Were I to cramp myself into my love, my heart would die, and I would have nothing left but hatred for him. And yet I love him!

The watchman beat his bronze gong and called his cry. "Four hours past midnight!" Suppose, she thought now, after Jung Lu is wed to Lady Mei, I could persuade him to meet me in some secret room of a forgotten palace. If a few times, say, over the years, I could meet my love as only a woman, then I could be happy. Ah, but while she sat on her throne another woman would lie in his bed. Her tears burned dry in sudden jealousy.

And then through her veins came the old powerful faith in what she was. Madness to imagine a secret room in some forgotten palace! If she would not give up all for love, he would be too proud to be her private lover. Once—yes, once, but only once. Well, she had that memory to keep, forever unforgotten. He would not yield again.

And now there came a thought so new that she was struck

with wonder. Grant that she could not forsake all and follow after love. Yet was it not a gift for him if she let him pour his love into her service? It may be that I love him best, she thought, when I accept his love for me and let it be my refuge.

She would set the wedding day as early as possible. Let it be soon, that it might be the sooner irrevocable!

With this wisdom a strange peace came flowing gently through her veins and stilled her restless heart. As she closed her eyes, the watchman's gong beat once again. "Dawn," he sang, "and all is well!"

"SUMMON THE chief eunuch," she commanded Li Lien-ying.

When he appeared before her in the imperial library, the empress mother looked up from her book and spoke with much distaste. "You, An Teh-hai, do you dare to let yourself become so fat?"

He tried a look of sadness. "Venerable, I am full of water. I am ill, Your Majesty, not fat."

"I know how you eat and drink," she said. "You grow rich, also. Take care. Remember that my eyes are on you."

The chief eunuch made a humble reply. "Majesty, we all know your eyes are everywhere at once." He began to sweat.

Suddenly she smiled. "You are too handsome to grow fat."

He laughed. "Majesty, I'll starve myself to please you."

In good humor then, she said, "I called to say it is my will that you arrange for the marriage of Lady Mei to Jung Lu, the commander of the guard. The lady has no parents. I must therefore stand in the place of parent to her. Yet my presence at her marriage would give her the appearance of a princess. Therefore, you are to take her to the house of my relative, the duke of Hui, with all honor and ceremony. From that house my kinsman, the commander, will receive her."

"Majesty, when is this day to be?" he inquired.

"Tomorrow she shall go to the duke. Bid the household prepare for her. His two old aunts can be her motherly companions. Then you shall go to the commander and announce that the marriage must take place two days from now. When it is over, you are to come and tell me."

"Majesty, I am your servant." He bowed and went away.

For two whole days until late at night she remained in the library and read.

On the morning of the third day the chief eunuch came and made his obeisance. "Majesty," he began, "all has been done with due honor and propriety." He paused, waiting for the most weighty question.

After a long time the question came. "Was the marriage—consummated?" Her voice was small and strange.

"It was," the chief eunuch said. "This morning the bride's serving woman came to tell me. The commander lifted the lady's bridal veil at midnight. The serving woman then withdrew, and the elder cousins gave her the stained cloth at dawn. The bride was virgin."

The empress mother sat silent now, until the chief eunuch coughed to show he was still there. She started as though she had forgot him. "Go," she said, "you have done well. I will send a reward tomorrow."

FROM THAT DAY on her son became the cause of all the empress mother did, the reason for all she had done. In the night when imagination presented scenes she could not share, she rose and went to find her little boy. While he slept she sat beside him, holding his warm hand.

He was strong and beautiful, and he had a mind that already the empress knew was brilliant. At five he could read not only his native Manchu, but Chinese books as well. His memory was prodigious. But she would not allow his tutors to spoil him with praise. "Say to him that his ancestor Ch'ien-lung did far better than he at five years of age," she said.

Had his been a smaller nature, surely he would have been ruined by power given him so young, but the genius of this child was that he could not be spoiled. He was tenderhearted, too, and would rescue a eunuch who was being whipped.

Yet at another time he could be imperious indeed. She once had to intervene because her eunuch, Li Lien-ying, had brought him some toy tigers instead of a foreign-made music box he had requested from a shop in the city. The little emperor rose from his small throne. "Throw them away!" he cried. "Am I an infant that I play with toy animals? I will have you sliced for this! Send me here my guardsmen!"

The guardsmen came and stood hesitating until a eunuch went in haste to find the empress mother. She came at once, her robes flying. "My son," she cried, "you may not put a man to death—not yet, my son!"

"Mother," her child said, very stately, "your eunuch has disobeyed not me but the emperor of China."

This small matter forced her to see that the boy needed a true man to take the place of the father he never had. Upon this she sent resolutely for Jung Lu. She had not seen him face to face since his marriage, and to shield her own heart she put on her robes of office and sat in her private throne room surrounded by her ladies. Jung Lu came in gowned as a councillor in a robe of gold brocaded satin.

"My son is old enough to ride a horse and draw a bow," she said. "I remember that you sit a horse well. As for the bow, I once did hear that you are a hunter better than the best. I command you, then, to teach my son, the emperor, to master a horse and to shoot an arrow straight to its target."

"Majesty, I will," he said and did not lift his eyes.

"Begin tomorrow," she commanded. "Each month I will see for myself and judge how able you are as a teacher."

From that day on, after his morning with his tutors, the little emperor spent his afternoon with Jung Lu. When the empress mother walked along the archery field, with what pride did he display the child! She spoke only a few words of cool praise. "My son does well, but so he should," she said. But her heart burned with joy to see these two as close as son and father.

"MAJESTY," PRINCE KUNG said one day, "I have summoned to the capital our two great generals, Tsêng Kuo-fan and Li Hung-chang."

The empress mother paused on the threshold of her private throne room. She was annoyed. He had come when she had not summoned him, and this was an offense. She turned and walked to the small throne in the middle of the hall. There she seated herself and waited for the prince to stand before her. She was not pleased when, having made his obeisance, he sat down uninvited on a chair to the right of the dais and began to say why he had come.

"Majesty, I have not troubled you day by day with the news of the war against the rebels."

"I am aware of that war," she said. Her voice was cold. "Did I not command Tsêng Kuo-fan to attack the rebels?"

"He did," Prince Kung replied, not seeing her anger, "and the rebels drove him back. Then the rebels announced plans to attack Shanghai itself. This has stirred up the rich merchants in that city—Chinese and white—and they are forming their own army. I therefore sent for our two generals that I might know their strategy."

"You take too much upon yourself," she said.

Prince Kung was amazed at this reproof. Until now the empress mother had been gracious and ready to approve what he did. In his zeal to serve the throne he had gradually assumed great responsibility for the conduct of a ferocious war.

"Majesty," he said, "if I have overreached myself, I ask your pardon and I excuse myself because what I did I have done for your sake."

She did not like this proud apology. "I do not excuse you," she said, "and so it scarcely matters if you excuse yourself."

Pride meeting pride, he rose and made his obeisance. "Majesty, I leave your presence. Forgive me that I came without your summons."

He went away, his noble head held high. She sent for the chief eunuch. "You are to summon the two generals, Tsêng

and Li, to the Audience Hall tomorrow," she told him. "Inform Prince Kung and the grand councillor Jung Lu that I shall require their presence. Invite the empress dowager of the Eastern Palace to come. We have grave matters to hear."

Then she rose, her ladies following her, and went to the archery field. How kingly handsome was her son! His short legs could barely touch the stirrups, yet he was bold enough to whip his horse to a gallop.

Suddenly the little emperor saw his mother. "My mother!" he cried. "See the saddle Jung Lu has given to me!" So she had to go and look at the saddle, and when she did, her eyes met Jung Lu's in mutual pride and laughter. On an impulse she said to him in a low voice, "Do you know that the two generals have come from the south?"

"I have heard it," he said.

"They propose to let the merchants of Shanghai build a stronger army under a new foreign leader. Is this wise?"

"The first task," he replied, "is to put an end to the rebellion. As it is, there are two wars at the same time, with the rebels and with the white men. Between them we cannot survive. Crush the rebels, using whatever means we can, and then with strength the white men can be driven away."

She, nodding and smiling all this time, watched the child gallop around the field. Jung Lu mounted his own horse to be at his side. She gazed at these two whom she loved, the child so small and gallant, the man straight and tall. The man's face was turned to watch the child, to speak a word of counsel. But the boy looked well ahead, his head high, his hands holding the reins with wonderful mastery. An emperor born, she thought, and he is my son!

IN THE CHILL gray dawn of the next day the two empress dowagers sat upon a raised dais behind the thin curtain of yellow silk. Sakota hated these audiences, and now, half drowsing, she waited to return to her bed. Meanwhile, the grand council assembled. They all knelt before the Dragon

Throne, their faces to the floor, and Prince Kung began to read from the memorial he held in both hands.

The empress mother was not pleased that Prince Kung had presented the memorial. She said, her voice clear and firm, "Let us hear the two generals themselves."

Prince Kung, thus rebuked, called for General Tsêng.

"I pray that my brother general, Li Hung-chang, may speak for both of us since his headquarters are in the city of Shanghai," Tsêng said.

Again without waiting for the empress mother to command, Prince Kung said, "Let Li Hung-chang come forward."

Behind the screen the empress mother's secret anger increased as Li Hung-chang prostrated himself before the empty Dragon Throne, and after greetings he said, "In the fourth month, I led my army into the city of Shanghai, under the command of my superior, General Tsêng Kuo-fan. There I found the city protected by the Ever-Victorious, who are mercenaries in the pay of the city merchants and now led by an American mercenary surnamed Bourgevine. Although he is well loved by the mercenaries, he is insubordinate to our command. When I commanded him to proceed to Nanking, Bourgevine refused to go. For this I deprived him of his post and threatened to disband the Ever-Victorious Army."

"This leaves the Ever-Victorious Army without a leader," Prince Kung observed.

"It does indeed, Highness," Li Hung-chang replied.

The empress mother was again displeased that Prince Kung had spoken without waiting for her reply, though she could not blame Li Hung-chang for answering his superior.

"Do you still wish to disband the mercenaries?" she inquired.

"Majesty," Li replied, "those soldiers are well trained, and though they are arrogant, we cannot afford to lose their skill against the rebels. I propose to invite the Englishman Gordon to lead the Ever-Victorious Army and proceed to battle."

"Does any one of you know this Gordon?" the empress mother now asked.

Prince Kung, unthinking, replied, "Majesty, when the invaders burned the Summer Palace and I stood there sick at heart, I saw a tall white man nearby in the uniform of an English officer. When I looked at his face, I saw to my amazement that he, too, was sorrowing. He came to me, and speaking very tolerably in Chinese, he told me that he was ashamed to see his compatriots so greedy for plunder, even destroying what they could not carry."

"Silence!" The voice of the empress mother came from behind the curtain.

Prince Kung was too proud to yield. "Majesty, I claim the right to speak. I then inquired of Gordon, 'Can you not call off your soldiers?' He said, 'Why did your emperor allow the torture and killing of our men, sent in good faith under a white flag to proclaim a truce?' Majesty, how could I answer?"

"Be quiet!" the voice of the empress mother cried out. She was bitter with fury, for Prince Kung was reproaching her publicly because she had persuaded the emperor, now dead, to send the Mongol general to seize the foreign truce party. She bit her lips and was silent for a full minute, while all waited for the voice of command from behind the yellow curtain. At last she said, "We give permission for this Englishman to serve us."

THOUSANDS OF YEARS ago the viscount Kê had advised the emperor Wu, then ruling, in this fashion: "In times of disorder, the government should be strong. In times of good order, it should be mild. But whatever the time, do not permit a prince or a minister to usurp the royal prerogatives." This thought came to the empress mother as though clouds parted above her. She would do more than bring a proud prince low. She would seat her son upon the Dragon Throne, and she behind the throne would whisper her commands for him to speak aloud as his own.

Yet this bold and most beautiful woman waited for the rebels to be quelled in the south, her plan ripening all the while within her mind. For the Englishman Gordon did not rush his soldiers into battle, but trained his men to strike sudden blows, changing his ground with vigor and speed until he had forced the rebels into defense. He converged upon the pivotal cities near Shanghai, and from there he advanced steadily toward victory.

Meanwhile, lulled by the empress mother's mildness during this crisis, Prince Kung more often than ever omitted small courtesies in her presence. She said nothing until one day, his mind upon affairs of state, he rose unbidden from his knees when holding audience with her. Swift as a tigress she pounced upon him. "You forget yourself, Prince! Is it not law and custom that all must kneel before the Dragon Throne? Dare you stand when every other must kneel? You plot treachery against the regents!" She turned to the eunuchs. "Summon the guards and let Prince Kung be seized!"

Now Prince Kung only smiled, thinking the empress mother jested. But the guards laid hold of him. He protested. "What— after all these years?" Then he gave her one long look and let himself be led away.

That same day she sent out an edict sealed with the imperial seal upon her own name and that of the empress of the Eastern Palace. "Inasmuch," she declared, "as Prince Kung has shown himself unworthy of our confidence, he is relieved of his duties as grand councillor. By this act we do sternly check his rebellious spirit and usurping ambition."

No one dared to plead the prince's cause, though many went secretly to Jung Lu to beg him to speak for this noble prince. But Jung Lu would not speak—not yet. "Let the people say what they think," he told them. "When she finds that the people do not approve her actions, she will change."

For a month they all waited. Everywhere the people complained that the empress mother had been unjust to the brother of the late emperor. The empress mother heard these complaints, seemingly without concern. Yet when she saw that Prince Kung submitted to his sentence and made no effort to oppose her, she restored him to the grand council but not to his place as adviser to the throne. In an edict she explained to the people that she must in duty punish with equal severity all who failed in humility before the throne. Of Prince Kung she wrote: "We admonish him to reward our leniency by greater faithfulness to duty." So Prince Kung returned and ever after did his work with proud dignity and correct humility.

From now on the empress mother set her son upon the Dragon Throne and taught him to hold his head high. Before dawn, they took their places, he on the throne and she so close behind the yellow curtain that her lips were at his ear.

When an ancient minister was droning his way through a long memorial, the little emperor often grew weary and sometimes forgot where he was. Then his mother's voice struck sharply across his ears. "Sit up! Do you forget you are the emperor?" He straightened, frightened by a power in her that he did not know. "What do I say now, Mother?" It was his constant question, and as often as he asked it, she answered.

In the summer of that same year, Tsêng Kuo-fan captured the outer ramparts of the rebel stronghold in Nanking, ordered gunpowder to be exploded beneath the city wall and so made breaches through which his men poured by the thousand. An iron bomb filled with gunpowder was thrown into the Palace of the Heavenly King, their last goal, and the last desperate defenders rushed out like rats from a burning house. They were all seized and put to death, except for the rebel leader, Hung, who had killed himself by poison some thirty days before.

The empress mother sent out the news in one edict after another so that all the people might know that the rebels were dead, and she proclaimed a month of feasting. Then she commanded that the body of Hung, the rebel leader, be dug up from its grave and the head cut off and sent everywhere throughout the provinces.

But first she announced that she wanted to look upon it with her own eyes.

Li Lien-ying received the head, wrapped in stained yellow satin, and brought it with his own hands to the empress mother. She gazed steadfastly while the satin fell away, transfixed by the staring eyes of the dead, which no one had taken time to close. The face was bloodless and made more pale by the sparse black beard around it, and the lips were drawn back from strong white teeth. Li Lien-ying could not suppress a groan. "A villain," he muttered.

"A strange wild face," the empress mother observed. "A desperate face, too sad to look upon. But it is not a villain's face. It is the face of a poet, gone mad because his faith was in vain. Ah me, it is the face of a man who knew himself lost when he was born." She sighed and covered her eyes with her hand for a moment. Then her hands fell and she lifted her head. "Take away the head of my enemy," she commanded Li Lien-ying, "and let it be shown everywhere to my people."

So ended the Taiping Rebellion in the year 1864.

THE IMPERIAL ARMIES, encouraged by what Gordon had taught them, put an end also to two lesser rebellions, one in the southern province of Yunnan, and the other a rebellion of Muslims in the province of Shensi. The empress mother, surveying the realm, now saw only peace, and in peace, prosperity. Her power rose high, and she knew it. But she did not forget the Englishman Gordon. Without him Nanking could not have fallen so easily, and Tsêng Kuo-fan was great enough to say so before the throne.

The empress mother commanded that the Order of Merit be awarded Gordon, and that he be given a gift of ten thousand taels. But when the imperial treasure bearers arrived, Gordon refused the gift and drove the bearers away. For when the city of Soochow was captured, Li Hung-chang had ordered the murder of many of the enemy leaders. Now Gordon had promised these leaders that their lives would be saved if they surrendered, and when he found that his promise had been voided, he fell into a frenzy of temper. Forever unforgiving, he sent this proud letter to the Dragon Throne:

> Major Gordon received the approbation of His Majesty with every gratification but regrets most sincerely that owing to the circumstances that occurred after the capture of Soochow, he is unable to accept any mark of the emperor's recognition, and therefore respectfully begs His Majesty to allow him to decline the same.

The empress mother read this document a few days later. She read it twice, considering what man this Gordon was, who could for so high a reason refuse vast treasure and great honor. For the first time it came into her mind that there could be good men among the foreign enemy. If righteous, the white men were stronger than she reckoned, and she kept this fear hidden in her as long as she lived.

But though the rebellion had been put down, the city of Nanking and the surrounding provinces were still so unruly and restless that the imperial viceroy had been assassinated. The empress mother sent in haste for Tsêng Kuo-fan and commanded him to take the dead man's place in Nanking. So powerful was the influence of the aging general that the restlessness of the people subsided when he entered the viceregal palace in Nanking.

Yet in early spring of the next year Tsêng Kuo-fan was struck down by the gods. He felt dazed and confused, and he lay silent upon his bed for three days. Then he seemed to rally and asked to be carried into the viceregal Audience Hall. There he sat on his throne as if he were conducting an audience and there he died. The empress mother, hearing the evil news, wept for a time in silence. Then she sent out a decree over the whole nation ordering that a temple be built in every province to the honor of this great and good man, who had brought peace to the realm.

Meanwhile, the board of imperial astrologers had finally proclaimed the day for the burial of the late emperor. During these years his jeweled casket had rested in a distant part of the palace. As a sign of her renewed confidence in Prince Kung, the empress mother had commanded him to be responsible for raising the vast sums needed to build the new tomb. He had collected ten million silver taels, levying taxes on every province and guild, and from this sum he allowed commissions to officials high and low.

Prince Kung spent four years in the building of the tomb, for time was needed to carve the great marble beasts and warriors who stood in pairs to guard its entrance. The tomb itself was domed and made of marble, and in its center stood a vast pedestal of gold inlaid with jewels upon which the imperial coffin was to rest. There one clear, cold autumn day the dead emperor was brought amid many mourners. In their presence, the great coffin was placed upon the pedestal while candles flamed and incense smoldered. Before the coffin was sealed, rubies and jade and emeralds and pearls were laid upon the dead emperor's wizened body. Then the lid was sealed with glue made from the tamarisk tree. Around the coffin eunuchs placed kneeling figures made of silk and paper so that he would not be alone beyond the Yellow Springs. When the priests had chanted prayers and the regents and the young emperor had prostrated themselves before the dead, they withdrew from the tomb, and the great bronze doors were sealed.

The day of the funeral the empress mother issued this edict of forgiveness for Prince Kung: "Prince Kung has for the last five years busied himself under our command with the funeral arrangements of the late emperor. He has shown decorum and diligence, and our grief has been somewhat assuaged by the splendor of the imperial tomb and the solemnity of the funeral ceremonies. So that Prince Kung's fair name may not be marred in the records of our reign, we decree that the record of his previous dismissal be erased and that he stand again in all his honor. Thus do we reward our good servant."

At the end of the day the empress mother walked alone in her favorite garden. She was melancholy but not sorrowful.

Loneliness was the price of greatness, and she paid it day after day. Yet now for a moment her mind, lit by her too vivid imagination, saw a house, a home, where a man lived with a woman and where he begat children. For on this day her eunuch had told her that a son had been born to Jung Lu. Before dawn, Lady Mei had given birth to a healthy male child. Again and again during the day the empress mother had thought of this child. Yet Jung Lu had stood among the mourners with no sign of joy upon his face. Tonight, when he returned to his home, could he refrain from joy? She would never know.

ON A CERTAIN day two summers later when the empress mother had moved to the Sea Palaces to enjoy the gardens, she sat before the imperial theater to watch a play written by a witty scholar two hundred years before. The villain was a big-nosed Portuguese sea captain with a great sword on his belt. The hero was the prime minister of the Chinese court, and this part was played by the chief eunuch, An Teh-hai.

Suddenly the eunuch Li Lien-ying, who had been laughing loudly, rose from his stool near his imperial mistress and endeavored to steal quietly away.

"Where are you going?" the empress mother demanded.

"Majesty," Li Lien-ying said in a whisper, "the sight of this foreign rascal has made me suddenly remember a promise I gave yesterday to the young emperor."

"What is it?" she asked.

"He has heard somewhere of a spirit cart that can run without horse or man, and he bade me buy him one. The chief eunuch said that it may be I can find it in the shop kept by a foreigner in the Street of the Legations. Thither I now go."

"I forbid it," the empress mother exclaimed.

"Majesty," the eunuch coaxed her, "I pray you remember that the young emperor has a temper and I shall be beaten."

"I forbid him to have a foreign object," the empress mother insisted. "Sit down again."

Li Lien-ying sat, not laughing anymore, although An Teh-hai

outdid himself on the stage. The empress mother did not laugh either, and after an hour or so, she signified to her ladies that she would withdraw. After proceeding to her own palace, she sent for the chief eunuch.

"How dare you plot with Li Lien-ying?" she inquired when he came.

"Majesty," he gasped. "I? Plot, Majesty?"

"To bring a foreign spirit cart to show my son!"

He tried to laugh. "Majesty, is this a plot? We all do what the emperor wishes, and is this not our duty?"

"Not if he wishes for what is wrong," she said, implacable. "I have told you that I will not have him learn such vices as his father learned. If you can be so foolish as to yield in this, where else have you not yielded?"

"Majesty—" he began.

But the empress mother frowned. "Get out of my sight, you faithless servant!"

He flung himself at her feet. "Majesty, my whole life is yours!" But she pushed him away with her foot. "Out of my sight—out of my sight!" He crept away then on his hands and knees and once beyond the door he fled to Jung Lu, whose palace was a mile distant.

In a few words An Teh-hai told of his trouble. "I beseech you to save me from the imperial wrath," he begged.

Jung Lu motioned the chief eunuch to a chair nearby and said, "I have been concerned at what I see in the emperor's palace."

"Venerable, what do you see?" the chief eunuch asked.

Jung Lu made his face stern. "The young emperor's father, Hsien Fêng, was ruined by his eunuchs. You had it in your power to persuade him to clean thoughts and righteous acts. Instead, you pandered to his weakness and his lusts so that he died an old man when he was hardly thirty. Now you have his son—" Jung Lu broke off. His face was moved, and he put his hand to his mouth.

An Teh-hai trembled with fright. He had come hoping for support and instead he was attacked anew. "Venerable," he said, "it is very hard to be a eunuch and disobey one's lord."

"Yet it can be done," Jung Lu said. "For there is in every man both good and evil. You chose the evil."

"Venerable," the eunuch stammered, "it was never given me to choose."

"You know," Jung Lu said yet more sternly, "that when the emperor, now dead, was fretful, you soothed him in evil ways. Before he was a man his manhood was destroyed."

An Teh-hai was not stupid. The time had come for him to use a dangerous weapon. "Venerable," he said, "if the emperor's manhood was destroyed, how is it that he begot a son and one so sturdy as the young emperor?"

Jung Lu looked steadfastly at the eunuch. "If this imperial house falls," he said, "you must fall with it and so must I, and with us, the dynasty. Shall we then destroy this young man, who is our only hope?"

Thus did Jung Lu put to one side the dagger that the chief eunuch thrust at him. And the chief eunuch pretended to be abashed, and he mumbled, "I came here only to ask that I be saved from the wrath of the empress mother."

Jung Lu passed his hand wearily over his eyes. "I will speak for you," he promised.

"Venerable, it is all I ask," the chief eunuch said, and he went quickly away. He was well content. His cruel question had served him better than a sword, and Jung Lu had only parried it.

In his library Jung Lu sat so long alone that his gentle wife came stealing in between the curtains.

She put her hand lightly on his shoulder. "It is nearly dawn," she said, "and still you do not come to bed?" Startled, he turned his face all naked to her eyes, and she saw such wild pain there that she threw her arms about his neck. "Oh, love," she cried, "what is wrong?"

He stiffened. "Old troubles," he muttered, "old problems, never to be solved! I am a fool to think upon them. Come, let's sleep."

291

At the door to her bedroom he took his leave, saying as though it had only come to his mind, "And are you better with this child within you than you were with the first?" For she was big with child for the second time.

"I thank you. I am well," she said.

To which he smiled and said, "Then we will have a daughter. It is the sons who struggle against the womb."

"And shall you mind if I give you a daughter?" she asked.

"Not if she looks like you," he said most courteously.

Next afternoon, Li Lien-ying announced to his royal mistress that the grand councillor Jung Lu sought an audience with her when it was her convenience. To which she said at once, "When is it not convenient for me to welcome my kinsman? Bid him come now." So in a brief time Jung Lu was in her private audience hall. Motioning the eunuch to stand at a distance, she bade Jung Lu rise from his knees and seat himself below her throne.

"Now pray you," she said, "put courtesy aside and say what is in your mind. You know that underneath the empress there is always the one you knew as child and maiden."

A long look passed between them. Then he forced his eyes away from hers. "I came to speak about the emperor." He used his own guile, knowing that only her son could divert those dark eyes from his face.

"What of him?" she cried. "Is something wrong?"

He was free again. "I am not pleased," he said. "These eunuchs pervert a young lad by their own perversion. You saw their evil wreak its doom upon the late emperor. Your son must be saved before it is too late."

She flushed, and then she said, "Being only a woman, what can I do? Can I foul my tongue to speak of deeds I should not so much as know about? These are men's affairs."

"So I am here," he said, "and I do advise you to betroth your son early. Though he is too young to wed, the image of the one he has chosen will keep him clean."

"How can you know that?" she inquired.

"I know it," he said bluntly.

She yielded to his stubborn goodness. "Well, I will do as you bid me. Let the maidens be called together soon, to be prepared—as I was. Now it is I who will sit, as the dowager mother once did, to mark the emperor's choice! Do you remember she did not like me?"

"You won her afterward as you do win all," he muttered.

She laughed softly and then rose, again the empress. "Well, let it be so, kinsman! And I thank you for advice." And so they parted yet again.

THE CHIEF EUNUCH was uneasy. Emperors came and went, but eunuchs remained, and above all eunuchs was the chief eunuch. Yet the empress mother could be angered even with him! He was shaken, and he longed to escape for a while from the walls of the Forbidden City.

He went to the empress mother. "Majesty," he said, "I know that it is against the law of the court for a eunuch to leave the capital. Yet it has been my secret longing all these years to sail on the Grand Canal southward and view the wonders of our land. I pray you let me go for such a pleasure."

When the empress mother heard this request, she was silent for a time. She knew that she was often blamed privately because she gave heed and honor to eunuchs.

"What a trouble you make for me," she now exclaimed to An Teh-hai; but she yielded, remembering his constant loyalty to her. "I might send you to Nanking," she said thoughtfully, "to inspect the imperial tapestries being woven there against the day of the emperor's marriage and accession."

In a few days the chief eunuch set sail for Nanking, his entourage on six great barges, each flying imperial banners. When they passed through the towns along the Grand Canal, the magistrates saw the banners and hastened to bring gifts to An Teh-hai. Thus encouraged, the proud eunuch demanded bribes not only of money but of lovely maidens, for though he was a eunuch, he used them in his own hateful ways.

Word of this soon reached northward to the ears of Prince Kung, and at the same time eunuchs who hated An Teh-hai for some past cruelty carried tales to Sakota, the empress of the Eastern Palace. She sent for Prince Kung, and when he knew that she had heard the rumors concerning the chief eunuch, he said boldly, "Now is the time, Majesty. With your permission I will arrest this An Teh-hai and have him beheaded."

Sakota made a small scream. "I do not like to see anyone killed," she faltered.

"It is the only way to rid the court of a favorite, and so it has always been in history," Prince Kung replied. "Moreover," he went on, "our late emperor was debauched while he was yet a child by this same eunuch. And now our young emperor is led in the same evil ways. If I prepare a decree, Majesty, will you sign it with your own imperial seal?"

She shuddered. "What—and brave the other one?"

"What can she do to you, Majesty?" Prince Kung urged.

Thus persuaded, she signed the decree that the prince had prepared, and in secret he swiftly dispatched it by courier.

By now An Teh-hai had gone beyond Nanking and had reached the city of Hangchow. The magistrate of that city sent secret memorials to Prince Kung, describing the orgies of the arrogant, handsome eunuch. To this magistrate, therefore, Prince Kung sent the secret decree of death. Immediately the magistrate invited An Teh-hai to a vast banquet. When he entered the hall of the magistrate's palace, An Teh-hai was seized while his eunuchs and guards were held in the outer court. The magistrate lifted his hand and thrust down his thumb. At the sign his headsman stepped forward and cut off An Teh-hai's head with one blow of his broadsword.

When the empress mother heard that her loyal servant was dead, her rage burned hot against her sister-regent and Prince Kung. "He alone could have made a lioness of that mouse!" she cried, and she would have ordered Prince Kung himself beheaded, except that Li Lien-ying, in terror at such madness, went secretly to Jung Lu.

Jung Lu came to the palace without delay and stood in the doorway of her bedchamber. Behind the curtain hanging between them, he said with sad patience, "If you value your place, you will do nothing. For it is true that the chief eunuch was a man of surpassing evil and that you broke tradition when you gave permission for him to leave the capital."

She said nothing for a while. Then she spoke, pleading for his mercy: "You know why I favor these eunuchs. I am alone in this place—a lonely woman."

To this he said but one word: "Majesty—" Then he was gone.

She went to her library with slow and weary steps and for many hours she read the memorials laid there on the table. When the day was done, she sent for Li Lien-ying and said to him, "You are now chief eunuch. But your life depends upon your loyalty to me and to me alone."

From this day on, the empress mother allowed herself to hate Prince Kung, and patiently she waited for the time when she could subdue his pride forever.

THE LONGER the empress mother pondered Jung Lu's counsel to betroth the young emperor soon, the more she found it to her liking, and this for a reason that no one but herself knew. Her son had one way to wound her, and so deeply that she could not speak of it even to him. Since his childhood he had preferred Sakota's palace to hers. Too proud to show her hurt, the empress mother never reproached him. She knew why her son went often to the other palace and stayed so long, whereas to her he came when called and left as soon as he could. The cruelty of a child! She, his mother, must often cross his will, for she must teach and train him for his future. But Sakota felt no duty to reprove or teach, and so with her he could be what he was—a merry, teasing, lounging boy.

Only this morning after the audience her son had been all eagerness to leave. But she had compelled him to remain in her library so that she might learn if he had listened to the memorials presented that day. He had not listened, and to her reproachful questions he had cried in a naughty voice, "Must I remember every day what some old man mumbles at me through his beard?"

She had been so angered by his insolence to her that she put out her hand and slapped his cheek. He fixed his great eyes on her in a rage; then, without a word, he had bowed stiffly to her and turned and left. Doubtless he had gone straight to Sakota. Doubtless she had comforted him and told him how often she, the gentler one, had been struck by his mother when they were children under one roof. At this the proud empress mother sobbed suddenly. If she had not her son's heart, then she had nothing. And she had given up all for him, had spent her life for him, had saved a nation for him!

Then she fell to thinking about how to get her way. Sakota must be supplanted by another woman, someone young and lovely, a wife who would enchant the man already budding in him. Yes, Jung Lu's counsel was wise and good. She would betroth her son against that woman who gave mild motherhood to a child not her own.

She clapped her hands for Li Lien-ying. Within an hour she had given commands for the parade of maidens—what day it was to be and where, and what the tests were. The new chief eunuch listened and begged for six months or so to do his best. But the empress mother gave him three.

When she had thus decided for her son, she set her mind again to those affairs of the realm from which she had no peace. The greatest danger was the invasion by the Christians. For hundreds of years the followers of Confucius, Buddha and Lao-tzu had lived together in peace and courtesy. Not so these Christians, who would cast out all gods except their own. And by now everyone knew that wherever the Christians went, traders and warships soon would follow.

To Prince Kung, the empress mother one day declared, "Sooner or later, we shall have to rid ourselves of foreigners, and first of all we must be rid of these Christians."

But Prince Kung cautioned her, saying, "Majesty, remember, if you please, that they possess weapons of which we know nothing. Let me, with your permission, draw up a set of rules to govern the behavior of the Christians so that our people may not be troubled."

Soon after, he presented a memorial containing several rules. "Today my head aches," she said. "Tell me what you have written and spare my eyes." So saying, she closed her eyes to listen.

"Majesty, I say that Christians may not take into their orphanages any save the children of their own converts." She nodded in approval, her eyes still closed.

"I also ask," Prince Kung went on, "that Chinese women shall not be allowed to sit in the foreign temples in the presence of men. This is against our custom and tradition."

"It is propriety," the empress mother observed.

"Moreover," Prince Kung went on, "I have asked that foreign missionaries shall not protect their converts from the laws of our land if they commit a crime."

"Entirely reasonable," the empress mother said, approving.

"And evil characters," Prince Kung concluded, "must not be received into their churches as a means of escape from just punishment."

"Justice must be free to work," the empress mother declared.

"Majesty," Prince Kung now said, "the foreign envoys do not accept these mild requests. They insist that all foreigners here shall remain entirely free to do what they like, without censure or arrest. Worse than this, they refuse so much as to read my document. The envoy from the United States alone has replied, not with agreement but at least with courtesy."

The empress mother could not restrain her feelings at such monstrous offense. Rising from her throne, she paced the floor, muttering angry words. "Have you asked them," the empress mother cried, "what they would do to us were we to go to their countries and refuse to obey their laws?"

"Majesty, I have so asked," Prince Kung said.

"And what is their reply?" she demanded.

"They say that our laws are inferior to theirs, and therefore they must protect their own citizens."

She ground her teeth together. "Yet they insist upon staying here, they will not leave us!" She sank upon her throne. "I see they will not be satisfied until they possess our land as they already possess India and Burma, the Philippines and Java."

To this Prince Kung did not reply. He, too, feared this was true.

She lifted her lovely face, now gone pale and stern. "I tell you, we must rid ourselves of foreigners! And to this I shall give my whole mind and heart from now until I die." She drew herself up straight and cold, and he knew himself dismissed.

IN THE AUTUMN of 1872, the seventeenth year of the young emperor T'ung Chih, the empress mother decreed that he should take his consort. Upon the day prescribed by the board of astrologers, therefore, six hundred beautiful maidens were called, of whom one hundred and one were chosen by the chief eunuch. It was a day of brilliant sunshine, and the courtyards and terraces blazed with chrysanthemums. In the middle of the Palace of Eternal Spring were set three thrones, and on the central one, higher than the rest, the emperor sat, while his mother and Sakota, as regents, sat on either side. The young emperor held his shoulders straight and his head high, but his mother knew that he was excited and pleased. His cheeks were scarlet and his great black eyes were bright. Surely he was the most beautiful young man under heaven, she thought.

A golden trumpet now blew three blasts to signify that the procession was about to begin. At the far end of the hall the maidens were coming over the smooth tiles of the floor, a moving, glittering line of beauties. One by one they came, some tall, some small, some proud, some childlike, some dainty, some handsome. The young emperor stared at each one and made no sign. The morning crept past, and a soft gray light filled the hall. The last maiden passed late in the afternoon and the trumpet blew again, three concluding notes.

The empress mother spoke. "Did you see one you like, my son?"

The emperor turned the sheets of the written records and put his finger on a name. "This one," he said.

His mother read the description of the maiden. "Alute, aged sixteen, daughter of the duke Chung Yi, bannerman and scholar of high learning. The maiden herself has the requirements of absolute beauty. Her measurements are correct, her body is sound, her breath is sweet. Moreover, she also is learned in books and in the arts. Her temper is mild, and she is inclined to silence rather than to speech."

"Alas, my son," the empress mother said, "I do not remember this one among the many others."

The emperor turned to the empress dowager, Sakota. "Do you remember her?"

To the surprise of all, the dowager replied, "I do remember her. She has a kind face, without pride."

The empress mother was secretly displeased, but she said, "How much better are your eyes than mine! It is I then who must see the maiden again."

Alute entered once more, and the imperial three stared at the slight young girl as she seemed to drift toward them, her head drooping and her hands half hidden in her sleeves.

"Come nearer to me, child," the empress mother commanded.

With exquisite modesty the young girl obeyed. The empress mother took the maiden's hand and examined the girl's face. It was oval, smoothly rounded, the eyes large, and the black lashes long and straight. She was pale, but the skin was glowing with health.

The empress mother continued to stare at the girl. Was there a hint of firmness about the chin? The lips were lovely but not childish. Indeed, the face was wiser than the face of one only sixteen years of age.

"She looks clever," Sakota ventured.

"I do not wish my son cursed with a clever wife," the empress mother said.

"You are clever enough for us all, Mother," the young emperor said, laughing.

The empress mother could not keep from smiling, and, willing to be good-natured on such a day, she said, "Well, choose this maiden, then, my son, and do not blame me if she is willful."

Alute knelt again and three times she bowed her head to the empress mother, three times to the emperor, now her lord, and three times to the empress dowager. Then she rose and walked away with the same drifting, graceful gait.

Four concubines were selected the next day, and it remained only for the board of astrologers to search the stars for the lucky date of marriage. Exactly at the chosen hour the emperor, waiting with his courtiers, the empress mother and the empress dowager, accepted Alute for his bride. She stepped from the wedding sedan, two matrons at her elbows, and two other matrons, the four being titled Teachers of the Marriage Bed, came forward to receive her and present her to the emperor.

Thirty days of feasting followed, during which the people of the nation were forbidden to work and commanded to enjoy their ease and pleasure. When these days were ended, the young emperor and his empress were ready to be declared the heads of the nation, but first the regents had to step down from their rule. The empress mother sent forth an edict that declared that the regents now requested the emperor to take the throne. He answered with his own edict saying that he in filial piety must receive it as a command from the older generation. After this, the empress mother announced she would retire to enjoy the accumulating years of her life. She declared that her goal was won, her duty done, for she gave the realm intact to her son, the emperor.

THESE WERE HER days of peace and pleasure. No longer did the empress mother rise in the darkness to hold an audience for those who came to appeal to the throne. She rose when she felt inclined, and when she awakened, she lay awhile thinking of the lovely empty days ahead in which she had no duty save to be herself. Weighted as she had been all these years with the cares of the realm, now when she awoke, she could think of her peony mountain, a hill she had commanded to be raised and then terraced with peony beds. The early buds were swelling into great flowers, rose-colored and crimson and pure white. Each morning hundreds of new blooms waited for her coming.

Today the empress mother was in a pleasant mood. It was the season of returning birds, and as she walked in her gardens she listened for the wild sweet music that she loved. When a bird called, she answered, pursing her lips and replying so perfectly that after a while a small yellow-breasted finch came fluttering down from among the bamboos to alight upon her outstretched hand. There it clung while on the empress mother's face there came a look so tender that her ladies were moved to see it, marveling that this same face could sometimes be so harsh and cruel.

When she had walked about her garden for an hour, she spoke amiably to her waiting ladies. "The air of this day is fine, the sun is warm, and it would be a pastime to see our court actors perform my play, *The Goddess of Mercy*. What do you say?"

At this all the ladies clapped their hands, but the chief eunuch, Li Lien-ying, made his obeisance. "Majesty," he said, "I fear the actors have not yet learned their lines."

"The actors have had plenty of time," the empress mother declared. "Go at once and tell them that I shall expect the curtain to rise before the beginning of the next period of the water clock. Meanwhile I will say my daily prayers."

Then the empress mother walked with her usual grace through a pavilion to her own private temple, where a white jade Buddha sat upon a great lotus leaf of green jade, holding in his right hand an uplifted lotus flower of rose jade. "*O mi t'o fu,*" she murmured for each of the sandalwood prayer beads until one hundred and eight were told. While she prayed first to the Buddha, she bowed too before the goddess of mercy, imagining in her secret thoughts that they two were sisters, one queen of heaven and the other the queen of earth. Sometimes in the middle of the night she even so addressed the goddess: "Sister in heaven, you know my kinsman Jung Lu, and how we would have been man and wife, except for my destiny. Tell me, shall we be free to wed in some other incarnation, or shall I still be too great? Sister, I pray you raise him up to me, so that at last we may be equals, even as my sister, the English queen, Victoria, once raised her consort."

When she came out from the temple she led her ladies and her dogs through a large courtyard and came to her theater.

She sat on a cushioned throne to watch the play that she had written. The actors did their best, achieving such wonders as a great lotus flower rising from the middle of the stage, wherein sat a living goddess of mercy, who was a young eunuch, his face so delicate and pretty that he made a lovely girl. The empress mother devised many pieces of magic in her plays, for she listened eagerly to legends told by the Buddhist priests in the imperial temple. And she liked best the tales of sacred rhymes and secret words that, when chanted, can make a human safe against a spear thrust or a blow. All this wonder and hope and longing to believe in heavenly power she put into her plays.

When the play ended, she clapped her hands, for indeed it was well done and she was pleased with herself as playwright. She declared that she was hungry, and so the serving eunuchs formed two long lines from kitchens several courtyards away and passed the covered dishes of hot food from hand to hand. Now the ladies stood back while the empress mother ate with good appetite. She was in high spirits as she told a eunuch she would drink her tea in the library and so withdrew.

It was as she sipped her tea that the present shadow of her life fell hard upon her. For she heard a dry cough at the door and recognized the voice of the chief eunuch, Li Lien-ying.

"Enter," she commanded. "Why am I disturbed?"

He lifted up his head. "Majesty, I ask to speak to you alone."

She made a gesture with her right hand dismissing the other eunuchs. "Get up," she said to Li Lien-ying. "Sit yonder."

The tall gaunt eunuch rose and sat down on the edge of a carved chair. "I have stolen this memorial from the archives. It has received the emperor's approval," he said. "I must return it within the hour."

He drew from his robe a folded paper and presented it with both hands. She knew the handwriting. It was that of Wu K'o-tu, a member of the board of imperial censors. The memorial was addressed to the emperor, her son.

> I, most humble slave, do now present this secret memorial beseeching the throne to end official conflict by granting permission to ministers of foreign governments to stand instead of kneel before the Dragon Throne, and by this permission to show imperial magnanimity and the prestige of the Superior Man.

The empress mother felt old fury stir in her breast. If the Dragon Throne was no longer venerated, what honor was left?

The empress mother's hands itched to tear the memorial into a thousand pieces, but she was too prudent. This Wu K'o-tu was a man of years and of high honor. He did more than preach the duties and the ceremonies. He practiced them most rigorously. The empress mother knew that such righteousness was rare indeed and she restrained her wrath. She folded the memorial and returned it to the chief eunuch. "Replace this where you found it," she said. "And bid my son attend me."

The minutes crept into an hour and the chief eunuch did not return. Twilight crept into the vast library. When the serving eunuchs came in to light the candles in the hanging lanterns, she said in a silver-cold voice, "Where is the chief eunuch?"

"Majesty," a eunuch replied, making his obeisance, "he stands outside. He is afraid to enter."

"Send him to me," she commanded.

In a moment Li Lien-ying flung himself upon the floor before her.

"Where is my son?" she asked.

"Majesty, he sent word that he is indisposed." His voice was muffled.

"And is he indisposed?" she inquired.

"Majesty—Majesty—"

"He is not indisposed," she said.

She rose. "If he will not come to me, I must go to him," she said, and walked away swiftly. She went straight to the emperor's palace. The doors were closed, but light streamed through the panes of silken gauze and she looked in. There sat her son, lounging in a great cushioned chair, and leaning over him was Alute. The young consort held a cluster of cherries to the emperor's lips, and he was reaching for them, his head thrown back, laughing as the empress mother had never seen him laugh. Around him were his eunuchs and the ladies of the young empress, and they were all laughing like children.

She wrenched the door open and stood there bright as a goddess against the darkness of the night. The light of a thousand candles fell upon her glittering robes of blue and gold and upon her beautiful, furious face.

"My son, I hear that you are ill," she said.

He sprang to his feet while Alute stood like a statue, the cherries still hanging in her hand.

He could not speak. He gazed at his mother, his eyes sick with fear.

"And you, Alute," the empress mother said, "I wonder that you do not consider your lord's health. He should not eat fresh fruit when he is ill. You are too careless of your duties to the Son of Heaven. I will have you punished."

"Mother," the emperor stammered, "I beg you, nothing is Alute's fault. I was weary—the audience lasted nearly all day. I did feel ill."

She put her terrible gaze upon him again and took three steps forward. "Down on your knees," she cried. "Do you think because you are emperor you are not my son?"

All this while Alute did not move. She stood straight and

tall, her delicate face proud and unafraid. Now she dropped the cherries and seized the emperor's arm. "No," she cried in a low soft voice. "No, you shall not kneel."

The empress mother took two more steps forward. "Kneel!" she commanded.

For a long instant the young emperor wavered. Then he loosed his arm from Alute's hand. "It is my duty," he said and fell to his knees.

The empress mother's gaze swept over eunuchs and ladies. "Away with you," she cried. "Leave me alone with my son." One by one they crept away until only Alute was left. "You, also," the empress mother insisted.

Alute hesitated, then she, too, went away. Alone with her son, the empress mother changed as suddenly as a day in spring. She smiled and went to him and passed her smooth, scented palm over his cheek. "Get up, my son," she said gently. "Let us sit down and reason together." But she took the thronelike chair and he sat on Alute's lower chair.

She made her voice calm and friendly. "It was necessary for me to establish the order of the generations before the eunuchs and in the presence of the consort."

He did not answer, but his tongue wet his dry lips.

"Now, my son," she went on, "I am told that you plan to receive the foreign ministers without their obeisance."

He summoned all his pride. "I am so advised," he said, "and even by my uncle, Prince Kung."

"And will you do it?" she inquired.

"I will do it," he said.

"I am your mother," she said. "I forbid you."

Her heart grew soft while she gazed at his handsome face, and in spite of his willfulness, she discerned, again, his secret fear of her. A pang of sadness passed through her heart. She would have him so strong that even her he would not fear, for any fear is weakness.

She sighed and seemed to yield. "What do I care whether the foreigners kneel? I am thinking only of you, my son."

"I know," he said. "Whatever you do is for me. I wish I could do something for you. Something to make you happy—a garden, or a mountain made into a garden."

She shrugged. Then she said slowly, "What I long for cannot be restored. Can you bring back life from ashes?"

He knew that she was thinking of the ruined Summer Palace. Ah, she would never forgive the foreigners for that.

"We could build a new Summer Palace, Mother," he said slowly, "one as like to the old one as you can remember. I will ask for a special tribute from the provinces."

"Ah," she said shrewdly, "you are bribing me to let you have your way."

"Perhaps," he said. He glanced at her sidewise.

Suddenly she laughed. "Ah, well," she said. "Why do I disturb myself? A summer palace? Why not?" And she rose to leave.

THERE IS NO end to the sorrows that children bring to their parents whether in a palace or in a hovel. The empress mother learned as the days passed that the emperor had lied to her when he said Prince Kung had advised him to receive the foreign ministers without demanding obeisance. Instead, Prince Kung had reminded the emperor how his ancestors had refused to allow a privilege to foreigners that they denied to their own citizens. Now Prince Kung made delay after delay to the foreign envoys, pleading illness, and this illness lingered through four months until the emperor himself commanded that the envoys be presented before the Dragon Throne. He thus proved that he alone was lenient and weak.

It was early summer, the loveliest season, and the empress mother was of no mind to cope with affairs of state. Enticed by the clear sunlight, she had walked into her library and was drawing a map of the new Summer Palace.

"Fetch me Prince Kung," she commanded Li Lien-ying when he had made his report.

The prince found her pacing up and down before the wide

doors open to the courtyard. Pomegranate trees were in full bloom, their red flowers studded among the dark green leaves. When he had made his obeisance, he spoke first of pomegranates. "Majesty, your trees are very fine. I do not see others like them. Whatever is near you takes on new life." He had learned by now to speak to her gracefully and with submission.

She inclined her head, ready to be newly generous to him because he did not approve of the emperor's will. "Let us talk here in the courtyard," she said. "Why should I waste your time? I hear that the emperor, my son, wishes to receive the foreign envoys without obeisance."

"Majesty, he is curious as a child," Prince Kung replied. "He cannot wait to look upon a foreign face."

"And did you not forbid him?" she cried.

Prince Kung raised his eyebrows. "Majesty, how can I refuse the emperor?"

He was silent for a while. Then he said, placating her, "Majesty, at least the foreign envoys should not be received in the imperial Audience Hall."

"Most surely not," she agreed, diverted as he had meant she should be. Suddenly she smiled. "I have it! Let them be received in the Pavilion of Purple Light. They will not know it is not the palace proper. Thus we keep to reality and give them illusion."

He could not resist her mischief. The Pavilion of Purple Light was on the western boundary of the Forbidden City, and in it the emperor received only the envoys of the outer tribes.

"Majesty," Prince Kung now said, "I do admire your skill and wit. I will so arrange."

Moved by his praise, she invited him to come and see her plans for the Summer Palace. There for an hour he heard of rivers winding among rockeries and spreading into lakes, of mountains moved from the western provinces and set with trees and gold-roofed palaces. He said not a word, so great was his dismay at such wasted money. He forced himself to murmur between his teeth at last, "Who but you, Majesty, could conceive so imperial a palace?" Then he begged to be excused and hastened straight to the grand councillor Jung Lu.

That same day, her eunuch came to say that Jung Lu waited for an audience. She was leaning over the map again, her brush pointed fine to ink in a slender pagoda. Knowing that Jung Lu would not approve what she did, she let him stand awhile behind her back before she spoke. "Who is there?" she asked after moments.

"Majesty, you know."

"Ah," she said indifferently, "and why have you come? Do you not see that I am busy?"

"It is the reason for my coming," he said. "You know there is no money in the treasury for a pleasure palace, and the people are already too much taxed."

She shrugged again. "It need not be money. It can be stone and wood and artisans. These are everywhere."

"Men must be paid," he said.

"They need not be," she answered carelessly. "The first emperor did not pay the peasants who built the Great Wall. And when they died, he put their bones among the bricks."

"In those days," he said, "the dynasty was strong. The emperor was Chinese, not Manchu, and the wall was to protect their own people against invading northern enemies. But will the people now be willing to send their goods and men only to build a Summer Palace for you? And could you find pleasure in a place where the walls are filled with bones of men? I think even you are not so hard."

The cords between the man and woman drew taut. She longed to hear his footsteps coming toward her, to see his hand put out to touch her own.

He did not move. He said, his voice still grave, "You should have told your son, the emperor, that it ill behooves him to give you a gift of palaces while the nation is beset with threats of war, with poverty and with floods."

She turned her head at this, and the tears shone in her tragic eyes. "Oh, this realm," she cried, "there is always misery!"

"What ails you?" he asked. "What more do you desire? You have made an emperor; you have given him a consort. He loves her, and she will give him an heir."

She lifted her head, her eyes startled. "Already?"

"Doubtless it will be so, for I know their mutual love." His eyes met hers, his own compassionate. "I saw them a few days ago, by accident. I saw them in the twilight, walking like two children, their arms about each other."

Her chin quivered and her tears welled up again. At the sight of her face, he could not restrain himself. He came closer to her than he had been in many years. "My heart," he said in a low voice, "they have what you and I can never have. Help them to keep it. Pour all your strength into this new reign, for it is based on love."

But she could bear no more and wept aloud. "Oh, go," she sobbed. "Leave me—leave me alone as I have always been!"

He took a step backward. When she saw him leaving her without comfort, her anger was so hot that her tears dried. "I suppose—I suppose—that you do not love anyone now except your own children! How many children have you with—with—"

He folded his arms. "Majesty, I have three," he said.

"Sons?" she demanded.

"I have no true sons," he said.

For a long moment their eyes met in mutual pain and longing. Then he went away, and she was left alone.

BEFORE THE END of the sixth month in the year 1873, the emperor T'ung Chih had received the envoys of the west in the Pavilion of Purple Light. Upon a raised dais the emperor sat cross-legged behind a low table. He gazed at the strange white faces of the tall men. Each walked forward from his place in line, bowed to the emperor and gave to Prince Kung a script of greeting to read aloud.

The emperor replied to each in the same fashion. Prince Kung mounted the dais and then fell on his knees and bent his head to the floor, careful before these foreigners to follow every law of conduct. He took from his imperial nephew the script already prepared, and gave it to each foreign envoy in turn. Then the envoys placed their credentials on a waiting table and, walking backward, withdrew from the imperial presence, pleased, doubtless, to think that they had won their way.

All this the empress mother heard from Li Lien-ying, and her heart hardened in her bosom. How dared her son defy her except that he was strengthened by Alute? She thought of the two of them as Jung Lu had seen them, their arms about each other, and her heart was stabbed again. A frightful thought crossed her brooding brain. If Alute bore a son, then Alute would be the empress mother! "Oh, stupid I," she muttered. "What shall I be then except an old woman in the palace?"

She must destroy the love that Jung Lu had bid her save. But how? She remembered suddenly the four concubines she had chosen for the emperor. They lived together in the Palace of Accumulated Elegance, waiting to be summoned. One of these concubines, the empress mother now remembered, was very beautiful. This girl could entice the emperor back to his old haunts outside his palace walls. Alute, too serious, too strong in conscience, would lose him.

As the empress mother so plotted she knew that she did evil, yet determined that she would do it. Was she not solitary in the whole world? Now while she was still beautiful, still strong, she must gain even the throne, if need be, to save herself from living death.

Her memory crept back through the years. She saw herself again as a small girl child, always working beyond her strength in her uncle Muyanga's great household, where she was no better than a bondmaid. Not even Jung Lu had been able to lighten her daily burdens. Had she married him, he would have stayed a guardsman, and in his house she would have worked again in the kitchen and courtyard, bearing children and quarreling with servants and slaves. How much more had she benefited even her lover by being his sovereign instead of his wife! Yet he used his power only to reproach her.

And her son, who ought always to love her, loved his wife better. For his sake she had spent weary hours with that childish emperor, and for what reason except to gain the throne for him, her son? She remembered the pallid yellow face and the hot sick hands always fumbling at her body and her gorge rose again.

Such thoughts forced a dark lonely strength into her mind. Her whole being rose up to battle against her present fate. So wounded was she that she forgot all love and set her will to cleave her way again to power.

AT HER COMMAND, the young concubines came fluttering into her palace as birds released from their cage. They had given up hope of being summoned before the emperor and now their hope was bright again. The empress mother looked from one face to the other, and she had not the heart to wound any of them. "How can I choose which is the pretty one?" she inquired. "You must choose among yourselves."

They laughed, four gay young voices joining together. "Our venerable ancestor," one cried, "how can you pretend that you do not know? Jasmine is the pretty one."

The empress mother studied the rosy face. There was boldness in the full curved lips and the large eyes. Instead of Alute's slender graceful body, Jasmine was small and plump, and her greatest beauty was a creamy skin without blemish.

The empress mother's mood changed suddenly. She waved the concubines away. "I will send for you when the day comes," she said half carelessly.

It only remained for the chief eunuch to inquire of Alute's woman what few days in the month the consort could not enter the royal bedchamber. These were seven days distant, and the empress mother sent word to Jasmine to be ready on the eighth day. Her robe, she commanded, must be peach-pink, and she was to use no perfume.

On the day that Jasmine came in, the empress mother observed her carefully. First she commanded the cheap jewels she wore to be taken away. "Bring me the case from my jewel room marked thirty-two," she said to her ladies. She lifted from the box two flowers shaped like peonies, made of rubies and pearls, and these she gave to Jasmine to fasten above her ears. The girl was beside herself with delight.

The empress mother now bade Jasmine rub a heavy musk perfume on her palms and under her chin, behind her ears and between her breasts and loins.

"Well enough," the empress mother said when all was done. "Since I know my son is alone today, I will invite him here for a feast of his favorite dishes. The day is fair. Let the tables be set under the trees in the courtyard, and let the court musicians attend us, and after we have dined, the court actors must give us a play. And you, Jasmine," she said, "you are to stand near me and tend my tea bowl, and be silent unless I bid you speak."

"Yes, Venerable Ancestor," the girl said.

In an hour or two the emperor entered wearing a robe of sky-blue satin embroidered with gold dragons.

"I heard you were alone today, my son," the empress mother said, "and to guard against your melancholy, I thought to keep you here for a while." She said this in a sweet and loving voice, her great eyes warm upon him.

The emperor smiled and was astonished, for of late his imperial mother had not been kind. "Thank you, my mother," he said. "It is true that I was casting about in my mind to know how to spend the day."

The empress mother spoke to Jasmine. "Pour tea, my child, for your lord."

The emperor lifted his head at these words and stared at Jasmine while with pretty grace she took the bowl of tea from a eunuch and presented it with both hands. "Who is this lady?" he inquired as though she were not there.

"What!" the empress mother cried in feigned surprise. "Do you not recognize your own concubine? She is one of the four I chose for you."

In some confusion the emperor shook his head. "I have not summoned them. The time has not yet come—"

The empress mother pursed her lips. "In courtesy you should have summoned them each at least once," she said.

The emperor lifted his bowl and drank, and Jasmine knelt and took the bowl again. He looked down for an instant into her face, so gay and vivid, so childlike in its hues of cream and rose that he could not look away.

Thus began the day. The empress mother summoned Jasmine again and again to wait upon the emperor, to fan him, to serve him when they dined at noon, to fetch him tea while the play went on. At last the emperor smiled openly at Jasmine, and she smiled at him as a child smiles at a playmate.

The empress mother was well pleased, and when the day was done, she said to the emperor, "Before you leave me, my son, I have a wish to tell you."

"Say on, Mother," he replied.

"For many months I have not stirred from these walls. Now why should we not go together, you and I, and worship at the tombs of our ancestors? It would not be fitting for you to take the consort with you upon so mournful a journey."

The emperor considered. "When shall we go?" he asked.

"A month from this very day," the empress mother said. "You will be alone then as now. The consort will welcome you the more when you return."

Again the emperor wondered why his imperial mother was so changed. Yet who could ever know her reasons? "We will go," he said. "It is indeed my duty to worship at the tombs."

"Who can say otherwise?" the empress mother replied.

She had already set her mind to take Jasmine as though to serve her, and it all came about as she had planned. On a certain night, in the shadow of the ancestral tombs, the emperor lay wakeful and lonely under the leather roof of his tent. He listened to the rain and fell into a fit of longing for his young wife. He had not made one sign throughout the solemn day that he saw Jasmine. But he had seen her as she moved about his mother's tent, where he had taken his night meal after the ceremonial fast. Now he could not put her image away.

To his eunuch he said, "I am chilled to my marrow. I never felt so cold as this before, a coldness strange as death."

The emperor's eunuchs had been well bribed by Li Lien-ying and this one said at once, "Sire, why do you not send for the first concubine? She will warm your bed and quickly drive the chill from your blood."

"Well—well," the emperor agreed.

He lay shivering while the eunuch ran through the wet darkness. And in a little while he saw the flash of lanterns and there in the tent door Jasmine stood, wrapped in a sheet of oiled silk against the rain. But rain glistened on her cheeks and hung on the lashes of her eyes. Her lips were red and her cheeks as red.

"I sent for you because I am cold," the emperor muttered.

"Here am I, my lord," she said. She put aside the oiled silk and then her garments one by one and she came into his bed, and her body was warm against his chilled flesh.

In her own tent the empress mother lay awake in the darkness. She needed now to do no more. Jasmine and Alute would carry on the war of love, and knowing her own son, she knew that Jasmine was already the victor.

THE SUMMER passed. The empress mother sighed and said that she was growing old and that when the Summer Palace was built, she would retire there for her last years. She said her bones ached, and there were mornings when she would not rise from bed. Her ladies did not know what to make of such pretended illness, for the empress mother seemed instead to be renewed in youth and beauty. Yet when Prince Kung came urging an audience, she refused him. Instead, she summoned her chief eunuch and demanded of him, "What does that prince want of me now?"

The chief eunuch grinned. He knew well that her illness was a pretense for some purpose that even he did not yet know. "Majesty," he said, "Prince Kung is much disturbed at the present behavior of the emperor."

"And why?" she asked, though she knew well enough.

"Majesty," the chief eunuch said, "all say the emperor has changed. He spends his days in gaming, and far into the night he roams the city streets dressed as a common man, and with him are but two eunuchs and the first concubine."

At this the empress mother made great show of horror. "The first concubine? It cannot be!" She raised herself on her pillows and then fell back and closed her eyes and moaned. "Oh, I am ill—very ill! Tell the prince I am likely to die because of this evil news. My son is emperor now and only princes can advise him. He does not hear me."

As for Prince Kung, he took her words as command, and he did so attack the emperor face to face that he roused a fury in his imperial nephew, and the emperor sent forth a decree declaring that Prince Kung and his son were stripped of all their ranks, degraded thus because Prince Kung had used unbecoming language before the Dragon Throne.

The next day the empress mother sent out another edict above her own name and Sakota's as her coregent, commanding all ranks and honors to be restored again to Prince Kung and his son. This she did without Sakota's knowledge, knowing that her cousin would not dare to speak a word in protest. No one dared to dispute this edict, and by its firmness she restored herself very much to power with this seeming favor to Prince Kung, who was much respected by all.

As for the emperor, before he could decide what next to do he fell ill of black smallpox, caught somewhere in the city. After many days of restless fever, he lay near death as the year 1874 drew to a close. The empress mother went often to his bedside, for long ago she had caught the smallpox and it left her immune, without one scar upon her faultless skin. She was wrung with a strange twisted sorrow. She longed to grieve with her whole heart, as mothers should, but she could not be only a mother even now. Her destiny was still her burden.

In a few days, however, the emperor improved, and his skin grew cool. He sent for the consort. Alute went to him with all speed, for indeed her heart had been desolate these many weeks apart from him, and her nights had been sleepless. When she entered the royal bedchamber, she was pale and thin, her delicate beauty gone for the moment. She entered all impatience, thinking to embrace her love, but there by her lord's bed sat the empress mother.

"Alas," Alute murmured, her hands fluttering to her heart.

"And why alas?" the empress mother answered sharply. "I do not see why you say alas when he is so much better. It is you who are alas, for you are as pale and yellow as an old woman."

"Mother," the emperor pleaded weakly, "I beg you to spare her—"

But Alute could not stop the rush of her own anger. "Do not spare me," she said, standing straight and slender in the doorway. "I ask no favor of the empress mother. Let her anger fall on me instead of you, my lord, since fall it must, for we cannot please her."

The empress mother rose to her feet and sped toward the luckless girl with both her hands upraised. She slapped Alute's cheeks again and again until her jeweled nail protectors brought blood.

The emperor wept aloud from weakness and despair. "Oh, let me die, you two," he sobbed. "Why should I live when I am caught between you like a mouse between two millstones?"

And he turned his face to the wall and could not stop his sobbing. Both women flew to his side, and the empress mother sent for the court physicians. The emperor sobbed on and on until he lost his reason and in extreme weakness his pulse faded and ceased to beat. Then the chief physician made his obeisance to the empress mother, waiting by the bedside in her carved chair.

"Majesty," he said sadly, "I fear no human skill can now avail. Evil has seized the destiny of the Son of Heaven, and it is not given to us to know the means to prevent his departure."

So on January 12, 1875, ended the brief life of the emperor T'ung Chih. When his breath ceased and his flesh grew cold, the empress sent everyone away. Even Alute she sent away. "Go," she told the young widow. "Leave me with my son." Her gaze was not cruel but desolate and cold, as though the sorrow of the mother was far beyond the sorrow of the wife.

What could Alute then do except obey? Her dead lord's mother was now her sovereign.

And when all were gone, the empress sat beside her son. She looked down on the face of her son, a young man's handsome face, proud in death, and calm. And while she looked she saw a little boy, the child she had adored. The tears welled up as hot as flame and she sobbed and took his dead hand and laid it against her cheek. Strange words came welling up. "Oh, child," she sobbed, "would that I had given you the little toy train—the foreign train you longed for and you never had!" She wept on and on, forgetting all she was, except a mother whose only child was dead.

Deep in the night, the door opened and a man came in. She did not hear the footsteps, but she felt her shoulders seized and she was lifted strongly to her feet. She turned her head and saw his face. "You—" she whispered.

"I," Jung Lu said. "I have waited outside the door these past three hours. Why do you delay? The clans are all astir to put an heir upon the throne by dawn, before the people know the emperor is dead. You must act first."

Within the instant she subdued her heart and made her mind clear to remember a plan she had long ago prepared for such an hour as this. "My sister's eldest son is three years old," she said. "He is the heir I choose. His father is the seventh brother of my own dead lord."

He met her eyes. They were deadly black against her pale face, but fearless. "Tonight you have a fearful beauty." His voice was strange and wondering. "You grow more beautiful in danger. Some magic in you—"

He shook his head, then gently took her hand. Side by side

these two looked down upon the great bed whereon the dead emperor lay. Through his hand she felt him quivering, his body trembling against his will.

"Oh, love," she whispered, "he is our—"

"Hush," he said. "We may not speak a word of what is past. The palace walls have ears—" After one long silent moment they unclasped their hands, he stepped back and made his obeisance. She was again the empress and he her subject.

"Majesty," he said, "go at once and fetch the child. Meanwhile, I have summoned General Li Hung-chang. His armies are already near the city gates. By sunrise you will have the child here in the palace and your loyal soldiers will crowd the streets. Who will then dare dispute your rule?"

Strong heart met strong heart. These two, in an accord made perfect by their hidden love, parted once more upon their common purpose.

IN HIS STRANGE nursery the new little emperor Kuang Hsü wailed his fright. Not even his mother could quiet him. For each time he lifted his head from her breast he saw the carved and gilded dragons crawling on the high beams above his head and he cried in fresh terror. When two days had past, his mother sent a eunuch to the empress to say the child had wept until he was ill.

"Let him weep," the empress replied. "Let him learn early that he will have nothing that he wants by weeping, though he be the emperor."

Without lifting her head she worked on her plans for the Summer Palace until the white light of the snowy day came to an end. The she beckoned to a waiting eunuch. "Fetch me the consort," she said. "And bid her come alone."

Within minutes Alute came and made her obeisance. The empress bade the young widow rise from her knees and sit on a carved stool nearby. There she stared awhile at the young figure, drooping in mourning robes of white sackcloth.

"There is nothing left in life for you," the empress said.

"Nothing, Venerable Ancestor," Alute said.

"Nor will there ever be," the empress continued, "and so were I you, I would follow my lord to where he is."

At this Alute lifted her bowed head and gazed at the stern, beautiful woman who sat so calmly on her thronelike chair.

"I pray you give me leave to die," she whispered.

"You have my leave," the empress said.

One more long look passed between them, and then Alute rose and walked toward the door, a sad young ghost.

That night at midnight the chief eunuch coughed at her door. He said, "Alute is no more."

"How did she die?" the empress asked.

"She swallowed opium," he said.

Their eyes met in a long and secret look.

"I am glad there was no pain," the empress said.

IV

THE EMPRESS

IT WAS THE DUTY of the court chief gardener to report to the empress the exact day upon which the wisteria vines would blossom. The empress then decreed that upon this day she would not appear in the Audience Hall. Instead, she would spend the day in the wisteria gardens with her ladies, and with due courtesy she also invited her cousin the empress dowager, since she and Sakota were coregents again.

"Amuse yourselves," she said to her ladies. "Walk where you will. Only do not mention sorrows."

They obeyed her but cautiously, careful that always some remained near her. But the empress did not seem to see them. Her eyes were always upon the little emperor, her nephew, who played with his toys on a terrace nearby, watched by two young eunuchs. Suddenly she beckoned to the child. "Come here, my son," she said.

The boy stared at her and then came slowly toward her,

and the toy he held in his hand dropped to the tiled path.

"Pick it up," she said. "Bring it to me that I may see what you have." She waited until the child took up the toy and came toward her. He knelt before her while he held up the toy for her to see.

"What is it?" she inquired.

"An engine," he replied, his voice so small that she could scarcely hear him. She looked at the child thoughtfully. "What else have you?" she asked.

"More trains," the child said eagerly. "And I have a great army of soldiers." He forgot to be afraid of her and even came close enough to lean upon her knees. She felt a strange pain where his arm rested and in her heart a yearning for something lost.

"Have you Chinese soldiers?" she asked.

"No Chinese soldiers," he said, "but English and French, German and Russian and American."

"All, all have white faces," she said in a strange voice. She pushed him away, and he stepped back, the light gone from his eyes. At this moment Sakota, the empress dowager, came in with four of her own ladies, her figure stooping under her heavy headdress.

The little emperor ran to meet her. "M-ma!" he cried. "I thought you were never coming!" While the empress watched he clung to Sakota's robe, walking beside her as she walked.

"Come and sit near me, Sister," the empress said. She pointed to a carved chair near her own.

Still the little emperor stood clinging to Sakota. She smoothed the thin childish hand she held. "This little Son of Heaven," Sakota murmured, "he does not eat enough."

"He eats the wrong foods," the empress said.

It was an old quarrel between the two of them. The empress commanded for the little emperor simple foods, vegetables cooked slightly, lean meats, few sweets. Yet she knew very well that when her back was turned, he ran to Sakota to be fed sweetened dough balls and rich dumplings. When he had pains in his belly, she knew that Sakota gave him whiffs of opium from her own pipe. Yet Sakota, foolish woman, believed that it was only she who truly loved the little emperor!

She sighed. Relentless even with herself, she perceived that she was jealous for the child's love, a strange old jealousy reaching into the past, when her dead son had been a child and had escaped her by loving Sakota. Yet it was I who loved him, she thought. Had he lived longer, he might have known.

She rose restlessly, never able to bear the thought of her son dead and in his tomb, and wandered out again into the wisteria gardens.

THE CHILD EMPEROR Kuang Hsü was in his ninth year, tall and slender as a new bamboo. His will was strong and he made no secret that he loved Sakota better than the empress. The rising strife between the aging empress and the young emperor divided the whole court, and in this division the weak and timid Sakota began to have faint dreams of power.

On that sacred day when the court made their obeisances at the Tombs of the Eight Emperors, Sakota set her will to be the first to offer a sacrifice before the dead emperor Hsien Fêng and thus take her rightful place as his consort.

Now the empress had come here fully prepared in mind and spirit. She had fasted the day before, and after meditating through the night, had risen at dawn to be escorted by Jung Lu and her princes and ministers to the tombs.

In such a grave mood, she was shocked to find that foolish one, Sakota, at the tombs before her! Indeed, Sakota stood ready before the marble altar and in the central place, and when the empress descended from her palanquin, she smiled a small, evil smile and motioned to her to stand at her right.

The empress gave one haughty stare and walked without a hint of haste into the pavilion nearby. There she seated herself and beckoned Jung Lu to her side. "I do not deign to question anyone," she said when he knelt before her. "I do but command you to bear this message to my coregent. If she does not yield her place at once, I will command the imperial guard to lift her from her feet and put her into prison."

Jung Lu bowed to the floor. Then, his handsome aging face cold and proud, he rose and bore the message to Sakota. He soon returned to make his obeisance before the empress and say, "The coregent replies that she is rightfully in her place, you being only the senior concubine."

The empress lifted up her head and said calmly, "Go back again to the coregent. If she does not yield, then command the imperial guardsmen to seize her. Henceforth I shall be merciful no more to anyone."

Jung Lu stood up and summoned the guardsmen, who had their spears lifted and glittering in their right hands. Then he approached Sakota again. In a few minutes he returned to announce that she had yielded. "Most High," he said, "your place waits. The coregent has moved to the right."

The life in the palace closed above this quarrel. Yet everyone knew that there could be no peace between these two ladies. The end was certain, but whether it would have come as it did had Jung Lu not committed a madness, who knows? For in the autumn of that same year a rumor crept up that Jung Lu was yielding to the love advances of a young concubine of the dead emperor T'ung Chih. When the empress first heard this report from her eunuch, she would not believe it. "What— my kinsman?" she exclaimed. "I would as soon say that I myself could play the fool!"

"Venerable," Li Lien-ying muttered, "I swear it is true. This imperial concubine is fair and he is at the age when a man likes his women as young as his own daughters. Remember, too, that he never did love the lady you gave to him, Majesty."

The eunuch brought her proof a few moons later, a letter of assignation from the young concubine to Jung Lu. "Come to me at one hour after midnight. The watchman is bribed, my woman will lead you to me. I am a flower awaiting rain."

The empress read and folded the letter again and put it

in her sleeve. Why delay, she asked herself, when proof was in her hands? "Bring me here the grand councillor Jung Lu," she commanded the eunuch. "And when he comes, then close the doors and draw the curtains and forbid entrance to everyone."

Li went in great haste. In less time than she needed to subdue her rage Jung Lu came in. He prepared to kneel but the empress forbade it. "Sit down, Prince," she said in her most silvery voice. "This is no formal summons. I speak to you in private to inquire of this letter placed in my hand an hour ago by my palace spies."

He would not sit but stood before her while she plucked the letter from her sleeve. "Do you know what this is?" she asked.

"I see what it is," he said, and his face did not change.

She let the letter flutter to the floor. "You feel no disloyalty to me?" she asked.

"No, for I am not disloyal," he replied. And then he said, "What you ask of me, I give. What you do not ask or need remains my own."

These words so confounded the empress that she could not answer. Jung Lu waited, and then he bowed and went away. She sat immobile while she pondered what he had said.

The next day, she sat on the Dragon Throne before sunrise, and announced by imperial edict that the grand councillor Jung Lu was from this moment relieved of all his posts and was now in retirement from the imperial court. No charge was made against him, nor needed to be made. Her ministers and princes heard their fellow thus condemned and their looks were grave, for if one so high could fall so low, then no one was safe. The empress saw their looks and made no sign. In loneliness she reigned and fear must be her weapon.

Yet fear was still not enough. One cool spring day in the next year, Prince Kung petitioned to be heard privately, a favor for which he had not asked in a long time. He made his usual brief obeisance and presented himself thus: "Majesty, I have not come to you on my own behalf, for I am rewarded enough by your past generosity. It is your greatness that

I invoke now on behalf of the empress, your coregent."

"Is she ill?" the empress asked with mild interest.

"Majesty, I do not know whether it has come to your ears that the eunuch Li Lien-ying has grown arrogant beyond all bearing. He even calls himself Lord of Nine Thousand Years. Majesty, you know that such a title means the eunuch Li Lien-ying holds himself second only to the emperor, who alone is Lord of Ten Thousand Years."

The empress smiled her cool smile. "Am I to be blamed for what the lesser folk of the palaces call him?"

Prince Kung's mouth was grim. "Majesty," he said, "if it were the lesser folk who were rebelling, I would not stand here before the Dragon Throne. But the one with whom this eunuch is most arrogant is the coregent herself."

"Indeed," the empress observed. "And why does she not complain to me herself? Am I not generous to her in all ways? Have I ever failed in my duty to her? I think not!" Upon this she dismissed the prince with her right hand uplifted, and he could only go, aware of her displeasure.

For the empress, nevertheless, the day was spoiled. She sent messengers to the Eastern Palace to announce her coming. She found Sakota lying in her bed beneath a quilt of amber satin. "I would rise, Sister," she said in her high complaining voice, "except that today I have such pains in my joints that I dare not move."

The empress sat down in a great chair that had been placed for her, and she sent away her ladies so that she could be alone with Sakota. Then she spoke bluntly, as she used to do when they were children. "Sakota," she said, "I will not accept complaints made to others. If you are not pleased, then tell me yourself what you would have. I will yield you what I can, but you are not to destroy my palace from within."

Sakota raised herself on her elbow. "You forget that I am above you, Orchid, and by every right and law. You are the usurper and there are those who tell me so. I have my friends and followers, though you think I have not!"

Had a kitten sprung into a tigress, the empress could not have been more surprised. She rose from her chair and ran and seized Sakota by the ears and shook her. "Why, you—you weak worm!" she cried. "You ungrateful, worthless fool—"

But Sakota, thus goaded, bit the empress on the fleshy part of her hand and her teeth clung there until the empress was compelled to loose her jaws by force.

"I am not sorry," Sakota babbled. "Now you know I am not helpless."

The empress answered not a word. She drew out her silk kerchief and wrapped it about her bloody hand. Then she turned and walked in her most stately fashion from the room.

In the dead of that night, her aching hand against her bosom, the empress struck the silver gong that summoned Li Lien-ying, who was always somewhere near her.

"Majesty, your hand pains you," he said.

"Yes," she said. "That female's teeth hold the poison of a viper."

She let him take the silk handkerchief away. Then he soaked the hardened blood in a basin of water, washed her hand clean and tenderly dried it on a towel.

"Can you bear more pain, Majesty?" he asked.

"Have you need to ask?" she answered.

With that he took a coal from the brazier and pressed it into her wound to cleanse it. Then he found a white silk kerchief to bind her hand again. "A little opium tonight, Majesty," he said, "and by tomorrow the pain will be gone."

"Yes," she said. He stood waiting then, while she seemed to muse. At last she spoke. "When there is a noxious weed within a garden, what is there to do but pluck it out by the root?"

"Indeed, what else?" he agreed.

"Alas," she said, "I can but depend on one who is most loyal."

"That am I, your servant," he said.

They exchanged one look, a long look, and he bowed and went away.

ON THE TENTH day of this same month Sakota fell ill of a strange and sudden illness, which could not be cured by the court physicians. An hour before her death, convulsed by inner agonies and certain of her fate, she roused herself and asked for a scribe. To him she spoke this edict: "Yesterday I was stricken with an unknown illness, and now it appears that I must depart this world. I do but ask that the twenty-seven months of usual mourning be reduced to twenty-seven days, in order that the thrift and sobriety in which I have lived may also mark my end. I have not desired vain display in all my life, nor do I wish it for my funeral."

This edict was sent forth by Prince Kung in the name of the dead. The empress said nothing, though she knew that such last words reproached her for her own extravagance. Nevertheless she kept the added bitterness within her heart and when, in yet another year, the French destroyed a fleet of Chinese junks she had sent to protect the province of Tonkin, she took the chance to blame Prince Kung. "We recognize his past merits," she wrote, "and therefore we will allow this prince to retain his hereditary princedom, but he is hereby deprived of all his offices and also of his double salary."

In his place the empress put Prince Ch'un, the husband of her sister and the father of the little emperor. Prince Ch'un's present appointment, she wrote, was only temporary. "We desire that in the future our ministers pay more respect to the motives behind their sovereign's actions and abstain from troubling us with their querulous complaints." When her ministers and princes received this edict, they were speechless. In such silence the empress ruled for seven years as a tyrant absolute.

THEY WERE GOOD years. Surrounded by the silence of her princes and her ministers, the empress gave few audiences. Heaven approved her reign, for in all these years there was neither flood nor drought and harvests were plenteous. Her foreign foes remained; but they did not come out for battle.

In such tranquility the empress could devote herself to the building of the new Summer Palace. She let her wish be known and the people sent gifts of gold and silver, the provinces doubled their tribute. She gave thanks to her subjects and declared that the Summer Palace would be her retreat when she had given the throne to its rightful heir, Kuang Hsü, the young emperor. This she would do, she promised, as soon as he had completed his seventeenth year.

For the new Summer Palace she chose to return to the site chosen by the emperor Ch'ien-lung, thus not only fulfilling her own dream but rebuilding those dreams of the imperial ancestors. With matchless taste she included in her plans the Temple of Ten Thousand Buddhas, which Ch'ien-lung had made and the foreigners had not destroyed. But the other ruins she would not rebuild or have removed. Let them stand, she said, to lead the minds of men to ponder on the end of life.

Near the southeastern region of the lake, she caused to be built her own palaces, where she and the emperor could live apart and yet not too far. There, too, she placed a vast theater, and near the marble gates, roofed with blue tiles, she set the Audience Hall, stately and very large, with wide marble steps leading to the lake. Along the lake she built a marble-pillared corridor, a mile long, and here she walked, to gaze upon a peony mountain, crab apple trees, oleanders and pomegranates.

Lulled by beauty, she let the years slip by, until one day her eunuch begged her to remember that the young emperor was now near the end of his seventeenth year. She perceived at once that Li Lien-ying was right and she must no longer delay the marriage of the heir. She would choose a woman always loyal to herself as empress.

"Name me some maidens you know who will not love my nephew as Alute loved my son. I will not be disturbed by love or hate," she said to Li Lien-ying.

"Majesty," he said after thinking awhile, "why not that good plain maiden, the daughter of your brother, the duke Kwei Hsiang?"

The empress clapped her hands softly in approval. "Why did I not think of her?" she replied. "She is the best among my younger ladies, silent, modest and always devoted to me. I will name her. Prepare the decree."

Thus directed, Li Lien-ying rose with great heaves and sighs, and he mumbled that his old Buddha must not disturb herself, for he would arrange everything.

"You!" she scolded. "You dare to call me Old Buddha!"

"Majesty," he said, "it is what the people call you everywhere since you prayed down the rains last summer."

It was gross flattery and she knew it was. Old Buddha! It was the highest name the people could bestow upon a ruler, for it meant they beheld in the ruler a god. By now, nearing the age of fifty-five, she was a being apart from men and women and beyond them all, as Buddha was. "Get away with you," she said, laughing. "What will you be saying next, you monstrous fat fellow!"

The wedding day drew near, an ill-omened day. The night before a mighty north wind tore away the matting roofs the eunuchs had built to cover the wedding courtyard. The dawn opened gray and dark, and the rain fell early. The red wedding candles would not light, and the sweetmeats were soft with the dampness. When the bride took her place beside the bridegroom, he turned his head away to show his dislike, and the empress, seeing him thus offend the one she had chosen, could not hide her rage. There he sat, a tall, pale reedy boy, his face not yet bearded, his hands too delicate and always trembling, and yet he was stubborn! His weakness was a rebuke to her, his stubborn will an enemy. Thus she raged in secret while tears ran down the young bride's sallow cheeks.

When the wedding day was ended, the empress returned to her Summer Palace. From there she later declared by edict that once more she had retired from the regency and that the emperor now sat alone upon the Dragon Throne. She moved all her treasures to the Summer Palace, with the intent to live and die there. Her princes and ministers besought her to keep

329

one hand at least on the reins, for the emperor, they declared, was headstrong and weak-willed, a dangerous combination.

She laughed at them. "It is your business now, my lords and princes," she declared.

"But may we come to you if our young emperor will not heed us?" they inquired. "Remember, Majesty, that he fears only you."

"I am not in another country," she said. "I am but nine miles away. I shall not let the emperor take away your heads, I daresay, so long as I know you are loyal to me."

She let the years glide by once more, though keeping secret hold upon her power through spies in every palace. Thus she learned that the young emperor and his plain consort quarreled, and that he turned to his two concubines, the Pearl and the Lustrous.

"They will debauch him," she said indifferently to her eunuch. "I have no hope of him or any man." She seemed not to care.

Yet she could be as sharp in her command as any ruler. When the princes of her own clan desired by memorial to raise the title of Prince Ch'un to father of the emperor, she would not allow it. No, the imperial line was still to be through her; she was the imperial ancestor.

THE YEARS DREW on to that most honorable dawn when the empress would celebrate her sixtieth birthday. With matchless vigor she had now completed the Summer Palace. Under her command, which even the young emperor dared not refuse, she had taken funds from all the government boards, and at the very last she had the final whim to build a vast white marble boat to stand in the midst of the lake, connected by a marble bridge to the land. But where was the money to come from for this?

This time the emperor dared to send his doubt back to her, couched in the most delicate words. She flew into one of her mighty rages and tore the sheets of silken paper and threw them into the air. "My idle nephew knows where the money is," she shouted.

In such moods only Li Lien-ying could calm her. "Say where the money is, Majesty," he said. "Say where it is, and you shall have it."

"Why, you big bag of wind," she cried. "There is all that unspent money in the treasury of the navy."

It was true that millions of dollars in silver bullion lay in the navy treasury, but there was a reason for it. In those years the men from the islands of Japan also threatened the Chinese shores, and they had learned how to make Western steamships of iron, upon whose decks they mounted cannons as the white men did. In much alarm worthy Chinese citizens had gathered funds together and given them to their ruler, saying that it was for the building of a new and modern navy.

"And why do we need fear those dwarfs?" the empress had said with rich contempt. "They can do no more than harass our shores, for our people will never let them march inland. It is folly to spend good gold on foreign ships."

So persistent was she that at last the emperor did yield, and so she had her marble boat. On this boat she now planned to hold the ceremonies of her sixtieth birthday. There would be thirty days of feasting, a holiday for the whole nation, and many prizes and honors to be awarded to her loyal subjects. To pay for such a vast celebration, officials were invited to give the empress one fourth of their annual salaries.

In her heart the empress planned a private pleasure for herself. In these years while Jung Lu had been banished, she had not seen his face. She was past the age of lovers and she and Jung Lu could be friends again, kinsman and kinswoman. It was sweet to think that she would see his face, that they could sit down together. She sent him a letter.

"I do not say this is a decree," she wrote with firm strokes. "Let it be a greeting and an invitation, a hope that we may meet again with quiet hearts and wise minds. Come, then, before the ceremonies for my sixtieth birthday."

The afternoon of the day she set was fair, the season late autumn, a warm day without wind. The sun shone upon the thousands of chrysanthemums in late bloom. In her library the empress sat at ease, in robes of yellow satin embroidered with blue phoenixes.

At the third hour in the afternoon she heard the tread of footsteps. Her ladies opened the doors wide and she looked down the corridor to see the tall figure of Jung Lu. To her dismay her old heart sprang to life again. Still the most handsome of all men! But he was grave, she saw that, and he had put on somber garments. In his hands a prince's scepter proclaimed a wall between them. When he stood before her, their eyes met, and then he made an effort to kneel in his usual obeisance. But she put out her hand to prevent him and motioned to two chairs nearby. "Put down your scepter," she said imperiously.

He put it down upon the small table between them and waited for her to speak again.

"How have you been?" she asked, and she looked at him sweetly, her eyes grown soft and tender.

"Majesty," he began.

"Do not call me Majesty," she said.

He bowed his head and began once more. "It is for me to ask how you are," he said. "But I see with my own eyes. You have not changed. Your face is the face I have carried all these years inside my heart."

She sighed and felt a gentle happiness pervade her.

"Why do you sigh?" he asked.

"I thought I had much to tell you," she replied. "But now, face to face as we are, I feel you know all of me."

"And you know all there is of me to know," he said. "I have not changed—not since the first day we knew what we were, I to you, and you to me."

She made no answer. Enough, enough was said. The years in the listening palace walls had set the habit of silence upon their lips, and they sat quietly for a space and felt renewed by such communion. When she spoke to put a question, her voice was humble. "Have you advice to give me? These many years I have listened to no prince's counsel, lacking yours."

He shook his head. "You have done well."

Yet she discerned something held back, words he would not say. "Come," she said, "you and I—have we not always spoken truthfully? What have I done that you do not approve?"

"I trust your own sense of wisdom," he replied unwillingly. "If, perchance, our forces are defeated by the Japanese enemy entrenched now in the weak state of Korea, it may be that you will not wish to allow rejoicing for yourself."

She sat motionless and thoughtful. Then slowly she rose and walked to her throne again. And he rose, too, and came toward her and knelt in obeisance. She said, "Sometimes I foresee such trouble ahead that I do not know where to turn for help. Once my birthday is past, I ought to summon soothsayers and know the evil, however monstrous."

He said in his strong deep voice, "Better than soothsayers, Majesty, is to be prepared."

"Then take command of my forces here in the capital," she urged. "Protect me as you used to. I do not forget the night you came to my tent when we were in the wild mountains near Jehol. Your sword saved my life that night—and my son's."

Bitter longing clutched her heart to speak aloud the words she thought: It was our son you saved. But he was dead, that son, and buried, as was the emperor before him.

"I accept the charge," Jung Lu said, rising.

ALAS THAT her birthday was never to be celebrated! Suddenly the enemy from Japan destroyed a fleet of Chinese junks and attacked Korea, which was under the suzerainty of the Dragon Throne. The Koreans sent out loud cries for help; unless they were aided they could no longer be a nation.

The empress, receiving messages of disaster by hourly couriers, was distracted into rage. She knew her own guilt—that she had spent the money from the treasury of the navy on the

Summer Palace—but she would not allow the knowledge to influence her before the eyes of others. The throne must be maintained inviolable, supreme. She prepared herself therefore for a mighty rage against her enemies, and in the ferment of her mind she chose the one to blame—the general whom she had most trusted, Li Hung-chang. She commanded all the doors to be left open so that listening ears could hear the tumult of her wrath and spread the news throughout the city and the nation.

"You!" she cried at the stout, tall general in obeisance before her. "You dare to lose our boats, even that good chartered troopship, the *Kowshing*! It lies at the bottom of the sea. See what your stupidity has done for our realm!"

The general knew better than to utter a word. He remained kneeling, his splendid robes spread out upon the floor. So she began again. "During these ten years France has seized Annam and attacked Taiwan. At the same time we have been distressed by the war in Korea with Japan. And how is it that all these foreign peoples dare to threaten us? It is because our armies and navies are weak, and whose fault is this weakness but yours? You shall stay by your post, traitor, for what you have not done you must now do. Like a slave you may not rest. Peace we must have, with whatever honor you can save for the Dragon Throne."

She ordered him to leave her and he rose and walked backward from her presence. On his full square face she saw a look of patience that struck her to the heart. For this man had saved her more than once and he had been obedient to her command, and she knew that he was still loyal. Someday she would be lenient toward him again, but not today.

One day in late afternoon as she sat playing games with her ladies on the great marble boat she saw Li Lien-ying come near. "Majesty, your tea is cold," the eunuch said. He took her bowl and whispered that he had news. She seemed not to hear and played her game out. Then she rose, and with a look she summoned him to follow her. When they were alone in her own palace, her ladies standing at a distance, she turned to him.

"Majesty," he said, "there is a plot." The plot was this: The young emperor now listened to his tutor, Weng T'ung-ho, who urged him that the nation must be made strong or it would surely fall at last into the hands of waiting enemies. The tutor recommended that the great scholar K'ang Yu-wei alone could advise how to build the ships and railroads and the schools for young men who could renew the nation. The emperor then sent for K'ang Yu-wei.

"He is daily with the emperor," the eunuch said. "They spend hours together and I hear that he declares the Chinese men must cut their queues off as the first reform."

At this the empress dropped her fan. "But their queues are the sign of subjection to our Manchu Dynasty!"

Li Lien-ying nodded. "Majesty, I have worse to tell. He bade our emperor send for Yüan Shih-k'ai, who commands our armies under Li Hung-chang. This Yüan now has imperial orders to seize you, Majesty, and keep you imprisoned."

"Indeed," she said. She felt a strange sweet strength invade her blood. She would do battle yet again. "Well, well," she said and laughed.

"There is none like you under heaven," Li Lien-ying said tenderly. "You are not male or female, Majesty, but more than either, greater than both."

They exchanged look for look in mutual mischief, and she struck him gaily on the face with her folded fan and bade him be off.

THE EMPRESS meditated much on what her spy had told her. Twice the men of Japan had been bought off from war, once by gold and again by yielding to them rights over the people of Korea. That, she now felt, was the weakness of Li Hung-chang. War must be her defense at last. And Yüan Shih-k'ai must begin the war in Korea and from there drive the Japanese into the sea. "You need no great armies or vast fleets," she told Li Hung-chang when he complained that his armies were too

335

weak, his ships too few. "Even if the enemy attack Chinese soil, the people will rise up and drive them into the sea."

"Ah, Majesty," he groaned, "you do not know these evil times! Here in your palaces you live apart."

Alas, the year was not spent before war was made and victory lost. The enemy came quickly and inside a few brief days their ships had crossed the seas. Yüan Shih-k'ai was driven from Korea and the enemy was next on Chinese soil. The empress for once was wrong. Her villagers stood silent when the men of Japan marched up their streets. They carried guns, these men, and the villagers had no guns.

The empress sent word to Li Hung-chang to surrender and to accept what terms he must. A bitter treaty then was forged, the terms of which shook even the haughty heart of the empress. Li Hung-chang himself went to the Summer Palace to comfort her. He told her that the treaty was indeed bitter, but the throne had a new friend to the north, the czar of Russia, who for his own sake would not have Japan grow strong.

The empress listened and took heart. "From now on I shall spend my whole strength to rid myself of every foreigner, white or yellow, upon our soil. As for the Chinese whom we Manchu rule, I will win them back again, save for those young men who have breathed in foreign winds and drunk down foreign waters. We should never have allowed the Christians to set up schools and colleges, for the young Chinese now are puffed up with false foreign knowledge." She struck her palms together and stamped her foot. "I swear I will not let myself grow old until I have restored the realm!"

The general could not but admire his sovereign. "If anyone can do this, it is only you, Majesty," he said, and then he swore to serve her always.

Again the empress seemed to play away the idle days. Yet she continued to weave her plans. From her spies she knew from day to day the plots of the emperor and his advisers. She prepared herself. First she lifted Jung Lu up again, this time to the rank of viceroy, and it was made easy by the death of Prince Kung, who had long not been her friend.

She learned that the emperor had summoned Yüan Shih-k'ai to be his general. She was of several minds when she heard this news. Should she wait still longer to seize back the throne or should she move at once? I will wait, she thought. I have found my wisdom always in waiting. My mind tells me that the hour is not yet here.

ON AN EARLY autumn day the empress sat in her library to compose a poem. Suddenly the chief eunuch appeared, unbidden, to say that a messenger had come to announce the arrival of the viceroy Jung Lu, from Tientsin. She knew he would not have come except for the gravest cause.

The empress waited for him in her central courtyard, in these months a vast outdoor living space. Tables and chairs were set out, and the empress seated herself upon a carved chair placed between her two favorite ancient cypress trees.

A summer warmth had returned that day and now a breeze wafted the fragrance of the late lotus flowers from the lake as through the dusk she saw him coming. When he reached her she put out her hand upon his forearm. "Here is your chair," she said.

He sat beside her in the sweet twilight, and through the gate they watched the torches flare upon the lake for the night's illumination. "I wish," he said at last, "that you could live your life here undisturbed. Yet I must tell you all the truth. The plot against you, Majesty, now nears its crisis."

"Impossible to believe," she murmured, "and yet I know I must believe, because you tell me."

He spoke on. "Yüan Shih-k'ai himself came to me four nights ago in secret, and I left my post in haste to tell you. The emperor sent for him twelve days ago."

"Who else was there?" she asked.

"The imperial tutor, Weng T'ung-ho."

She moved restlessly and put her fan against her cheek, a screen between them. "And was no one else there?"

"The Pearl, the emperor's favorite concubine. You know that the emperor will not receive his consort. Therefore her heart has turned to hate. She is your ally."

"I know," she said.

"We must count every ally," he went on, "for the court is divided. Even the people on the streets know it. One party is called Venerable Mother and the other is called Small Boy."

"Disgraceful," she muttered. "We should keep our family secrets private. My nephew is a fool," she said sadly.

"But those about him are not fools," he said. "These edicts that he sends forth—have you read them?"

"I let him have his way," she said.

"One reason that he hates you," he said bluntly, "is that your eunuch keeps him waiting on his knees outside your doors when he comes to call on you."

"It is his duty to his elder," she said indifferently.

Jung Lu spoke on. "This is not fitting and well you know it."

"I know it," she said, half laughing, "but he is so meek, so frightened of me, that he tempts me to torture."

"Not as frightened as you think," Jung Lu retorted. "The hundred edicts are not the work of a weak man."

She turned her head away and would not look at him. "The plot," she murmured.

"The plot is to surround this palace," he said, "and force you to promise never to decree again, promise to put away your spies, to yield the great imperial seal, and employ yourself henceforth with flowers, your favorite dogs—"

"But why?" she cried.

"You are the obstacle," he told her. "But for you they could bring a new nation into being, a nation shaped and modeled on the west—"

"Railroads, I suppose," she cried, "guns, navies, wars, armies—" She leaped from her carved chair. "No—I will not see our realm destroyed! I love these people whom I rule. For two hundred years the Dragon Throne was ours and now is mine. My nephew has betrayed me and all our ancestors."

Jung Lu rose beside her. "Command me, Majesty—"

His words restored her. "Hear me, then. Summon to me at once my grand council. Let the leaders of our imperial clan come also. They will implore me to return to the Dragon Throne. They will say my nephew has betrayed the country to our enemies. This time I will make ready to do what they ask. Your own armies must replace the imperial guardsmen at the Forbidden Palace. When the emperor enters Chung Ho Hall tomorrow at dawn, let him be seized and brought here and placed upon that small island in the middle of the lake. There let him wait, imprisoned, for my coming."

She was herself again, her mind at work. "You wonder!" Jung Lu murmured. "What man's mind can run like yours from yesterday beyond tomorrow? The plan is perfect."

In two hours the grand councillors arrived. The empress sat upon her throne robed in phoenix-gilded satin. Two tall torches flamed beside her and glittered on her jewels and blazed in her eyes.

"Great princes, kinsmen, ministers and councillors," she said, "there is a plot against me in the imperial city. My nephew, whom I made the emperor, designs to put me into prison and kill me. When I am dead, he plans to rout you all and set up new men who will obey his will. Our ancient habits are to end, our wisdom is to be flouted. New ways, new thoughts, are now to be put in their place. Our enemies, the foreigners, are to be our guides. Is this not treason?"

"Treason, treason!" they shouted one and all.

She put out her hands. "Rise, I pray you," she said. "Sit down as though you were my brothers, and let us reason together how to foil this hideous plot."

At this Jung Lu stood up. "Majesty," he said, "your general, Yüan Shih-k'ai, is here. I beg that he may tell the plot."

Yüan Shih-k'ai came forward, wearing his warrior robes, and made his obeisance.

"On the morning of the fifth day of this month," he said, "I was summoned before the Son of Heaven. The emperor bade me make all haste to Tientsin and there put to death the viceroy Jung Lu. When this was done, I was to hasten homeward again to Peking and, bringing all my soldiers with me, I was to seize you, Majesty, and lock you in your palace. Then I was to find the imperial seal and myself take it to the Son of Heaven."

The grand councillors groaned to hear such perfidy. When the general had finished, they fell on their knees and begged the empress to take back the Dragon Throne.

"I swear I will grant your request," she said graciously.

They rose again and took counsel and decided that Jung Lu must return secretly to his post as soon as he had replaced the guards at the Forbidden City with his own men. At dawn these guards were to seize the emperor and bring him to the island to await his aunt's arrival.

When she woke the next morning the sun was high, the air was sweet and chill. She rose as usual and summoned Li Lien-ying.

"Is all well?" she asked when he appeared. "Is our guest on the island?" Her red lips quivered with secret laughter.

"Majesty, two guests," he said. "Pearl ran after us and clung to her lord's waist with both her arms. We dared not delay to part them, nor could we take the liberty of killing her without your order."

"Shame on you," she said, "when did I ever order—ah, well, if he is there, she matters nothing. I go to face him with his treason. You will accompany me and only you. I need no guard—he's helpless."

She snapped her fingers toward her favorite dog, and the creature loped to her side. Behind them followed Li Lien-ying. In silence they walked toward the lake, crossed the marble bridge, and entered the pavilion. The emperor rose to receive her. His narrow face was pale, his large eyes sad, his delicate mouth trembling.

"Down on your knees," she said, and sat herself upon the central seat. In every chamber, this central seat was hers.

He fell on his knees before her. The dog smelled him

carefully from head to foot, and then lay down across her feet.

"You!" the empress said most bitterly. "You should be strangled, sliced and thrown to wild beasts!"

He did not speak or move.

"Who put you on the Dragon Throne?" she asked. "Who went at night and took you from your bed, a whining child, and made you emperor?"

He lifted up his head. "I wish you had not taken that child from his bed."

"You weakling!" she retorted. "I tell you, there is not a Manchu prince or commoner who does not pray that I take back the throne! And who supports you? Fool, who but Chinese rebels? It is their plot to coax and flatter you, and when they have you in their power, they will depose you and end our dynasty. You have betrayed not only me but all our sacred ancestors. Reforms! I spit upon reforms!"

Her breath came suddenly too tight. She stopped and put her hand upon her heart. Her dog looked up and growled, and she tried to smile. "A beast is faithful, but a man is not," she said. "Yet I will not kill you. You shall even keep the name of emperor. But you shall be a prisoner. You shall implore me to sit in your place and rule. And I will yield, though unwilling, for how proud I might have been if you had ruled as a ruler should. Yet since you are not fit to rule—"

At this moment curtains parted and Pearl ran in and threw herself upon the floor beside the emperor. Sobbing loudly, she besought the empress to blame him no more. "I do assure you, Holy Mother," she cried out, "a man more kind and gentle never lived. Why, Imperial Mother, my cat caught a mouse the other day—"

"Be silent, silly girl," the empress said.

But Pearl shrieked at the haughty empress, "I will not be silent, and you may kill me if you like! You have no right to take him from the throne. He is the emperor by will of Heaven and you were but a tool of destiny."

"Enough," the empress said. Her handsome face was stern.

"You have passed beyond the boundaries. You shall never see your lord again." She turned imperiously to Li Lien-ying. "Remove the concubine. In the Palace of Forgotten Concubines there are two small inner rooms. These shall be her prison until she dies. She shall have no change of clothing until the garments that she wears fall from her in rags. Her food shall be coarse rice and beggar's cabbage. Her name must not be mentioned in my presence. When she dies, do not inform me."

"Yes, Majesty," he said. He took Pearl by the wrist and dragged her away. When she was gone, the emperor crumpled senseless at his sovereign's feet. Above him the white dog stood and growled, and the empress sat motionless in silence.

V

OLD BUDDHA

Once more the empress ruled, and now because she was old, she put aside the screen that shielded her from the eyes of men. She sat on the Dragon Throne as though she were a man, in the full light of torch or sun. Since she had accomplished what she had planned, she could be merciful; thus, at the autumn festival, she allowed her nephew to make the imperial sacrifices at the Altar of the Moon, to thank Heaven for the harvests and for peace. Let him deal with gods while she dealt with men.

And she had much to do with men. First she put to death the rebels whose advice had led the emperor astray. When she had no enemies left inside her court, she set herself to make what she had done seem right to all the people. For she knew the people were divided, that some took the emperor's part and said that the nation should be shaped to new times, while others declared themselves for the ancient ways and wisdom.

Both must be persuaded. By edicts and by skillful gossip

leaking from the court the people were informed that the emperor had plotted against his ancient aunt and that he was supported by foreigners and was too simple to see that they hoped to seize the whole country for themselves. These two sins convinced them that the empress did well to resume the imperial seat. Before long, even foreigners said that it was better to deal with a strong female than a weak male ruler.

And here was the wile and wit of this Old Buddha. She made a feast and invited the wives of all seven ambassadors from Western lands. The empress had never seen a white face before. If she won the women, she said, the men would follow. She chose the time of her sixty-fourth birthday celebrations in 1898 for the meeting.

The whole court was stirred, for none had seen a foreigner. Only the empress was calm, and she planned every courtesy. At midmorning she sent mounted Chinese guards in scarlet and yellow to accompany the sedan chairs that would carry the foreign ladies to the first gate of the Winter Palace. Here seven court sedans waited, each borne by six eunuchs garbed in bright yellow satin. With mounted escorts following, the ladies were now carried to the second gate, there to dismount again.

The empress had commanded that they be ushered into a small foreign train of cars, drawn by a steam engine, which the emperor had bought some years before. The train carried them through the Forbidden City to the entrance hall of the main palace. Here the guests drank tea and rested. The highest princes then invited them to the great Audience Hall. The empress had willed her nephew to sit at her right hand this day so that in the eyes of all they might appear united.

According to the length of their stay in Peking, an interpreter presented each guest in turn to Prince Ch'ing, who then presented her to the empress. The empress gazed at each face, and however much she was amazed by what she saw, she leaned down and put out her hands and clasped the right hand of each lady and on each forefinger she placed a ring of heavy Chinese gold, set with a large round pearl. Then, followed by

her nephew, she rose and left the room. The four eunuchs who were his guard by day and night led the emperor again to his prison.

In her dining hall the empress ate her noon meal, surrounded by her favorite ladies, while her foreign guests dined in the banquet hall. She was in good spirits, laughing much at the strange faces of the foreigners. Her ladies laughed and applauded all she said, declaring they had never seen her in better wit.

Now the empress changed her robes and returned to her guests. She had meanwhile sent for the young empress, and now presented her to each guest in turn. She perceived that they discerned the quality of satins and jewels, and she decided privately that when she received them at the end of the day she would astonish them with her own apparel. She rose and held out her hands to her guests as they came near, one by one, and put her hands on her own breast and then on theirs and repeated the words of an ancient sage: "All under Heaven are one family," interpreters explaining what she said in English and in French. When this was done, she sent them to her theater, saying that she had chosen her favorite play for their amusement.

Again she withdrew and went to her chambers. This time she chose her costliest robe of gold-encrusted satin embroidered in phoenixes of every shade and hue, and she wore her famous great collar of matched pearls. She wore a high headdress of pearls and rubies inset with diamonds from Africa. Never, so her ladies said, had they seen her more beautiful.

In the banquet hall, the guests were now drinking tea and eating sweetmeats. The empress came in state, borne in her palace chair, and eunuchs lifted her to her throne. The foreign ladies rose, and she smiled at all, and raised up her bowl of tea and drank from one side, and summoning each lady to her, she put the other side of the bowl to the lady's lips. Again she said, "All one family—under Heaven, all are one." And feeling bold and free, she commanded gifts to be brought and given to the ladies: a fan, a scroll of her own painting, and a piece of jade, to each alike. When this was done, she bade them all farewell, and so the day was over.

The foreign ladies praised the empress much to their lords, saying that no one so gentle and beautiful could also be evil or cruel. She was well pleased and she felt that she was indeed what they had said she was. Now she set herself to clean away the rebels and reformers. The more she pondered this task the more she perceived that it could not be done so long as the emperor, her nephew, lived. His pensive ways, his very submission, had won those who surrounded him, even while they obeyed her.

"So long as he lives, Majesty," Li Lien-ying whispered, "the nation will remain divided. They love dissent, these Chinese, and never are they happier than when they plot and plan against their rulers. Only you can keep the peace, because the people trust you, though you are Manchu."

That day she paced her terrace and gazed across to the island upon which her nephew was imprisoned. She could see him even now as he wandered about the narrow island, and with him, though at a distance, the ever watchful eunuchs who guarded him. She considered what Li Lien-ying had hinted this day and abruptly rejected it. No, it was not time yet for her nephew to die. The blame for his death must not lie on her. When next the eunuch came into her presence, she was cold to him and said, "Do not speak to me again of the emperor's journey to the Yellow Springs. What Heaven wills, Heaven itself will do."

Yet who could have dreamed that the Chinese rebels would somehow contrive to find their secret way to the ear of the lonely young emperor? One morning he escaped from his guards and fled through the pine woods on the island to where a boat waited. The eunuch guards ran and caught up with him as he was about to step into the boat, and they besought him not to escape. "If you escape, Son of Heaven," they pleaded, "Old Buddha will have us all beheaded."

No other plea would have served as well. The emperor hesitated while the boatman, a rebel in disguise, shouted to him that he must not delay. But among the imploring eunuchs was one youth, scarcely more than a child, gentle and kind, who had always stayed near his royal master to serve him. And looking down at this weeping boy, the emperor could not step into the boat. He shook his head and the boatman, not daring to delay longer, rowed off into the mists of dawn.

The sad tale was carried to the ears of the empress. She put to death all the emperor's supporters, but him she let live. For her mercy Jung Lu commended her. "Majesty," he said, "the people would never condone a plot against you, yet they would not revere you were you to allow the life of the emperor to be taken. He must be imprisoned, I acknowledge, but grant him every courtesy. You, Most High, can afford every act of grace and kindness. Let me even suggest that the concubine—"

But here she put up her two hands to signify silence. The concubine's name was not to be said in her presence.

"I will speak of other matters," he said. "While there is peace now in the realm, yet the people show anger against the white men. An English priest has been murdered by mobs in the province of Kweichow. This will bring the English hornets again about the throne."

The empress clenched her hands and struck her knees. "Again these foreign priests!" she cried. "How is it they will not stay at home?"

"They are the fruit of the defeats we have suffered in battle with the Western men," Jung Lu reminded her.

In the last month of that year still another foreign priest was murdered in the western province of Hupei. In the same month mobs rose against foreign priests in the province of Szechwan, and this was because of old rumors that the priests stole children and made medicine from their eyes and bones. The empress was beside herself, for the foreign envoys became arrogant and threatening. France, whose priests had been several times killed, now sent word that she would attack with her ships of war unless she was granted land in Shanghai. Portugal demanded more land surrounding Macao, and Belgium, Spain and Italy also demanded compensation for their murdered priests.

The empress summoned her ministers and princes for a special audience to deal with these disasters and sent for her general, Li Hung-chang. The day of audience was hot, and a sandstorm blew from the northwest. But when the empress appeared, she seemed unaware of the storm. She walked to the Dragon Throne, compelling all by her proud indifference to take the kerchiefs from their faces and fall in obeisance before her.

"Where is the grand councillor Jung Lu, my kinsman?" she demanded of Li Lien-ying.

"Majesty, he sent word that he is ill. I think he is ill because you have sent for Li Hung-chang."

Having implanted this dart of malice in her mind, he stepped back. One by one she called on each prince and minister to give his opinion upon the crisis. Last of all she called on the aged general, Li Hung-chang, who came forward with unsteady steps and with difficulty knelt to make his obeisance.

"And what have you to say, most honored protector of our throne?" she inquired in a pleasant voice.

To which Li Hung-chang replied, "Most High, we must avoid war at all costs, for against so many angry enemies it would be indeed to mount the tiger. It is prudent therefore to entice one enemy to become our ally. Let this one be the northern enemy, Russia. Among them all, Russia is most Asian, like ourselves."

"And what is the price to make an enemy our friend?" she asked. The old man trembled under the sweet coldness of her voice. He could not speak.

"I will answer my own question," she continued. "The price is too great. What benefit if we conquer our other enemies only to become the vassal of one? Does any nation give something for nothing? Instead we will repel all enemies. I will not rest until every white man and woman and child is driven from our shores. I will not yield."

She rose from the throne as she spoke, her eyes blazing, her cheeks flushed. Power streamed from her; the very air grew sharp and needled through with angry heat. She let her eyes roam over the bent figures of the men, their brilliant robes outspread on the tiled floor, and her eyes chose the form of the grand councillor Kang Yi, a man who had spent his strength through all his years in preserving what was ancient.

"You, my grand councillor Kang Yi," she said in loud clear tones, "you shall remain for a private audience. You, my lords and princes, are dismissed."

An hour later the grand councillor Kang Yi stood to hear her commands in her private audience hall. "I vacillate no more," the empress said. "I shall reclaim our land. I shall take it back, foot by foot, without counting the cost."

"Majesty," Kang Yi said, "for the first time I feel hope."

"What is your advice?" the empress asked.

"Majesty," he said, "Prince Tuan and I have often spoken of this. We agree that we should use the anger of the Chinese against the Western men. The Chinese are sick with fury over their stolen land, over the gold they pay in indemnity because of the priests the mobs have killed. They have made secret bands among themselves, sworn to destroy these enemies. Majesty, I do not claim wisdom, but since these roving bands exist, why not use them? When they are added to the five-pronged armies that Jung Lu has built, who can resist us?"

The empress heard and pondered. The plan seemed good. She asked a few questions more, she praised him once or twice, and then she dismissed him.

In a few days she sent for Jung Lu, ready to reprove him for what her spies said he had done. For the first time she thought he looked old and tired. "I hear you have allowed the foreign ministers to augment their guard."

"I was compelled," he said. "Their spies brought them word that you, Majesty, have listened to Kang Yi, and intend to

349

approve the bands of secret rebels whose purpose is to destroy the foreigners. Majesty, I said I would not believe that you could approve such folly. Indeed, do you think that you can fight against the whole world?"

"Kang Yi says that the secret rebels who belong to the order of the Boxers have magic that prevents their death. Even when guns are fired against them they are not wounded."

Jung Lu cried out in anguish, "Oh, Majesty, can you believe such nonsense?"

"It is you who are foolish," she retorted. "Do you forget that at the end of the Han Dynasty, Chang Chou led the Yellow Turban Rebels against the throne and that they, too, knew magic against wound and death. I tell you, there are spirits who aid the righteous."

Jung Lu was beside himself by now. He wrenched his hat from his head and threw it on the floor before her. "I will not forget your place," he said between set teeth. "But still you are my kinswoman, that one to whom I long ago gave up my life. Surely, I deserve the right to say you are a fool. I warn you, if you listen to that stone-head, Kang Yi, who lives in centuries now dead, then I say you do destroy yourself and with you the whole dynasty. Oh, hear me—hear me—" He gazed into the face he still adored. Their eyes met and clung, and he saw her will waver.

"It is only I who dare to speak the truth to you," he said. "What man worships you as I do?" His voice sank and his words came out a reluctant whisper.

She dropped her head. The old power still held. All through their lives his love had stayed her.

"Promise me at least that you will do nothing without telling me," he said. "It is a small reward—the only one I ask."

He kept his eyes fixed upon her drooping head. And she kept her head down and saw his two feet planted on the floor before her, strong feet in velvet boots. Faithful in her service, those two feet—stubborn, brave and strong.

She lifted up her head. "I promise."

"Majesty," Kang Yi said, "you do wrong. Your heart grows soft with age. One word from you and the foreigners would be gone." His spies had told him that Jung Lu was his enemy and he had made haste to seek an audience.

She turned away her head. "I am weary of you all," she said.

"But, Majesty," he urged, "now is the hour of victory. Only speak, and the Boxers do your work. We await your word, Majesty."

She shook her head. "I cannot speak it," she said.

The empress sat on her throne in the Winter Palace. She had returned to the Forbidden City the day before, leaving the autumn beauty of the Summer Palace behind her. The Boxers, without permission, had burned the railway to Tientsin. Were they invulnerable? Who could know? She glanced toward the assembled council.

"Majesty," Kang Yi said again, "yesterday I went to the birthday celebration of the first lady in the household of the duke Lan. More than a hundred Boxers live in his outer courtyard, under their own commander. I saw youths no more than fourteen or fifteen years old who went into trances and spoke strange languages. The duke says that when the time comes, these spirits will lead the Boxers to the houses of Christians to destroy them."

"I have not seen it with my own eyes," the empress declared. She raised her hand to end the audience.

"Majesty," Li Lien-ying said in the twilight, "many citizens are sheltering the Boxers. Many people are leaving, fearing a war. All await your word, Majesty."

"I cannot give it," the empress said.

At last she sent Li Lien-ying to find Jung Lu and bring him to her. She must take back her promise. This morning brought news that still more foreign soldiers were marching overland from the coast. This was to avenge the death of yet another foreigner, killed by angry Chinese in the province of Kansu.

When Jung Lu arrived, she said, "Am I still to be silent

351

while the city fills with foreign soldiers? The people will rise against the throne."

"Majesty, I agree that we must not allow more foreign soldiers to enter the city," Jung Lu replied. "Nevertheless, it will disgrace us if we attack the envoys of foreign nations."

"What would you have me do?" she inquired bitterly.

"Invite the foreign ministers to leave the city," Jung Lu said. "When they are gone, their troops will go with them."

"And if they will not go?"

"Perhaps they will go," he said calmly. "If they do not, then you cannot be blamed."

"Do you release me from my promise?" she demanded.

"Tomorrow," he said, "tomorrow—tomorrow."

That night, in the deepest darkness, she was suddenly awakened by a bright light shining through the windows. It fell from the sky itself, crimson and on fire. From behind the door Li Lien-ying shouted that a foreign temple was in flames, the fire lit by unknown hands.

The empress rose and dressed at once. With her eunuchs she went out and climbed her peony mountain, where she could look down into the city. Smoke mingled with flames and soon a fearful stench of roasting flesh spread into the air. The Boxers were burning the French church nearby, Li Lien-ying told her, and inside were hundreds of Christian Chinese— men, women and children.

"What horror," the empress moaned. "Oh, that I had forbidden the foreigners from the very beginning!" She turned away and refused to look anymore.

"Majesty," her princes and ministers urged, "unless you would see all lost, you must use the magic of Boxers. The foreign soldiers are filling the streets like floodwaters—"

"Now, now, Majesty, without delay—"

They clamored before her in the small throne room. They had come in haste at her summons, and they stood in disarray. This was no time for ceremony.

At her right the emperor sat upon a low carved chair, his

head bowed, his face pale. "Son of Heaven," she said to him, "shall we use the Boxer horde against our enemies?" If he said yes, was not his the blame?

"Whatever you will, Holy Mother," he said and did not lift his head.

She looked at Jung Lu. He stood apart, his head bowed, his arms folded. "Majesty, Majesty!" the voices cried about her. She rose to her feet and raised her arms for silence in the early-morning twilight. She had eaten nothing and she had not slept while the fires burned on. Foreign soldiers converged from the four corners of the earth upon her city. What remained except war?

"The hour has come," she cried. "We must destroy the foreigners in their legations! One brick must not be left upon another nor one human being allowed to live!"

She had broken her promise to Jung Lu. He strode forward and fell before her in obeisance. "Majesty," he cried, and the tears ran down his cheeks, "Majesty, though these foreigners are indeed our enemies, though they have only themselves to blame for their own destruction, yet I beseech you to consider what you do. If we destroy these few buildings, this handful of foreigners, their armies, their navies, will fly across land and sea to attack us. Our ancestral shrines will be crushed into dust, and the people's altars will be razed to the ground!"

She had never shown herself afraid and the old strong habit held, though her fear was monstrous and near despair. "I cannot restrain the people," she declared. "If they do not rend our enemies, they will rend even me. I have no choice. As for you, Grand Councillor, if you have no better advice than this to bestow upon the throne, you are excused from further attendance." Immediately Jung Lu rose and left her presence.

When he was gone the councillor Ch'i Hsiu approached the throne and in obeisance he presented a folded paper. "Majesty," he said, "I have presumed to suggest a decree. If I am permitted, I will read it aloud."

"Do so," the empress commanded.

He began to read a decree of war against the foreigners, to be approved by the empress. He read in silence so deep that his voice echoed to the roof. When he had finished, he waited for her will.

"It is excellent," the empress said in a calm, cold voice. "Let it be sent forth as a decree from the throne."

It was now dawn. Li Lien-ying came forward and held out his arm, and the empress stepped down from the throne and into the sedan that waited on the terrace. From there she was carried to her own palace. "I will sleep this whole day," she told her ladies. "Let no one wake me." But it was only an hour after noon when she was awakened suddenly by the voice of Li Lien-ying outside her door.

"Majesty," he called, "Prince Ch'ing waits and with him is Kang Yi." The empress could not evade such a summons, and so she went out to receive the two.

"Majesty," Kang Yi exclaimed, "war has begun already. A Manchu sergeant this morning killed two foreigners. One was the German minister coming, it was said, to beg you for a special audience."

The empress felt fear clutch her heart dry. "Oh, horror!" she cried. "Where is Jung Lu? Make haste—fetch him here—the war begins too soon—we are not ready." She turned and fled into her own chamber again. There she waited for Jung Lu and in two hours he came, looking grave.

"Leave me," she told her ladies. "And do not let another enter," she told her eunuch. When all were gone, she looked up at Jung Lu and said faintly, "Speak. Tell me what to do."

"I had the guards ready to escort the foreigners to the coast," he said sadly. "Why did you not obey me?"

She wiped the corners of her eyes with a kerchief.

"Now having disobeyed me," he went on, "you ask me what to do."

She sobbed softly.

"Where will you find the money to pay these Boxers?" he demanded. "Do you think they work for nothing?"

Lifting up her eyes to his face, she saw him suddenly turn ashen gray and clutch his left side and then sink to the floor. She ran to him and lifted his hands. They were listless and cold. The pupils of his eyes were fixed and staring, and he drew his breath in great gasps.

"Oh, alas, alas!" she cried in a loud voice, and her ladies and eunuchs came running into the chamber. "Lift him up," the empress commanded. They laid Jung Lu on a couch at the far end of the hall, while the empress sent a eunuch flying for the court physicians.

"Majesty," the chief physician said, "the grand councillor rose from his sickbed to come to you."

The empress turned on Li Lien-ying with terrible eyes. "Why was I not told?"

"Most High," Li Lien-ying said, "the grand councillor forbade it."

She controlled the turmoil of her heart, and made her voice calm. "Let him be carried to his own palace, and you, imperial physicians, stay by him night and day. And send me news of his health every hour, day and night. As for me, I shall go to the temple to pray."

WAR RAGED ABOUT the empress, and each day seemed a month long. "Majesty," Prince Tuan implored her, "these Boxers have a secret talisman, a circle of yellow paper that each carries on his person. On this paper are written these magic words: 'I am Buddha of the Cold Cloud. Before me the Black God of Fire leads my way. Behind me Lao-tzu himself supports me.' Whoever learns these mystic words destroys by each incantation a foreign life somewhere in our country. Surely, Majesty, it does no harm to learn the magic words."

"It does no harm," the empress agreed, and she learned the mystic words and repeated them seventy times a day while Li Lien-ying counted how many foreign devils were gone.

As if the angry foreigners were not woe enough, the people rose up throughout the realm, plundering the rich and robbing those who had a little food, including a few white priests. The foreign ministers protested every death, and they declared that unless the people were put down, their governments would send still more armies and warships. While Jung Lu lay helpless on his bed, speechless and deaf, the empress asked General Yüan Shih-k'ai what could be done. He replied only that he had ordered twenty of the Boxers to be shot and he himself had seen them fall and die like common men. And he begged the empress not to put her faith in these charlatans.

Meanwhile, Prince Tuan was always boasting that he could drive the foreigners into the sea and he begged for her command. While she delayed, he began to force her secretly by allowing angry men here and there to attack the foreigners. Her loyal viceroy in Nanking sent a memorial beseeching her not to allow such attacks:

"The present war," he wrote, "is due to bandits spreading slaughter and arson on the pretext of paying off a grudge against Christianity. The foreign governments are already uniting to send troops to attack China on the pretense of protecting their subjects. Nevertheless, Majesty, let benevolence and power move together. Respectfully, I suggest that you inflict stern and exemplary punishment on all those rebels who attack innocent officials and missionaries."

The empress replied by special courier: "We would not willingly be aggressors. You are to inform the various foreign legations that we have only kindly feelings toward them and urge them to devise some plan whereby we may make a peaceful settlement, in the interest of all."

Next she wrote an edict in which she spoke to the whole world: "We have endured a succession of unfortunate circumstances following one upon another in rapid confusion, and we are at a loss to account for the situation that has brought about hostilities between China and the Western powers. A state of war has been created, but it is none of our doing. How could China be so foolish, conscious as she is of her weakness, as to declare war on the whole world at once? We will and do instruct our military commanders to protect the legations meanwhile. We can only do our best."

Yet the empress was not satisfied that she had done all she could and sent telegrams to the most powerful sovereigns of the outer world, pleading "circumstances beyond our control" and asking them to act as peacemakers.

To all these messages the empress received no reply. She waited unbelieving, sitting in her Throne Hall day after day, but silent were the majesties abroad and silent was Jung Lu upon his bed. The summer days passed by, one after the other, equal in brilliance, and no rain fell. Last year there were floods and now came drought, and the people cried out that it was the wrath of Heaven. And while the empress meditated, outwardly calm, within she was numb with confusion and despair.

The city was now filled with rebels and Boxers, and people hid inside their houses. The foreign legations were preparing for attack, their gates were locked, and guards waited with their guns ready. More than a thousand shops were set on fire and rich merchants fled the city with their families. Now the war was not only against the foreigners but also against the throne.

One early morning soon after that the empress was drinking her tea when suddenly she heard loud shouts and the beat of tramping feet. She hastened to the gate of her palace, and there she saw a horde of noisy drunken men, their broadswords drawn. At their front, half frightened, half boastful, she saw the form of Prince Tuan himself.

He motioned to his followers to be silent and arrogantly addressed her. "Majesty! I cannot hold back these true patriots. They hear that you are sheltering those devils' pupils, the Christian converts. More than that, they are told that the emperor himself is a Christian. I cannot be responsible, Majesty. I will not be responsible—"

Her jade tea bowl was still in her hands and she lifted it high above her head and crashed it to the stone floor. Her huge eyes shone with cold fire. "You traitor! Stand forth!"

Thus she commanded Prince Tuan. "How dare you behave in this insolent fashion? Your head sits no more tightly on your shoulders than the head of any commoner! It is I and I alone who rule! Do you think that you can approach the Dragon Throne unless I speak?"

"Majesty—Majesty," Prince Tuan stammered, and such was the power of her presence that one by one his followers went away. Then she sent word to the imperial guards that these men were to be caught and beheaded and their heads hung on the city gates because they had dared to come into her presence when she had not commanded them.

On this same day came news that foreign soldiers had captured Tientsin and were marching now to the capital to rescue their beleaguered countrymen. The imperial army was in retreat. What could she do but wait and pray.

Now in answer to her daily prayers, the empress received word that Jung Lu had awakened from his stupor. She sent special foods to strengthen him. Nevertheless, it was four more days before he could be carried into her presence in a palanquin. When she saw his pallor and the weakness of his limbs, she cried out and descended from her throne and sat down beside him in a chair.

"Where have you been, kinsman?" she inquired tenderly. "Your soul and mind have wandered far away."

"Wherever I have been I cannot remember now." His voice was high and weak. "But I am returned by whose will I do not know, unless it was your prayers that brought me back."

"It was my prayers," she said, "for I have been alone indeed. Tell me what I must do. Do you know that a war rages in the city and that Tientsin has fallen? The enemy approaches the city—"

"I know all," he said. "There is no time to prepare. You must seize Prince Tuan, whom the foreigners blame for everything, and you must order him beheaded. This will prove your innocence and your will for peace."

"What—and yield to the enemy?" she cried in outrage. "To behead Prince Tuan is a small matter, but to yield to the foreign enemy—no, that is too much! The meaning of my whole life crumbles into dust."

He groaned. "Oh, stubborn woman," he sighed. "When will you learn that you cannot stay the tides of the future?" And he motioned to his bearers to carry him away again.

Day pressed on day, and often she summoned her princes and ministers to the Hall of Peaceful Longevity. To these audiences Jung Lu also came, forcing himself to rise from his palanquin and take his place. They remained silent, their faces lined with weariness.

In this silence Prince Tuan again boasted that the Boxers had prepared their secret incantations, and when the foreign troops reached the moat outside the city wall, they would all fall in the water and be drowned. To this Jung Lu shouted, "The Boxers are no more than thistledown, and when the foreigners approach, they will fly away like thistledown!"

His words were fulfilled. At midafternoon one day, the duke Lan rushed into the empress's library and cried out, "Old Buddha, they are here—the foreign devils have broken through the gates as fire through wax!"

She looked up. "Then my kinsman was right," she said in a small, wondering voice. She closed her book and rose.

"You must flee, Majesty," the old duke cried. "You and the Son of Heaven together! You must flee northward."

She shook her head, and so he made haste to find Jung Lu, who alone could persuade her. Jung Lu came in shortly, walking now with a cane and still uncertainly, but strengthened to do what he could for her. He spoke to her in low and tender tones: "My love, you must hear me. You cannot stay here. You are still the symbol of the throne. Where you are is the heart of the nation. Tonight after midnight you must escape."

"Again," she whispered. "And you?"

"I must stay to rally our forces. For you will come back, as you did before, and I must save the throne for you."

She lifted up her face and he saw that she had yielded to terror, if not to him. In pitying love he took her hand and held it for a moment. He put it to his cheek and pressed it there for a moment. Then he stepped back.

"Majesty," he said, "there is no time to lose. I must select those who shall guard you. You must dress as a Chinese peasant and leave the palace by the hidden gate. Two ladies only—more will seem too many. The emperor must go with you dressed as a peasant, too. The concubines must be left behind."

When he was gone, she opened a book and her eyes fell upon words written centuries before by Confucius: "For lack of a broad mind and true understanding, a great purpose has been lost."

She stared at the words and received them humbly. Her mind was not broad enough, she had not understood the times she lived in. Her purpose was lost—her purpose to save the country. She surrendered her spirit. From now on she would not shape the times but be shaped by them.

THEY MARVELED at her proud calm. She gave commands to everyone concerning the safe disposal of her books, her paintings, her scrolls, her jewels. For the hiding of her treasure, she commanded Li Lien-ying to build a false wall in a certain chamber and behind this wall the treasure was concealed. When all was done, she summoned first the emperor, and then the concubines.

"I must preserve the emperor and myself," she said, "not for our worth, but because we must protect the throne. Here you will remain and you need not fear, for the grand councillor Jung Lu will rally all our armies. Moreover, I do not believe that the enemy will penetrate these palaces. Continue then as though I were here."

The concubines wept softly. None spoke except Pearl, whom the eunuchs had dared to bring from her prison. There she stood, her beauty gone, her body clad in faded rags. But still she was rebellious. Her onyx eyes still flamed. She cried out to the empress, "I will not stay, Imperial Mother! I claim my right to go with my lord."

The empress rose up. "You! Could he have thought of so much evil had you not whispered in his ears?"

She turned to Li Lien-ying and gave command. "Take this woman and cast her into the well by the Eastern Gate!"

The emperor fell on his knees, but the empress would not allow him to speak. "Not a word," she cried at him. "This concubine was hatched from the egg of an owl." She looked at Li Lien-ying and immediately he beckoned to a eunuch and the two of them carried the concubine away, silent and pale as stone.

"Get you into your cart," the empress said to the kneeling emperor. "I will lead in my own cart. The mule is for Li Lien-ying. If anyone stops us, say that we are poor country folk fleeing into the mountains."

So said, so done. Behind her curtains the empress sat on the cushion in her cart, straight as a Buddha, her eyes resolute. "Westward," she commanded, "westward to the city of Sian."

The journey proceeded day by day for ninety days. When they reached the next province, it was no longer necessary to maintain their disguise, and her spirits rose. On the very first evening there a general who had come north with his troops gave to the empress a basket of fresh eggs and a jeweled girdle. This cheered her, too. It was a good omen of the love that her subjects still felt for her, and she was comforted.

Never was autumn more glorious than now. Day after day the sun shone down upon land and people. Further west, harvests were plentiful and the war was far away. In peace and plenty the people gave her homage and declared that indeed she was their Old Buddha. Again her heart was robust with courage, the more because many of her princes and ministers now followed her and slowly the court assembled itself.

Her mood was dimmed suddenly by a letter from Jung Lu telling her that their cause was lost. The empress commanded Jung Lu to come to her to make a full report. While he journeyed to her, his wife was taken suddenly ill and died in a strange city. This news the empress heard by courier.

When he was announced upon the day after her own arrival at the city of Taiyuan, she sent word that he rest only an hour and then appear before her. Jung Lu came in, tall and gaunt from sorrow and fatigue, but always fastidious in her presence. As usual he made a feint of obeisance, and as usual she put out her hand to prevent him. She rose, and they exchanged a long lingering look. "I grieve that your wife has left you for the Yellow Springs," she said in a low voice.

He acknowledged this by a slight bow. "Majesty, she was a good woman," he said, "and she served me faithfully."

They waited, one for the other. "You are tired," she observed. "Let us sit down together. I have need of your wisdom." She crossed the room with her old grace and they sat down in two straight wooden chairs on either side of a small table. He waited for her to speak. "Is all lost?" she asked at last and looked sidewise at him from her long eyes.

"All is lost," he said firmly. He sat with his large beautiful hands planted upon his knees.

"What is your counsel?" she asked.

"Majesty," he said, "you must return to your capital and yield to the demands of the enemy and so again save the throne. I have left Li Hung-chang behind to negotiate the peace. But before you return you must order Prince Tuan to be beheaded, as an earnest of your repentance."

"Never!" she exclaimed.

"Then you can never return," he replied. "So great is the hatred of the foreigners against Prince Tuan that they will destroy the imperial city rather than let you come back to it. They will pursue you even here if you do not show submission."

"I can move westward again," she insisted. "Our imperial ancestors did so before me."

"As Your Majesty wills," he said. "Yet the whole world will know then that you are in flight."

But she would not yield, not instantly, even to him. Rising, she bade him leave her and go to rest. The next day the court continued its journey westward to the distant city of Sian in the province of Shensi. It was there, the empress had decided, that she would declare her capital.

By her command Jung Lu rode beside her palanquin, and he said no more of her return to Peking and she asked no counsel. When they came to Sian, she took residence with the court in the viceroy's palace, which had been cleaned and furnished for her anew.

Settled in her exile capital, she again gave audiences and sent couriers daily to the distant imperial city for news. She bore all until they told her that the Summer Palace was desecrated once more. Soldiers of several Western nations had made merry in her sacred palaces, she heard. They had carried her throne to the lake and cast it into the waters, they had stolen her robes and paintings, and they had drawn lewd pictures on the walls of the halls and the chambers. When she heard this, she knew that she must return to the capital, and that before she could return, she must yield to the demands of the enemy that all who had aided the Boxer band must die. Through all this Jung Lu was at her side, impassive, silent, pale.

"Is there no other escape from my enemies except to yield?" she asked one day.

"Majesty, none," he said.

One night when she sat in her courtyard alone in the twilight, he stood before her unannounced and said, "I come as your kinsman. Why do you not yield to your destiny? Will you live your life here in eternal exile?"

She had upon her knees a small cinnamon dog, born in exile, and as she spoke she played with its long ears. "I am unwilling to kill those who have been loyal to me. Of the lesser ones I will not speak . . . But how can I kill my good ministers? Yet the foreigners insist. And I am told to order the death of Prince Tuan . . . Eh, alas—all those loyal to me. Am I now to destroy them?"

Jung Lu's face, thin with age and sorrow, was gentle beyond the face of any man. "You know that you cannot be happy here," he said.

"Long ago I cast my happiness away," she said,

"Then think of your realm," he argued. "How can the realm be saved and the people united again if you remain in exile? The rebels will seize the city if the foreigners do not hold it. The people will live in terror and danger and they will curse you ten thousand times because for a few lives you were not willing to return to the throne."

The little dog whined upon her knees; she put it down and rose to meet Jung Lu's waiting gaze. "I have been thinking only of myself," she said. "Now I will think of my people. I return again to my throne."

IN THE AUTUMN of 1901, the empress began the long journey home. She commanded steady marching, at the pace of twenty-five miles a day, day after day.

It was soon to be seen that Jung Lu was correct in his counsel. Everywhere the people welcomed the empress, believing, now that the exile was over, their country was safe. At Kaifeng, the capital of the province of Honan, she commanded the court to rest. And when she reached the Yellow River, again she paused. The autumn skies were violet-blue, and the dry air was warm by day and cool by night. "I shall offer sacrifices to the river god," she declared, "and I shall make absolution and give thanks."

This she did with much pomp and magnificence, and the brilliant noonday sun glittered on the splendid colors of the court. And while she worshiped, the empress was pleased to see among the crowds a few white-skinned persons. Now that she had decided to be courteous to her enemies, she sent two eunuchs to take wine, dried fruits and watermelon as gifts to the white persons.

But proof of her new resolution was that she came down from her palanquin and entered a train of iron cars that ran on iron rails. The railway was a toy of the emperor's, which she had always forbidden to be used. Now, however, she would use it to show the foreigners how changed she was, how modern, how able to understand their ways. Thirty iron cars were needed for the court and their possessions.

Nevertheless, in respect for the imperial ancestors, she commanded that the train stop outside the imperial city that she might be carried through the gate in her royal palanquin. At the station the empress looked out at a great crowd of her subjects, princes and officials of the city in front. To one side she saw foreign envoys in their strange dark coats and trousers. She forced a courteous smile.

Supported by her princes, the empress came down the steps and stood in the brilliant sunshine while her subjects knelt with their foreheads on the clean-swept earth. The foreigners stood together, their heads bared but not bowed, and she was amazed at their number. She smiled graciously in their direction and then stood talking with her usual liveliness to the managers of her imperial household. They all praised her, saying that she looked in health and youthful for her many years, and indeed, her skin was flawless under the relentless sun.

This done, she entered her gold palanquin and was lifted up by the bearers and carried into the city, and from there to the great entrance gate of the imperial inner city. Here she came down from her palanquin and knelt before the god of war while the priests chanted their rituals. She chanced to lift her eyes as she came from the shrine and saw standing on the walls a hundred or more foreigners who had come to look at her. At first she was angry and was about to have them scattered. Then she remembered. She was ruler only by the mercy of these same foreigners. Forcing herself, she bowed to them. Then she was carried once more into her own palace.

How beautiful was this ancestral palace to her now, saved by her surrender! She went from room to room, and into the great Throne Hall which the emperor Ch'ien-lung had built. And behind this Throne Hall were her courtyards, all as they had been, the gardens safe, the pools calm and clear. And beyond them was her small private throne room, and beyond it her sleeping chamber. Everything was just as she had left it.

Here I live and die in peace, she thought—but her first care was to know if her treasure was still safe. Accompanied by Li Lien-ying, she stood before the wall where they had hidden her treasure and examined every crack. "Not one brick has been moved," she said, much pleased. She commanded Li Lien-ying to tear the wall down and examine and check every parcel and report to her. Then she went away again to her own chamber.

Ah, the peace here, the joy of return! The price was high and it was not yet all paid. Before the sun was set, she announced that she would invite the wives of foreign envoys to visit her again, and she herself wrote the invitation. Then, that every stain might be removed, she commanded honors for the concubine Pearl, decreeing that because this lady was unwilling to watch the desecration of the imperial shrines by foreign enemies, she had leaped into a deep well.

This done, the empress summoned Jung Lu for a report. Soon he was there, leaning heavily upon two tall young eunuchs; and between these youths he looked so aged, so infirm, that the joy of her return drained from the heart of the empress.

"Enter, kinsman," she said, and to the eunuchs she said, "Lead him here to this cushioned seat. And you, Li Lien-ying, bring a bowl of strong hot broth and a jug of hot wine. My kinsman is too weary in my service."

The eunuchs ran to obey. When they were alone, the empress rose and went to Jung Lu and felt his brow and smoothed his hands. Oh, how thin his hands were, the skin hot to her touch!

"I pray," he whispered, "I pray you stand away from me."

"Shall I never be able to minister to you?" she pleaded.

But he was so troubled for fear that her honor be soiled that she sighed and went back to her throne. Then he drew a scroll from his bosom and read from it slowly and with difficulty, reporting that after she had gone from the train, he had supervised the ladies of the court and the removal of the boxes of bullion, each marked with the name of the province and the city that had sent tribute. "Majesty, the baggage alone filled three thousand carts. I fear the anger of the people when they learn the cost of this long journey."

Here the empress stopped him with tender kindness. "Rest yourself now. We are home again."

"Alas, a thousand burdens remain to be carried," he murmured.

"But not by you," she declared.

She scanned his aging handsome face with love and he submitted to her searching eyes. They were closer now, these two, than marriage itself could have made them. Flesh denied, their minds had interwoven in every thought, and knowledge was complete. She put out her hand and stroked his right hand gently. In such communion a moment passed. Then they interchanged a long deep look and he left her.

How could she know that it was the last time she was to see his living face? He fell ill in that same night. The empress sent her court physicians to him, but Jung Lu remained unconscious, and he died, still silent and unknowing, before dawn one day in April 1903. The empress decreed full mourning for the court.

Had she been only a woman, she could have sat the night out in his dead presence and worn white mourning to signify her loss, and wept and wailed aloud to ease her heart. But she was an imperial woman, and she could not leave her palace nor show herself moved beyond the point of lofty grief for a loyal servant of the throne. Her one comfort was to be alone.

One night she lay sleepless, so desperate with sorrow that she fell into a dream, a trance, and felt her soul taken from her body. She dreamed she saw Jung Lu, young again except that he spoke with old wisdom. He took her in his arms and held her for so long that her sorrow lifted and she felt light and free. And then she seemed to hear him speak. "I am with you always." This was his voice. "And when you are most gentle and most wise, I am with you, my being in your being."

The warmth of certainty welled through her soul and into

her body. When she awoke, the weariness was gone. She who had been loved could never be alone. This was the meaning of the dream.

THERE CAME such a change in the life of the empress thereafter that none could comprehend it. She was possessed by ancient wisdom and she made defeat a victory. She fought no more but yielded with grace. To the amazement of all, she even encouraged young Chinese men to go abroad to Japan, and also to Europe and America, and learn the skills and knowledge of the West. This she did one year after the death of Jung Lu.

Before another year had passed, she decreed against the use of opium, not suddenly, for she was mindful of aged men and women who were used to a pipe or two at night to waft them to sleep. No, she said, within ten years, year by year, the importation and the manufacture of opium must be stopped.

And in that same year, she decreed that law and not force must judge the crime. Dismemberment and slicing, she commanded, must be no more, and branding and flogging and the punishment of innocent relatives must cease. Once, long ago, Jung Lu had so adjured her, but she had not heeded him then. Now she remembered.

And who, she asked herself, would take her place when she died? Never would she leave the realm to the weak young emperor who was her eternal prisoner. No, strong young hands must be raised up, but where was the child?

"Alas," she said with plaintive grace, "I am very old. My end is near."

When she spoke thus, her ladies protested much, saying that she was more beautiful than any woman, her skin still fresh and fair, her long eyes black and bright, her lips unwithered. "Ten thousand thousand years, Old Buddha," they replied. "Ten thousand thousand years!"

But she was not deceived. She felt the magic of the future, and her next decree was to send the best of her ministers to the countries of the West. "Go to all countries and see in which the people are most happy and content with their rulers. Choose the four best, and stay a year in each. Study how their rulers govern and what is meant by constitutions and people's rule, and bring back to us a full understanding of these matters."

She had her enemies among her own subjects, who said that she was bowing down before the foreign conquerors, that she had lost her pride.

To all her judges the empress smiled. "I know well what I do," she said. "Nothing now is strange to me. I heard of such things long ago, but only now I heed them. I was told—but only now I believe." Those who listened to her did not understand, but this, too, she knew, and she did not change.

WHEN THE DAYS of mourning for Jung Lu were finished, the empress sent out edicts of invitation to all the foreign envoys and their ladies and their children for a great feast on the first day of the New Year. The envoys themselves were to assemble in the great banquet hall; the emperor was to remain with them and she would appear after the feast. The dishes were to be both Eastern and Western.

The empress commanded the daughter of her plenipotentiary to Europe, a lady who was both young and beautiful, to teach her to give greetings in a foreign language. France, the empress declared after studying maps, was too small a country for her to heed its language. America was too new and uncouth. But the British Empire, she declared, was ruled also by a great woman, for whom she had always had a fondness. Therefore she chose the language of the English queen. Indeed, she had commanded a portrait of Queen Victoria to be hung in her own chamber.

How astonished, then, were the foreign envoys when the empress welcomed them in the English tongue! She was borne into the great hall in her imperial sedan, and the emperor stepped forward to assist her. She came down, her jeweled hand upon his forearm, glittering from head to foot. She inclined her head to the right and to the left as she walked to the throne with her old youthful grace. What was she saying? One envoy after another, bowing before her, heard words which their ears could not at first recognize, but which repeated again and again became clear: "Hao ti diu—" she said, "Ha-p'i niu yerh! Te'-rin-ko t'i!"

They comprehended that the empress asked how they did; she wished them a happy New Year; she invited them to drink tea. These foreign envoys were so moved that they burst into applause, which at first bewildered the empress, who had not in her life before seen men clapping their hands palm to palm. But gazing at the foreign faces, she saw only approval of her effort and she laughed gently, much pleased.

In such a mood the feast day ended, and when gifts had been bestowed, the empress retired to her own chamber. She had done well this day, she mused. She had laid foundations of accord and friendship. And she thought of Victoria, the Western queen, and she wished that they two could meet. All under Heaven are one family, she would tell Victoria.

Alas, before such dreams could grow the news was cried across the seas that Victoria was dead. The empress was aghast. "How did my sister die?" she cried.

When she heard that the queen had died of old age as any common mortal does, the knowledge struck like a sword. If Victoria was dead, then anyone could die. Though she herself was strong, it was indeed her duty once again to find an heir, a child, for whom she must rule while she trained him to be the emperor. But this time she would let the heir be taught what the world was. She would summon teachers from the West to teach him. He must learn to make Western war, and then in his time, when she was gone, he would do what she had failed to do. He would drive the enemy into the sea.

What child, what child? The question was a torment until suddenly she remembered that a child had been born in Jung Lu's palace. His daughter, wed to Prince Ch'un, had given birth to a son but a few days before. This child, this boy, was Jung Lu's grandson. She bent her head to hide her smile from Heaven. This would lift her beloved even to the Dragon Throne! It was her will and Heaven must approve.

Yet she would placate the gods and preserve the child's life by keeping her plan secret until the emperor lay upon his deathbed—not far off, surely, for pains and ills consumed his flesh.

For two months the country had been cursed by a dry cold that reached the very roots of trees and winter wheat. No snow fell that winter, and now, in the last seventeen days, a most unseasonable warmth had crept up from the south. Even the peonies, bewildered, had sent up shoots. The people had flocked to temples to reproach the gods, and seven days ago the empress had commanded the Buddhist priests to take the gods out daily in procession to see for themselves what damage was abroad. And then one day she heard a sound of rushing wind and lifted up her head.

"What wind is this," she now inquired of her ladies, "and from what corner of the earth does it arise?" Even as she spoke all heard a clap of thunder, unseasonable and unexpected. A roar came from the streets, the people running out from every house to look at the skies.

The wind rose higher. It shrieked through the palaces, and great gusts tore at the doors and windows. But this wind was a clean wind from the sea, dustless and pure. The empress rose from her throne and walked into the court beyond. She lifted up her face toward the swirling sky and smelled the wind. At this same instant the skies opened and rain came down, a cool strong rain, strange in winter but how welcome!

While the rain fell on her, a great voice rose from far beyond the walls, the sound of many people crying out together, "Old Buddha! Old Buddha sends the rain!"

She turned and walked to her private throne room again and stood there inside the doorway, her satin garments dripping on the tiled floor. While her ladies made themselves busy wiping her dry, she laughed at their sweet reproaches. "I have not been so happy since I was a child," she told them. "I remember now that when I was a child I loved to run into the rain."

"Old Buddha," her ladies murmured fondly.

The empress turned to reprove her ladies with all grace and gentleness. "Heaven sends the rain," she said. "How can I, a mortal, command the clouds?"

But they insisted. "It is for your sake, Old Buddha, that the rain comes down, the fortunate rain, blessing us all because of you."

"Well, well," she said, and laughed to indulge them. "Perhaps," she said, "perhaps."

THE CHINA
I KNEW

THE CHINA I KNEW

A CONDENSATION FROM THE BOOK *MY SEVERAL WORLDS* BY

Pearl S. Buck

TITLE PAGE ILLUSTRATION BY NITA ENGLE

As Pearl Buck was growing up, her missionary parents refused to shelter her in the protected compounds where other foreign families lived. Instead, she was raised in a largely Chinese world, speaking the language and making friends among all classes of people.

She chronicled this unique experience in her first autobiography, *My Several Worlds*, from which *The China I Knew* has been condensed. It is a remarkably candid personal story, and even more, it documents the tumultuous story of the making of modern China as Mrs. Buck saw it and lived it.

1

THIS MORNING I rose early, as is my habit, and as usual I went to the open window and looked out over the Pennsylvania land that is the fairest I know. I have seen these hills and fields at dawn and dark, in sunshine and in moonlight, in summer green and winter snow, and yet there is always a new view before my eyes. Today I looked at sunrise upon a scene so Chinese that it might have been from my childhood. A mist lay over the big pond under the weeping willows, a frail cloud through which the water shone a silvered gray, and against this background stood a great white heron, profiled upon one stalk of leg. Centuries of Chinese artists have painted that scene, and here it was before my eyes, upon my land, as American a piece of earth as can be imagined. Had I prayed Heaven, I could not have asked for a picture more suited to the mood for this day's work, which is to begin my book.

The reader is warned that this is not a complete autobiography. My private life has been uneventfully happy except for a few incidents whose disaster I was able to accept. I have had a happy childhood, marriage in its time, love and home and children, friends, and more than enough success.

The fortunate chance I have had has been the age into which I was born. Never, or so it seems to me as I read history, has there been a more stirring and germinal period than the one I have seen passing before my eyes. I might have grown up secure in the pleasant small town of my ancestors, taking for granted the advantages of families accustomed to more than their share, perhaps, of comfort. Instead I had as my parents two enterprising, idealistic young people who felt impelled to leave their astonished relatives to take up life in China and there proclaim the advantages of their religion. To them the task seemed inevitable and satisfying, and they were devoted to it for more than half a century.

As a result, I grew up on the Asian side of the globe instead of on the American side, although I was born, quite accidentally, in my own country. My young mother, who was only twenty-three years old when she went as a bride to China, had four children rather rapidly, and as rapidly lost three of them to tropical diseases, which at that time no one understood how to prevent or cure. She was distracted enough so that the doctors ordered my father to take her to her home in West Virginia for two years. It was in the last few months of this long rest, on June 26, 1892, that I was born, and thereby became an American citizen by birth as well as by two centuries of ancestry.

Had I been given the choice of place for my birth, I would have chosen exactly where I was born, my grandfather's large white house with its pillared double portico, set in a beautiful landscape of rich green plains and with the Allegheny Mountains as a background. I had a happy beginning in a pleasant place, and at the age of three months, my mother's health being restored, I was transported across the seas to live and grow up in China.

Thereafter the world in which I lived was Asian. The actual earth was Chinese, but around China clustered a host of other nations and peoples. Thus I learned about India very early indeed, because our family physician was Indian. High on the hillside across the valley above which we lived in our low brick house, a Japanese lady lived with her English husband, and among our friends were other Asians from the Philippines, Thailand, Indonesia, Burma and Korea.

To the Western world belonged the English friends we had and the few French and Italian families who lived behind the barred gates of the British Concession in our port city of Chinkiang on the great Yangtze River.

In the secret thoughts of the Chinese, confided to me by my Chinese playmates, these Westerners were "foreigners" and potential enemies. "Foreigners" had done evil things in Asia—not the Americans, my small and even then tactful friends declared, for Americans, they said, were "good." They had taken no land from Asian countries, and they sent food in famine time. I accepted the distinction and felt no part with those other Western peoples, whom at that time I considered also my enemies. Our version of the universal game of cops and robbers in those days was the endless war of the Chinese against the imperial powers of the West, and as the sole American in the game, it was my duty to come forward at the height of battle and provide food and succor for the ever-victorious Chinese.

Halfway between my two worlds, Chinese and American, were the children of my Chinese adopted sister. Years before I was born, my mother was called one night to the house of a Chinese lady who was dying. My mother would never tell me her name, but I knew that she was the first wife of the head of an old and wealthy Chinese family. My father had become acquainted with the head of this family through their mutual scholarly interests and had asked my mother to call upon his friend's wife. The lady was attracted to my mother, and my mother to her, so that when a sudden illness became obviously mortal for the lady, she called my mother to her bedside and asked her to take her small daughter, who she feared would suffer if left alone with her husband's concubines. My parents adopted the child. Her name was Ts'ai Yün, or Beautiful Cloud, and I remember her as a gentle young woman with a soft, pretty face. She was already married by the time I was born, and she had begun to bear the large family of girls that became such an embarrassment for her.

My mother had followed the Chinese tradition for Beautiful Cloud and, when she had finished her education in the mission school for girls, betrothed her to a handsome young man, the son of my father's assistant pastor. It was a happy marriage and a suitable one; the young man followed in his father's footsteps and became a pillar of the church in a mild and agreeable way. The only embarrassment was the regularity with which the girl babies appeared in their home. A first girl they accepted with welcome, a second one a year later with equanimity, a third with gravity, a fourth with consternation. By the time the sixth one came, the situation was critical. People were asking, How is it that Christians have nothing but girls? Inasmuch as the matter had become a subject of prayer for the church members after the third girl, the next question was, How is it that our prayers are not heard? Actual doubt of the foreign God began to arise and my father, who had tried to take no notice, exclaimed "Oh, pshaw" several times a day, as was his habit when perplexed. No one suffered more than my pretty adopted sister, who felt that all was her fault, and never was her husband's goodness more manifest than when he refused to allow her to take the blame. He was an example of Christian fortitude, as my father remarked.

The story had a happy ending, for after six girls my distracted Chinese sister did give birth to a fine boy. This ended the family. Neither she nor her husband dared to risk an eighth child that might be another girl.

It was a happy world for a child, in spite of lepers and beggars and occasional famines; and our ruler, if you please, was a proud old woman in Peking, the empress dowager, or, as her own people called her, the Venerable Ancestor.

I cannot remember when I first learned that the empress dowager was not Chinese and that many Chinese thought of the dynasty as alien. I knew the Manchu, for every important city had a special reservation for them and we had one in Chinkiang, too. It was on the edge of the city and a high wall surrounded all the Manchu houses. At the front gate stood Chinese guards, and no one was allowed to go in without their permission. It was not imprisonment, supposedly, but simply that all Manchu needed special protection because they were related to the royal house and so were part of officialdom. Actually it was a luxurious imprisonment, for this was the Chinese way of conquering enemies. When the Manchu invasion of 1644 was successful in a military sense—and almost any people could invade China successfully, it seemed, in a military sense—the people were apparently passive, mildly curious, and even courteous to their conquerors. The real struggle came afterward, but so subtly that the conquerors never knew they were being conquered. The technique of victory was that as soon as the invaders laid down their arms, the philosophical but intensely practical Chinese persuaded them to move into palaces and begin to enjoy themselves. The more the new rulers ate and drank, the better pleased the Chinese were, and if they also learned to enjoy gambling and opium and many wives, so much the better. Since the Manchu were encouraged to do no work, the tedious details of government were performed by Chinese, ostensibly for them. The Manchu were like pet cats, and the Chinese kept them so, knowing that when the degeneration was complete, a Chinese revolutionary would overthrow the rotten structure.

As a child, of course, I did not know how near the end was for the Manchu. Those early years were carefree ones for me. The Chinese servants spoiled me dangerously, always taking my side against discipline. When my mother set me a task as a much-needed punishment, I had only to look sorrowful and my Chinese amah would secretly perform the task, or, if it had to do with the outdoors, the gardener or the second boy would do it.

THE CHINA I KNEW

The cook himself was not above helping me in a pinch. My mother discovered this eventually and tried to show them that they were preventing me from learning the proper lessons of self-discipline, to which their reply was bewilderment and murmurings that I was only a child and must not be expected to know everything at once. Discipline, in their estimation, was the expression of adult anger and the child must as a matter of course be protected from it, since anger was merely a sort of dangerous seizure. My mother learned to set me tasks that the loving Chinese could not perform for me, such as looking up words in the English dictionary and writing down their meanings. And then how the agitated Chinese tried to help anyway and comforted me in the cruel labor by smuggling in a toy that one of them had rushed out to buy in the marketplace—a pottery doll dressed in bright robes of paper or a bamboo whistle—or sweetmeats or a sugar tiger stuck on the end of a stick!

Once, before I was eight, my father whipped me for telling a lie, and horror spread through the servants' quarters and even among the neighbors. I had broken the gardener's hoe and then said that I had not, and in his grief, in order to stave off the whipping, the gardener swore that it was he who had done it. My father had seen the event, however, and the whipping was swift and hard. The gardener stood weeping in the doorway with peanut candy bulging in his pocket. Such foods were forbidden, for the germs of tropical diseases were hidden in them, but they were fed to me secretly and I ate them without qualms because the Chinese did, and built up a like immunity, I suppose, for I was the healthiest child imaginable. Nor did I consciously deceive my parents, I think, for although I believed what they said about white people, who seemed to die or at least to fall ill with amazing ease, I did not consider myself a white person in those days. Even though I knew I was not altogether Chinese, still I was Chinese enough to eat sweets from the marketplace with impunity.

Thus I grew up in a double world, the small, white, clean,

382

Presbyterian American world of my parents and the big, loving, merry, not-too-clean Chinese world, and there was little communication between them. When I was in the Chinese world, I spoke Chinese and behaved like a Chinese. I ate as the Chinese did, and I shared their thoughts and feelings. When I was in the American world, I shut the door between.

In the Chinese world, it is true, we often discussed the Americans. My parents fortunately were beloved by the Chinese, and except for a few unfortunate facts, such as my father's absurdly large feet and immense height, and my mother's quick temper, I had nothing to be ashamed of. But other white people did not always fare so well, and their characters were sometimes dissected with mirth and thoroughness. I knew what no other Americans knew about the white people and their secret lives. I knew that a certain man kept a secret whisky bottle in his closet, and that a certain woman would not sleep with her husband, and that a certain lonely young man tried to make love to any woman who would allow it, even to the gateman's wife. Nothing was private in the Chinese world, nothing could be kept secret—the very word for secret also meant unlawful. It was a richly human world, steeped in humor and pathos, for more often than not, when the laughter was over, some kindly old Chinese would say tolerantly, "But these Christians are good, nevertheless. They do their best and we must not blame them for what they do not know. After all, they were not born Chinese. Heaven did not ordain."

WHEN I THINK of the world of my childhood, I see a circle of green hills with purple mountains beyond. Between the green hills were the greener valleys, tilled to the last inch by farmers for four thousand years. Farm families rolled up the legs of their blue cotton trousers and planted their rice seedlings together; there was poetry in every movement of the blue-clad peasants. Ponds full of fish lay outside the gates of farmhouses around us, and every family had a pig and some hens and a cock and a water buffalo.

Beggars were on the city streets, but unless there was a famine in the north, those beggars were as professional as the city thieves. They were organized under a beggar king and they exacted alms from all shopkeepers. If any shopkeeper failed to pay, the most hideous of the lepers and the deformed would station themselves outside his doors to scare away his customers. To be a beggar was to accept the lowliest life, unless one went still lower and became a professional soldier. We had no beggars in the villages, but we did have soldiers. There was an earth-walled fort near our house, and the terror of my life was that I might meet a soldier on the road to the Chinese girls' school where I went every day. If I saw one lounging along the road in his yellow uniform, I ran more fleetly than any deer through the big clanging gate of our compound.

"What is the matter?" my mother inquired one afternoon.

"A soldier!" I gasped.

"What of that?" she asked too innocently.

I could not explain. She belonged to the little white world and she could not understand. But in my other world I had been taught that a soldier is separated from the laws of life and home, and it is well for a girl child to run fast if he comes near.

"True," old Madame Shen said one day when she was instructing me with her granddaughters, "not every soldier is a devil, but it is hard for him not to be. He has a devilish trade."

Madame Shen was a neighbor, a matriarch in her own domain as much as the empress dowager was in the palaces of Peking. Her granddaughters were my schoolmates, for the Shen family was enlightened and there was already talk of not binding the feet of their youngest girls. The older girls had bound feet, and while I did not envy the pains and aches of that dire process whereby the toes of each foot were turned under into the sole, and the heel and the ball of the foot brought together under the arch, still there were times in those early days when I wondered if I was jeopardizing my chances for a good husband by having big feet, that is, un-bound feet. In that world small feet were a beauty that any woman could have, whatever her face.

Speaking of cruelty, this is perhaps the place to mention the cruelty to animals that shocks so many foreigners when they visit China. I used to wonder why my Chinese friends, whom I knew to be merciful and considerate toward people, could be quite indifferent to suffering animals. The cause, I discovered as I grew older, lay in the permeation of Chinese thought by Buddhist theory. Part of the doctrine of the reincarnation of the human soul is that an evil human being becomes an animal in his next incarnation. Therefore every animal was once a wicked human being. While the average Chinese might deny direct belief in this theory, the pervading belief would lead him to feel contempt for animals.

Another seeming cruelty among the Chinese, also very shocking to Westerners, was that if a person fell into danger— for example, if he were drowning—only a very rare Chinese would rescue him. Cruel? Yes, but again, centuries of Buddhism had persuaded the people generally to believe that fate pursued the sufferer, that his hour of death had come. If someone defied fate and saved him, the rescuer must assume the responsibilities of the one saved. A man, however kind, might hesitate to save a person if thereafter he had to care for this person, and even perhaps his whole family, because he had given new life to one who was supposed to die.

IT WAS perhaps because the Manchu rulers were always careful not to disturb such beliefs and customs of the Chinese that their dynasty survived so long. Certainly we were scarcely conscious of being ruled at all. There was a magistrate in each county seat, and at the head of each province was a viceroy, the representative of the throne in Peking, but the main duty of these officials was to see that every family continued free to live its life. They interfered only when some injustice was done. I never saw a policeman in that early world of China.

Each family maintained firm discipline, and if a crime was committed, the family elders sat in conference to decide the punishment, which sometimes was even death. For the honor of the family the young were taught how to behave, and though they were treated with the utmost leniency until they were seven or eight years old, after that they learned to respect the code of human relationships so clearly set forth by Confucius.

Chinese children were alarmingly spoiled when they were small, my Western parents thought. No one stopped tantrums or willfulness, and a baby was picked up whenever he cried—indeed he was carried by somebody or other most of the time. The Chinese believed that it was important to allow a child to cry his fill and vent all his tempers and humors while he was small, for if these were suppressed by force or fright, then anger entered into the blood and poisoned the heart, and would surely come forth later to make adult trouble. It was a knowledge as ancient as a thousand years, and yet something of the same philosophy is considered modern in the Western world in which I live today. Somehow these spoiled children emerged like butterflies from cocoons at about the age of seven or eight, amazingly adult, sweet-tempered and self-disciplined. The Chinese believed that there is an age for learning each law of life, and to teach a child too young was simply to wear out the teacher and frustrate the child. It was a delightful and lenient world in which a child could live his own life. Instead of the hard-pressed father and mother of the Western child, the children of my early world had grandparents, innumerable aunts, uncles, cousins and servants to love them and indulge them.

If the child was a boy, when he reached the age of seven a person outside his family became important in his life. This was his schoolteacher. In that Chinese world the teacher had the responsibility not only for the mental education of the child but for his moral welfare, too. Education included the learning of self-discipline and proper conduct, and proper conduct meant perfecting and practicing how to behave to all other persons in their various stations and relationships. The fruit of such education was inner security. A child learned in the home how to conduct himself toward the different generations, and in school he learned how to conduct himself toward teachers, friends, officials, neighbors and acquaintances. Being so taught, the young were never ill at ease. We young persons knew where to sit when we came into a room. We did not take the seats of our elders until we ourselves became the elders. We were taught not to sit until our elders sat, not to eat until they had eaten, not to drink tea until their bowls were lifted. If there were not enough chairs, we stood, and when an elder spoke to us, however playfully, we answered with the proper title. Did we feel oppressed? I am sure we did not. We knew where we were, and we knew, too, that someday we would be elders.

I am glad that my first years were in an ordered world where children knew the boundaries beyond which they could not go and yet within which they lived secure. My parents had their work of teaching and preaching their religion, and this kept them busy and happy and out of their child's way. I had lessons to do, but a solitary child learns lessons quickly and most of my day was free for play and dreaming.

How sorry I feel nowadays for the overcrowded lives of my own children, whose every hour is filled with school and sports and social events of various kinds! They have no chance to know the delight of long days empty except for what one puts into them. Then the imagination grows like the tree of life, enchanting the air. No wonder I was a happy child, and that my parents were happy, too. We met briefly, we smiled and communicated about necessary matters of food and clothing and the small tasks of my day. My mother bade me hold my shoulders straight, and my father reminded me at table to hold my knife and fork as he did. Upon this subject of the knife and fork my mind was divided, for my mother ate her food as Americans do, cutting her meat and then putting down the knife to take up her fork, but my father ate as English people

THE CHINA I KNEW

do, holding the fork in his left hand and the knife in his right, and piling the chopped food against his fork. Each gave me directions, and sometimes I obeyed one and sometimes the other, accepting, as children do, the peculiarities of parents. Meanwhile my private choice was chopsticks.

MY EARLY MEMORIES are not of parents, however, but of places. Our big whitewashed brick bungalow, encircled by deep arched verandas for coolness, was honeycombed with places that I loved. Under the verandas the beaten earth was cool and dry, and I had my haunts there. The gardener made a stove for me from a large Standard Oil tin with one side cut away. He lined the sides with mud mixed with lime and then set into it a coarse iron grating. When I lit a fire beneath this and put in charcoal, I could really cook, and of course I cooked the easy Chinese dishes I liked best and that my amah had taught me. I had a few dolls, but my "children" were the small folk of the servants' quarters or the neighbors' houses. We had wonderful hours of play, unsupervised by adults. I remember going to bed at night replete with solid satisfaction because the day had been so packed with pleasurable play.

Under those verandas, too, I kept my pet pheasants and there I smoked my first corn-silk cigarette, an unknown sin in my world, but introduced to me by the small red-haired son of a visiting missionary who had lately returned from America.

"All the kids smoke in America," the rascal said, and so we smoked in the latticed cellars while our elders talked theology upstairs. It was not exciting enough for me, however, for in my other world any child could take a puff from a Chinese grand-parent's water pipe and adults only laughed when children choked on the raw Chinese tobacco smoke. Opium I knew I must never taste. My parents had spent weary hours trying to help some addict break the chain that bound him, and I feared the sweet and sickish stuff, imagining that if once I tasted it, I would grow thin and yellow, like the father of my next-door playmate, and never be myself again.

There was more than that to opium. Our city had been captured in 1842 by the British during the Opium Wars, when China tried to stop the entrance of opium from India and failed. The English insisted on their right to trade, maintaining that it was not they who had introduced the opium habit to the Chinese, that opium was grown on Chinese soil and greedy Chinese traders merely wanted all the income for themselves. Probably this was partly true, yet there were many Chinese who were not traders and who were frightened at the tremendous increase of opium smoking among their people. It was also true that most of the opium, especially the cheaper kind, came from India, and not only under the English flag but also under the Dutch and the American flags.

Opium was first brought to China by Arab traders during the Middle Ages as a drug beneficial for diarrhea and intestinal diseases. The Chinese did not begin smoking it until the Portuguese traders taught them to do so in the seventeenth century, when it became a fashionable pastime for officials and rich people. Most Chinese, even in my childhood, considered it a foreign custom.

The Chinese lost the Opium Wars, and the price was heavy. Treaty ports were yielded, the rights of trade and commerce were demanded and given, and high indemnities had to be paid. Chinkiang, my home city, was deeply affected by the wars. It became a treaty port and the stretch of land along the river's edge was a British Concession. High walls surrounded it, broken by two great iron gates that were always locked at night. Within the boundaries lived the British consul and all the other foreigners, except for a few missionary families who preferred to live among the Chinese. My parents were among these. They were constitutionally unable to preach a gospel of love and brotherhood they did not practice, and they could not live happily behind the high walls and the iron gates. Happy for me that I had such parents, for instead of the narrow and conventional life of the white man in Asia, I lived with the Chinese people and spoke their tongue as I spoke my own.

Did I not see sights that children should not see and hear talk not fit for children's ears? If I did, I cannot remember. I saw poor and starving people in a famine year, but my parents bade me help them. Thus I learned early that suffering can always be relieved, if there is the will to do it, and in that knowledge I have found escape from despair throughout my life. Often I saw lepers, their flesh eaten away from their bones. I saw dead children lying on the hillsides and wild dogs gnawing at their flesh, and I saw rascals enough and heard rich cursing when men and women quarreled. I cannot remember anything evil from these sights and sounds. It is better to learn early of the inevitable depths, for then sorrow and death take their proper place in life and one is not afraid.

And how much joy I saw and shared in! We were the only missionary family I knew in those days who welcomed Chinese guests to spend the night with us. I am sure this was partly because my parents were themselves cultivated persons and drew to them Chinese of like nature. They disliked a crude and ignorant Chinese as much as they disliked such a person were he white. Thus we learned early by their example to judge a man or woman by character and intelligence rather than by race or sect.

How shall I conjure those childhood days? I rose early in the morning because my father demanded it. He got up at five o'clock, and when he had bathed and dressed, he prayed for an hour in his study. He expected then to find the family waiting for him at the breakfast table. If any one was not there, he would not seat himself at the end of our oval teakwood dining table but would stand, tall and immovable, his blue eyes gazing across the room at the landscape beyond the high windows. When a small girl hurried through the door and slipped panting into her chair, he sat down, and with him all of us. He then asked grace, not carelessly gabbling, but with a moment's preceding silence. In a solemn voice peculiar to his prayers, he asked for the divine blessing and prayed that the food might strengthen us to do God's will.

The food itself was simple, but it seems to me that it was always good. In the morning, except in the summer, we had oranges, brought by ship and bearer from Fukien, where such oranges grow as I have never seen elsewhere. When the oranges were gone, we had loquats, and then apricots, perhaps fresh litchis, and of course peaches, bananas, pineapples and melons of many kinds. Melons were summer fruits and we never ate them if they had been cut in the streets, for we knew that flies were deadly enemies, carrying dysentery and cholera and typhoid on their tiny feet.

After the fruit at breakfast we always had a special sort of porridge made of whole wheat and ground at home on a Chinese stone hand mill. We ate it with sugar and white buffalo cream, which was richer than cow's cream. It was followed by eggs and hot rolls or biscuits.

Breakfasts were always solid and American, for my parents worked hard and expected their children to do so, but the other two meals were less hearty. I usually ate first within the servants' quarters, and my mother was often astonished at my lack of appetite without apparently ever guessing its cause. The servants' food was plain but delicious: even their breakfast I liked much better than my own. In our region it was rice gruel served very hot, with a few small dishes of salt fish, salted dried turnips and pickled mustard greens, and now and then a hard-boiled egg. But the servants' midday meal was the best: rice, cooked dry and light, a bowl of soup of some sort, another bowl with Chinese cabbage and fresh white bean curd, and still another with a bit of meat or fowl. We needed no dessert, for fruits and sweets were considered between-meal dainties.

The gala days in my Chinese world were the days when we were invited to wedding and birthday feasts. Then the menu included a score or more of different dishes, each perfected by centuries of gourmets. The best of these Chinese dishes were always seasonal as well as local. In my earliest world I ate rice-flour cakes at New Year's, and in the spring I ate glutinous rice wrapped in green leaves from the river reeds and steamed, and with it hard-boiled duck eggs or red sugar, which I now know is full of vitamins, but which I ate then merely because it was delicious. The only delicacy I ate at any time of the year was the barley taffy covered with sesame seeds that the traveling vendor sold as he wandered along the narrow earthen roads of our hills and valleys. Whenever I heard his small bronze gong struck by a minute wooden hammer, I gathered a few coppers from my store and ran to beckon to him. The taffy, dusted with flour to keep it from becoming sticky, lay in a big round slab on the lid of one of the baskets he carried suspended on a bamboo pole across his shoulders. After we had settled the size of the piece I could buy with my coins, each of which was worth a tenth of a penny, he took his sharp chisel and chipped off the portion. It was a delicious sweet, long lasting and very healthy, since it contained no white cane sugar.

One of the benefits of sharing the food of the poor—and how generous they always were—was that I ate brown rice and brown flour and brown sugar. Yet the strange human passion for whiteness possessed the Chinese, too. When a poor man became rich, he immediately took to eating white polished rice and flour and imported white cane sugar, and then wondered why he did not feel as well as he used to in his days of poverty.

And though I was pitied for my blue eyes and yellow hair, my white skin was always praised. It was counted a misfortune if a daughter in a Chinese family was born with brown skin instead of skin the color of light cream. The northern Chinese are tall and fair in comparison to the dark, short brown people of the south, and so the women of the north are much admired.

Throughout those glorious days of my early childhood there was always something to see and to do. Behind our compound walls, whose gates were never locked except at night, a warm and changeful life went on. Many Chinese ladies came to see my mother, curious to meet a foreigner and see a foreign house. My own friends came and went, and our favorite playing place was the hillside in front of the gate, where the pampas grass grew above our heads. There in the green shadows we pretended jungles one day and housekeeping the next. In a sunny corner of the south veranda I spent many winter afternoons reading alone. It was in that spot that I read and reread our set of Charles Dickens, refreshing myself meanwhile with oranges or peanuts.

For change and excitement we went on rare occasions to the hills or to Silver Island for picnics. Or we might go to Golden Island, where there lived a giant who froze my heart when I looked into his fat, bland face. He stayed in an inner room of the vast and famous Buddhist monastery, an immense figure in the gray robes of a priest, eight and a half feet tall and broad in proportion. He sat with huge hands placed on his knees, and he would not get up to show how tall he was unless he was paid to do so. Even then he would not always get up, for he was often in a surly mood, but kept the money anyhow. If I had nightmares, it was about that hideous gigantic priest.

The Chinese year was rich with treasures of feast days, each with its particular dainty to be made and eaten, and each with its special toys and delightful occupations. Thus at the Feast of Lanterns our faithful servants bought us paper rabbits pulled upon little wheels and lit within by candles, or lotus flowers and butterflies, or even horses, split in two, one half of which I carried on my front and the other strapped upon my back, so that to my great joy I looked like a horse walking in the dark. And in the spring there were kites in every imaginable shape. Sometimes we made them ourselves of split reeds, rice paste and thin red paper. Then we spent our days out on the hills, watching the huge and intricate ones that even grown men flew: a mighty dragon or a thirty-foot centipede or a pagoda that needed a dozen men to get it aloft. We played with birds in cages and birds that could talk if we taught them carefully enough, black macaws and white-vested magpies, and we had nightingales for music. We listened to the wandering storytellers who beat their little gongs while traveling the country roads, or stopped at villages at night and gathered their crowds on a threshing floor. We went to see the troupes of traveling actors who performed their plays in front of the temples, and thus I early learned my Chinese history and became familiar with its heroes. The Chinese New Year was, of course, the crown of all the year's joys. On that day we exchanged gifts with our Chinese friends and received calls and went calling, dressed in our best and bowing and wishing "Happy New Year and riches" everywhere we went.

Yet there was always the other world on the fringe of my Chinese world, the white world, which had its own holidays and pleasures. Halloween, for instance, I faithfully observed with a jack-o'-lantern made from a yellow Chinese gourd, and the kindly Chinese neighbors pretended to be terrified when a fiery, grinning face shone through their windows on the October night. Christmas, too, was a foreign festival, a family joy, and so were the Fourth of July and Thanksgiving. My parents were careful to observe all such days and to teach us what they meant.

It was in the year 1900, when I was eight years old, that the two worlds of my childhood first split apart. In an academic fashion I had always known, of course, that I was American and not Chinese. I even felt a rough justice in street urchins' calling me "little foreign devil," or in their pretending when they saw me that it would soon rain, since devils, they said, come out only when it is going to rain. I knew that I was no devil, but to be called one did not trouble me because I was still secure in my Chinese world. I merely replied that those urchins were the children of turtles—that is to say, they were bastards—a remark that sent them into shocked silence. My parents did not know for years the significance of my retort, and by that time I was old enough to be ashamed of it myself.

In that year of 1900, however, throughout the beautiful springtime of the Yangtze River valley, I felt my world splitting. The stream of visitors thinned and sometimes days passed without a single Chinese friend appearing before our gates. My playmates were often silent, and at last they, too, ceased to climb the hill from the valley.

I was bewildered at first, and then sorely wounded. When my mother saw this, she explained to me as best she could what was happening. It had nothing to do with our being Americans, she said, for we had never been cruel to the Chinese nor had we taken their land or their river ports. Other white people had done the evil, and our Chinese friends, she promised me, understood this and felt as warmly toward us as before, only they did not dare to show their feelings for fear of being blamed. It was then that I felt the first and primary injustice of life. I was innocent, but because I had blue eyes and blond hair, I was hated, and because of fear of me and my kind, I walked in danger.

Danger! Its meaning had been unknown to me, but now we were in danger, I and my family and all white men, women and children like us. For there came creeping down from Peking to our midcountry province the most sickening rumors about the empress dowager. The Venerable Ancestor had turned against us. Because greedy Europeans were gnawing at the shores of China, she wanted to rid herself of all white people and lock the gates of China forever against us. She was scarcely to be blamed, my grave father said, for wanting to free China of its plunderers. How would we like it if our own country, the United States, were fastened upon by strangers and stolen away from us bit by bit, by nagging petty wars and huge indemnities in money and land and railroad rights? He sympathized with the empress dowager, but his sympathy could not save us.

I remember the faultless summer day when we heard of the first massacre of missionaries in Shantung and that the little children had been murdered with their parents. It was the death of the children that made my mother's face turn pale and made my father decide that we must all be sent away. He had not believed until then that the empress dowager could

Pearl Buck grew up in China during the turbulent last years of the reign of Empress Tzu Hsi, the center figure in the picture at right, which was taken in 1903. When Pearl was eight years old, the Boxer Rebellion broke out. It pitted Chinese fanatics against foreign troops stationed in China, such as the American contingent marching past a Peking temple below.

The fighting forced Pearl's family to flee from their home in Chinkiang for the safety of the well-protected foreign enclaves in coastal Shanghai.

Pearl's parents, Absalom and Carie Sydenstricker, were Presbyterian missionaries. They sat for this formal portrait in Shanghai, with older son Edgar (standing), Pearl (at her father's knee) and baby Clyde, who died of diphtheria when he was four. Pearl (above right) was nine when she returned to America for the first time. Back in China she continued her education at a Chinese mission school like the one shown at right.

be so foolish as to trust herself to the Boxers,* that clan of monstrous impostors who pretended to her that they could by their secret magic withstand the foreign guns. But by this time hysteria was raging over the whole nation. The foreign powers had demanded one concession after another from the weak young emperor. France had taken Annam, England insisted upon Weihai, France upon Kwangchowan, Germany upon Tsingtao and Russia upon Dairen. These were called "leased territories," but actually they were colonies. And where were the army and the navy for which the Chinese people had been paying so heavily through taxes? It was clear that the money had been absorbed, spent, squandered, not only by the old empress dowager herself upon such follies as a marble boat on the lake by the Summer Palace, but also through the private hoardings of her officials. When her full guilt began to be suspected, she was glad to turn the attention of the angry people to the plundering foreigners, and so she listened to the Boxers, against the advice of her best ministers. The young emperor now had no power at all, for the empress dowager had had him taken prisoner and locked up on an island. All the leading reformers who had advocated that China modernize to defend herself were decapitated or gone.

Into this storm and fury our quiet bungalow was swept one day like a leaf upon a whirlpool. The air that summer's day was hot and still, and from the verandas the landscape was beautiful, the valleys green as jade with their earthen farmhouses shaded beneath the willow trees. White geese walked the paths between the fields and children played on the threshing floors while their parents in blue cotton peasant garb tilled the fields. Beyond the dark city the shining river flowed toward the sea. I remember, though I was only eight

---

*The I Ho Ch'üan, or "Boxers"—literally translated, the "Righteous Harmony Fists"—who gave their name to the so-called Boxer Rebellion of 1900, sprang up during the late 1890s as secret groups of nationalists and terrorists. One of their slogans was: "Protect the country, destroy the foreigners." They used a combination of special exercises and self-hypnotism to make themselves, they claimed, invulnerable to bullets.

years old, that long moment I stood on the veranda, gazing upon the scene that was home to me because I knew no other. It was the same, and yet I knew, child though I was, that it could never be the same again.

We left our home on that perfect summer's day and boarded one of the sturdy steamboats that plied the Yangtze down to Shanghai. There had been plenty of argument in the mission bungalow before we left, for my mother and father did not leave their post easily. Even now there was no thought of my father's remaining with us: he was to take us to Shanghai and then return alone. We left the house as it was, but my mother took some of the family silver she had brought from her West Virginia home and buried it in a corner of the yard to save it. She had learned such lessons long ago in her childhood when her family had hidden their treasures during the Civil War.

The actual leave-taking was entirely unreal. The signal for instant flight had long been planned. When the flag on the American consulate was changed to one of solid red, we must go, and it had changed at noon. I said farewell to the house, and to my favorite haunts inside our compound: the big Chinese elm, three feet in diameter, that I had climbed so often, the garden bench under the bamboos where I went to read, and the little play kitchen under the verandas. And there were the animals: my pheasants, a rabbit, and an old gray dog, Nebuchadnezzar, whom we called Neb, a humble, mangy, pleading, too-affectionate creature that no one could love except me. I could not be sure that anyone would feed him when I was gone, for our amah was going with us, and she alone had the heart to keep old Neb alive for my sake.

And yet I could not believe that I was never to return. My father would be here, I could not imagine him not living, and there was the buried silver to be dug up. The trees must remain, and the permanent hills and the valleys. With irrepressible hope, I followed my family to the embankment along the river and crossed the wooden bridge to the steamer.

We reached Shanghai, but for the next months—I think it

was almost a year—my memory falters and whatever happened seems accidental and disjointed. We were merely refugees. Shanghai was breathlessly hot, but I was used to semitropical heat. At home our daily baths were in a painted tin tub filled with buckets of water that the water bearer brought in. Here I saw for the first time water coming out of the wall from faucets. It was pure magic, the self-coming water that I had heard about. The tub was a big one, and it was set in a wide shallow wooden platform fenced about with board and lined with tin, at one end of which was a drain. My mother stopped the drain with a big cork and then let cool water run into the walled platform, and there on hot afternoons my baby sister Grace and I played.

One incident of that refugee period is rooted in my mind. We were walking along a street, my mother and I. It was crowded, and ahead of me, stifling me, I thought, was a stout Chinese gentleman in a blue satin robe and a black sleeveless jacket. Straight in front of my face was the swinging end of his queue, a black silk woven cord ending in a large tassel. The heat became unbearable, the gentleman seemed immovable, and at last in a sort of willful impatience I did what I had never done before. I pulled the tassel gently, as a hint that he walk a little faster. Instantly he turned around and directed a look of black wrath at me. He did not frighten me, but my mother did. For I saw her face go white, and quickly she begged the Chinese to forgive me.

"She is only a child." I remember her very words. "But she is a naughty child, and I will punish her. Please overlook her fault."

The gentleman did not reply but he did not look mollified, and my mother drew me down another street. "Never," she said more sternly than I had ever heard her speak, "never do such a thing again! It might be very dangerous."

What frightened me was the look on her face. She was afraid, afraid of a Chinese! I had never seen her afraid before in my life. It was indeed the end of an era.

2

MY FATHER was not killed during the Boxer troubles, nor were any of the white men in our province of Kiangsu. This was the result of the wisdom and courage of one man, our viceroy, who, when he received the edict of the empress dowager, refused to obey it. It was more than mercy, it was also foresight, for our viceroy understood what our old empress did not: that it was not white men alone who had bred revolution in China. Their presence and deeds had only hastened the awakening of the Chinese people. Why, the people asked themselves, had they no weapons to resist the Westerners, who were different from past invaders? These white men had seized lands and rivers instead of the throne and did not yield as the other invaders had to the superior civilization of China. On the contrary, the Westerners considered their own civilizations superior, and they tried to prove them so by guns and cannons. Such weapons were terrifying to the unarmed Chinese people.

I now see myself, a child of ten, the Boxer troubles ended, returned to China with my parents after a furlough in America. It is the year 1902 and I am in the small dining room of an old mission bungalow on the hills above the Yangtze River. I am listening to the grave voice of the old Chinese gentleman who is my tutor, Mr. Kung. He is a Confucian, which seems not to trouble my Christian parents, although he instills Confucian ethics into me while he teaches me Chinese reading and writing. He prides himself on the surname Kung, which was also the surname of Confucius, this name being a corruption of the Chinese K'ung Fu-tzŭ, or Father Kung. But I, as a Christian child, suppose that Confucius is the same as Our Father in Heaven.

The most important lesson, says Mr. Kung, is that if one would be happy, one must not raise one's head above one's neighbors'. "He who raises his head above the heads of others," Mr. Kung observes, "will sooner or later be decapitated."

It was true in China as elsewhere that when a man became too successful, too powerful, mysterious forces went to work and the earth began to crumble under his pinnacle. The Chinese are proud and envious, both as a nation and as individuals. They do not love their superiors and never did, and the truth is they have never believed that people superior to them could exist. This fact partly explains the anti-Americanism of recent years, this and the attitudes of earlier missionaries, traders and diplomats who considered themselves, consciously or unconsciously, superior to the Chinese.

In those days after 1900 when white men punished the old empress so bitterly, when her palaces were looted and incalculable treasures stolen from Peking, Americans were among the white men.

After the storm was over—so strangely called in Western history the Boxer Rebellion, but rebellion against what ruler except the white man?—after the storm and after the defeat, the white men returned to China without a lesson learned. They returned in complacency, thinking that by force they had taught the Chinese a lesson so that never again would they rebel against the white man's rule.

It made me unhappy even in the days when Mr. Kung was my teacher. He explained it to me gently, and I remember one afternoon that I wept. We had only just come back from America and a year in my kindly grandfather's house, and I wept because I knew that if men like Mr. Kung and my grandfather could meet and talk things over, they would understand each other.

What Mr. Kung said in his beautiful polished Peking Mandarin was something like this: "It will be peaceful for you here again, Little Sister, but not for long. This storm is still rising. You must go to America and not come back, lest next time you be killed with all your kind."

"There must be a next time?" I asked, terrified.

"Until justice is done," he said gravely and with infinite pity.

And I could say nothing, for I knew that his ancestral home in Peking had been destroyed by German soldiers, men to whom the kaiser had given the imperial command in some such words as these: "Germans, so behave that forever when a Chinese hears the name of Germany he will quake with fear and run to save himself." And the Germans had obeyed their kaiser.

Yet as the days passed, I forgot my fears as a child forgets, though my worlds were now sharply clear, one from the other. I was American, not Chinese, and although China was as dear to me as my native land, I knew it was not my land.

Notwithstanding, they were good years in many ways for a child. The emperor, Kuang Hsü, was now dead, and so was the old empress. But before she died, she had declared a little child her successor, P'u-yi. We saw pictures of him sometimes in the papers, a plump baby with an astonished wooden little face above his stiff satin robe and sleeveless jacket. There was a regent, and life went on as usual apparently.

Those were strange, conflicting days, for in the morning I sat over my American schoolbooks and learned the lessons assigned to me by my mother, while in the afternoon I studied under the wholly different tutelage of Mr. Kung. I became mentally bifocal, and so I learned early that there is no such condition in human affairs as absolute truth. There is only truth as people see it, and truth may be kaleidoscopic in its variety. This is why I could never belong entirely to one side of any question. To be a Communist would be absurd to me, as absurd as to be entirely anything. I straddled the globe too young.

All this learning went on quite pleasantly and painlessly. Indeed, I had a happy life, though my days would perhaps have seemed slow and boring to my own children. I see Mr. Kung as he arrived on all afternoons, except Sundays, carrying his treasure of books wrapped in an old piece of soft black silk. This he unfolded, but only after he had given greeting to me and received from me a suitable bow and salutation, after which I, too, could seat myself. Then he opened the silk with tender care and brought forth the book that we were studying. For two hours we read and he expounded, not alone the past contained within the book, but also the relation of that past, however dim and distant, to the present and even to the future.

It was from him that I learned the first axiom of human life: that nothing, not the least wind that blows, is accidental or causeless. Fate, Mr. Kung taught me in my early youth, is unalterable only in the sense that, given a cause, a certain result must follow. But no cause is inevitable in itself, and man can shape his world if he does not resign himself to ignorance. Mr. Kung liked to quote also from the Christian Bible, partly, I imagine, to prove to me his liberal Confucian mind. His favorite text was the one about reaping the whirl-wind if one sowed the wind, and he reminded me often, in his gently lofty manner, that one could not expect figs from thistles.

When four o'clock came, the lesson was over. He covered his tea bowl and wrapped the book again in the soft black silk. We rose and I bowed and he inclined his head, reminding me of tomorrow's preparation and of the few mistakes I might have made. So we parted, I following him to the gate, as a pupil should follow a teacher, and standing there until his swaying robes and black silk queue had disappeared. Years later the revolution demanded that the queue be cut away as the last sign of servitude to the dying Manchu Empire. But Mr. Kung was dead by then, taking his queue with him.

I WAS TOO old by now to play in the pampas grass outside the gate. I was getting to be what was called "a big girl," and if my mother was not with me, then my Chinese nurse accompanied me when I went outside the gate. She was far more strict than any mother, and she pursed her wrinkled lips if I stopped to buy a sweet from a vendor or some bit of jewelry that took my fancy at a silversmith's. The Chinese silver was beautiful, soft and pure, and the smiths carved it in delicate patterns for a bracelet or a heavy chain, or they twisted hair-fine wires into exquisite filigree as delicate as cobweb and studded it with plum blossoms and butterflies inlaid with blue kingfishers' feathers.

For the first time, during these post-Boxer years, I tried to find a few friends among people of my own race. I remember a sweet-faced, brown-eyed English girl named Agnes, whose father worked for the English Bible Society. She was a gentle creature who lived the secluded, almost empty life of most white families, entirely unaware of the rich culture of the Chinese people. Nothing was more delightful than to sit down with her family on a chill winter's afternoon, when we gathered in a little dining room stuffed with ugly English furniture and had an English tea. There was no dainty nonsense about that meal. The big rectangular table was covered with a solid white linen cloth, and upon this were set silver-covered plates of hot scones and dishes of Australian butter and Crosse & Blackwell English strawberry jam. We had strong black Indian tea, stout empire stuff, enriched with white sugar and proper English condensed milk.

This good English meal was prepared in a little Chinese kitchen by a thin Chinese man who consoled himself for the scoldings of his foreign mistress by cheating her richly when he shopped. Meanwhile he learned to cook so well that when the white folk departed, he found a job as head cook for a famous warlord. We were served by a table boy who afterward burned down the house in which we sat.

Still, living today with electric household appliances, I find myself nostalgic for a house where the servants are human, at the same time hating the poverty that makes human labor cheap. And yet the servants in our own Chinese home enjoyed their life, and they respected themselves and their work and us. How lonely might I have been at evening had I not been free to sit in the servants' court, to play with their babies and listen to the music of a country flute or a two-stringed violin!

Certainly machines are not so companionable. Not long ago I went to call upon a young farmer's wife, a neighbor of mine in Pennsylvania. I entered the kitchen, and encircling it, I saw monumental machines: washing machine, drier, mangle, two freezers, refrigerator, electric stove, sink. With such help her daily work was soon done. We went into the neat living room where there were no books, but where a television set was carrying on. She paid no heed to it and, inviting me to sit down, took her fat baby, immaculate and well fed, on her knee, and we talked until I had to leave. Said she, real disappointment in her voice, "Oh, can't you stay? I thought you'd spend the afternoon. I get so bored after dinner—I haven't a thing to do."

I thought of Chinese farm wives who took their laundry to the pond and chattered and laughed together while they beat their garments with a wooden paddle upon a flat rock. With their talk and merriment they were more amused, I do believe, than was that young neighbor of mine with her television rattling all day long.

Two worlds, and one cannot be the other, and each has its ways and blessings, I suppose.

As I LOOK back upon those years between 1901 and 1911, they seem to be strangely hesitant years. Peace covered China like a sheet of thin ice beneath which a river boiled. Outwardly our life was better than ever. My mother had dug up the buried family silver, our faithful servants had gathered around us again, and there was little cursing at my father as he came and went on the street. For after the Boxers had been dispelled and disgraced, new treaties guaranteed the safety of the white man wherever he might choose to live, to preach, to trade. In addition, China was compelled to pay vast indemnities for the desperate folly of the old dead empress, though my own country later chose to spend its share in scholarships for young Chinese in American universities.

The Chinese are a practical people. They knew their own defeat and could not then risk another. For ten years at least they must recuperate, reflect and plan. In those ten years I passed from childhood into adolescence in a freedom that perhaps no white child had ever known before in China and certainly could not know again. Sometimes, to be sure, a child would still shout *"Yang kwei-tse!"*—"Foreign devil!"—as I passed, but if he did, his mother clapped her hand across his mouth, frightened because she had heard how cruel was the revenge that white folk took.

This fear always broke my heart and, wherever I found it, I stopped and spoke gently to the mothers and asked them not to be afraid. I told them about my country and how my people did not hate them, and how much I wished that we could be friends, because indeed our hearts were all the same.

Mr. Kung died in 1905, and my parents sent me to a mission school for girls. But I never again learned as much as I had learned from Mr. Kung. I wept at his funeral and wore a white band of mourning on my sleeve, and I bowed before his coffin with the lesser members of his family. He died of cholera in September. He had risen as usual in the morning, but he was dead by night. My mother did not want me to go to his funeral because of the danger of contagion. When I insisted, she let me go with my father only on the promise that we would not touch our lips even to so much as a bowl of tea. She had good reason to demand such promises, for she had nearly died of cholera in Shanghai once, before I was born, and had on the same day lost my sister, whom I never saw, a child of four. My father, having found a doctor, was forced to decide which life was to be saved, his daughter's or his wife's.

"I cannot save them both," the doctor had said.

He chose his wife, but sometimes I wonder if my mother forgave him for it. It would have been like her to have insisted on saving both and somehow getting it done.

Day by day through these years I had plenty of love and kindness and I knew no personal unhappiness. I was healthy and full of good spirits and never idle or bored, a curious child plaguing everyone with questions. I was entangled in every human story going on about me, and spent hours listening to anyone who would talk to me. Of course I absorbed much useless information, and yet I wonder if it was really useless. I took a deep interest, for example, in the farming problems of our Chinese neighbors, who raised crops on five acres or so of land. Every rice plant had to be thrust into the paddy field by hand, by farmers and their wives and daughters and sons and sons' wives and their children. All this knowledge was useful to me when I began to write.

I had decided well before I was ten to be a novelist, but Mr. Kung confused my mind. He had been trained in the early Chinese classical tradition that said no reputable writer condescends to produce novels. Novels, he taught me, are designed only to amuse the idle and the illiterate, that is, those persons who cannot appreciate a true literary style and moral and philosophical content. This discouragement was increased by the religious feeling of my parents, who considered novel reading an idle pastime. Indeed, my mother and I played a sort of hide-and-seek all through my childhood, although neither of us ever referred to it. She hid the novels I read and I hunted for them until I found them. I cannot remember that I bore her any ill will for this, she was far too lovable and good; nor did she, apparently, feel any anger toward me for almost invariably finding her hiding places. The whole performance was carried on in silence by both of us. When I grew up, I forgot about it, though I have since wished that I had asked her why she hid the books in such easy places. But she died too young. There were many questions I meant to ask her and did not remember until it was too late.

The result of all this was that I grew up feeling that the writing of novels was a lesser work than it is. When *The Good Earth* took on a life of its own, no one was more astonished than I. I was even apologetic that my first appearance in the world of literature should be with a novel.

I WAS TOO young when I was ready for college, so my mother, always sensitive and observant, decided that I must spend a year in a boarding school. I was to go to Shanghai, to

Miss Jewell's School. It was, at that time, the most fashionable and supposedly the only good school for Western boys and girls in our part of the China coast.

When I look back on the months spent at Miss Jewell's, the memory is unreal, fantastic. In the first place, Shanghai was a city altogether unlike any Chinese city, created by foreigners and for foreigners. Decades earlier, Manchu emperors had assigned a living space to the intruding Westerners, and in contempt had allowed them nothing better than mud flats on the Hwang Pu River, where the Yangtze flows into the sea. Out of this malarial waste the foreigners had made a city. Great buildings lifted their bulk along the riverside. Parks were opened, the famous parks that later provided a slogan for the simmering revolution: "No Chinese, No Dogs."

Miss Jewell's School was established in buildings of somber and indestructible gray brick. On the ground floor by the front door was the parlor, and there on the day upon which I was to be received, my mother and I sat waiting for Miss Jewell. Shades of *Nicholas Nickleby* enveloped me as I looked around that dreary parlor. The windows were partly sunken beneath the pavement of the street outside and they were heavily barred against thieves, a reasonable condition but one that added something dreadful to my impression of the room. Texts from the Bible, framed in dark oak, hung upon the pallid walls, and in a small English grate a handful of coals was carefully arranged to smolder rather than burn.

There we sat, and I felt my own misgivings growing deeper as I saw my mother's usually cheerful face gradually losing its cheer. Presently into the room came a short, heavyset, white-haired, black-eyed woman. It was Miss Jewell herself. She wore a dark full dress whose skirt came to the floor, and she entered silently because, as I was to discover, she always wore soft-soled shoes, partly so that no one would know when she was coming and partly because she suffered grievously from corns. She greeted us in a low voice, and I noticed that although her hands were beautiful, they were cold. No

409

warmth came from her. In fairness I must admit that she was already an aging woman and always tired. In spite of her seeming coldness, she did many good works, but it took time for me to discover the hidden goodness. On that first day I felt only a sort of fright.

I kissed my mother good-by and reminded her in a whisper that she had promised that I need not stay if I did not like it. When she had gone, I followed Miss Jewell up a dark stairway behind a Chinese houseboy who carried my bags.

I was assigned an attic room, which I shared with two other girls, both daughters of missionaries. Their lives had been wholly different from mine, and although we were soon acquainted, we remained strangers. My roommates came of orthodox folk, and they despised me somewhat, I think, because I had been taught by Mr. Kung and wrote letters regularly to Chinese friends.

The nearest that we ever came to quarreling, however, was on the subject of Buddhism, about which they knew nothing. I, on the other hand, knew a good deal because my father had studied Buddhism for many years and had written an interesting monograph on the similarities between it and Christianity. One of his ideas was that the likeness between Buddhism and Christianity was not accidental but historical since it is quite possible that Jesus visited the Himalayan kingdom of Nepal when He was a young man, during the eighteen unrecorded years of His life. Such tradition is widespread in northern India and is even mentioned in *Vishnu Purana*, the ancient Hindu scripture.

My father believed that Jesus also knew the teachings of Confucius, for the almost identical expression by Confucius and by Jesus of the Golden Rule, to take one example among many, could scarcely be accidental similarity of thought. In short, although my father was a conservative Christian, he had come to the conclusion that all religions in Asia had contributed their share to the profound and steady movement of mankind toward God.

These were shocking ideas to my two roommates, and they reported me to Miss Jewell as being a heretic. I, in turn, was shocked that they could call the Chinese people heathen, a term my parents never allowed to be spoken in our house. Miss Jewell, informed of my monstrous views, removed me from the attic room, lest I contaminate the others, and put me in a little room alone. Then, feeling that I needed a stricter Christian theology, she endeavored to instill it in me by taking me to prayer meetings and to places of good works. Both terrified me.

The prayer meetings were unlike any I had ever seen. I do not know to what sect Miss Jewell belonged, but for her prayers she went to meetings in one private house or another. She was a busy woman and we usually arrived late, after the meeting had begun. In the room of prayer it was always dark and we stumbled over legs until we found a space wherein to kneel. There we stayed as long as Miss Jewell could spare the time and, stiff with repulsion, I listened to voices in the darkness pleading for the forgiveness of unmentioned sins, accompanied by moans and groans and sighs.

The experience became so frightening, so intolerable, to me that I asked my mother to let me come home. Religion I was used to but not this dark form of it. In my father's house religion was a normal exercise, a combination of creed and practice, accompanied by music. My father's sermons inclined to scholarly dryness but did not contain any talk of hell. Infant damnation was in those days still part of the normal creed, but my father would have none of it, and my mother, having lost four beautiful little children, was raised to fury at the very mention of any child descending into hell. I had heard her comfort more than one young missionary mother beside the body of a dead child, "Your baby is in heaven," she declared. "There are no babies in hell—no, not one. They are all gathered round the throne of God the Father, and Jesus takes them in His bosom when they first come in, when they still feel strange to heaven." On the common tombstone of three of her children, who died before I was born, she had their names inscribed and then the text, "He gathered them like lambs in His bosom."

My parents were alarmed, then, when I told them of the dark rooms and the strange prayers. They wrote my headmistress requesting that I be taken to no church services except those held on Sunday mornings in the Community Church, where Mr. Darwent, a stout little Englishman, could be trusted to preach harmless sermons, sincere and brief.

Miss Jewell, however, did not give me up. She felt that I was old enough to have some share in her good works. So I took her turn, when she was busy, at the Door of Hope, a rescue home for Chinese slave girls who had had cruel mistresses. I was supposed to teach the girls to sew and knit and embroider, all of which tasks I disliked, but which my own beautifully educated mother had taught me to do well.

The girls at the Door of Hope were eager to learn. They were wretched children, bought young in some time of famine and reared to serve in rich households. We had only the ones from evil households, of course, for a bondmaid in a kindly family received good treatment, and at the age of eighteen she was freed and given in marriage to some lowly good man. But these were ones who had run away because they had been beaten with whips and burned with live coals from pipes and cigarettes by cruel and bad-tempered mistresses, or ravished by adolescent sons in the family or by lecherous masters and their menservants.

Such slavery was an old system and perhaps no one was entirely to blame for it. In famine times the desperate starving families sold their daughters not only to buy a little food for themselves but also to allow the child to enter a rich family rather than die of starvation. The girl was sold instead of the boy because the family still hoped to survive somehow and the son must be kept to carry on the family name. There are many romantic and beautiful love stories in Chinese literature centering about the lovely bondmaid who becomes the savior and the darling of the rich family, and these perhaps added to the hopefulness of the starving family when they sold their girl child. As with all systems in human life, everything depended upon the good or evil of the persons concerned.

SOMETIMES IN America today I hear a train rushing past, making its mournful cry, a cry nearly human, so wild, so lost. It makes me think of human voices I have heard in the night elsewhere: the mournful monotony of voices singing in some village in India, a few notes repeated over and over, thin and high, until at last one's very heart is caught and twisted into it; or, most clearly, the cry of a Chinese mother whose child is dying, his soul wandering away from home, she thinks, and so she seizes the child's little coat and lights a lantern and runs out into the street, calling the wailing pitiful cry, "Sha-lai, sha-lai!" ("Child, come back, come back!"). How often have I heard that cry, and always with a pang of the heart! Lying in my comfortable bed and safe under our own roof, I see too vividly the stricken Chinese family and the little child lying dead or dying, whose soul all the calling in the world can never bring home again.

The Shanghai streets had their own noises. Often wakeful at Miss Jewell's School, I heard the creak of a late ricksha rolling along and the call of voices, girls' laughter sometimes, or a hearty English voice, a man saying good-by to someone. And deep in the night I woke to hear the endless slip-slip of Chinese feet in their cloth shoes, walking along the pavements, and I wondered where they went and why they never seemed to go home but always on and on.

In the spring of that strange year I spent at Miss Jewell's School she took me with her to still another of her good works, a shelter for destitute white women, many of them prostitutes. This place struck me with a profound horror. Here, for the first time in my life, I saw people of my own race, and women at that, so low in poverty and disease and loneliness that they were worse off than the Chinese slave girls at the Door of

Hope. I suppose my horror must have been plain, for the women fell silent when I came near, although I did my best with them.

When I went home for the spring holidays my mother said I was pale and thin, and when I told her of Miss Jewell's good works and my part in them, she pressed her lips together and her dark eyes sparkled with anger and I knew that I would not be sent to boarding school again. In the summer my parents were to take me to America to college. The few months at home passed in a sort of sweet melancholy while I wondered if this time was a sort of last farewell to China.

I have not mentioned the sound I liked best at night, but perhaps the memory belongs here. It was the voice of the great bronze bell that stood on a pedestal in the Buddhist temple halfway down our hill. When I was small I used to be afraid of it; the sound was melancholy and made me feel alone. But in the years of my childhood I had often visited the temple in the daytime and had seen for myself how the bell was struck by a small, kind old priest who grasped with both hands a piece of wood, the end of which was wrapped into a club with cloth. He swung out his arms and let this club fall against the bell, and out rolled the great pure sound.

I remember the last night at home with all the bags packed and ready to close. I was sleepless, and when I heard the bell strike its last note at dawn as we left the house, I had a strange premonition that I would never hear it again. I never did.

ON THE SHIP crossing to America I spent more thoughtful hours, perhaps, than I ever had before. We had come through Russia and Western Europe, and my mind was full of all I had seen. When I talked with my father one evening while we were still on the ship, he said something that I never forgot. "The uprising," he said, "will begin in Russia, for there the people are oppressed not by foreigners but by their own rulers. The Russians are the most miserable and wretched people on earth today, and there the world upheaval will first show itself. Out of Russia will come the Antichrist; it is clearly foretold in the Scriptures and it will come to pass. The uprising will spread to other countries of Asia, and because men of the white race have been the oppressors there, all the white race must suffer."

I said to my father, "Can't we tell them? Can't we warn them?"

He shook his head. "They have their prophets," he said.

I knew he was thinking of the biblical story of the man who, in hell for his sins, wanted to send a warning to those he loved who were still on earth, but God sternly replied that they had their prophets and would not heed them.

My father and I did not often talk together. He was in some ways an unbending man. One had to enter his world of intellect and religion, for he never left it. But that evening we understood each other.

I entered America in September 1910, with a sober heart and a mind too old for my years. I had hoped to go to Wellesley, but my southern relatives, still haunted by the Civil War, had objected, so a southern college for women, Randolph-Macon at Lynchburg, Virginia, was chosen for me. My mother approved of it because the education there was planned to be exactly what a man would get. After being married to my father for thirty years she had developed into an ardent feminist, and I must say with cause. My father, who based all his acts on biblical precedent, followed strictly some remarks made by St. Paul, in which that saint stated flatly that, as Christ was head of the Church, so man was head of the woman. My mother had an intrepid and passionate nature, but my father was a monument of calm, and as usual the monument won. To her eloquent and sometimes angry assaults, such as when she felt that the family bank account, always slim, should be a joint account so that she could draw checks as well as he, he never answered anything more violent than "Oh, now, Carie, don't talk that way!"

The result of years of defeat, although she never acknowledged subjection, was that my mother determined to give her daughters every possible advantage. So she was charmed by the idea of educating me exactly as though I were a boy.

When I look back from this distance upon those four college years, I see them as an experience divided again by my different worlds. I had grown up in Asia, and this fact lent me an aura of strangeness, more unkindly called queerness, which I perceived well enough in the attitude of my college mates toward me. I wanted to belong to my own kind, and I soon saw I must learn to talk about the things that American girls talked about, and I must look like them. I bought a few American dresses and I put up my hair, which I had been wearing in a thick braid doubled up and tied with a ribbon. By the end of my freshman year I was indistinguishable from any other girl of my age and class, and so I joined my American world. By my junior year I was sufficiently American to be elected president of my class.

Of my senior year I can remember very little that is pleasant. I lived off campus at my brother's house, for he had married and settled in Lynchburg, and I was burdened with a secret he now shared with me, that he had decided upon a divorce. He asked me to write to my parents, and I did so. They wrote back in such horror and shock that he postponed the whole matter for several more years. Indeed, he did not seek a divorce until after their death, although he separated from his wife and lived alone in the intervening years.

This crisis so near me was an isolating experience, for it meant that the normal life I might have had in my brother's home was denied me. Finally I took my place in the long procession of graduates and was faced with a choice between my two worlds. Should I stay to become permanently American, or should I go home again to China?

I wanted to stay, for between the two countries my heart chose my own. I could decide among several teaching jobs, including one in the college as an assistant in psychology with the professor under whom I had majored. Yet my conscience moved me to return to my parents, though I did not want to be a missionary, for I knew I could never persuade people to change their religion. I had seen too many good people who were not Christian, and, as my father used to remark, it took the arrogance out of anybody to have to acknowledge that the best Christian converts were always good people anyway, the best Buddhists or Moslems or Taoists or what not.

One day a letter came from my father telling me that my dearly loved mother had been taken with sprue, a slowly fatal tropical disease that no physician knew how to cure at that time. My mind was made up on the instant. I wrote to the Presbyterian Board of Foreign Missions, under whom my parents worked, and asked to be sent to China as a teacher. I packed my bags and sailed as soon as I could get passage. I did not think of my return as permanent, but only until my mother was well again, or if she did not get well—but that end I could not face.

REALITY BEGAN for me in China when the tall thin figure of my father and the little figure of my younger sister appeared upon the pier to meet me. The very fact of my mother's absence struck me to the heart. She had not been well enough to come to Shanghai, but she hoped to meet me at the train in Chinkiang.

I read many warnings nowadays against too deep an attachment between parents and children, but I am sure that such dangers are overrated. There should be a deep attachment, heart should be tied to heart between parent and child, for unless the child learns how to love a parent profoundly, I believe that he will never learn how to love anyone else profoundly, and not knowing how to love means the loss of the meaning of life and its fulfillment.

I loved both my parents but at different times and in different ways. During my childhood all my love went to my mother, and I felt very little for my father, even going to the extent of remarking one day at the age of eleven that I hated him. My mother rebuked me, but my father, although he had overheard me, said nothing. I continued to hate my father mildly until I was old enough to appreciate him, which was not until I was grown. During the years when he was seventy to eighty years old, I adored him and he knew it and expanded in the friendly atmosphere between us. It was not my fault nor his that we had both to wait until such an age for mutual understanding. We had to grow together in time and maturity, and I am glad he lived long enough for that.

My love for my mother was a thing apart. It was rooted in my blood and my bones. I felt her every pain, I knew when she was wounded, and she was wounded always too easily. I discerned, although she never acknowledged it, that as she grew older she was desperately homesick for the land she had left too young. It was impossible for her to return: she could not leave my father, and anyway she could not cross the ocean again with her weak heart and enfeebled frame.

How weakened she was I had not been able to imagine until I saw her at the railway station in Chinkiang. Instead of the strong upright figure I had remembered, wearing her thick white hair like a crown, I saw a lady, very dainty in dress as she always was, but shrunken and tiny, so tiny that I lifted her up in my arms when I ran to her.

"Mother, how little you are!" I cried.

"Daughter, how big you are!" she retorted, laughing.

My heart trembled at her fragility and I tried not to weep. She saw it and made me turn to greet the crowd that had come to welcome me: my old Chinese friends, my English friend, Agnes, and her family, a few American missionaries, our servants and neighbors. What a heartwarming homecoming it was, with all of them trying to hug me at once and clinging to my hands and making speeches and giving me flowers and little gifts and packages of Chinese sponge cakes and sesame cookies! I was home again, even though during the years I had been away, the compound in which I had grown up had been given over to a boys' school and my parents had moved to another hill and another modest mission house. The hills and the valleys were the same, and as we walked along the familiar roads of beaten earth, the farmers put down their hoes and came to speak to me and their wives and children ran out of the earthen houses to call to me. "And have you come back?" they shouted. "It is good—it is good."

When we came to the new house, I found that my mother had set aside for me the pleasantest upstairs room, facing the distant river and overlooking the green valley. It was a bare room, I suppose, with the minimum of plain furniture, but bowls of late roses stood on the desk and the dressing table, and my mother had made white curtains for the windows. My old bed was there and my childhood books were in a little bookcase built in the wall.

That night my mother and I sat long in talk, and I made her tell me about herself and how it was that sprue had fastened itself on her. Unwillingly she showed me her poor mouth, sore and red, and told me that the vicious disease, a sort of fungus growth, was destroying the mucous membranes of her mouth and throat and intestines, so that it was painful for her to speak very much or to eat anything but the mildest of bland foods. And this she had hidden from me! I put my arms about her and wept, and she comforted me, saying that she intended to fight the disease with all her strength and get well again now that I was home. I dried my eyes and swore myself to the task with her. I was sure now that I had decided rightly to leave America. It was not so much China that I chose. It was my mother's life.

MY OWN LIFE now was divided. My daily duty, besides teaching in the new boys' school and supervising seventeen to twenty young Chinese women who were being trained for various types of work in other schools, was to care for my mother. I took over the management of the house in order to relieve her, and I made a fierce and determined attack upon her disease. Nothing but diet was then tried as a cure, and we experimented with all the known foods to find the one most suitable for her. Some victims professed to recover upon bananas, and my long-suffering mother fed for months upon bananas, never her favorite food. Then we heard that fresh strawberries were helpful, so we set about the cultivation of strawberries. Milk, however, fresh unwatered raw milk, seemed to be the most approved food, and how to get it became my problem.

In those days it seemed impossible to find an honest milkman. The Chinese had never been used to drinking cow's milk. Indeed the very idea of it was repulsive to them, partly because Buddhists considered that to drink milk was to rob the calf of its life, and partly because of the cow smell of those who drank milk, or so they declared. Yet cow's milk was beginning to be thought of as a Western source of health, and the more modern among the Chinese eagerly bought canned milk from American stores in Shanghai for their children. A few enterprising Chinese even bought a cow or two and sold raw milk to foreigners. I conceived the idea of having the milkman lead his cow up the hill to our backyard and there milk her product into a pan before my eyes, after I had seen his hands scrubbed with hot water and soap and dipped into disinfectant. We did this for a few days, and still the milk seemed disconcertingly blue and thin. It was our faithful cook who asked me to observe closely one day that the milkman's cotton sleeves hung down over his wrists. I did so, and discovered under his right wrist a thin rubber tube from which a small stream of water ran into the milk pail. I stooped and twitched back the wide sleeve and disclosed a rubber hot-water bag that he had bought from some servant of a foreigner. I was speechless and for a moment could only look my reproach.

He was ashamed enough, though only for the moment, I fear. Then he said, "But I boiled the water, Little Sister—truly I boiled it, knowing that foreigners always drink only boiled water. Besides, the milk is so rich I feared it would make your honored mother ill."

We gave up on raw milk after that. Experimenting further, we worked out a diet of rice gruel, fresh fruit juice, soft-boiled eggs and liver that served at least to prolong my mother's life, though she was never really well again during her few remaining years. Now, of course, doctors know that sprue is a deficiency disease, and while the bananas and fresh strawberries and raw milk and liver were useful in providing some vitamins, far more were needed. But the knowledge came too late for my mother.

Outside this home battle I lived another life. My senior high school students were far more mature than Western boys of the same age. Many of them were already married men and some had children. My task was to teach them English, and in this tongue we attempted to converse on the profound subjects that interested them. They taught me far more than I taught them, for great things were happening in China. I had left in a period of confusion. The weak little Emperor P'u-yi still sat upon the throne, but since the passing of the doughty old empress dowager, there had been no real ruler and the Manchu Dynasty was near its end. As usual in such times, the Chinese people were waiting philosophically for a new head to appear and various local leaders were developing into warlords. It was a thoroughly Chinese process.

This historical process was now disturbed. The warlords were swarming as usual when the dynasty came to an end, but there was no throne for a prize. While I had been peacefully at college a real revolution had been going on, fed by a dozen fires, but chiefly by the intrepid Sun Yat-sen. He was the son of a village farmer in South China, but he had been sent to a mission school. When only a boy, he had been taken to Honolulu by his elder brother, who was a merchant, and there, too, he had attended a Christian school and had seen American government at work. He was no mean missionary himself, for he soon conceived the vast notion of modernizing his country, not by education but by inciting other Chinese to help him overthrow the throne and set up a republic based on the constitutional form of the government of the United States. With this idea in his head, he had given up his profession as a doctor of medicine and set out as a sort of patriotic pilgrim to find Chinese in every part of the world and collect funds from them for his revolution. Meanwhile he hoped to persuade foreign governments to help him with the new China. The foreign governments, as was to be expected, only shrugged Sun Yat-sen off, but the overseas Chinese gave him all they had and put their faith in him.

During my sophomore year in college Sun Yat-sen's dream actually did succeed. While he was traveling in the United States collecting his funds, the revolutionaries he had left behind him became impatient and rose up and overthrew the dynasty representatives in the province of Kiangsi and declared Sun Yat-sen the first president of the Republic of China. He saw the news in an American newspaper while he was on a train in Missouri, traveling toward New York. No one recognized him, of course, and it is fascinating to imagine his thoughts as he saw his own name in great headlines while he sat in the dingy day coach, lonely and unknown. The anger of the Chinese people, meanwhile, had risen to its height and everywhere they killed the Manchu whom hitherto they had protected in contempt. In a letter my mother had written to me in 1911 she said, "I look from the window this morning and see poor Manchu women and children hiding for their lives behind the graves on the hillside. I shall have to go out and see what I can do." It was characteristic of my parents that while the American consul had warned all Americans to leave for Shanghai and stay there until the trouble was over, lest the revolution take the usual antiforeign turn, they did not go.

All these doings had seemed vague enough to me while I was at college. Now, however, the struggle of Sun Yat-sen was a matter of daily study in the newspaper and daily talk with my Chinese friends. Could he organize a republic? Or would we have a new emperor, and if so, who would he be?

Meanwhile, the life of the Chinese people went on in its accustomed ways. The greatest outward change that I could see was that most men and boys had their queues cut off. The queue had been a sign of subjection to the Manchu Dynasty and that dynasty was ended. Even so, many a Chinese peasant clung to his queue. He did not know why he had it, but his father and forefathers for generations had worn the queue and therefore it must be good. But young men, some of them my own students, stationed themselves at the city gates through which the farmers had to pass to carry their vegetable baskets and bundles of fuel to the markets, and when they saw one who wore a queue, they sat him down on a stool, lectured him and cut off his appendage, even though he wept while they did so. In a short time all the queues seemed to be gone, although when I was living in North China after my marriage a few years later, I still occasionally saw dusty-haired farmers from the back country with modest little queues curled under their felt caps.

There were many conservative and well-educated old Chinese who heartily disapproved of Sun Yat-sen and wished the emperor back again. Some of them were friends of my parents, so while I heard the arguments of the young during the day in my classes, I had the other side from these older Chinese.

Young as I was in those years, I tried very hard to understand what was going on in my worlds. I was lonely, and my years in college had separated me from the Chinese girls with whom I had once been such close friends. They were all married and busy with household affairs, and they felt strange with me, perhaps because I had been away to college. They asked me a thousand questions, for the Chinese are full of curiosity about other peoples and will stop at nothing in the way of intimate detail. I answered as best I could, but invariably our sessions together ended with the one important question—"When are you going to be married?"

"I don't know," I always replied.

The next question was also invariable. "Are your parents doing nothing about finding a husband for you?"

Without exception their parents had found husbands for them in the approved old Chinese fashion; a Chinese girl or young man would have been astonished and embarrassed to be told that she or he must find a mate. Marriage was a family affair, and the parents pondered with much care upon the nature of their child and the sort of person that should be found to complete his or her life. It was also essential that this person fit into the family group, for where the generations lived together in the old Chinese custom, it could only bring unhappiness if the new person did not fit into the circle. The results of these arranged marriages were usually good. Most of them were happy, and usually love did develop after marriage, sometimes even romantic and passionate love. But it was not an essential. Such marriages had perhaps a greater chance for survival in China because the expectations of romantic love were not as high as they are in the West.

At any rate, my Chinese friends were happily married and busy with babies, and although I was still young, they were troubled about my solitary state. There were a few young white men in the British Concession in our city, among them two or three Americans with the Standard Oil Company or one of the tobacco companies, but when I accepted their invitations, one of the older missionary women in the narrow circle lectured me severely. "You cannot continue in both ways of life," she said solemnly. "If you go with the business people, you must leave the missionary circle."

"I am not a missionary," I insisted. "I am a teacher."

"You are a teacher in a missionary school," she reminded me, "and your parents are missionaries."

"My parents don't mind," I persisted.

"The rest of us do," she retorted.

So for the sake of my parents I refused all invitations from then on and scheduled my days severely between work and home. My Chinese friends were still concerned, and I know they talked with my parents about arranging a marriage for me. This resulted in a curious argument between my father, who had become far more Chinese than American in his mentality, and my mother. My father, it seemed, would have been pleased to have me marry a young Chinese gentleman of his own choice but my mother was wholeheartedly against it. I took no sides, for I saw no danger from the handsome and brilliant young Chinese whom my father had in mind, since his family would not have tolerated his marriage to an American. I decided, instead, since my mother's health seemed to be improving, that I would like to go to some other part of China and carve out my career alone.

Casting about, I thought of a woman who had stirred my imagination ever since I had first heard of her. She lived alone in a distant and ancient city of the province of Yunnan, a supremely beautiful part of a beautiful country. I sat down one day at the little Chinese desk in my room and wrote to Cornelia Morgan to ask her if she would let me come and work with her. Somehow or other, a week later, her friendly reply fell into my mother's hands, and then I saw a new aspect of my mother. She broke down and wept and said that if I went away she did not want to live. Why was I dissatisfied here, where everyone loved me so much? And what would the Chinese, who believed in filial piety, say if I deserted my parents?

I said, "But you left your home when your father did not want you to do it. Grandfather even forbade your marriage."

Her dark eyes were tragic. "I know it," she said, "and I did wrong. I wish I had obeyed him."

This was a terrifying revelation, and I was struck speechless. I neither promised to stay nor insisted upon going. I was simply silent, and a few days later she fell seriously ill again and the doctor said that someone must take her up the mountains of Lu, to the summer resort of Kuling. I asked for a leave of absence from my school and my mother and I boarded one of the clean little English river steamers and set sail for Chiu-Chiang, where we would take sedan chairs for the climb up the mountains. My fate, for the time being, was settled.

KULING WAS more than a summer resort for white families; it was a lifesaving station, especially in the early years of my childhood before it was known how some of the worst of the tropical diseases, against which white people seemed to have no immunity whatever, were carried. The death of children from these diseases had compelled white parents to find some place where families could go for the worst months of our tropically hot summers. My father had been one of the white men who explored the famous Lu Mountains in Kiangsi, where the climate was so salubrious that it was said the priests in the old stone temples lived forever. I can still remember the day when my father came home from the expedition and reported that high in those mountains, six thousand feet above sea level, he had found the air as cold as in early winter, though the season was midsummer. "The air up there is like the Alleghenies," he said, "and the brooks run clear."

We were among the first, then, to buy a plot of ground in Kuling—a long lease it was, actually, for foreigners could not own the soil of China. Gradually a beautiful little town developed there at the top of the mountains. A church was built, and shrewd Chinese merchants opened shops.

To me Kuling meant a kind of beauty I knew nowhere else, the beauty of clear brooks and wild ferns and lilies, a place where I could explore to my content. Each morning during the years when I was small it was my task to climb the mountain behind our house and come back with fresh ferns and flowers, and never have I seen so many flowers growing wild as I found there.

One fearful aspect of the valleys between those beautiful mountains of Lu was the flash floods. A cloudburst on the top of a mountain could pour water into a gorge so suddenly that within minutes a great wall of water was built up, although below the sun might be shining. Every summer some lives were lost in these floods. Picnickers enjoying their meal by the side of a small and peaceful brook looked up to see descending upon them a mass of water twenty feet high, and before they could escape, they were swept away, sometimes over high falls. I remember the tragedy of a neighbor, an American woman whose husband was dead and who had only one child. On the child's sixth birthday she had put their supper in a basket and the two of them had gone to a nearby brook to have a little celebration. In the midst of their meal she heard a roar, and looking up, she saw the flood rushing toward her. In her fright she seized what she thought was the child's frock and clambered up the side of the gorge, only to discover that what she had grasped was her own skirt and that the child was gone. The possibility of death always at hand lent an undertone of terror to the pleasantest summer day in Kuling.

All that was in my childhood. Now, in early June, I went to Kuling as a young woman with my mother. Kuling was changed, too. Wealthy Chinese wanted to buy land in the white concession, and it had become a point of hot disagreement among the white people as to whether Chinese could or should be kept out any longer. Kuling had developed very much, I discovered, and I did not like it so well, although the journey up the mountain had been even more beautiful than I remembered. We had left the ship at the river port of Chiu-Chiang the day before and had gone by ricksha to the rest house in the city to spend the night. Early the next morning we were waked as usual by the chair bearers, clamoring to get off. We rose and ate a hearty breakfast of rice and eggs, and then climbed into our chairs, made of wood and rattan. We set off across the plains and up into the foothills to the second rest house, where other chairs waited with mountain bearers, for the plainsmen could not climb.

Now came, as always, the magical part of the journey. One caught the first hint of it at the rest house, where a clear mountain brook tumbled past and the village houses were made of stone instead of the gray brick of the plains. We seated ourselves in our chairs. Four bearers carried each chair, suspended by ropes from poles across their shoulders, and thus they mounted the first flight of stone steps with light rhythmic stride. Up the mountain we climbed and soon the frothing bamboos changed to pines and dwarf chestnuts and oaks. The road wound around the rocky folds of the cliffs, and beneath us were gorges and rushing mountain rivers and falls. Higher

The China of Pearl Buck's youth was a land of dramatic contrasts. Her family spent summers at a mountain retreat in Kuling. It was reached by the primitive stone stairway at left that spiraled up from a country town like the one below. Parts of Shanghai, on the other hand, reflected the foreign presence and were European in style, especially along the famous waterfront Bund (right). A more typical Chinese city scene was the narrow, colorful thoroughfare in the port city of Canton pictured at lower right.

and higher the road crawled, twisting so that sometimes our chairs swung clear over the precipices as the front bearers went on beyond the rear ones, still behind the bend. One misstep and the chair would have been thrown down a thousand feet into the rocks and swirling waters. But I never heard of an accident, even though the bearers went at an astonishing speed.

Somewhere near the top of the mountain we turned a certain corner and were met, as I had remembered, by a strong cold current of mountain air. Until then the air had gradually cooled, but at this spot it changed suddenly and the bearers welcomed it with loud hallooing calls and a spurt of running, the chair swaying between them. As a child I could never keep from laughing, and this time I still felt exhilaration.

So we reached our old stone house, my mother and I, and very small it looked to my grown-up eyes. But the trees were big and the ferns had grown thick on the terrace walls. We settled in, my mother to rest in bed for a while and I to care for her and read to her. I studied my Chinese books while she slept and every day I went for a long solitary walk. It was interesting to see the changes in the settlement. The streets were named and the atmosphere of the place had become cosmopolitan.

"We must let the Chinese come in—I can see it," my mother said. "Perhaps we white people ought never to have built a separate place for ourselves, but we did it so that we could keep our children. We lost so many little children."

She could never mention the lost children without thinking, I knew, of our four buried in little walled cemeteries, three in Shanghai, and one, who died when I was six, in Chinkiang. The eldest, my sister Edith, my mother considered her most beautiful and brilliant child. She was the one who had died of cholera when she was four. There was a portrait of her in my mother's bedroom in the mission house, a handsome, sturdy blue-eyed child, her dark hair in bangs across her fine forehead and hanging in thick curls on her shoulders.

"Someday," my mother was saying, "the Chinese will take everything back again."

And so they did, though not until she was dead. Then Kuling became a stronghold for Generalissimo Chiang Kai-shek and Madame Chiang and their many relatives, and the new officials were more rigorous than the white people had been about keeping out poorer Chinese. But it was no more our business.

THE FIRST World War was raging that summer we spent in Kuling, but I knew nothing of it except through the newspaper that reached us weekly from Shanghai, an English paper that gave few reports of American forces. I had no idea until years later, when I was visiting Europe again, how many Americans had fought and died on foreign soil in the First World War. And then when I wandered through the cemeteries in France and saw little white crosses set as closely as human bodies could lie, the magnitude of what my country had done overwhelmed me and I wept belated tears for the young men whose flesh was already dust.

We stayed that wartime summer through in Kuling, and my sister came up from boarding school in Shanghai. An English doctor had my mother in charge, and he changed her diet again, so that she now fed upon an obnoxious mixture of boiled liver and spinach, consuming it with a fortitude that was amazing. She was slow to get well, and after my father had come for his brief vacation and gone, and my sister had returned to school, I began the loneliest winter of my life. The nearest person to my age was a young man in a nearby sanatorium recovering from tuberculosis; but our friendship was brief, ended by the alarm of his missionary parents at his growing interest in a young woman.

Meanwhile, as the winter passed, my mother grew better. My school was clamoring for my return, and so, with the doctor's permission and on her own insistence, I left her surrounded by a few good friends and cared for by our servants, and one cold February day I walked down the mountain. It was strange to get back to the mission house and take charge of it alone, my father its only other occupant. I enjoyed my independence, in spite of my great love for my mother, and I busied myself.

There was plenty with which to be concerned. Sun Yat-sen and his followers were still struggling with political problems. Yüan Shih-k'ai, the military leader, had finally assumed the presidency of the new Republic of China as a compromise between the old guard, who rejected Sun Yat-sen, and the impetuous radicals, who would not acknowledge P'u-yi as emperor. Sun Yat-sen had been set back, but he had accepted the situation with Chinese grace. Now, however, it became apparent that the ambitions of Yüan Shih-k'ai were leading him to try to establish a new dynasty with himself as the first emperor, though it was doubtful whether the people would allow this.

It was a wonderful time in which to live in China, and I was at the right age for it. True, the center of new revolutionary movements was far from our quiet, rather old-fashioned city and countryside, but we knew what was going on. Even the church was growing, and my father was surprised at the number of businessmen and farmers who were interested in becoming Christians. None were scholars of the old-fashioned sort, and few were young students in schools and colleges, and this grieved him. Yet a solid group of Chinese was becoming interested to some extent in the Christian religion, and it was, I am sure, because this religion gave promise of creating a new society where all men could be equally valuable as human beings.

The mission schools, too, had a very strong part in the social and political revolution. They insisted upon unbinding the feet of girl students; they taught Western subjects, including science and mathematics, rather than the old classical and literary subjects of Chinese schools; more, they taught the revolutionary and world-shaking principles of Christ. The wonder is that none of them realized how revolutionary those principles were. They had been reared in the Western atmosphere where church members practiced the teachings of Jesus only so far as was convenient in the total framework of their society.

Perhaps the most powerful revolutionary force in China came from the graduates of mission schools. They had not been allowed to compete in the old imperial examinations for government jobs, and even after these were abolished in 1905, they were still not considered sufficiently educated in Chinese ways to apply for high political positions. These new young scholars were determined to build a society where they and not the men they considered old fogies would be in power. Sun Yat-sen had many of them among his followers.

Everywhere a phrase, "the new people," used by a Chinese intellectual leader, Liang Ch'i-chao, became fire set to tinder in China. Sun Yat-sen had thought that when the Manchu Dynasty was overthrown, the people would inevitably become "new." The Manchu were overthrown too easily and quickly, however, before anyone had had time to think out exactly how to make the people new.

What does one do with a vast country and hundreds of millions of people without rulers? It is dangerous, perhaps the supreme danger, for persons or parties to destroy the framework of government that a people has built for itself by the slow and profound processes of life and time. No one had a plan after the revolution of 1911, and so Sun Yat-sen was able to put forth his ideas of a republican form of government. The common man, peasant or merchant, was glad to think that he would not be taxed anymore to keep up expensive palaces and pleasure gardens for officials. There was, too, a great deal of democracy in China, deep and inherent in the people.

As a matter of fact, the Chinese had always governed themselves. They distrusted governments and even held them in contempt. They were cynical to the last degree about official honesty; an ancient Chinese adage was that the best government is the one that governs least. A folk song runs thus:

> *When the sun rises I work;*
> *When the sun sets I rest.*
> *I dig the well to drink;*
> *I plow the field to eat.*
> *What has the emperor to do with me!*

And the Chinese people were quite capable of self-govern-ment. Their traditional family system was a sound basis for a new kind of modern democracy. In China, before Commu-nism began its destructive work on the family system, there was no need for the institutional expenses that lie so heavily upon our own democracy. There were no orphanages, for the family as a whole remained responsible for the care of the child who had lost his immediate parents. There were no insane asylums, for the family cared for its insane. As a matter of fact, there were very few insane Chinese, for the family system provided security for individuals without disgrace, and thus removed one of the main causes of modern insanity, the lost individual. There needed to be no relief rolls, for again, the family as a whole cared for its members who were jobless. Only in times of widespread famine and catastrophe did the people need outside help.

If Sun Yat-sen and his followers, and this includes the later Nationalist government under Chiang Kai-shek, had under-stood the value of this family system and built upon it, I have no doubt that Communism would not be ruling in China today.

THE FAILURE of the early revolution was not evident at first. Sun Yat-sen continued to struggle for political unity, although the country was drifting toward the old trend of warlords, who became the real rulers in their own regions. I lived under warlords for many years in that period, and peacefully enough, although we had always to watch their moods and temper. They were usually uneducated and given as much to pleasure as to war. After a combat, whether they were victors or vanquished, they tended to settle down for a while, take a few new concubines and perhaps yield to opium or some such diversion. Then we would have peace again until the next time. Warlords seldom disturbed white people because they did not want trouble with Western governments, but they had another vice, maddening to the young radicals. Since they needed endless amounts of money to support their ever-increasing armies of ne'er-do-wells and malcontents, they sold off bits of their country. Japan leased or bought many mines, ports and concessions from these greedy warlords.

Educated Chinese despised the warlords, but ordinary folk were, more often than not, amused by them so long as they kept off bandits and let other people alone. The warlords were usually rough-and-ready individuals, afraid of no one and often very funny. One of our neighboring warlords was famous because of the three things he did not know—how many soldiers he had, how much money he had and how many wives he had. I remember the warlord in the province next to ours who was twice defeated by another warlord. At last he declared in loud public tones that he intended to fight once more, and if he was defeated, he would come home in his coffin. We all waited the outcome of this much-touted battle. When it ended as the others had, in defeat, an elaborate funeral was prepared for the return of the body. The funeral went off in high humor with every detail complete, except that instead of a corpse, the old warlord, very much alive though vanquished, was seated in the enormous coffin, dressed in his best robes and grinning at the astonished crowds. The people burst into laughter and instantly forgave the old ruler all his sins because he had made such a good joke.

Meanwhile young Chinese, many of them the husbands of my friends, or even my own students, were trying their best to create the new China. They attacked first the written language of the old scholars, the classical wen-li, which was the only language used for literature. Years of study were necessary in

THE CHINA I KNEW

order to become proficient in wen-li, and the young intellectuals, who had spent those years in studying science and therefore were poor in classical Chinese, declared themselves against it. From now on, they said, they would write with simple clarity in the language of the people. A new intellectual life began to flow with a strength and an influence far out of proportion to the numbers who were actually engaged in it. The young Chinese searched the world in their hunger for new ideas, new intellectual companionship. So alive were they that my faith in China was born again. Compared to my young Chinese friends, my American college mates seemed puerile indeed.

From all this fascinating new life I was suddenly removed, or removed myself, by my marriage to a young American employed as an agriculturist by the Presbyterian Board of Foreign Missions. I have no interest now in the personal aspects of that marriage, which continued for seventeen years in its dogged fashion before it ended in divorce, but I do remember as freshly as though it were yesterday the northern Chinese world into which it transported me, a world centuries distant from the one I was living in. This was the world of the Chinese peasant.

3

THE DECISION to marry was the result of one of those human coincidences that cannot be explained except to say in the words of the wise man of Ecclesiastes that there is "a time to marry." When this time comes in the life of any healthy and normal creature, marriage is inevitable, and to the most likely person who happens to be in the environment. My parents did not approve of my marriage, but they maintained silence on the subject. This was amazing, for they were an articulate pair. I took my mother aside one day and asked why they disapproved. She replied that they felt that this young man, while a good sort of person, would not fit into our rather intellectual family. His interests were obviously not intellectual, she said, and when I reminded her that at least he was the graduate of an American college, she retorted that it was an agricultural college and this was not what our family considered education.

"You two are behaving like Chinese parents," I said. "You think whomever I marry has to suit the family first."

"No," she declared, "it is you we think of. We know you better than you imagine, and how can you be happy unless you live with someone who understands what you are talking about?"

I was as willful as any other member of our willful family, however, and so in a few months I was married, with a very simple ceremony, in the garden of our mission house. Soon thereafter I was settled in my own first home, a little four-room Chinese house of gray brick and black tile within the walled town of Nanhsüchou, in Anhwei province, many miles north of my childhood province of Kiangsu.

It was a complete change of scene. I had never lived in North China before, and the very landscape was strange to me. Instead of our green valleys and lovely blue hills beside the wide Yangtze River, I now looked from my windows upon a high embankment where stood the city wall, foursquare, with a brick tower at each corner, surrounded by a moat. Huge wooden gates braced with iron were locked against bandits and wandering soldiers at night and opened in the morning. Outside the walls the countryside stretched as flat as any desert, broken only by what appeared to be heaps of mud but which were actually villages whose houses were built of the pale sand-colored earth of the region. In winter there was no green of any kind. Earth and houses were all one color, and even the people were of the same dun hue, for the fine sandy soil was dusted into their hair and skin by the incessant winds.

The women seemed never to clean themselves, and this I found was intentional, for if a woman was tidy, her hair brushed back and coiled smoothly and her garments any color but the universal sand color or faded blue cotton, then she was

437

suspected of being a prostitute. Honest women took pride in being unkempt as a sign that they did not care how they appeared to men and were therefore virtuous. It was impossible to distinguish between the rich and the poor, for a rich lady wore her satin coat underneath a dull cotton one and was no better to look at than any farm woman.

In the spring the whole landscape suddenly grew beautiful. The bare willow trees around the villages put forth soft green leaves, the wheat turned green in the fields and the blossoms of the fruit trees were rose-colored and white. Most beautiful of all were the mirages. When the earth was still cold but the air was warm and dry and bright, wherever I looked I could see mirages of lakes and trees and hills between me and the horizon. A fairy atmosphere surrounded me, and I felt half in a dream.

But what my parents had feared about my marriage proved to be true, and my inner life in Nanhsüchou was lived alone. There were only two other white people in the compound, a missionary couple much older than I, and for long periods of time they were absent. Then we were the only white people there.

We did, however, have for a short time an American doctor, and I had often to help him in one way or another. One night, long after midnight, I heard a knocking on my door. When I opened it, there stood the doctor, a tall thin figure with a lighted lantern in one hand and in the other his bag.

"I've had a call to go to a young woman who may be dying in childbirth," he said. "I'll have to operate and I need someone to give the anesthetic. But especially I need someone to explain things to them."

His Chinese was limited and an operation was a dangerous risk if the people could not understand what he was doing. I put on my coat and we walked through the silent streets on that bitter cold night to a cluster of small houses crowded with people. Everybody there was awake, it seemed. Smoky oil lamps were lit and faces stared at us out of the darkness. All was silence, and I knew that the people did not trust the foreign doctor. I followed him to the very back of an alleyway, where the young husband met us. With him were an old woman, his mother, and various relatives.

The husband was distracted with terror, for, as he soon explained to me, a wife was expensive for a man in his situation, and he had only been married a year. If she died, the whole business of another wife, a wedding and so on would have to be undertaken afresh. Moreover, his parents were old and they wanted the assurance of a grandson before they died. I expressed my understanding and sympathy, and asked that the doctor be allowed to see the patient. He led the way and we all crowded into a small unventilated room, where upon a big wooden bed, behind heavy curtains, a young woman lay near her death. The agitated midwife stood by her, declaring that no one could save the woman, and that she believed the child was already dead.

"You understand that your wife will certainly die if this foreign doctor does nothing?" I said to the young husband.

"I do understand," he said.

This was not enough. I asked all the relatives who stood silent and watchful if they also understood. They nodded. Last of all I asked the mother-in-law if she understood that she was not to blame the foreign doctor if it was too late to save the young wife. She, too, agreed that he could not be blamed. With so many witnesses it was safe to proceed. The doctor, who had been chafing at the necessary delay, handed me his bag and told me to sterilize the instruments while he prepared the patient.

I went into the courtyard and found a few bricks and built a fire of some straw and charcoal between them. Then I put a tin can of water on the bricks and sat down on a stool to wait for it to boil. Around me in the cold darkness stood the family, fearful of what was to happen. The water boiled quickly and I dropped in the instruments and let them boil. Then I took them, tin can and all, into the stuffy bedroom again, where the doctor gave me my instructions.

"Pour off some of the water into a basin," he said. He looked around the room impatiently. "Can't you get these people out?"

"We can't get them all out," I said. "We must have witnesses."

After some argument the relatives did go out, except for the husband and the mother-in-law.

"Now," my doctor said to me, "put this cotton lightly over the patient's nose and begin dropping chloroform from this bottle."

"How shall I know when she has too much?" I asked, trying not to be afraid.

"Watch her breathing," he ordered. "And don't ask me anything. I have enough to do."

We worked in silence then, the husband and the mother-in-law leaning to see what we did. I concentrated only on the woman's breathing. Was it weaker? Surely it was more faint. Once it stopped.

"She's dead," I whispered.

The doctor reached for a hypodermic and stabbed her arm. She began to breathe again unwillingly.

The ordeal came to an end somehow and there was the little dead child.

"A boy!" the mother-in-law wailed.

"Never mind," I said. "She will get well and bear you another."

It was a rash promise, but it was fulfilled a year later. The incredible strength of the Chinese woman pulled the young wife through. We stayed until she came out of the anesthetic and the husband had fed her a bowl of hot water with red sugar melted in it. By morning she ate a raw egg in rice gruel. It was enough. If someone can eat, the Chinese believe, that person will not die.

As FAR AS Chinese friends went, I was never lonely in Nanhsüchou. My little house was so accessible that a fairly steady stream of visitors came and went, and I was pressed with invitations to birthday feasts, weddings and family affairs. None of my new friends knew how to read or write, yet so learned were they in the ways of life that I loved to listen to their talk. I delighted especially in their humor and in their freedom from inhibitions. As time went on, I made new friends and visited the homes of proud old families where no white person had ever been. One such house I remember especially was small and totally untouched by modern times. The family was surnamed Li, and I became friends with the wife of the youngest son, a woman about my own age.

She was intensely curious about me and about the life I lived, and yet she never spoke a word in the presence of her husband's mother and her elder sisters-in-law. I always noticed her sweet and gentle face, however, and always smiled at her. One day she came to my room alone and begged me to go to her part of the vast compound. We went through small lanes and hidden ways to the little courtyard and rooms where she and her husband lived. No one was there, and she seized my hand and led me into her bedroom and barred the door. It was an old-fashioned Chinese bedroom with an enormous bed, hung with embroidered curtains of red satin, filling one entire end of the room.

"Sit on the bed so we can talk," she begged.

She stepped up on a footstool, for the bed was high, and patted the red satin mattress. I sat down beside her.

"Tell me," she said earnestly, "is it true your husband speaks to you in the presence of other people?"

"Quite true," I said.

"Not shameful?" she persisted.

"We do not consider it so," I assured her.

"Ah," she sighed enviously. "I dare not speak to mine except at night here. If I am with the family and he comes in, then I must leave the room, otherwise it would be shameful. I have been here two years, yet I have never once spoken to my father-in-law. I bow to him if we meet, and then I must leave the room."

We talked a long time. She adored her young husband, I could see, and was sorrowful because they could be together so little, for when he came home at night from the family business, duty compelled him to spend hours with his parents. It was always late when he came to bed, and she was afraid to ask him for too much talk. And yet there was no one else, for custom forbade her to speak to the elder women unless she was spoken to.

This rigorous family decorum was not to be found except in the oldest, richest and most conservative Chinese families. Eventually even my friend would have more freedom, for when her mother-in-law died and her elder sister-in-law became the head of the inner family, her own position would improve until someday she herself might be the head, with daughters-in-law of her own. I am sure it was hard to wait, and she listened enchanted to what I told her about American women.

The longer I lived in our northern city, the more deeply impressed I was, not by the rich folk but by the farmers and their families. They were the most real, the closest to the earth, to birth and death, to laughter and weeping. They were not all good, by any means, nor honest, and it was inevitable that their lives made them sometimes cruel. A farm woman was capable of strangling her own newborn girl baby if she was desperate enough at the thought of another mouth added to the family. But she wept while she did it and the weeping was raw sorrow, not simply at what she did, but, far deeper, over the necessity she felt to do it.

Once, in a small gathering of friends, and not all of them poor or farm folk, we fell to talking of killing girl babies. There were eleven women present and all except two confessed that at least one girl child had been killed in each home. They still wept when they spoke of it, and most of them had not done the deed themselves. Indeed they declared that they could not have done it, but that their husbands or mothers-in-law had ordered the midwife to do it because there were too many girls in the family already. The excuse was that a girl becomes part of another family when she marries. Poor families could not afford to rear too many children who brought nothing to the family but, instead, took from it to another family when they married.

I have heard proud young Chinese abroad declare that such things never happened in their country, just as I have heard them deny that Chinese women have had bound feet in recent decades. But I, within my adult life, have seen girl children with bound feet. A Nanhsüchou neighbor of ours, Madame Chang, had bound feet, and when she walked, it was as though she went on pegs. Another neighbor, Madame Wu, had always to lean on two bondmaids when she came to see me. Her feet were only three inches long. Yet the granddaughters of Madame Chang and Madame Wu were not having their feet bound because they were going to school. Madame Chang put it in practical terms: "I am glad for every girl who does not have her feet bound, for I spent my nights in weeping when I was a girl before my feet grew numb. Yet if she is not bound-footed, she must be educated. Otherwise she will not get a husband. Small feet or schooling she must have, one or the other."

AT LAST we, too, in our quiet northern town, became embroiled in the national troubles. Warlords had the country firmly in their rude clutches by now and in our own region battles began to break out between them. It was never called war but always "attacking the bandits." That is, each warlord would claim that he was the real ruler and the other one was the "bandit chief." At least once or twice a year bullets would fly over our town in brief but alarming scuffles, and we learned to run for the inner corners of a room and stay there until the battle moved on. The battle usually ended at sundown, or if we were lucky enough to have a rainstorm come up, the soldiers on both sides prudently called a truce and returned to their encampments outside the city wall so that they would not get wet.

One further change came into my life: the building of a new house. My little four-room Chinese home was needed for expansion of the boys' school. The mission bought a piece of land outside the city and we were told to design a modest house and build it. I wanted a Chinese house, all on one floor, but this I was forbidden by the mission authorities. No, it must be a two-story house after the Western fashion. I planned a story-and-a-half structure, very simple, but with stairs. When it was finished, my Chinese friends came to see the foreign house. They were fascinated and terrified by the stairs. They went up fairly easily, but looking down that steep decline, they could not risk descending.

"This is the way I shall do it," Madame Chang declared, and she sat herself without more ado on the top step and gravely bumped her way down the steps on her seat, her padded winter garments protecting her nicely. And after her came all the other ladies without the slightest self-consciousness, until the last one was safely on the first floor. The most delightful quality the Chinese had, I do believe, was a total lack of self-consciousness in all they did. It did not occur to them to wonder or to care what anybody else thought.

The years passed tranquilly in our town in spite of the sporadic skirmishes between warlords, and my days were absorbed in small human events. There is much humor in Chinese life, together with a strong sense of drama.

How can I ever forget the trials of old Mr. Hsü, our town's rich man, whose life was enlivened and beset by his wife and three concubines, and the clamor with which they surrounded him! When he traveled on the train to Pengpu, he dared not do what he wished, which was to take only his youngest, and therefore his favorite, concubine with him. She was a pretty woman in her late twenties, the only one still slender enough to wear the long, tight and very fashionable Shanghai dress. He began each journey determined to take only the youngest woman with him, but he was never allowed that luxury, for each woman complained until he had unwillingly agreed to take all four. For economy's sake, however, he distributed them through the train, the third and the youngest concubine with him in second class, the second concubine in third class, and his wife and the first concubine in fourth class. Alas, he still had no peace, for the three who had been assigned the lower classes were continually around him, demanding the same food and tidbits that he bought for his favorite.

Then there was Mrs. Liu, a tall thin woman who was in much suffering because her husband, a "good-for-nothing," as she called him, had gone to France as a laborer during the First World War and she had heard through another friend, whose husband had also gone to France, that he was living with a Frenchwoman. Mrs. Liu was torn between grief and pride.

"To think," she cried, the tears streaming down her face, "that my old good-for-nothing should have got himself a foreign woman! But what sort of woman, I ask you? Anyone can see that my old piece-of-baggage is no use. Why, I was even glad when he came home last year from Shanghai and said he was going for a soldier! And now he has got a foreign woman! What if he brings her home? How can we feed her? What do Frenchwomen eat?"

The term good-for-nothing, I later discovered, was the usual name for a husband in our region, where women prided themselves on their virtue. "My *yao-yieh*," or "my good-for-nothing"—the women began most of their sentences with these words. It was true that, generally speaking, the men were not as strong as the women. I suppose this was because boys were so spoiled in Chinese homes, whereas the girls knew that they had their own way to make and would get very little spoiling indeed. Whatever the reason, the Chinese woman usually became the stronger character. Chinese women are witty, brave and resourceful, and they have learned to live freely behind their restrictions. They are the most realistic and least sentimental of human beings, capable of absolute devotion to those they love and of implacable hatred, not always concealed, toward those they hate. The Communists could never have taken China, I believe, if they had not prudently given so many advantages to Chinese women.

My years in Nanhsüchou came rather abruptly to an end one

day when the man in the house announced that there was a vacancy in the University of Nanking and that he intended to apply for it. He had been floundering, I knew, unable to find a way of applying Western farm methods to an old, established agriculture. Now he could teach agricultural students in a university and let them make the practical application.

I was sad to leave my northern town where I had been so warmly befriended, and yet in a way I was glad to get back into the midst of modern China. There were feasts and farewells, exchanges of gifts and considerable weeping and many promises to visit before I finally closed the new brick house and took the train southward.

NANKING, AN ancient capital of the Ming Dynasty, lies seven miles from the Yangtze River, a vast walled area. Its city wall is one of the handsomest in China, made of large brick as strong as stone, and so wide at the top that several automobiles can travel abreast. This wall is twenty-five miles in circumference. During the famines that befell North China periodically the refugees flooded into Nanking and, lacking other space, built their matting huts on top of the city wall where the winter winds were the most bitter. One of the few angry discussions I ever had with a Chinese friend was with a young woman of Nanking who had graduated from the University of Chicago, where she had specialized in social service. We had a famine that first winter in Nanking, a very bad one, and I tried to do my share in getting food and clothing for the thousands of wretched people huddled on the city wall. Thus I went to Mrs. Yang, only that was not her name. She was a young and a very pretty woman, in a hard, smart modern fashion. Her satin dresses were Chinese but cut tight to her slender figure, and her hair was short. Her house was a two-story Western brick building, furnished in semiforeign fashion. I told her of the plight of the refugees on the city wall. She would not believe that conditions were as I portrayed them, nor could I persuade her to climb the city wall and see for herself.

"I saw such things in Chicago slums," she said complacently, "but I am sure they are not here."

In my memory she is embalmed as the typical Western-educated Chinese who is no longer Chinese. She had created a little tight nice world of her own, whose citizens were all like herself.

In the spring, when the refugees had gone back to their land, the city wall became a pleasant place to walk where I could gaze out over the countryside and the mountains. One mountain stood high and clear against the sky, Tze-ch'ing Shan, or Purple Mountain. Temples were hidden in it, beautiful shaded spots of repose, and nearby were the tombs of the Ming emperors, approached by avenues of huge stone beasts and men on guard.

And I remember Lotus Lake outside the city wall, where, at the end of a long hot summer day, I would go with a friend or two and engage a little boat, in which we were rowed through the watery lanes of the lotus plants. The great rosy fragrant blossoms lay open upon the surface of the lake until the sun set and they slowly closed, their fragrance lingering sweetly on the air. In the dusk the boatman would reach under the huge heavy leaves and pluck off lotus pods for us secretly, for the lotus-seed concession was rented out, such seeds being a delicacy used for feast dishes. If we were really hungry, the boatman's wife would cook a dish of noodles for us, and while we ate we listened to the sounds of singing over the water, a pretty courtesan, perhaps a "flower girl," strumming her lute for her lover.

It was in Nanking that I saw my first motion pictures, mainly comedies with Charlie Chaplin and Harold Lloyd. I enjoyed them vastly, sitting on a hard, backless wooden bench in a big mat shed. Part of my enjoyment lay in the running comments of the crowded Chinese audiences, their roars of laughter at the jokes, their lively horror at the kisses, the old ladies decently holding their sleeves before their eyes and peeping from behind while they exclaimed with delighted repulsion at the disgusting sight of mouth upon mouth. So that was the way foreigners behaved! How pleasant, then, the audience implied, to be a Chinese and a superior person!

I WAS GRATEFUL when I found that my windows in Nanking opened to Purple Mountain. I chose for my own an attic room from which I could look over the compound wall toward the curved roofs of the university and beyond them a pagoda, the city wall, and then the mountain. The city was full of trees and gardens because it had been designed centuries ago to contain within its walls sufficient space so that, if enemies attacked, the gates could be locked and the besieged live indefinitely upon the land inside.

Within my own wall was a gray brick house surrounded by a lawn, a bamboo grove and a vegetable garden. The servants' quarters were in one corner at the back of the house. I set myself joyfully to make a rose garden, for the lovely Chinese tea roses had refused to grow in the dry northern climate. The gardener, who had been there before, begged to be kept on. I was willing, and he led me about the place, explaining its difficulties. When he came to the bamboo grove, he gave me grave looks and sighed.

"There is something very strange about these bamboos, Learned Mother," he said.

"Indeed," I replied with interest. "What is peculiar?"

"They never have sprouts," he replied sadly. "Each spring I look for the sprouts and, alas, there are none."

"That is strange," I agreed. "I have lived in China since I was very small and never did I hear of bamboos with no sprouts in the spring. We must get up early in the morning when the season comes again and perhaps we shall find them. I like to eat bamboo sprouts in the spring."

He gave me the flicker of an eye and nodded, and thereafter we had no trouble at all about sprouts. Each spring they came up thickly and inevitably, and the cook made delicious dishes from them. As for the gardener, he stayed with me faithfully until a revolutionary army drove all white people from the city. Then he disappeared and I never saw him again. With him, I was told, disappeared various valuables, and I suppose that he paid himself back for the bamboo sprouts he no longer ate. But I was fond of him, for he made me laugh very often, rascal and wild-witted fellow that he was, and his wife, a small harassed woman, was my devoted friend. She was older than he, and nothing that either of us could do could prevent him from gambling his wages away, so I often gave her secret money to keep her children from starving. Much to his own and his wife's misery, they averaged more than a child a year. Indeed, as the poor little bedraggled mother said to me once, "It is mercy that we women must have nine months to make a child, for if it were only a day, I should have a new one every day, that man being what he is."

During the long hot summers there was always a new and ailing baby to keep alive somehow. As the mother's milk was never enough, each morning I made up bottles of formula and the mother came for them. Each year I remonstrated with the gardener and urged self-control, and he agreed with all that I said, but the new baby arrived as promptly as ever.

Then one day he came in and said he had a favor to ask of me. "Please, Learned Mother," he said plaintively, "find me a job on the opposite side of the city so that I cannot come home."

I knew too well what this meant. "Which is it this time?" I inquired. "Boy or girl?"

"Both," he said in a whisper.

"Twins!" I gasped.

He nodded his miserable head, speechless.

NANKING WAS another world, familiar and yet new. My parents were only two hours away by rail, and I went home as often as I could, for I was increasingly anxious about my mother.

My first child was born that first year in Nanking, and after that I was not so free to come and go. I did not mind, for to have a child was a miracle to me and I did not dream of the dark future in store for us both. During that same year my mother died, not suddenly, but slowly and unwillingly, and I am glad that she never knew what lay ahead for me. But let me tell of the year of birth and death.

It was 1921 and I was in full touch again with what was going on in China. In 1915 Japan had begun the conquest of China in earnest. While the Western powers were busy with the First World War, Japan made the infamous demands that would have reduced China almost to a colony. The nine-power Washington Conference, in 1922, returned to China the province of Shantung, which Japan had seized, and restored a measure of China's independence. It soon became evident, however, that unless China could organize herself and establish a unified government, she would eventually be swallowed up by Japan.

Three dates are monuments in my memory of the next decade. On a gray October afternoon in 1921 a nurse told my father, my sister and me that my mother was dying. I alone could not go to her bedside. She was in a coma, and whether I went or not she would never know. So I let them enter her bedroom without me and I stood in the hall outside and gazed out of the window at a landscape dimmed by tears. My father opened the door at last and said in a strange calm voice that she was gone. Then he walked wearily down the hall and the stairs to his own study. A few minutes later my sister came out, but I cannot remember beyond that.

The funeral was the next day, a gray autumnal day, dripping rain. Our little procession made its way down the hill and across the valley to the small walled cemetery of the white people. Oh, those sad cemeteries of the white people in alien lands! We used to walk about those very paths, my mother and I, when we came to bring flowers to my dead baby brother, buried there years before, and here we brought her, too, to lie in an empty corner where the sun shone down and wild purple violets clung to the crannies of the high brick wall.

When I went back to Nanking I was filled with the need to keep my mother alive, so I began to write about her. I thought and said it was for my own children, that they might have a portrait of her. I did not know that this portrait was to be my first book. When it was written, I put it in a box and sealed it and placed it in a high wall closet to wait until my children were old enough to read it for themselves. I did not dream that because I put it so securely away it would be almost the only possession to survive the revolution that broke over our heads a few years later. It went to America with me eventually and was put away again in my farmhouse to wait still longer, for by then I knew that my eldest child would never be able to read it. I have told her story in a little book, *The Child Who Never Grew*, for the mothers of other children whose mental growth is retarded for reasons that have never been discovered.

When a family need arose, after still more years, I thought of my mother and how she would have wanted to help and I dedicated her portrait to the cause; it was published under the title *The Exile*. It was the seventh of my published books, but actually it was the first one to be written.

When it was done, I found I wanted to keep on writing. The summer after my mother's death, while I was in Kuling with my sister and my child, I remember quite clearly saying suddenly one August afternoon, "This very day I am going to begin to write. I am ready for it at last."

Though it was the hour sacred to the semitropical siesta, an hour that, however, I always devoted to reading, I sat down as I was, in my robe of blue Chinese silk, and wrote a little essay expressing some of the experiences of my world at that time and sent it off to *The Atlantic Monthly*. When this was done, I enjoyed a delightful exhilaration. At last I had begun to do what I had always known I would do as soon as I felt rich enough in human experience. And after the essay was accepted and published, I had a letter from *The Forum* asking for an article. The year was 1922, and I was thirty years old. It was high time, indeed.

I had no illusions about the importance of these two little essays, but their acceptance induced a mood of happiness and I began to write in earnest on what was to be my first big novel, though I told no one about this.

MY LIFE IN my northern town had been simple indeed compared to the one I now led. I began to teach again and had classes not only in the Christian university but also in the provincial one. The young men in the Christian university were the sons of Christians and had scholarships, or they were the sons of the rich who could afford to pay substantial tuition fees. All of them understood English at least fairly well. The students in the provincial university, on the other hand, were nearly all poor, knew little English and paid no tuition. Most of them had not much to eat and they wore a sort of blue cotton garb later known as the Sun Yat-sen uniform. In winter they were bitterly cold, and so was I, for we had no heat in the buildings and when windowpanes were broken they were not replaced. Yet I enjoyed my work in the provincial university far more because there my students were desperate for learning. They waited eagerly for my arrival and tried to keep me from leaving at the end of our classes. I came away frozen with cold in my body but warm in my heart and stimulated in mind.

In those days Sun Yat-sen was still alive and working to bring unity to the country, but he was in retreat in the south. In Nanking we lived under one of the young and more temperamental warlords, Sun Chuan-fang, but the people were patient as usual and waited for things to work themselves out. Family life went on, the center and the core of the nation as it had always been, and our warlord did not interfere with our affairs.

AND NOW CAME the second monumental date of the decade between 1920 and 1930. In the year 1925 Sun Yat-sen died in Peking of cancer of the liver.

To look back upon this single-hearted man is to feel pity,

sorrow and an unwilling admiration. He was a man who won the affection of all who knew him, a man of goodness and unshakable integrity. There was never a wind of evil rumor about Sun Yat-sen, and the story of his life was that of a consecrated, tragic and lonely man. Many years have passed, yet as clearly as though it were this morning I remember the newspapers that detailed his last hours. He had gasped out these tragic words: "I thought I would come here to set up our national unity and peace. Instead I have been seized by a stupid disease and now I am past all cure. . . . To live or die makes no difference to me as a person, but not to achieve all that I have struggled for through so many years grieves me to the very heart. . . . I have tried to be a messenger of God—to help my people get equality—and freedom. You who live, strive—to put into practice—"

A foreign doctor had begged Sun Yat-sen to rest and he fell asleep for a while. When he woke in the early evening his hands and feet were cold. Yet he lived through the night, still clinging to his dream. They heard him murmuring, "Peace—struggle—save my country—" He died in the morning. His young wife was with him, and upon her his last look rested.

In China the last words of a good man are precious; they are carved upon wood and written into the records. We read Sun Yat-sen's last words again and again and wept. We forgot that he had not been able to do all that he dreamed. His goodness and integrity still stand unimpaired, but we know now that those qualities were not enough. He had no understanding of history, so when Soviet Russia alone had offered her friendship, he had declared that it was to Russia that the Chinese people must henceforth look.

After the First World War Japan, which had allied itself with England, was allowed to take over Germany's possessions in China. This so outraged the Chinese people that the Chinese delegate at Geneva did not dare to sign the Treaty of Versailles. By 1920 the Russian Communists had consolidated their hold on all Russian territory, and then they made a clever and farsighted move. They offered to renounce extraterritorial rights in China and henceforth to treat China as a respected equal. Meanwhile no Western power had paid any heed to Sun Yat-sen's appeals for help. In 1921 he ceased asking and formally accepted the aid of the Soviet Union, though he did not believe that Communism, in the Soviet sense, was suited to the Chinese people. With the aid of Russian advisers, the Kuomintang, or Nationalist party, was completely reorganized on the Communist pattern, with the same discipline, the same techniques of propaganda and the same ruthless political commissars.

It is interesting to know that at that very moment a certain young man, the son of a well-to-do peasant, was working as an assistant in a university library in Peking. His name was Mao Tse-tung. And in Paris, Chou En-lai was a member of the first Chinese Communist group of students. But as for me and my house, in spite of my fears, there were two more years of strange peace after the death of Sun Yat-sen.

AFTER MY mother's death it was necessary to arrange for my father, then seventy years old, to come and live with me. This meant a great deal more than mere living, for he had no idea of retirement and his work had to be moved with him. His new life had to be most delicately and carefully arranged, for it did not occur to him that he might not be the head of any house in which he lived. The illusion was not lessened by the unfortunate fact that he did not like his son-in-law and made no bones of letting me know it in considerable private I-told-you-so conversation. I had been reared with the Chinese sense of duty to my parents, however, and I can remember only once when I allowed my occasional impatience to escape me.

One hot summer's afternoon, when the sun had set, I opened the windows to allow the cool air of an approaching but still distant storm to make the house comfortable before we had to close all doors and windows against the storm. As soon as I opened one window, my father quietly followed and closed it. Upon discovering this, I turned and said a few reproachful words. His mild reply was that he felt chilled as he rested upon a couch. Then I heard him repeat the old words he used to my mother when her robust temper got the better of her: "Oh, don't talk that way!" I did not let him get beyond the "don't." I flew to him, embraced him and begged him to forgive me, and promised that the windows would be closed. It is a small thing, and yet to this day I wish it had never happened. Life is so pitifully short, the years with parents especially, that not one second should be misused.

Among the Nanking white community I tried to take my place as neighbor and friend, but my reality, the warm relationship between human beings that alone makes life, was still with my Chinese friends and neighbors.

One Chinese friend I remember especially, among all the ones I loved. One wintry morning, sometime in those years of uneasy peace after the death of Sun Yat-sen, I heard a knock at my door. I opened it and saw a woman standing there, a ragged, dusty figure whom I could not recognize. She came from the north, that I could see, for her half-bound feet and baggy trousers, her old-fashioned knee-length padded jacket and disheveled hair could only belong to a northern peasant.

"Wise Mother," she said, "do you not remember me?"

"No," I said, "but please come in."

She came in then and sat on the edge of a chair and told me who she was. In the north I had had for a while a rascal of a young fellow for a gardener. He knew nothing and worked little, so we soon parted company. He was her husband, she now told me, but he had run away and left her when the famine came. And she was pregnant, that I could now see.

"Have you no children?" I asked.

She patted her belly. "Only this one. The others all died of the ten-day madness—five of them."

This ten-day madness was simply tetanus, a disease from which many Chinese babies died within the first fortnight of their lives. It was the result of infection at birth, and I had spent a good deal of effort in teaching young Chinese women how to boil the scissors and the bits of cloth or cotton that they used for the children when born. In the north, however, scissors were not used. Instead a child's cord was cut with a strip of reed or leaf.

"I came to you," the woman said, adding with touching and, I must say, annoying naiveté, "I have no one else."

I cannot pretend that I was at all happy about this. Where could I put a pregnant peasant woman in my already too complex household? She could not live outside the compound, for a woman alone would be molested by any idle man in the neighborhood, and we had plenty of such in these times of warlords and wandering soldiers. My guest must have seen what was going on in my mind, for she said humbly, "There is a little house behind your garden, Wise Mother. I could live there until the child is born, not troubling anyone except for a handful of rice. Then, when I am able, I will find work."

The little house was a hen house and in no way fit for a human being, and I told her so. Besides, there was a room in our house, used for storage but quite good, and it could be prepared for her. "But you had better have your child in the hospital," I concluded. "Then you will have good care."

Mrs. Lu was a sweetly stubborn woman, as I was to discover. She wanted the hen house, where she could be alone, and she would not, under any persuasion, go to a foreign hospital. She had had so many children, she insisted, that she knew exactly what to do and she wanted no one with her when the baby was born.

I yielded at last, and the hen house was cleaned and whitewashed, and the floor relaid with fresh clean brick. I put a bed and a table and a chair or two in the little room and curtained the windows so that men would not look in at night. I also gave her a strong padlock for the door. Thereafter Mrs. Lu was part of the compound and she remained almost unseen while she waited for the child. Meanwhile, troubled that she would not go to the hospital or even have our good amah with her, I made up a small sterile kit for her, containing bandages, scissors and a bottle of iodine.

One crisp December morning our amah came with good news. Mrs. Lu had come out of her little house long enough to tell her that the baby had arrived during the night. I ordered the usual nourishing food and liquids for the mother: a bowl of hot water strongly mixed with red sugar, followed in an hour or so by chicken soup and noodles. This was accepted northern practice, the red sugar supposedly replenishing the blood, and the chicken and noodles insuring a good supply of milk. Then I went to visit mother and baby. Mrs. Lu was lying in bed, her large flat face rapturous, and wrapped in the clean baby blankets I had given her was a small very fat boy. She had put on him the usual Chinese arrangements for diapers and then encased him in the blankets. All seemed in order and I gave her a birth gift of two silver dollars wrapped in red paper.

The next day while I was at breakfast the amah came in to tell me that the baby was dying. I could not believe it.

"Didn't she use the boiled scissors to cut his cord?" I asked.

"Oh, yes, Wise Mother," the amah said. "But his belly is burned."

What mystery was this? I went out at once to the little house and found the baby very ill indeed. Mrs. Lu unwrapped him and there upon his tiny belly I saw iodine burns.

"But I told you not to pour the iodine on the baby," I exclaimed.

"Ah, so you said, Wise Mother," Mrs. Lu moaned. "But I thought if the medicine is good, why not use it all?"

I said I would take the baby at once to the hospital, but this Mrs. Lu would not hear of, nor would she have the foreign doctor touch the child. But she let me take him to my own house, and after a few days in my bedroom his robust peasant ancestry came to his aid and he decided to live. I returned him to his mother. Before he was a month old his father, the runaway husband, appeared at the gate and the family was united again. I found a job for the father on the university farms and Mrs. Lu rented a small earthen house just over the compound wall.

Once again the baby came near death before he was a year old. Mrs. Lu walked in with him one day, weeping and declaring that the child was doomed to die for some past sin in another incarnation. She turned him over to display his naked bottom and there I saw broken blisters and raw flesh.

"How is it he is burned again?" I inquired, astounded.

"He is not burned, Wise Mother," Mrs. Lu said. "I said to myself that now he is so big I should not use the water cloths you gave me but lay him on a bed of sand as we do in the north. But here there is no sand. So I laid him on ashes from the stove."

Ashes? Of course the urine had combined with the wood ashes to make lye. Again I took Little Meatball, as his milk name was, and after a few weeks of nursing he was well again.

THOUGH SUN Yat-sen was dead, in a powerful way he was more than ever the leader. He had, in 1921, sent a gifted young soldier to Moscow for military and revolutionary training. This man was Chiang Kai-shek, and in 1926 he began a triumphant northern march from Canton with the revolutionaries—known as the Kuomintang. He was flanked by Communist Russian advisers, both political and military. The warlords of the southern provinces made a pretense of resisting, then fell to bargaining and finally to yielding and "joining" the revolution. It was far more than a military victory. As soon as a region fell, the Communist cadres spread through the country and organized the peasants against the landlords and the workers against their employers. I say "Communist" and yet I do not believe that Communism itself was meaningful in those days to the Chinese revolutionists. The driving force behind the Chinese was not political unrest but a passionate determination to get rid of the foreigners who had fastened themselves upon China.

I pause here to reflect. Over and over again in recent years

Americans have said to me with real sadness that they cannot understand why the Chinese hate us "when we have done so much for them." Actually, of course, the Chinese did not ask us to send missionaries nor did they seek our trade.

The Chinese attitude toward the whole business of the missionary may best be exemplified by a little incident I once saw take place in my father's church in an interior city. He was preaching earnestly and somewhat long, and the people in the congregation were growing restless. One by one they rose and went away. There is nothing in Chinese custom that forbids a person to leave an audience: he saunters away from the temple, the public storyteller or the theater when he feels like it. My father was disturbed, however, and a kindly old lady on the front seat, seeing this, was moved to turn her head and address the people thus: "Do not offend this good foreigner! He is making a pilgrimage in our country so that he may acquire merit in heaven. Let us help him to save his soul!" This reversal so astonished my father, and yet he so perfectly understood its sincerity, that he begged the pardon of the assembly and instantly stopped his sermon.

It did not occur to the Chinese that missionaries were in China for any purpose except their own. Moreover, it must be remembered that while Americans took little part in the wars, yet whenever any other country, usually England, forced a new treaty, we demanded that its benefits be extended also to us. The famous Open Door Policy of the United States was useful to China, but certainly it was as useful to us. In short, we have no honest claim to gratitude from the Chinese.

An interlude in these years was spent in the United States. In 1925, the year in which Sun Yat-sen died, I went to the United States and took my child to one doctor after another, and when I was told of the hopelessness of her case, I felt it wise to plunge into some sort of absorbing mental effort that would leave me no time to think of myself. The child's father had been granted a year's leave of absence and he decided to spend it at Cornell University, where I, too, decided to study for my master's degree.

I had to live, that year, on the single salary of the man, in order that I could study while he did. This meant an economy so severe that, for example, I bought only two eggs a day, one for the child and one for the man. Once a week I bought a small piece of meat. I paid a farmer to bring me a cartload of potatoes, onions, carrots and apples, and these I piled in the cellar to provide most of the winter's food, except for a quart of milk a day and a loaf of bread. The only other expenditure was a small sum paid to a kindly neighbor woman to stay with my child two or three times a week for an hour, when I had to be at classes.

Even my stringent economy, however, was not enough, and after Christmas I saw that something had to be done to earn some money. I thought of a story I had written on the ship coming over, the story of a Chinese family whose son brings home an American wife. I sent it to *Asia* magazine and almost at once I had a letter of acceptance and the promise of one hundred dollars. That sum seemed as good as a thousand. Should I buy a much-needed winter coat with part of it or use it all to pay school fees and bills? I decided to let the coat wait and to start another story, a sequel to the first.

The second story went slowly, burdened as I was with schoolwork and housekeeping and caring for my child, and I began to despair of being able to finish it. I remembered then certain money prizes that the university offered. Quite cold-bloodedly I asked which was the largest and was told that it was awarded for the best essay on some international subject. My professor told me that it was always won by a graduate student in the history department and he discouraged me from trying for it.

I decided to try for it anyway. The prize was two hundred dollars, and this sum of money would see me safely through the year. I chose as my subject the impact of the West upon Chinese life and civilization, and my essay grew into a small book before it was finished. All manuscripts were handed in without names, though our names, of course, were given to the office. A fortnight passed and I began to think I had failed. Then someone told me that he had heard that a Chinese had won the prize, for only a Chinese could have written the winning essay. A weak hope rose in my bosom but I repressed it, for there were several brilliant Chinese students at Cornell. In a few days, however, I received a letter telling me that I had won.

Ah well, it is not often that need and grant meet so neatly. I finished my second story in a good mood and sent it to *Asia* magazine and it was accepted also. Now I was quite rich, and I bought my warm coat, a soft dark green one that lasted me until I lost it in the revolution, of which I shall tell hereafter. And I got back my faith in myself, which was all but gone in the sorry circumstances of my life.

I returned to China in the summer, not only with what I needed in material goods but also with a second child, my first adopted daughter, a tiny creature of three months whom the orphanage had given up because she had not gained an ounce since she was born. Nothing, they told me, agreed with her. I said, "Give her to me," and as soon as they did, she began to eat and grow fat. How easily happiness can be made, and when it is made, how wonderfully it works!

These events bring me to the last of the three dates that I remember as monuments of the events that changed my world: March 27, 1927.

4

THE WINTER after my return to China, the fateful year of 1926–1927, was mild, as most of our winters were in the Yangtze valley. Yet we had enough snow to enhance the green bamboos and leafless branches of the elms and the prickly oranges that made a hedge to hide the compound wall. It was a strange, uneasy winter. The Communist-led forces had dug in, and we waited for the spring when they would march again.

White people were hopeful or distrustful, depending upon their feeling for the Chinese people. My sister's little family was in far Hunan, and the Communists had settled across the lake from her home. Bandits and brigands had joined their ranks, but bandits and brigands were an inevitable part of all warlord regimes. What we heard about the Communists was what we had always heard about the bandits and brigands. Which was which? No one knew.

In spite of the mild winter, the spring was slow that year of 1927. The *la-mei* trees bloomed after the Chinese New Year, and they had never been more beautiful, with their fairy cups of clear and waxlike yellow upon the bare and angular branches. They were scarcely gone, I remember, when my sister and her family left Hunan and came for refuge to my house in Nanking, for they had heard disquieting stories of the antiforeign behavior of the revolutionary troops, who were on the march again.

When I recall the fateful morning of March 27, 1927, I see it in a scene, as though I had nothing to do with it. A little group of white people stands, uncertain and alone, on the early green lawn of a gray brick house, three men, two women, three small children. The wind blows damp and chill over the compound wall. The sky is dark with clouds. They hold their coats about them, shivering, and they stare at one another.

"Where can we hide?" This is what they are whispering.

One of those women is me, two of the children are mine. The other woman is my sister. The two younger men are our husbands, and the tall dignified old gentleman is our father. The nightmare of my life has come true. We are in danger of our lives because we are white people in a Chinese city. Today we suffer for those we have never known, the white men who fought the wars and seized the booty, the empire builders. The weight of history falls heavily upon us now, upon my kind old father, who has been only good to every Chinese he has ever met.

"Where shall we hide?" we keep asking, and we cannot answer.

The pleasant house that until now has been our home can shelter us no more. The rooms stand as we left them a few minutes ago, the big stove still burning in the hall, the breakfast table set, the food half eaten. I was just pouring the coffee when our neighbor, a tailor, came running in to tell us that the revolutionists, who in the night had captured the city, were now killing the white people. He stood there at the table where we were all sitting, and he wrung his hands and the tears ran down his cheeks while he talked.

"Do not delay, there is no time—Teacher Williams lies dead already in the street outside the gate!"

Dr. Williams? He was the vice-president of the Christian university!

My father had breakfasted early and had gone to his classes at the seminary, but only just gone, so immediately the houseboy ran to bring him back. My sister and I got up quickly and found the children's coats and caps and our own coats, and we all hastened outside the house that was no longer a shelter. Here we stand in the chill wet winds.

Where can we hide?

"There is no use in hiding in our quarters," the amah says. "They will find you there." She falls to her knees and puts her arms around one of my children and sobs aloud.

Oh, where can we go? There is nowhere. We hear the sound of howling voices in the distant streets and we look at one another and clasp the children's hands. My old father's lips move and I know he is praying. But there is nowhere to go.

Suddenly the back gate squeaks on its hinges, the little back gate in the corner of the compound wall, and we all turn our heads. It is Mrs. Lu, who still lives in a cluster of little mud houses in the alley just over the wall. She comes hobbling toward us on her badly bound feet, her loose trousers hanging over her ankles. Her hair is uncombed as usual, and her kind, stupid face is all alarm and love.

"Wise Mother," she gasps, "you and your family, come and hide in my little half-room! Nobody will look for you there. Who would harm a woman like me? My good-for-nothing has left me again and I and my son are alone. Come—come—there is no time!"

She pulls at me, she embraces all the children at once, and we follow her blindly, half running, through an open space of grassland and old graves until on the far side of our wall we reach the handful of mud houses, in one of which Mrs. Lu lives. The people are waiting for us there, the kind poor people, and they receive us, her friends and neighbors, and hurry us into the little half-room that is her home. There is no window, only a hole under the thatched roof, and it is almost entirely dark. Into this narrow place we all crowd ourselves and Mrs. Lu closes the door.

"I will come back," she whispers. "And if the children cry, do not be afraid. We have so many children here, those wild soldiers will not know if it is your child or ours that cries."

She goes away and we are left in the strange silence. Our children do not cry. No one speaks. We are all trying to realize what is happening. It has been too quick. Then my father looks out of the little hole under the roof. We can see a light, a glow from a reddening sky.

"They are burning the seminary," my father says. It is where he goes every day to teach and to do his work of translating the New Testament from Greek into Chinese. Nobody answers him. We are quiet again.

I remember thinking on two levels. On one, I felt nothing but sympathy for the Chinese. Were I a young Chinese, I too would have wanted to be rid of the white man forever. But on the other level, I was thinking of the children. My father would meet his fate with calm, and the two young men must handle themselves as best they could. My sister and I were strong enough to bear ourselves proudly. But what of the little children? Somehow we two mothers must contrive to see them dead before we ourselves must die.

For by now the mobs had risen. Outside the little hut we heard the firing of guns, screams and loud laughter, yells and sounds of blows. We heard the heavy front door of our house beaten in and then the shout of greedy joy when the crowd burst into the hall.

I could see it as clearly as though I stood there watching the rooms I had made and loved. I had nursed for weeks the bulbs of the white sacred lilies and they were in full bloom, scenting the house. A coal fire burned in the grate in the living room, and upstairs were the bedrooms and the children's nursery. In the attic was my own special place, where I did my work. And I remembered that in that attic room was the finished manuscript of my first novel.

It was all gone. The crowd was surging through the rooms, snatching everything they could take, quarreling over garments and bedding and rugs and all else that had been mine. And I, by some irony that almost made me smile, was sitting on a board bed in a hut wearing my oldest clothes.

In that crowded hut we sat the hours through while one foreign house after another went up in flames. The door opened at last and Mrs. Lu crept in with a teapot and some bowls.

"The wild people are looting," she whispered to me while she poured the tea, "but they have not burned your house."

"It doesn't matter," I whispered back.

She whispered again. "The cook and the amah and the gardener—they are pretending to loot but they are taking the things for you. I and the neighbors here—we have taken, too, but it is for you." She patted my cheek. "You helped me when I had no home. Twice you saved my son's life."

It may sound strange but at this moment I felt such a peace come over me that I remember it still. Here was a human being who was only good. At the risk of her life she was saving ours. "You know that if we are found, they will kill you, too?" I whispered.

"Let them try," she said robustly under her breath. "The wild beasts! Not knowing the difference between good people and bad!" She hugged one of my children. "Little precious," she whispered tenderly and went away again.

The day dragged on, and the madness continued unabated. Once again the door opened. This time it was a young friend who came to whisper that many Chinese—university professors, students, neighbors and friends—were working for the white people. They had gone to the Communist commander in chief, they would beseech him to spare us. "Take courage," he told us. "We are trying to save you." He hesitated, I remember, and then he said, "I have been a long time finding you because Mrs. Lu would not tell me where you were until a few minutes ago. One does not know now who is friend and who is enemy—these Communists!"

He went away and the hours passed. Again the door opened and a kind Chinese face peered in, an old woman who lived in the cluster of huts, a stranger to me then. She came in with bowls of hot soup and noodles and set them on the table.

"Eat," she said in a loud whisper. "Eat, good foreign devils, and let down your hearts. They will not find you. If I hear your child cry, I will strike my grandchild and make him cry outside the door. All children cry the same noise—"

She went away, nodding and smiling to reassure us. We fed the children, and again the day dragged on.

Alas, the madness grew. We could not hide from ourselves that the uproar and the frenzy were worsening, and that with the night ahead and the darkness, our chances were small. What, I wondered, was happening to the other white people in the city? For the first time in my life I realized fully what I was, a white woman. No matter how wide my sympathies with my adopted people, nothing could change the fact of my ancestry. In a way, I suppose, I changed my world then and there, in that tiny dark hut.

No one opened the door now, not even Mrs. Lu. I knew the soldiers must be very near, so that she dared not make the slightest move to betray our presence. We could hear the rude voices, the hoarse chanting of the Communist songs, the endless crackling of the burning houses, the rumbling of falling walls.

Sometime in the afternoon, before twilight fell, the door did open once more. It was the young Chinese who had come in the morning. He entered now and fell at once on his knees. "We can do nothing," he told us, the tears wet upon his cheeks. "We are helpless. We have been told that all will be killed before nightfall. Forgive us, forgive us, we have greatly harmed you, we sin against you."

We begged him to get up, saying that we understood he had done all he could for us and indeed had risked his own life. "Thank you," we said, bowing to him as he bowed to us.

He went away and now indeed we were alone, each of us in his own way trying to face what lay ahead.

In this strange speechless waiting the afternoon wore on, the dreadful wild noise unabated. It grew dark in the hut. It was five o'clock when we last were able to see our watches. Then I took off the little gold watch I wore and slipped it under the pillow on Mrs. Lu's bed. At least she would have that. Loud feet passed and repassed the door and at every instant we expected to hear it burst open. In the midst of this desperate waiting suddenly we heard a frightful noise, a thunder, rumbling over the roof. It could only be cannon. But the Chinese had no such cannon as this. Foreign cannon—the warships in the river! We had not imagined such a possibility. The river was seven miles away, but the powerful weapons were dropping their loads not far from where we were hidden.

The booming lasted for what seemed a long time but was only a few minutes. When it was over, we heard no sound whatever. The shouting had ceased, the footsteps were gone. Only the falling of a burning beam from some house or the crumbling of a wall broke the sudden silence.

How I wished Mrs. Lu would come in! But no one came. We remained alone in the silence for two hours or more, so we guessed, but it was hard to know in the darkness how slowly the time went. And what did the silence mean?

The door opened at last and by the light of a torch flying in the night wind we saw again our Chinese friend. He was surrounded by Communist soldiers and he did not bow or show any formal politeness.

"You are all to go to the university buildings," he commanded harshly. "All white people are to gather there by command of the new general."

In the light of the torch I saw his lips move and his eyebrows lift. His harshness meant nothing except protection. "Forgive me," his lips were silently saying.

I rose at once, and taking a child by each hand, I led the way out of the hut. In the shadows outside I saw Mrs. Lu among the watching people. She was crying and the torchlight shone on her wet cheeks. But the others made no sign, and we spoke to no one, lest we mark them as our friends. Out of the little cluster of houses we went, and along narrow paths between vegetable fields, and then over grassy grave lands to the road that led to the university. In the darkness my helpless child grew impatient and pushed against the young soldier who was ahead. He turned on her with a frightful snarl, his bayonet pointed.

"Please," I cried, as once my mother had cried for me. "She is only a child. I ask pardon for her."

He went on sullenly, and thus led we entered the campus and marched between enemy guards to enter the big university building where other white people were already waiting. As we passed, the light of the flaming torches fell on the revolutionists' faces and I looked to see what sort of men they were. Every face was young, and I saw among them not one face I knew. They were ignorant faces, drunk faces, red and wild-eyed. Perhaps they were drunk with wine, but perhaps only with triumph and with hate.

We went upstairs and into a big room, and there we found the other white people saved by heroic Chinese who had worked without thought of their own danger. Never had I loved the Chinese so well or honored them so much. I was sure now that, somewhere and sometime, my two great peoples would come together in enduring friendship, and so the dreadful day closed.

We bedded the children down in overcoats and quilts that the Chinese had gathered and at last we slept. One by one through the night and the next day the few remaining white people were brought to join our number. We knew now the dead, and among them was a gentle old Catholic priest, an Italian, who had been a teacher at the Chinese university where I, too, had taught.

A steady flow of Chinese friends continued to brave the harsh revolutionary guards to bring us food and clothing. They came weeping and heartbroken. We had to cheer them up and thank them over and over and assure them that we bore no one ill will.

Still we did not know what was to happen, although we heard rumors that the commanders on the foreign warships were negotiating for our release. Late in the afternoon of that second day we were told to gather together and march to the embankment, where we were to be taken off on the warships. When we reached the gate, we found that several broken-down carriages had been provided for the old people and women with little children, and so I, with other mothers, climbed in and drove off down the familiar streets, lined with watching silent people. The miles were slow, but at last we reached the river's edge. There we were met by American sailors, who took us aboard the gunboats.

All my life I had seen those gunboats on the river, and I had wished that they were not there, foreign warships in Chinese interior waters. Now such a ship was saving me and mine. I was glad not to die, but I wished that I had not needed to justify, against my will, what still I knew to be wrong.

I HAD A curious sense of pleasant recklessness when I stepped off the ship at Shanghai. There is something to be said for losing one's possessions, after nothing can be done about it. I had loved my Nanking home and the little treasures it had contained. Well, that was over. Nothing was ever as valuable to me again—nothing, that is, in the way of place or beloved objects, for I knew now that anything material can be destroyed.

Room had been found for us all in Shanghai, but I felt that the city was intolerable and that I must go away, somewhere into high mountains, where there were few people, and if possible no one that I knew. I said to my family, "Let's go to Japan, into those mountains above Nagasaki and the sea. We could rent a little Japanese house."

I cannot remember how it was done except that the mission head let us draw on salary for funds. Then we all found space in a crowded little Japanese ship and crossed the sea to Nagasaki, on the island of Kyushu, Japan.

What comfort it was to walk on quiet clean streets again, among friendly courteous people, and watch the evening mists gather over the mountains that seemed almost to push the houses into the sea! A Japanese cabman drove us up the winding roads into the mountains and we took rooms at an inn until we could find a house. The mountainside around us was pierced with hot medicinal springs, little curls of steam rising from the rocks. Japanese woodcutters and tourists cooked their eggs and heated their rice and vegetables in the steam.

My sister and her family went on to Kobe, for she expected a child and needed to be near a doctor, and my father decided to go to Korea by himself, so there were only the four of us in Unzen. Within a few days we moved to a little Japanese house. It was made of wood, as all such houses are, and it was deep in a pine forest. The house itself was one big room whose whole front could be slid back at either side. Behind it were three cubbyhole bedrooms, and a tiny room with a large oval wooden tub for a bath. On the narrow back porch, on a rough table, stood a charcoal stove, and there I cooked our meals.

I did not want a servant nor any stranger in the house. Indeed there was nothing to do except to prepare the meals and sweep the floors with a bamboo broom and, when this was done, to wash our few garments in the brook. The nights were long and still, and in the morning I was waked by the soft rustling and whispering of the crab women. When I had washed and dressed, I went out and found five or six old souls sitting in a row on the edge of the floor of our living room as it opened directly into the trees. They had been too kind to wake me, but once they saw me, they held up their baskets of fresh crabs and fish so that I might make my choice for the day. I tried to buy first from one, then the other, in justice to all. They made no complaint, but they always came together and went away together, leaving me with a grass string of frantic crabs or pulsing fish in my hand. Rice, boiled dry and flaky, and a green of some sort was enough for a meal. We grew healthy and clear-eyed on the fare.

Sometimes we went off for the day to climb a mountain or explore a valley, and often we found ourselves part of a procession, for the Japanese love their mountains and beauty spots and are indefatigable about picnics. I must have been very happy and idle, for I cannot remember anything else about our months in the mountains of Japan, except one incident. I was taking my daily bath in the wooden tub, and when my glance happened to fall upon a familiar knothole in the wooden wall, I saw it not green, as usual, with the immediate forest, but filled with an unblinking black eye. I stared at this eye for an instant, then put my forefinger into the knothole, whereupon it withdrew. I pondered upon the sex of the eye's owner but could come to no conclusion. When I had finished my bath and had dressed and come out again, I found that the eye belonged to a young woman with six eggs that she wished to sell. She had heard the splashing of water in the tub and had merely wanted to know if I was at home.

I enjoyed doing my own housework, or supposed I did, until one morning I heard a loud familiar female voice from the back porch. Slipping into a kimono, I went out and found one of our faithful womenservants, Li Sau-tse, from Nanking. This hearty and indomitable creature had decided that it was her duty to find me, because, she said, she was sure that I needed her. She had gone to Shanghai, had inquired of friends where I was, and then with her own money she had bought a steerage ticket and found her way, not speaking a word of Japanese, to our mountaintop. I have no idea how she accomplished all this, but when I saw her standing there on the back porch in her blue cotton jacket and trousers, her belongings tied up in a flowered kerchief and her round lively face all smiles, I suddenly knew that I did need her, and that I was glad to see her. We fell into each other's arms and within minutes she was managing everything as usual.

Since she had no one to talk to except me, I had to listen to her long monologues on the Japanese, who, she declared, were much better than the Chinese.

"Look, Wise Mother," she would say, "when two Chinese ricksha men bump together, what do they do? They curse and howl and one calls the other's mother dirty names. But when two ricksha men bump together here in Japan, what happens? They stop, they bow to each other, they are not angry, each says he is wrong, and then they go their way. Is this not better than the Chinese?"

I always agreed with her as the easiest way to silence.

By this time my sister's baby was born and she and her family needed a place to stay. So after a little time together in the small house, I decided upon a sight-seeing journey. My children and I took a train, any train, and all through the lovely autumn days we sat with Japanese traveling companions who were kind and courteous, interested and interesting. When we were hungry we bought little lunch boxes at a station: cold rice and pickle and a bit of fish daintily packed in a clean wooden box with a pair of new bamboo chopsticks, and bottles of hot pasteurized milk for the children and persimmons and pears and small red apples for dessert. Sometime before darkness we got off the train, just anywhere, and found a Japanese inn, clean and welcoming. There I slept as I had not slept since I was a child.

It was like a dream to wake in the night and lie under the soft quilts upon the tatami mats, and gaze into the dim moonlight of the garden. There was always a garden and we always drew back the paper-paned sliding doors so that the soft damp air of outside filled the little room where we slept. And in the morning we waked at the minute sounds of the maid bringing in the breakfast trays of rice and fish and pickled radishes. I remember the wonderfully controlled beauty of Japan and, above all, the kindness of the people. Their self-discipline was exquisite and it broke only when a man was drunk. Then, instead of growing mellow and humorous as the Chinese did when drunk, the Japanese turned wild and ferocious.

The Nationalists, under General Chiang Kai-shek, were setting up a government in Nanking, my home city, and it was only a matter of months, we were told, until order would be restored enough for us to return. For, as all now know, Chiang Kai-shek, who disliked the increasing arrogance of the Russian Communists, separated himself from them in 1927. He was determined to put an end to Chinese Communism, declared himself friendly to the West and invited foreigners to return to Nanking.

But the next winter, when we went back to China, we were not allowed to return to Nanking after all, so we had to find quarters in Shanghai. The city was more repulsive than ever that year, filled as it was with refugees of every sort. There were warlords and their families living in magnificence in the French and British concessions, and decadent Chinese intellectuals, educated abroad: artists from the Latin Quarter in Paris, Johns Hopkins–trained surgeons who did not practice, Columbia Ph.D.s who could not bear life in "the interior." Most of them spent their time in literary clubs and pretended that the common Chinese did not exist. In such groups there were also a few American women who had come to China for adventure, women who took Chinese lovers and about whom the Chinese lovers boasted.

There was nothing healthy or good about Shanghai. Its Chinese city was filthy and crowded, and the foreign concessions were hiding places for criminals of all countries. If I had to draw a cartoon of Shanghai during that period, I would draw a wretched ricksha puller, his vehicle piled with five or six factory workers on their way home after work, being threatened by a tall English policeman or a turbaned Sikh in the British Concession, while he made way for a carful of satin-clothed people of any nationality, usually Chinese. I am not one of those who think the poor are always right, for I know they are often stupid and wrong, and the rich are not wrong merely because they are rich. Yet that is what I see when I think of Shanghai. I felt as though I were living in the capital of Louis of France before the French Revolution.

Of that winter in Shanghai I can remember little except Li Sau-tse and her romance, which in its small way was connected with the romance of Chiang Kai-shek and Soong Mei-ling, then a young Shanghai debutante.

The redoubtable Li Sau-tse had, of course, accompanied us from Japan. She established herself in the basement kitchen of the three-family house in which we then lived and proceeded to cook our meals. With the three amahs, she declared, she could manage, although she might in the future want a table boy, but it would be one of her own choosing. We were willing to be managed and gave no more thought to the table boy. One morning, however, we heard a violent noise in the basement and a man's voice protesting loudly. A man? Our servants were all women. I sent for Li Sau-tse, and after a few minutes she came up breathless and red-faced while the man's voice continued to bellow from below.

"Li Sau-tse," I exclaimed, "what is going on?"

She explained. Since these were modern times, she had fallen in love with a neighbor's table boy the winter before and there had been some amorous passages and promises. Then the man had disappeared.

"It was those Communists," she declared. "When they

came and you all left, my man went crazy. Everything was upset, you understand. There were no law and custom anymore. In this time another woman seized him from me, and he could not be found. So I went to Japan to serve you. But yesterday when I was at the market to buy your vegetables, I saw the woman, older than I am and uglier. He was with her, and I seized him before her eyes and brought him here and locked him in my room. We are going to be married."

"Bring him here," I said. "I will see whether he wishes to marry you. We cannot have this noise in the house."

She looked unwilling, but she went away and returned soon with a tall good-looking young man.

"How is this?" I asked him as severely as I could.

He was quite willing to tell me how it had happened. "It is difficult for me now that we are having a revolution," he said. "Two women want me for a husband. They are both widows, it is true, but such women are shameless nowadays."

"Do you want either of them for a wife?" I asked.

"Either would do," he said quite honestly. "I would like a wife, but to get a virgin still costs money. A widow can be had for nothing. I am willing."

"But which?" I urged.

"Li Sau-tse is as good as the other," he replied. "Yet I do not wish to be locked up."

Li Sau-tse, who was supposed to be in the kitchen, now thrust her head in the door to bawl at him. "If I do not lock you up, you good-for-nothing, you will go back to the other woman!"

The man grinned rather nicely. "Let's get married," he suggested.

This was all entirely unorthodox, but it was symbolic of the upset times, at least in coastal China. Marriages were being made independently, divorces were easy (a mere newspaper notice was enough), and the incident in my own house made me realize suddenly that the old China was really gone.

So they were married. We gave the wedding feast, and for a few days all went well. Li Sau-tse managed the table boy who was now her husband as she managed everyone, and since she had the best heart in the world, I let it go. Alas, the other woman's charms became brighter in the bridegroom's memory as he continued to live under Li Sau-tse's oppressive love, and one night he told her he wanted to leave. She locked him up immediately and we were wakened at dawn by his shouting and thumping on the door. Once more I summoned the strong-minded bride.

"You cannot keep a grown man locked up," I protested.

She looked grim and folded her arms across her full bosom. "Do you know what he wants?" she demanded. "He wants the other woman, too—both of us!"

"Many Chinese men have more than one wife."

"No," she said impressively, "not since the revolution. And he is only a common man. He is not Chiang Kai-shek."

While this kitchen romance had been going on, Chiang Kai-shek had been carrying on his courtship of Soong Mei-ling. Although it was supposed to be private, everybody knew that old Mother Soong objected, as a stout Methodist Christian, to his reportedly having three wives already. The young lady herself, having been reared in America, also objected, one heard. The three earlier Madame Chiangs were to be divorced, gossip said, although Chiang Kai-shek, it seemed, was reluctant to be so severe, and compromise was being talked of. It was this compromise that disgusted Li Sau-tse. A Chiang Kai-shek could have what he wanted, the old and the new, but not her common fellow. Nevertheless, she released her bridegroom upon my insistence. He fled instantly and she went about weeping for several days. Suddenly, when she had given up hope of seeing him again, he returned one day without explanation, and from then on was an exemplary husband.

It was a happy ending, and quite unexpected. When last I saw Li Sau-tse she was the proud mother of a child, not her own, for a tragic miscarriage in earlier life had made motherhood impossible for her, to her great grief. Out of necessity she had returned to the ways of old China and chosen a nice ugly concubine for her husband. The obliging girl promptly produced a fine baby boy, whom Li Sau-tse instantly appropriated for her own. She adored him and kept him beautifully dressed, exhibited him with maternal conceit and boasted of his intelligence.

As for Chiang Kai-shek, he was obliged to sacrifice his wives, or so we were told. There was a great wedding, very fashionable and Christian, and Soong Mei-ling became the first lady of the land.

Meanwhile, the Communist Party was firmly expelled from the Kuomintang and all Soviet advisers were sent back to Russia, while the Nationalist Army forced its way triumphantly to Peking. This was very satisfactory for the white people, and they gave up some of the smaller of their advantages, like the concessions at Hankow and the lesser ports. The Communists, however, were not so easily vanquished. Part of the Fourth Army mutinied against Chiang in Kiangsi and was immediately organized into the Red Army, dangerous because it provided a nucleus around which all discontented persons could gather. Still more dangerous was the fact that while most of the intellectuals, the Western-trained scholars, left the Reds and flocked about Chiang Kai-shek, who promised them government jobs, the peasants had nowhere to turn. Those who had been organized for the first time by the Communists remained for the most part with the Communists, for Chiang Kai-shek had made no promises to peasants. This division between peasant and intellectual was the first threat to the new government.

But this I did not comprehend immediately. The American consul had granted us permission to return to Nanking. Our house, I heard, had been used recently as a government cholera base and it would have to be thoroughly disinfected. But kind Chinese friends, the family Chao, invited us to stay in their house as long as we needed to do so.

So we went back, the first American family to return, although my unconquerable old father had returned alone some months before and had been living quietly with a Chinese family in the city. How strange it was to ride again through the city gates! The carriage was as dirty and decrepit as ever, the horse as disconsolate, and the streets as crowded and filthy. Yet I quickly felt a change. It was in the people. The city was crowded with new people who looked at us with curious and unfriendly stares. I saw familiar faces, too: the peanut vendor who had always stood at the corner of the Drum Tower, the gatekeeper at the Li Family Gardens, an occasional ricksha puller, passersby on the street. But they did not smile.

And so we went jogging along with our few bags to the Chao house, a modest place in a valley below the university buildings. There we found Mr. and Mrs. Chao, their recently born baby girl and their old parents waiting for us. They were in the tiny living room, and I felt that they had not dared to come outside to greet us. But they were kind and as warm as ever, and Mrs. Chao led us to two small rooms set aside for us.

We stayed there a month, and I shall never forget the unfailing daily courtesy of this Chinese family. If they were inconvenienced or in danger from our presence, they never let me know. If my two children were troublesome, I heard nothing of it, except that one day my amah told me that my elder child had thrown mud into the jar of soy sauce, that prized possession of every family. Mrs. Chao, being an old-fashioned housewife, made her own soy sauce and it always stood for a whole year fermenting in the yard under the eaves of the house, the jar covered with a wooden lid.

"Do not speak of it," the amah said. "She made me promise not to tell you. But I do tell you because it will be necessary to show her some special kindness in return when the opportunity comes."

The opportunity came a few days later when I happened to see in the glass-covered foreign china closet of Mrs. Chao's living room a fine large platter that had belonged to my set of Haviland china. There it was, quite obvious, and when I first noticed it, I almost cried out, "Oh, where did you find my platter?" Remembering my amah's warning, however, I kept silent. As the days passed, I found other possessions that had once been in my house, a set of tea service stands, a sewing machine and so on.

"Where did she get them?" I asked my amah in the privacy of our own rooms.

"She got them honestly by buying them at the thieves' market," the amah said. "That is where the looters sold the foreigners' goods when the Communists came in."

"Isn't it strange she doesn't ask me if I want them back?" I inquired. I had thought that I understood my Chinese friends, but this was a new experience.

The amah looked surprised. "But you lost them," she reminded me. "They do not belong to you anymore. And she is your friend—why should they not belong to her?"

I could not explain why this seemed wrong reasoning, and yet it did. I was more American than I thought. "I don't mind anything except my Haviland platter," I said stubbornly. "I do want that back."

"Remember the soy sauce, please," my amah advised. "If you are patient," she added, "someday you may be able to have the plate again without losing friendship."

I knew the amah was right. To lose friendship is a human disaster, so I held my peace and pretended not to see the platter. Meanwhile I spent every day in my own house. All the walls had to be whitewashed and every bit of woodwork and stone scrubbed with Lysol. The house smelled hideous, but at last it was safe to live in again. Some of the household objects that our good servants had saved for us were returned from their hiding places in friends' houses. And the manuscript that I had left in my attic room had been overlooked by the mobs and saved later by students of mine who had gone to my house to salvage my books. Those books now stand upon the shelves of the library here in my American home, their pages torn and their backs soiled, but they are precious to me.

It was next to our last day with the Chaos, I think, when

absentmindedly I let my eyes rest on the platter. I was not thinking of it anymore, but unguardedly my eyes had fallen upon it and Mrs. Chao noticed. She said in her sweet calm voice, "I bought that big platter of yours so that I might have a dish upon which to place a whole fish. But it is too flat—the sauce runs off."

"You have been so kind to us," I said, trying to seem indifferent. "Let me buy you a big fish plate in South City."

"Do not trouble yourself," she said. "Are we not friends?"

It was true that our friendship was deeper than ever. We had enjoyed the month together, and not by the slightest sign had the Chao family showed the least weariness, although there must have been times when our presence was a burden. When we moved at last to our own house, we left gifts behind us, and among the gifts was a fine big fish dish that my amah had gone to South City to buy for me. The day after we moved, Mrs. Chao's amah came up the hill with my Haviland platter.

"My mistress asks me to thank you especially for the fish dish," she said as she stood before me. "She asks me to say that since she now has the fish dish, she would like to present you with this plate."

With both hands she presented to me my plate, wrapped in red paper, and I received it with both hands, as a valuable gift, and certainly as one that I had never seen before.

"You see," my amah said later, "if relationships are conducted with honor, the reward is sure."

"Thank you for teaching me," I said.

My friendship with Mrs. Chao continued throughout the years, and although we discussed the most intimate details of one family crisis or another, we never violated courtesy by talking of the platter that had been mine, then hers, and now mine again.

MY FATHER CAME back to his own rooms, my children were happy in their nurseries, and to all appearances my life was as it had been before, except that it was not and never could be again. We were living in another world, not the old world of our warlord and our ancient city. I soon saw that the Nationalist government of Chiang Kai-shek was like none I had known. Chiang Kai-shek was already a presence in the city, a force, a personality. I heard him talked about on the streets as well as by my friends.

Once, for example, there was to be a procession for a visiting prince from Europe, and vast preparations were made, even to the extent of tearing down hundreds of the mat huts in which the beggars lived along the foot of the city wall, clustered together like wasps' nests. But the old shops and slums could not be torn down, so walls of mats, thirty feet high, were built to hide the worst of the ancient buildings from the eyes of the foreign prince. Well, on the morning of the day of the procession I went out early to buy a length of raw silk to make a curtain for the dining room. The common people were already gathering for the show, and on my way back I was caught in the crowd. Next to me was an ancient man, a vendor of small bread loaves. He held his basket on his arm, and over the loaves was the usual filthy gray rag to keep the dust and flies away.

As usual, too, he talked. Everybody always talked to anybody on the streets in China. "This old Chiang Kai-shek," the vendor declared, "he is winning all the battles with bandit warlords. As soon as the foreign prince is gone, he will fight in the north."

"Will he win?" I inquired.

"It depends on the weather," the vendor replied judiciously.

"The weather?" I repeated.

"Certainly the weather," he replied. "This Chiang is a river god, reincarnated in a human body. How do I know? He was born by a river in Fukien. Before he was born, that river flooded every year. Since he was born, it has not flooded once. Therefore if the sun shines, he always loses in battles. If it is a rainy day, he always wins. We shall have to wait and see what Heaven decrees."

Chiang Kai-shek had already become a legend, then!

There were more legends and stories every day, not only about him, but about his new young wife, too. The people of Nanking relished the situation of a strong man, essentially old-fashioned in his outlook, married to a strong woman, new-fashioned. Bets were made as to who would win on anticipated occasions. Would the lady be allowed to attend the sessions of the government executives? Bets were only slightly in Chiang's favor. The guards had been ordered not to admit the lady, but would they dare to refuse her? Which did they fear more, the male or the female tiger?

In this particular incident, those who bet on Chiang Kai-shek won. After that, the bets were always in his favor. He lost once, however, years later, when the lady wanted to visit the United States. An eyewitness, whose name cannot matter, told me that one day the great man came out of his personal rooms looking pettish.

"Such trouble," he said in effect. "Every day it is the same thing. She wants to go to America." That morning, the great man went on, she had produced a new argument. The president of the United States, she told him, allowed Mrs. Roosevelt to go anywhere she pleased. This was because the president of the United States was a modern man. At this very moment, she said, Mrs. Roosevelt was in England, having a wonderful time. Whereas she, surely no less in position, could not go anywhere abroad to have a good time! The great man then told her to go, but he made more than one word out of it.

WE WERE PROUD that Nanking had been chosen as the capital of the new government. It was, we were told, to be made into a modern city with wide streets, electricity, telephones, automobiles and great department stores. But our city was as old-fashioned as ancient Jerusalem. Its cobbled streets were narrow and winding, and if a ricksha and a sedan chair had to pass, the people were obliged to flatten themselves against the walls of the houses. And what about the shops? The heaps of vegetables and fruits and fish and meats were piled to the very edge of the streets, and any space left was taken by the tables of fortune-tellers and the stalls of second-hand booksellers.

I could not imagine how a modern city could be made from our old capital. Then one day I understood. Our tailor came to tell me that "they" were pushing down the homes of the people with a monstrous machine. "They" by this time meant the new government.

I put on my jacket and went into the city to see for myself. I saw a monster machine, with a man guiding it slowly along one side of the street and then the other. He was pushing down the old one-story houses, made of hand-shaped brick and cemented together with soft lime plaster, that had stood for hundreds of years, while a crowd of Chinese people watched, silent, stricken. Then an old grandmother who had lived in one house since she was born began to cry wildly. I asked her son in a whisper if the families had been paid for the loss of their homes, and he whispered back they had been promised pay. But no money could compensate for the homes that were gone, with all their traditions and memories.

I knew from that day on that the new government was doomed to fail in the end. Why? Because it had failed already in understanding the people whom it purposed to govern. The Communists in China gained their first victory that day, when the young Nationalists sowed the first seeds of resentment in the hearts of their own people.

In these days, too, a strange change was taking place on the flank of our beautiful Purple Mountain. From my distant attic window I could see what looked like a white scar daily growing larger among the pines and the bamboos. It was the tomb for the embalmed body of Sun Yat-sen. A gatehouse stood at the foot, and from there a vast flight of white marble steps led up the mountain to a memorial hall, with the tomb itself behind it.

The climax of that building was on a hot summer's day. I had as guests Dr. Alfred Sze, the Chinese ambassador in

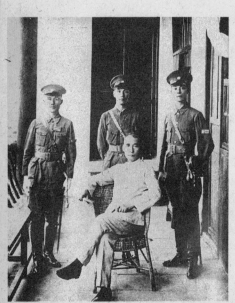

Dr. Sun Yat-sen (seated, left) led eleven unsuccessful attempts to overthrow the Manchu Dynasty before succeeding in 1911. He was elected provisional president of the Chinese Republic in 1912, but stability eluded the new government and Sun Yat-sen turned increasingly to his talented military adviser Chiang Kai-shek (standing behind Sun Yat-sen) to maintain order. Four years after Sun Yat-sen's death, his remains were enshrined in a great tomb at Nanking (above) and Chiang had become recognized as China's leader.

As China's capital, Nanking (left and below) was a major objective in the Japanese invasion of 1937; the infamous "Rape of Nanking" resulted in the death of 100,000 civilians. Earlier, Mao Tse-tung (left) had led his followers on the Long March to Communist strongholds in northwestern China, where they strengthened their ranks and awaited the war's end.

Washington, and Dr. Taylor, the missionary physician who
had embalmed the body of Sun Yat-sen. Dr. Sze was a tall
handsome man, polished in the cultures of East and West
alike, and he could scarcely conceal his dismay at the discom-
forts of Nanking. But what I remember most clearly about his
visit was a brisk after-dinner conversation between me and
the unquenchable Li Sau-tse, still managing our household.

"It is a pity," she said in her loud, practical voice, "that so
pretty a man as this guest of ours was fed too many chicken
feet when he was little."

"How do you know he was fed chicken feet?" I inquired.

"Don't you see how his hands tremble all the time? That is
because he was fed too many chicken feet when he was little."

"Indeed," I observed. I knew better than to contradict her:
she would cheerfully spend hours to prove that I was wrong.

I HAVE NO memories of peace under Chiang Kai-shek. Those
were the years when his army was pursuing the Communists
across the country. Often there were vacant seats in my classes,
and when I inquired where my missing pupils were, the
others told me the unfortunate ones were under arrest as
Communists. I suppose that there were Communists among
them, but many of them were not, as I very well knew. They
were arrested for reading liberal magazines, for associating,
perhaps accidentally, with a classmate who was a Communist, or
for criticizing the new government. With every such injustice,
the Nationalist government was further weakened, and as
early as 1930, behind closed doors and in the villages, the
people were singing secret songs of revolt. They were not
Communists; they were against injustice, knowing that a government built upon injustice cannot stand.

And so in silence and with bland faces the people in our city
watched the brave young Nationalist officials, the Western-
trained specialists and earnest intellectuals, go the way of all
flesh. Government officials grew haughty and domineering
and there were already whispers of widespread graft. The old

evils were still with us. I had in my own classes the handsome son of a high official family. He came every day in an American car, wearing a uniform, his bright spurs clanking as he walked. When the end of the term came, he did not appear for his examination and I failed him on the semester's work. He was indignant.

"Do you not know that I am a lieutenant in the Nationalist Army of the Chinese Republic?" he demanded. "My father is—"

He was one of many. And somehow the Chinese people could not forgive the new officials because they were so much like the old. They had hoped for more than a new government. They had hoped for a new world.

5

IN THE MIDST of these years I made a swift journey to the United States to put my invalid child into a permanent school. It was during those few months that I heard my first novel, *East Wind: West Wind*, had been accepted for publication. I took this news in a properly humble frame of mind—long ago Mr. Kung had seen to that.

Such was my own small estimate of my powers, indeed, that one day much later, in the autumn of the year 1938, when I heard that I had just been awarded the Nobel Prize in Literature, I did not believe it until a telephone call to Stockholm confirmed it.

And if I had doubts about myself, they were doubled by my fellow writers who were men. The gist of their criticisms was that no woman, except possibly the veteran writer Willa Cather, deserved the Nobel Prize, and that of all women I deserved it the least because I was too young, had written too few books of note, and was scarcely even to be considered an American, since I wrote about the Chinese and had lived only in their outlandish part of the world. I was only too ready to agree with all this, and yet I did not know how to refuse the award without seeming even more presumptuous.

I am sure the blast from my fellow writers fell upon me with a severity they scarcely intended. I had for years worked so entirely alone in my writing that I was oversensitive to criticism and almost absurdly worshipful toward my elders in the golden field of American letters.

All this leads me to the kindly memory of Sinclair Lewis, himself a winner of the Nobel Prize in Literature. I sat next to him at a writers' dinner and said very little to him because I felt reticent before so great a writer. He was already sad and disillusioned, and I felt a sort of reckless honesty in his words, spoken with his fine homely face turned away from me most of the time so that I had to listen carefully.

Suddenly my turn came to make a little speech. I told the audience that I had learned as a child in China that a mere teller of tales is not to be considered a literary figure, and that my novels were only stories to make a heavy hour pass a little more easily. Mr. Kung would have approved of all I said.

Sinclair Lewis, however, did not. When I sat down again, he turned to me with an animation sparkling with anger. "You must not minimize yourself," he declared. "A novelist has a noble function." And he went on to speak of that function, and how a writer must not heed what others say. I would weary, he said, of the very name of *The Good Earth*, for people would act as though it were the only book I had ever written. He had often wished, he said, that he had never written *Main Street*, so sick was he of hearing people speak of it as "your book."

"You must write many novels," he cried. "Let people say their little say! They have nothing else to say, damn them!"

What comfort that was, and how warmly I felt toward him ever after! Years later, when I heard that he had died in Italy so alone that he was reduced to playing his beloved chess games with his maidservant, I wished that I had known of his loneliness so I could have made some return for his kindness to me. But I had supposed that a man so famous would be surrounded by old and faithful friends, and I still cannot understand why he was not. I had heard of his faults and difficulties, but his genius was a heavy burden for him to bear, and because of it all his sins should have been forgiven, certainly by his friends.

ALL THIS WAS still in the future when I returned to China from America. The house in Nanking was empty without my little elder daughter, and this, I decided, was the time to begin really to write. So one day I put my attic room in order and faced my big Chinese desk to the mountain, and there, each morning when the household was in running order for the day, I sat myself down at my typewriter to work on *The Good Earth*. The story had long been clear in my mind, and its energy was the anger I felt for the sake of the peasants and the common folk of China, whom I loved and admired, and still do. For the scene of my book I chose the north country, and for the rich southern city, Nanking. My material was therefore close at hand, and I knew the people as I knew myself. "Are your characters real people?" A hundred times and again I am asked that question. Of course they are real people, created from the dust of memory and breathed upon by love. Yet none of them lived outside my books exactly as they do within them.

How long the days were now, in the separation from my older child, although I crammed them full! My father always spent the two hottest months of summer with my sister's family in the mountains, and when he left, the house was emptier than ever.

As a bystander, I watched my Chinese world change before my eyes. Chiang Kai-shek was having a hard time as president of a republic. He knew nothing about any government except a military one. He was used to men who came when he said come and who went when he said go. There was a hot-springs resort not far from Nanking, and he used a house there as a place of confinement for the members of his cabinet who disagreed with him. There they went and there they stayed until they saw reason. I remember passing by the house sometimes when I was riding outside the city wall and asking the villagers who was now in prison there. They always knew.

I do not propose to blame Chiang now. He sincerely did the best he knew, but he did not know enough. I do not know whether ignorance can be called a crime. If so, then many in this world are guilty, and I see them here in my own country, too, in high places.

Meanwhile I was still writing *The Good Earth*. This I did in three months, typing the manuscript twice myself in that time. When it was finished, I felt very doubtful indeed of its value, but I tied up the pages and mailed them off to New York and prepared to wait, while I busied myself with other work.

At this period I was especially aware of the Chinese peasant, of his wonderful strength and goodness, his amusing and often alarming shrewdness and wisdom. Nothing in Communist theory enrages me more than Trotsky's callous remark that the peasants are the "packhorses" of a nation. In all my years in China I never ceased to feel pain and anger when I looked at the thin face of some Chinese peasant twisted into sheer physical agony because on his back he bore a burden too much even for a beast. I have seen his slender legs quiver under the weight of a two-hundred-pound bag of rice, or under the huge wardrobe trunk of some tourist. Few Asian leaders have understood the quality of their own peasant, and among them the Communists are the most guilty, for despite all their talk, their condescension makes my soul sick.

THE YEAR 1931 was a monumental one in many ways for me. In that year my dear old father died in the eightieth year of his life. In that year the Yangtze River swelled with unusual rains and flooded our whole countryside, a sight no one living had ever seen before. And in that year the Japanese empire builders seized Manchuria.

For me, of course, the most moving event of 1931 was my father's death. During the last two years his tall ascetic frame had grown more and more frail, his nature more completely saintly, and I feared, observing these changes, that he had not many more years to live. That summer, however, he went to my sister in Kuling as usual and spent a happy two months there. It was when he was preparing to come back to me that he was suddenly seized by dysentery. He weakened rapidly and in a few days was gone. I could not even get to his funeral, for the river was flooding at a frightening speed.

I did not tell my father's story until years after he died, when I wrote *Fighting Angel: Portrait of a Soul*. I wrote that book because some of my American readers were so bemused by my mother's story in *The Exile* that they thought I did not love my father. On the contrary, I had learned to love him with warmth and reverence. His soul can perhaps be best expressed in two quotations I placed at the beginning of my book about him:

ANGEL — One of an order of spiritual beings, attendants and messengers of God, usually spoken of as employed by Him in ordering the affairs of the universe, and particularly of mankind. They are commonly regarded as bodiless intelligences.—*Century Dictionary*

Who maketh his angels spirits
And his ministers a flame of fire.—*The Epistle to the Hebrews*

BEFORE MY FATHER died and the floods came, *The Good Earth* was published. I remember when the first copy of it reached me. I felt shy about it, but I went to my father's room and showed the book to him, not expecting much, to be sure, since he read no novels. He was very kind about it. He complimented me upon the appearance of the book and inquired when I had had time to write it. Then a few days later he returned it to me, saying mildly that he had glanced at it but had not felt equal to reading it.

And I remember that my first letter from the United States about the book was from an official on a mission board, who sent me several pages of blistering rebuke because I had been so frank about human life. Reared as I had been in the naturalism of Chinese life, I did not know for a long time what he meant, but now I know. The worlds in which I have lived have made me what must be called a controversial figure, and this is because, inescapably, I see the other side of every human being. If he be good, then there is that other side, and if he be evil, there is again another side.

BEYOND THE LOCAL disaster of the flood, there was the gnawing awareness of the Japanese militarists, now firmly entrenched in Manchuria. They moved into the vital province of Jehol in 1931–1933, and finally virtually took over North China. The American consul now advised all American families in Nanking to send their women and children away.

I took my little younger daughter and went to Peking. It was there that I became convinced that sooner or later I must leave China and return permanently to my own country, for such wars and upheavals lay ahead that no white people would be allowed to remain. While Japan continued her aggressions, Chiang Kai-shek was still fighting against the Communists, who had simply retreated strategically to the northwest where he could not reach them. He was right, of course, in believing that Communism was a basic enemy of the Chinese way of life. But what he did not understand was that by ignoring the terrifying growth of Japanese domination, he was alienating his own people, who did not yet gauge the dangers of Communism.

As for the Communists, whom he was pursuing at all costs, they, too, behaved stupidly while advised by the Russians. The Russian Communists had urged the Chinese Communists, under their military leader, Chu Teh, to capture the cities, where, they said, the factory workers or "true proletariat" would gather to their aid. But few Chinese cities had factories and there was no proletariat in the orthodox Communist sense.

In the end, the Communists were completely routed, so that they were compelled to hide in the mountains. There in a famous meeting place, Ching-kang Shan, Chu Teh met Mao Tse-tung and together they reorganized the Chinese Communist Party, this time without help from Soviet Russia. The reorganized party under Mao and Chu proceeded then to entrench itself among the peasantry, for as Chu said, "The people are the sea, we are the fish, and as long as we can swim in that sea we can survive."

To win the favor of the peasants, the Communists announced as their enemies those whom the peasants considered enemies—landlords, tax gatherers, moneylenders and middlemen. The peasants were won over by this policy and they helped the Communists in every way they could, telling them when the Nationalist soldiers were coming and generally defeating the purposes of Chiang Kai-shek, without really knowing what they did.

Whether Communist or Nationalist would finally win depended, I believed, on which one first recognized the menace of Japan. Unfortunately it was the Communists who were the first to do this and who virtually compelled Chiang to fight Japan. They adopted as their new watchword, "Chinese do not fight Chinese," meaning that they were willing to unite with the Nationalists in order to fight the common enemy.

It was tragic in those days to watch the decay of the Nationalist government. While the nation was being torn by dissension and struggle, the intellectuals and party members were quarreling among themselves over a constitution and new laws and what form labor unions should take—all good concerns but irrelevant in the face of the immediate danger. Meanwhile Chiang Kai-shek, irritated and desperate, was trying to establish some sort of order, not only among his own government officials, but also among rebellious warlords whom he could not actually conquer and with whom he therefore had to bargain. Dissidence had risen to such a point that Feng Yü-hsiang, the most spectacular of the warlords, had in 1930 withdrawn from all bargaining, and had set up a rival government in Peking, further to confound the president.

While I was in Peking, then, it became clear that unless I wanted to spend my life in a turmoil that I could neither prevent nor help, I would have to change my country. I remember how long I pondered in those days of the Peking spring, for nowhere is China greater and more manifest in beauty than in Peking. I felt the nobility of the wide streets, designed for a princely people, and the palaces and tombs remained as splendid monuments. Yet the monuments were falling into decay, and I remember my sadness one day when I visited the very palace where the old empress had liked best to live.

It was under military guard, and the idle soldiers stared at me curiously as I lingered. At last one of them beckoned me to follow him around a corner of the palace. When I reached the place where he stood, he put up his hand and pulled down a magnificent porcelain tile from the edge of a low roof, a tile of the old imperial yellow, stamped with a dragon.

"One silver dollar," he said in Chinese.

I shook my head and went away. What use was it to accuse him? He did not feel the idealism that alone would have made him perform his duty.

Idealism? There was the weakness. The new government never gave its people an idealism to live by, and the Chinese, like all of us, cannot live by bread alone. There had to be something to live for. There had, above all, to be a leader whom they could revere. The Chinese do not object to a dictator if he is strong enough as a man to command their respect. Their conception of democracy is totally different from that of Americans, for their conception of a nation is different. The head of the Chinese government, whether emperor or president or Communist dictator, stands in the position of father of the people. As a father he must be worthy of their honor and obedience. He must also be a good provider, for the Chinese proverb has it, "When the price of rice is beyond the ability of the common man to pay, then Heaven decrees a change of rulers."

When the Chinese people began to reject Chiang Kai-shek, the whole process was in accord with the tradition of Chinese history. Corruption and dissolution began when it was apparent that Chiang could not hold the people. This corruption was not the cause of the downfall of the Nationalists, although it has often been said that it was. The truth is that any declining government falls into corruption, and the very fact is a proof of its approaching end.

Still, I did not decide quickly or easily to leave China; in fact, the decision was not final for two years. We had a sabbatical year in 1932 and spent it in the United States. When we returned, the gray house in Nanking stood as I had left it, but I must say that when I walked in the front door, it looked empty to me. Somehow it was no longer home. I had changed more than I knew.

The outlook was not good. I found an ever-deepening gulf between the white people and the Chinese. Both groups of white people, businessmen and missionaries, were unhappy. Mission schools were forced to comply with government regulations decreeing obeisance before the portrait of Sun Yat-sen, which was required to hang on every chapel or assembly hall wall. His famous *Will*, now a sacred document, had to be read aloud once a week, the audience standing. In the Christian churches the Chinese members were pressing for self-government and control of foreign funds.

Yes, it was time for me to leave China forever. There were personal reasons, too, why I should go. My invalid child had become ill after I left her in America, and it was obvious that for her sake I should live near enough to be with her from time to time. The gray house, too, had ceased to be a home for family life, for the distance between the man and the woman there had long ago become insuperable. There was a difference so vast that communication was impossible, in spite of honest effort over many years. Now the difference had come to include the child who could not grow and what should be done for her, and there was no bridge left to build between.

Yet I had decided that before I finally went back to America I would travel in the countries of Asia as far as I could go. I went first to parts of China that I had not seen, and then farther

495

to Indochina and Thailand, to India and Indonesia. Of this journey, I remember first the beautiful province of Fukien in South China. It is a seacoast province whose undulating shores are infested with pirates; their nests centuries old. The little steamer that carried me had a strong iron fence and a barred gate on the stairway between the upper decks where the white folk traveled and the lower decks where the rest of the world ate and slept. Fence and gate, the English captain told me, were made so that if pirates were hidden among the lower-deck passengers, the white people could defend themselves from above. What, I asked, if the pirates set a fire below?

The captain shrugged. "We have the lifeboats."

I was glad to get ashore from that vessel and settle myself in a Chinese inn. And from there, with Chinese friends, I traveled slowly by bus into the back country through handsome citrus groves, the trees rich with oranges and grapefruits that the kindly farmers plucked for us as we passed. Every hour or two the bus broke down and we all got out and waited while the driver patched up the engine with bits of wire and string. I observed that there was no hood to the engine.

"Where is the hood?" I asked.

The driver looked up, his face streaked with oil. "That lid," he said with contempt, "it was take-it-up, take-it-down, and for what? I took it off altogether."

I went on southward to Canton. I walked its ancient narrow streets where the ivory dealers, the jade lapidaries, the gold- and silversmiths had their one-story shops. There was jade of every color: yellow, rust-red, blue, and the green of spring rice. It was as mottled as marble, or as smooth and cold and white as mutton fat. And every variety was exquisite and put to exquisite use! I had seen triumphs of such art in the palaces of Peking, whole landscapes carved from a single huge lump of jade, but here in a Canton street I saw it actually done by men who had spent a lifetime upon one work. The southern jades came usually from Burma, whereas the jade in Peking was brought by camel from Turkestan. Chinese and Burmese jade miners alike believe that jade has miraculous qualities. The Kachins, or Burmese hillmen, locate the mines with a bamboo divining rod, set afire, and then, when jade is found, they perform old rituals and ceremonies for opening the mines.

In China jade became a divine gem, a sign of imperial power, in the third century before Christ when the first great imperial seal was made for the Emperor Ch'in Shih Huang Ti. That seal was preserved throughout the dynasties, so that whoever was strong enough to gain it and to keep it became by that very sign the Heaven-ordained ruler.

BACK IN Nanking again after my journey, I saw no change for the better. The Communists were soon to be locked in the far northwest, the Long March taking place from October 1934 to October 1935, but the warlords were still not conquered, not all bought and bargained with, and Japan was ominous indeed. And there was more bad news about my child across the sea. I must go back to the land of my ancestors.

Before I left, I went once more to Peking, simply to impress upon my memory the last scenes of what had been the heart of my childhood China. It was not a private return, for by that time too many people knew me and there were invitations I could not refuse. I do not remember them now—what I do remember is the blind musician I met one twilight evening in a lonely street. I was walking just for pleasure when I heard the melody of an accomplished hand on the two-stringed Chinese violin, and there against the soft lights of the street was the figure of a big man in a long gray cotton robe. His massive head was high, his dark eyes wide open but blind, as I could see when he came near. He held his violin across his breast, and as he played on the two strings with his bow, he strode alone, too absorbed to feel my presence. I have never forgotten that man, nor his melody.

Thus I filled my cup full, perhaps for all my life, for who could know whether it would ever be possible to return? Yet when the last moment came, the final departure from house and garden, I took nothing with me. I could take nothing. I felt compelled to leave it all exactly as it was, as though I might be coming back. Thus, in the spring of 1934, I went to my own country.

To CHANGE countries is an overwhelming experience, but I have accomplished it somehow during the years that have passed since I left China; and I have never returned there.

Back in America, I spent my first summer in New York, and I learned that I could never really understand my country unless I became a part of it somewhere else and not merely a city visitor. After some musing and traveling, I decided upon Pennsylvania, where I found an old stone house and a farm, cheap then, at the end of the Depression. And it was there that I came to live and take root after my second marriage, and there that my husband and I brought up our family.

For me, a house without children cannot be a home. I do not know why people who love children are so often prevented by accident from having them, but, God be thanked, there are many who have children and leave them, for one reason or another, and then others can take them for love's sake. As soon, then, as the old Pennsylvania house was ready for us, we approached our one adopted child, then eleven years old, and asked her what she thought of our adopting two little boys, and then, a year or so later, a girl and a boy. She reflected for some weeks and months, and only when she decided it would be "nice" to have babies did we adopt our three boys and a girl.

The years have been rich with living, with the writing of many books, and with a quiet, steady background of farming, home, children and work. I have shared my friends from other worlds with family and neighbors, and in my American world I have found friends and neighbors, too, who have hearts as wide as the globe itself. Many of these people have helped us work for the place we have christened Welcome House, and for the children who live there—and in this way my several worlds are indeed united.

Welcome House began when my children were all but grown up. One cold December day, when our house was all in ferment with approaching Christmas and long-legged boys and girls with their skis and their dances and glorious hodge-podge of Christmas presents and holly wreaths, the postman brought me a special-delivery letter from a distant child-adoption agency, asking if I could help them place a little baby, the son of an American white mother and an East Indian father, but rejected by both families on both sides of the globe. Do not ask why a child is rejected, for I cannot understand it, whatever the reason. The agency workers had exhausted every possibility in the whole of the United States, they told me, and they had even tried to place him in India, but no one wanted him. They enclosed his picture. I looked into the sad little face of a lonely child, and the happy world in which I lived dropped away. What I saw was hundreds of little faces like his in India, hundreds and thousands of young men and women, born of the white man and the Indian woman, not wanted by either and therefore lost, for the unwanted child is always the lost child. But this little boy was American, and for me it was unendurable that he should be as lost here as he would have been in India. I hastened to the telephone and called every friend I had who was Indian, or partly Indian, everyone, too, who I knew had been to India and might know other Indians, and over and over again I told the baby's story. Still nobody wanted him.

Hastily I gathered my family around me and told them the story. What should we do? There was not one dissenting voice, from the father to the youngest daughter. All of them said, "Bring him here."

Thus authorized, I telephoned the agency. Soon after Christmas, in the darkness of a winter's night, a small dark boy was deposited in my arms, his enormous brown eyes quietly terrified and he utterly silent because his thumb was buried permanently in his mouth. I took him upstairs to the crib we had prepared and put him to bed, but he did not sleep much that night and neither did I. He did not cry aloud, but now and then he cried in a small voice subdued by fear, and then I held him until he slept.

Astounding as this advent was, yet another came and in the same month. A friend wrote me that a little half-Chinese child was to be born in a certain city hospital. The child would have nowhere to go, for the Chinese father, already married, could not acknowledge it and had returned to China, the American mother had no way to keep it, and the local adoption agency could not accept it. By now I felt that I was under some guidance I did not understand. My family said, "We may as well have another," and so, on a cold January day, we brought home from the big city hospital a little baby boy, nine days old.

We all took care of our babies together, and we all shared the joy of seeing them grow strong and happy. The little American-Chinese never knew anything but love and he thrived from the first, but the little American–East Indian had to be won into believing that we loved him. Yet that did not take long. The months passed and our family did a great deal of thinking. If there were these two children, there must be many others. I began to inquire among child-adoption agencies and found that the American child of Asian or part-Asian ancestry was their greatest problem at that time, greater even than the black child. Many agencies would not accept them at all, feeling their adoption was impossible.

I reported back to my family. Behind our two babies were perhaps hundreds of others. We could not take all of them, that was obvious. Besides, these little American Asians needed special love and care right through the years and we were no longer young. Then I asked myself, Why not find younger parents in our own community for our two American Asian babies, and let theirs be the home center while we helped as grandparents? And why not plan for all such children until other agencies were convinced that they are "adoptable"? I invited the leading men and women of our community one evening to talk over the plan. "If you will stand behind it with us," I said, "I believe we can do something really useful, not only for this small group of children, but also for our nation. Communist propaganda in Asia says that we Americans despise people with Asian blood. But we will show them that we care for these exactly as we care for all."

The man who keeps our general store spoke for everybody. He was a big Pennsylvania Dutchman, our oldest citizen and our most respected and influential one. He said, "We won'dt only be willin', we will be proudt to have the childtern."

Thus began Welcome House, Incorporated. It has grown through the years to gather many children. A few live permanently in our community, but the others, the babies, now go to adoptive parents. For there are many parents, after all, who want American children of Asian blood; some of these parents are white Americans, some Asian, some part Asian. All of them are people who have unusual backgrounds, advantages in understanding, education and experience. We are particular about our parents. They must want our babies for what they are, value the Asian heritage and be able to teach the child to value it. Once a prospective mother, looking at a lovely little part-Japanese girl, asked me, "Will her eyes slant more as she grows older?" My heart hardened. That woman would not be given one of our children. She had to think the tilted eyes were beautiful, and if she did not, then she was not the right one.

We have at last a long list of waiting parents who want our babies. And when they are approved, our babies go with them into their communities and successfully make their way, for the blood of Asia adds a gentle charm to the American child.

The job has not been easy. Has it been worth doing? Yes; and I hope I am not too selfish in finding comfort in the children for myself. In the solitary hours before dawn I find myself thinking of all our Welcome House children, each one of them belonging now to an American family, loving and loved, and I remind myself that thousands, maybe millions, of people in Asia know about them, too. As I wrote these very words, I was stopped by the ringing of the telephone, and when I answered it, I heard the voice of a man from Indo-china, a Vietnamese, who broadcasts regularly to his own country against Communism and for democracy. He put a familiar question to me. "May I come and visit Welcome House? I want to tell my countrymen about it. This is what they ought to know about the United States."

And how true that is! There was never a more generous or spontaneously unselfish people than the Americans, and this same spirit would work, I am sure, if it had the freedom and the knowledge, anywhere in the world. Our contribution to the solution of the world's problems will come only from the working of the American spirit: practical, though sometimes impatient; optimistic, though humorously rueful; and energetic, though occasionally reluctant.

In short, if I am sometimes critical of my own people, it is in excess of love, for I perceive so clearly our own amazing ability to aid in fulfilling the needs of humanity that I grow restless with delays. Yet the advance in our national thinking since the end of the Second World War should encourage even the most exacting critic. In spite of mistakes and mis-steps, I see the American spirit reaching new levels of common sense and enlightenment, generous, decent and sane.

In this mood of faith and hope my own work goes on. A ream of fresh paper lies on my desk waiting for the next book. I am a writer and I take up my pen to write. . . .

ACKNOWLEDGMENTS

The condensations in this volume have been created by The Reader's Digest Association, Inc., and are used by permission of and special arrangement with the publishers and the holders of the respective copyrights.

The following works by Pearl S. Buck, originally published by The John Day Company, are reprinted by permission of the Pearl S. Buck Family Trust, Harper & Row, Publishers, Inc., and Methuen London, Limited:

THE GOOD EARTH
Copyright 1931; renewed © 1959 by Pearl S. Buck.
Copyright 1949 by Pearl S. Buck; renewed © 1977 by Janice C. Walsh, Chieko C. Singer, Richard S. Walsh, Jean C. Lippincott, John S. Walsh, Edgar S. Walsh, Henriette C. Teush and Carol Buck.

IMPERIAL WOMAN
Copyright 1956 by Pearl S. Buck; renewed © 1984 by Janice C. Walsh, Chieko C. Walsh, Richard S. Walsh, Jean C. Lippincott, John S. Walsh, Edgar S. Walsh, Henriette C. Walsh and Carol Buck.

MY SEVERAL WORLDS: A Personal Record
Copyright 1954 by Pearl S. Buck; renewed © 1982 by Janice C. Walsh, Chieko C. Singer, Richard S. Walsh, Jean C. Lippincott, John S. Walsh, Edgar S. Walsh, Henriette C. Walsh and Carol Buck.

ILLUSTRATION CREDITS

Frontispiece: Illustration by Hodges Soileau.

THE CHINA I KNEW
Page 396 (top): Harringa Collection.
Pages 396 (bottom), 397 (bottom), 429, 484, 485 (top): The Bettmann Archive.
Pages 397 (top), 428 (top): By permission of the Pearl S. Buck Family Trust.
Page 428 (bottom): U.P.I.
Page 485 (center): Wide World Photos.
Page 485 (bottom): Brown Brothers.